About the Authors

Lindsay Armstrong was born in South Africa. She grew up with three ambitions: to become a writer, to travel the world, and to be a game ranger. She managed two out of three! When Lindsay went to work it was in travel and this started her on the road to seeing the world. It wasn't until her youngest child started school that Lindsay sat down at the kitchen table determined to tackle her other ambition – to stop dreaming about writing and do it! She hasn't stopped since.

Amy Woods believes that real love, while not always easy, is absolutely worth the work. She enjoys writing about imperfect characters who deserve to be loved for all the weird and wonderful things that make up who they are. When she's not busy writing, Amy likes taking walks with her senior rescue dog and watching movies with a husband she adores.

Katie Meyer is a Florida native with a firm belief in happy endings. She studied English and Religion before getting a degree in Veterinary Technology. A former Veterinary Technician and dog trainer, she now spends her days homeschooling her children, writing, and snuggling with her many pets. Her guilty pleasures include chocolate, Downton Abbey, and cheap champagne. Credit for her romance writing goes to her parents and her husband, who taught her what true love really is.

Animal Magnetism

Animal Magnetism: Rescued by Love

LINDSAY ARMSTRONG

AMY WOODS

KATIE MEYER

MILLS & BOON

First Published in Great Britain 2021
by Mills & Boon, an imprint of HarperCollins*Publishers* Ltd,
1 London Bridge Street, London, SE1 9GF

www.harpercollins.co.uk

HarperCollins*Publishers*
1st Floor, Watermarque Building,
Ringsend Road, Dublin 4, Ireland

ANIMAL MAGNETISM: RESCUED BY LOVE
© 2021 Harlequin Books S.A.

The Socialite and the Cattle King © 2010 Lindsay Armstrong
Puppy Love for the Veterinarian © 2016 Amy Woods
The Puppy Proposal © 2015 Katie Meyer

ISBN: 978-0-263-28198-9

MIX
Paper from
responsible sources
FSC™ C007454

This book is produced from independently certified FSC™ paper to ensure responsible forest management.

For more information visit: www.harpercollins.co.uk/green

Printed and bound in Spain
by CPI, Barcelona

THE SOCIALITE AND THE CATTLE KING

LINDSAY ARMSTRONG

CHAPTER ONE

HOLLY HARDING had the world at her feet—or she should have had.

The only child of wealthy parents—although her father had died—she could have rested on her laurels and fulfilled her mother's dearest ambition for her, that she settle down and make an appropriate, although of course happy, marriage.

Holly, however, had other ideas. Not that she was against wedlock in general, but she knew she wasn't ready for it. Sometimes she doubted she ever would be, but she went out of her way not to dwell on the reason for that...

Instead, she concentrated on her career. She was a journalist, although occasionally she partook of the social scene so dear to her mother's heart; Sylvia Harding was a well-known socialite. It was on two such occasions that Holly had encountered Brett Wyndham, with disastrous consequences.

'A masked fancy-dress ball and a charity lunch? You must be out of your mind,' Brett Wyndham said to his sister Sue.

He'd just flown in from India, on a delayed flight that

had also been diverted, so he was tired and irritable. His sister's plans for his social life did not appear to improve his mood.

'Oh, they're not so bad,' Sue said. She was in her late twenties, dark-haired like her brother, but petite and pretty—quite unlike her brother. She was also looking a bit pale and strained, whilst trying to strike an enthusiastic note. 'And it is a good cause—the lunch, anyway. What's wrong with raising money for animal shelters? I thought that might appeal to you. I mean, I know they may only be cats and dogs...'

Brett said wearily, 'I can't stand them. I can't stand the food, I can't stand the women—'

'The women?' Sue interrupted with a frown. 'You don't usually have a problem there. What's wrong with them?'

Brett opened his mouth to say, *They are usually the most ferociously groomed set of women you've ever seen in your life, from their dyed hair, their fake eyelashes, their plucked eyebrows, their fake nails and tans; they're ghastly.* But he didn't say it. Although she didn't have a fake tan or fake eyelashes, his sister was exquisitely groomed and most expensively dressed.

He shrugged. 'Their perfume alone is enough to give me hay fever,' he said moodily instead. 'And, honestly, I have a problem with the concept of turning fund-raising into society events that bring out all the social climbers and publicity seekers.' He stopped and shook his head.

'Brett, please!'

But Brett Wyndham was not to be placated. 'As for masked fancy-dress balls,' he went on, 'I can't stand the fools men make of themselves. And the women; something about being disguised, or thinking they are, seems to bring out the worst in them.'

'What do you mean?'

'I mean, beloved,' he said dryly, 'They develop almost predator-like tendencies.' For the first time a glint of humour lit his dark eyes. 'You need to be particularly careful or you can find yourself shackled, roped and on the way to the altar.'

Sue smiled. 'I don't think you would ever have that problem.'

He shrugged. 'Then there's Mark and Aria's wedding coming up shortly—the reason I'm home, anyway.' Mark was their brother. 'I've no idea what's planned but I'm sure there'll be plenty of partying involved.'

Sue's smile faded as she nodded, and tears came to her eyes.

Brett frowned down at her. 'Susie? What's wrong?'

'I've left Brendan.' Brendan was her husband of three years. 'I found out he was being unfaithful to me.'

Brett closed his eyes briefly. He could have said, *I told you so*, but he didn't. He put his arms around his sister instead.

'You were right about him.' Sue wept. 'I think all he was after was my money.'

'I guess we have to make our own mistakes.'

'Yes, but I feel so stupid. And—' she gulped back some tears '—I feel everyone must be laughing at me. Apparently it was no big secret. I was the last person to know,' she said tragically.

'It's often the way.'

'It may be, but it doesn't make it any easier.'

'Are you still in love with him?' Brett queried.

'No! Well, how could I be?'

Brett smiled absently.

'But one thing I do know,' Sue said with utter conviction. 'I refuse to go into a decline, I refuse to run away and hide and I refuse to be a laughing stock!'

'Susie—'

But his sister overrode him, with tears in her eyes still, but determination too. 'I'm patron of the Animal Shelter Society so I will be at the lunch. The ball is one of the festivities planned for the Winter Racing Carnival; I'm on the committee, so I'll be there too, and I'll make sure everyone knows who I am! But—' she sagged a little against him 'I—would dearly love some moral support.'

'I beg your pardon?' Mike Rafferty said to his boss, Brett Wyndham.

They were in Brett's apartment high above the Brisbane River and the elegant curves of the William Jolly Bridge. Sue, who'd insisted on picking him up from the airport, had just left.

'You heard,' Brett replied shortly.

'Well, I thought I did. You asked me to make a note of the fact that you were going to a charity lunch tomorrow and a masked fancy-dress ball on Friday night. I just couldn't believe my ears.'

'Don't make too big a thing of this, Mike,' Brett warned. 'I'm not in the mood.'

'Of course not. They could even be—quite enjoyable.'

Brett cast him a dark glance and got up to walk over

to the window with his familiar long-legged prowl. With his short, ruffled dark hair, blue shadows on his jaw, a kind of eagle intensity about his dark eyes, his cargo pants and black sweatshirt, his height and broad shoulders, he could have been anything.

What did come to mind was a trained-to-perfection daredevil member of a SWAT team.

In fact, Brett Wyndham was a vet and he specialized in saving endangered species, the more dangerous the better, such as the black rhino, elephants and tigers.

He dropped out of helicopters with tranquilizer guns, he parachuted into jungles—all in a day's work. He also managed the family fortunes that included some huge cattle-stations, and since he'd taken over the reins of the Wyndham empire he'd tripled that fortune so he was now a billionaire, although a very reclusive one. He did not give interviews but word of his work had filtered out and he'd captured the public's imagination.

As Brett's PA, it fell to Mike Rafferty to ensure his privacy here in Brisbane, amongst other duties at Haywire—one of the cattle stations in Far North Queensland the Wyndham dynasty called home—and at Palm Cove where they owned a resort.

'So will you be saying anything to the press?' he queried. 'There's bound to be some coverage of the lunch tomorrow, even if you'll be incognito at the ball.'

'No. I'm not saying anything to anyone although, according to my sister, my presence alone will invest the proceedings with quite some clout.' He grimaced.

'It probably will,' Mike agreed. 'And what will you be going to the masked ball as?'

'I have no idea. I'll leave that up to you—but

something discreet, Mike,' Brett growled. 'No monkey suit, no toga and laurel wreath, no Tarzan or *anything* like that.' He stopped and yawned. 'And now I'm going to bed.'

'Mum,' Holly said to her mother the next morning, 'I'm not sure about this outfit. Isn't the lunch supposed to be a fundraiser?' She glanced down at herself. She wore a fitted little black jacket with a low vee-neck over a very short black-and-white skirt. Black high-heeled sandals exposed newly painted pink toenails, matching her fingernails. She wore her mother's pearl choker and matching pendant earrings.

'It certainly is,' Sylvia replied. 'And a very exclusive one. The tickets cost a fortune, although of course they are tax deductible,' she assured her daughter. 'But you look stunning, darling!'

Holly grimaced and twirled in front of the mirror. They were in her bedroom in the family home, a lovely old house high on a hill in Balmoral. She still lived at home, or rather had moved back in after her father had died to keep her mother company. There were plenty of advantages to this arrangement that Holly was most appreciative of, which was why she humoured her mother now and then and attended these kinds of function.

Quite how she'd got roped into going to a charity lunch and a masked fancy-dress ball within a few days of each other she wasn't sure, but she knew it did give her mother a lot of pleasure to have her company. It also gave her a lot of pleasure to dress her daughter up to the nines.

Holly was quite tall and very slim, two things that

lent themselves to wearing clothes well, although when left to her own devices she favoured 'very casual'. She herself thought her looks were unexceptional, although she did have deep-blue eyes and a thick cloud of fair but hard-to-manage hair.

Today her hair was up in an elaborate chignon, and sprayed and pinned within in inch of its life to stay that way. Sylvia's hairdresser, who made house calls, had also done their nails.

Sylvia herself was resplendent in diamonds and a fuchsia linen suit.

Despite her mother's preoccupation with the social scene, Holly loved Sylvia and felt for her in her loneliness now she was a widow. But the most formative person in Holly's life had been her father, imbuing her not only with his love of the different but his love of writing.

Richard Harding, had he been born in another era, would have been a Dr Livingstone or Mr Stanley. He'd inherited considerable means and had loved nothing better than to travel, to explore out-of-the-way places and different cultures, and to write about them. The fact that he'd married someone almost the exact opposite had been something of a mystery to Holly, yet when they'd been together her parents had been happy.

But it was Holly who Richard had taken more and more on his expeditions. Amongst the results for Holly had been a well-rounded informal education alongside her formal one and fluency in French, plus some Spanish and a smattering of Swahili.

All of it had contributed towards Holly's present job. She was a travel reporter for an upmarket magazine but with a slight difference: hard-to-get-to places were her speciality. As a consequence, to bring to life her destinations, she'd used bad-tempered camels, stubborn donkeys, dangerous-looking vehicles driven by manic individuals and overcrowded ferries.

According to her editor, Glenn Shepherd, she might look as if a good puff of wind would blow her away but she had a hint of inner steel. She had to, to have coped with some of the situations she'd landed herself in.

She'd shrugged when he'd said this to her and had responded, 'Oh, I don't know. Sometimes looking and playing dumb works wonders.'

He'd grinned at her. 'What about the sheikh fellow who introduced you to all his wives with a view to you joining the clan? Or the Mexican bandit who wanted to marry you?'

'Ah, that required a bit of ingenuity. I actually had to steal his vehicle,' Holly had confessed. 'But I did have it returned to him. Glenn, I've been doing travel for a couple of years now—any chance of a change?'

'Thought you loved it?'

'I do, but I also want to spread my wings journalistically. I'd love to be given something I could *investigate* or someone I could get the definitive interview from.'

Glenn had sat forward. 'Holly, I'm not saying you're not capable of it, but you are only twenty-four; some kinds of—insight, I guess, take a bit longer than that to develop. It will come, but keep up the good work in the meantime. More and more people out there are getting to love your pieces. Also, re the definitive interview, we have a policy; any of our staff can try for one, so long as they pull it off ethically, and if it's good enough we'll publish it. But I must warn you, it has to be outstanding.'

'As in?'

'Mostly as in, well, surprise factor.' He'd shrugged. 'Brett Wyndham, for example.'

Holly had grimaced. 'That's like asking for the moon.'

Holly came back to the present and took one last look at herself. 'If you're sure,' she said to her mother, 'We're not terribly over-dressed?'

'We're not,' Sylvia said simply.

Holly saw that she was right when she took her place in the upmarket Milton restaurant that had been turned into a tropical greenhouse. She was amidst a noisy throng of very upmarket-looking guests. Almost without exception, the women were exquisitely groomed, expensively dressed and their jewellery flashed beneath the overhead lighting; many of them wore hats. Not only that, a lot of them seemed to know each other, so it was a convivial gathering helped along by the wine that started to flow. Recent cruises, skiing holidays and tropical islands featured in the snippets of conversation Holly heard around her, as well as the difficulties attached to finding really good housekeepers.

There were men present but they were rather outnumbered. One of them took his place beside Holly.

Goodness, gracious me! was Holly's first, startled reaction.

The man who sat down beside her was tall and beautifully proportioned; he was dark and satanic looking. He had a suppressed air of vitality combined with an arrogance that was repressed, but nevertheless you couldn't help but know it was there in the tilt of his head and the set of his mouth. All in all he made the little hairs on her arms stand up in a way that made her blink.

He was casually dressed in khaki trousers, a sports jacket and a navy-blue shirt. He looked out moodily over the assembled throng then concentrated on the first speaker of the day.

The patron of the shelter society introduced herself as Sue Murray. She was petite and dark, and clearly under some strain, as she stumbled a couple of times, then looked straight at the man beside Holly, drew a deep breath, and continued her speech smoothly. She gave a short résumé of the shelter society's activities and plans for the future, then she thanked everyone for coming. There was loud applause as she stepped down.

'Poor thing,' Sylvia whispered into Holly's ear. 'Her husband's been playing around. Darling, would you mind if I popped over to another table? I've just spied an old friend I haven't seen for ages. I'll be back when they start serving lunch.'

'Of course not,' Holly whispered back, and turned automatically to the man beside her as she unfolded her napkin. The seat on the other side of him was empty too, so they were like a little island in the throng. 'How do you do?'

'How do you do?' he replied coolly and studied all he could see of her, from her upswept hair, her pearls, the vee between her breasts exposed by her jacket and her slim waist. But it was worse than that. She got the distinct feeling he was viewing her without her clothes and with a view to assessing her potential as a partner in his bed.

She lowered her lashes swiftly as her blue eyes blazed at the sheer insolence of this unexpected appraisal, and at the inexplicable reaction it aroused in her. A wholly unexpected ripple of awareness touched her nerve ends.

Her lips parted on a stinging retort, but before she could frame it he smiled slightly, a lethally insolent twisting of his lips as if he was quite aware of his effect on her, and posed a question to her with an air of patent scepticism.

'Are you a great supporter of animal shelters?'

Holly looked taken aback for a moment but she recovered swiftly and said, 'No—not that I'm against them.' She shrugged. 'But that's not why I'm here.'

His eyes left her face briefly and she realized he was keeping tabs on the progress of Sue Murray as she moved from table to table introducing herself to everyone. When his gaze came back to her, he posed another question. 'Why *are* you here?'

'I came with my mother.'

A glint of amusement lit his dark eyes. 'That sounds as if it came from a list of excuses the Department of Transport publishes occasionally: "my mother told me to hurry up, that's why I was exceeding the speed limit".'

If she hadn't been so annoyed, if it hadn't been so apt, Holly would have seen the humour of this.

'Clever,' she said coldly. 'But I have to tell you, I'm already regretting it. And, for your further information, I don't approve of this kind of fund-raising.'

He lifted a lazy eyebrow. 'Strange, that. You look so very much the part.'

'What *part*?' she asked arctically.

He shrugged. 'The professional, serial socialite. The embodiment of conspicuous philanthropy in order to climb the social ladder.' He glanced at her left hand, which happened to be bare of rings. 'Maybe even in the market for a rich husband?' he added with soft but lethal irony.

Holly gasped, and gasped again, as his gaze flickered over her and came back to rest squarely on her décolletage; she had no doubt that he was mentally undressing her.

Then she clenched her teeth as it crossed her mind that she should have stuck to her guns. She should not be sitting there all dolled up to the nines, with her hair strangled up and starting to give her a headache, all to support a cause but giving off the wrong messages entirely. Obviously!

On the other hand, she thought swiftly, that did not give this man the right to insult her.

'If you'll forgive me for saying so,' she retorted, 'I think your manners are atrocious.'

'Oh. In what way?'

'How or why I'm here has nothing whatsoever to do with you and if you mentally undress me once more who knows what I might be prompted to do? I am,' she added, 'quite able to take care of myself, and I'm not wet behind the ears.'

'Fighting words,' he murmured. 'But there is this—'

'I know what you're going to say,' she broke in. 'It's

chemistry.' She looked at him scornfully. 'That is such an old, dead one! Even my Mexican bandit didn't use that one although, come to think of it, the sheikh did. Well, I think that's what he was saying.' She tipped her hand as if to say, 'you win some, you lose some'.

He blinked. 'Sounds as if you have an interesting life.'

'I do.'

'You're not making it all up?'

'No.' Holly folded her arms and waited.

'What?' he queried after a moment, with utterly false trepidation.

'I thought an apology might be appropriate.'

He said nothing, just gazed at her, and after a pensive moment on her part they were exchanging a long, telling look which came as quite a surprise to Holly. The luncheon and its environs receded and it was if there was only the two of them...

Whatever was happening for him, for Holly it became a drawing-in, not only visually but through her pores, of the essence of this man and the acknowledgement that his physical properties were extremely fine. He was not only tall, he was tanned, and he looked exceedingly fit, as if sitting at charity luncheons did not come naturally to him. His hands were long and well-shaped. His dark hair was crisp and short, and the lines and angles of his face were interesting but not easy to read.

In fact, she summarized to herself, there was something inherently dangerous but dynamically attractive about him that made you think of him having his hands on your body, his exciting, expert, mind-blowing way with you.

That's ridiculous, she told herself as a strange little thrill ran through her. *That's such a* girlish *fantasy!*

Nevertheless, it continued to do strange things to her.

It altered the rate of her breathing, for example. It caused a little pulse to beat rather wildly at the base of her throat so that her pearls jumped. To her amazement, it even caused her nipples to become sensitive and make the lace of her black bra feel almost intolerably scratchy.

Her lips parted, then she made a concerted attempt to gather her composure as his dark gaze raked her again, but he broke the spell.

He said very quietly, 'I don't know about the bandit or the sheikh, ma'am, but I can't help thinking chemistry is actually alive and well—between us.'

Holly came back to earth with a thud and rose to her feet. 'I'm leaving,' she said baldly.

He sat back and shrugged. 'Please don't on my account. I'll say no more. Anyway, what about your mother?' he queried with just a shadow of disbelief.

Holly looked around a little wildly. 'I'll take her with me. Yes!' And she strode away from the table.

'I'm sorry, I'm so sorry,' Holly said as she clutched the steering wheel and started to drive them home. Her mother still looked stunned. 'But he was—impossible, the man sitting next to me! Talk about making a pass!' she marvelled.

'Brett Wyndham made a pass at you?' Sylvia said in faint accents as she clutched the arm rest. 'Holly, slow down, darling!'

Holly did more, she stamped on the brakes then pulled off the road. 'Brett Wyndham,' she repeated incredulously. '*That* was Brett Wyndham?'

'Yes. Sue Murray's his sister. We can only assume that's why he's there. I told you, she's having husband troubles, and perhaps he's providing moral support or something like that. I've never seen him at such a function before, or any kind of function for that matter.'

Holly released the wheel and clutched her head, then she started shedding hairpins haphazardly into her lap. 'If only I'd known! But would I have done anything differently? He was exceedingly—he was— That's why he was watching her.'

'Who?'

'His sister. In between watching me,' Holly said bitterly. 'On the other hand, I could maybe have seen the funny side of it. I could have deflected him humorously and—who knows?'

'If I had the faintest idea what you were talking about I might be able to agree or disagree,' her mother said plaintively.

Holly turned to her then hugged her. 'I am sorry. On all counts. And don't mind me; it's just that an interview with Brett Wyndham could have been the real boost my career needs.'

CHAPTER TWO

A COUPLE of days later, Holly found she couldn't get out of the masked fancy-dress ball she'd agreed to attend with her mother, much as she would have loved to.

When she raised the matter, Sylvia pointed out that it would make the table numbers uneven, for one thing, and for another wasn't her costume inspired—especially for a girl called Holly?

'So, who are we going with?' Holly queried.

'Two married couples and a gentleman friend of mind, plus his son: a nice table of eight,' Sylvia said contentedly.

Holly had met the gentleman friend, a widower, but not the son. In answer to her query on that subject, she received the news that the son was only twenty-one but a very nice, mature boy. Holly digested this information with inward scepticism. 'Mature and twenty-one' in young men did not always go together, in her opinion, but then she consoled herself with the thought that her mother couldn't have any expectations of a twenty-one-year-old as in husband material for Holly, surely?

Still, she wasn't brimming with keenness to go—but she remembered how she'd probably embarrassed the life out of her mother a few days ago, and she decided to bite the bullet.

Unfortunately, the memory of the lunch brought Brett Wyndham back to mind and demonstrated to her that she didn't have an unequivocal stance on the memory. Yes, she'd been outraged at his approach at the time—who wouldn't have been? He'd accused her of being a serial socialite and a gold-digger.

Of course, there'd been an intrinsic undercurrent to that in his own fairly obvious distaste for the lunch and all it stood for. Why else would he challenge her motives for being there? But—another but—how did that fit in with his sister being the patron of the shelter society?

Ironic, however, was the fact that two things had chipped away at her absolute outrage, making it not quite so severe: the undoubted frisson he'd aroused in her being one. Put simply, it translated into the fact that he'd been the first man to excite her physically since, well, in quite a long time...

She looked into the distance and shivered before bringing herself back to the present and forcing herself to face the second factor that had slightly lessened her outrage. Had she mucked up a golden opportunity to get the interview that would have boosted her career?

Yes, she answered herself, well and truly mucked it up. But there was no way she would have done anything differently so she just had to live with it!

All the same, militant as she felt on the subject of Brett Wyndham on one hand, on the other she had an impulse, one that actually made her fingers itch—to look him up on the Internet.

She shook her head and fought it but it was a fight

she lost, and her fingers flew over the keys of her laptop, only to find that not a lot personal came to light. He was thirty-five, the oldest of three. There was a brother between him and his sister Sue, a brother who was getting married shortly. In fact, there was more about this brother Mark, his fiancée Aria and Sue Murray than there was about Brett Wyndham, so far as personal lives went.

She dug a bit further and established that the Wyndhams had been pioneers in the savannah country of Far North Queensland where they'd established their cattle stations. She learnt that Haywire, situated between Georgetown and Croydon, was the station they called home. And she learnt that the red-basalt soil in the area produced grass that cattle thrived upon—quite beside the point. Well, the treacherous little thought crept into her mind, not so much beside the point if she ever got to interview the man!

She also learnt that Brett Wyndham was a powerful figure in other ways. The empire was no longer based solely on pastoralism. He had mining interests in the area, marble from Chillagoe, zinc and transport companies. He employed a significant amount of people in these enterprises, and he was respected for his environmental views, as well as views on endangered species.

Then she turned up gold, from her point of view—a rather bitchy little article about one Natasha Hewson, who was described as extraordinarily beautiful and extremely talented. Apparently she ran an agency that specialized in organizing events and functions down to the last exquisite detail for the rich and famous. But, the article went on to say, if Natasha had hoped to be last in the long line of beautiful women Brett Wyndham had squired when they'd got engaged, her hopes had been dashed when they'd broken off the engagement recently...

Holly checked the date and saw that it was only nine months ago.

She sat back and tapped her teeth with the end of her pen. She had to admit that he'd got to her in a way that had reawakened her from a couple of years of mental and physical celibacy—but had she wanted to be reawakened? Not by a man who could have any woman he wanted, and had had a long line of them, she thought swiftly.

Mind you—she smiled a rueful smile—there was no hope of her getting an interview with him anyway, so it was best just to forget it all.

Brett Wyndham wondered how soon he'd be able to leave the ball. He'd come partnerless—well, he'd come with his sister. True to her word, she was looking stunning in a lavender crinoline, but otherwise apart from her tiny mask was quite recognizable as Sue Murray. Moreover she was putting a brave face on even if her heart was breaking and, whether it was his presence or not, no-one appeared to be making a laughing stock of her.

He watched her dance past—he'd left their table and was standing at the bar—and he found himself pondering the nature of love. Sue felt she shouldn't be able to love Brendan Murray now but was that all it took in matters of the heart? Dictating to yourself what you should or should not feel?

Which led him in turn to ponder his own love life. The nature of his life seemed to ensure that the women in it were only passing companions, but there had been no shortage of them. The problem was, he couldn't seem to drum up much enthusiasm for any of them.

Not only that, perhaps it was the inability of those partners to disguise their expectations that he was getting tired of, he reflected. Or the fact that none of them ever said 'no.' Well, one had quite recently, now he came to think of it. His lips twisted with amusement at the memory.

He shrugged and turned to watch the passing parade.

He'd come, courtesy of Mike Rafferty, as a masked Spanish aristocrat with a dark cropped jacket, dark, trousers, soft boots and white, frilled shirt, complete with scarlet cummerbund and black felt hat.

Dinner was over and the serious part of the evening under way—the serious dancing, that was. They were all there, strutting their stuff to the powerful beat of the music under the chandelier: the Cleopatras, the Marie Antoinettes, the belly dancers, the harem girls, the Lone Rangers, the Lawrences of Arabia, the three Elvises, a Joan of Arc and a Lady Godiva in a body stocking who looked as if she was regretting her choice of costume.

Some of them he recognized despite the masks and towering wigs. All of them, he reflected, bored him to tears.

He was just about to turn away when one girl he didn't recognize danced past in the arms of an eager pirate complete with eye patch, one gold earring and a stuffed macaw on his shoulder.

She was quite tall, very slim and dressed almost all in black. Something about her, probably her outfit, stirred something in his memory, but he couldn't pin it down.

'Who's she supposed to be?' he enquired of an elderly milkmaid standing beside him. He indicated the girl in black.

The milkmaid beamed. 'Isn't she perfect? So different. Of course, it's Holly Golightly—don't you remember? Audrey Hepburn in *Breakfast at Tiffany's*. That gorgeous black hat with the wide, downturned brim and the light, floaty hat-band; the earrings, the classic little black dress and gloves—even the alligator shoes. And to think of using her sunglasses as a mask!'

'Ah. Yes, she is rather perfect. You wouldn't happen to know who she is in real life?'

The milkmaid had no idea and Brett watched Holly Golightly dance past again.

She looked cool and detached, even slightly superior, but that could be because the pirate was having trouble containing his enthusiasm for her.

In fact, as he watched she detached herself from her partner as he attempted to maul her, swung on her heel and swept away towards the ballroom balcony with a hand to her hat.

The pirate looked so crestfallen, Brett could only assume he was either very young or very drunk.

Without giving it much thought, he took a fresh glass of champagne off the bar and followed the girl onto the balcony.

She was leaning against the balustrade, breathing deeply.

'Maybe this'll help to remove the taste of the pirate?' he suggested and offered the champagne to her.

Holly straightened and wondered if she was imagining things. She'd been rather darkly contemplating the fact that she'd been right about very young men such as the pirate who was the son of her mother's friend; he hadn't been able to keep his hands off her!

But could this tall, arrogant-looking Spaniard be who she thought he was? Could you ever forget Brett Wyndham's voice, or his athletic build? Or the pass he'd made at her? More importantly, did she want to be recognized? As a serious journalist, perhaps, but like this? As a *serial socialite*…?

In a lightning decision that she did not want to be recognized, she lowered her voice a notch and assumed a French accent. '*Merci*. I was of a mind to punch his parrot.'

Brett laughed then narrowed his eyes behind the mask. 'You sound as if you've just stepped out of France.'

'Not France, Tahiti.' It wasn't exactly a lie. She'd returned from her last travel assignment, Papeete, a bare week ago.

'So, a Tahitian Holly Golightly?'

'You may say so.' Holly sipped some champagne. 'What have we with you? An Aussie *señor*?'

He looked down at his attire. 'You could say so. Are you into horses, Miss Golightly?'

Holly gazed at him blankly.

'It *is* the kick-off to the Winter Racing Carnival, this ball,' he elaborated.

'Of course! But no, you could say not, although I

have done some riding in my time. Generally, though, on inferior beasts such as asses and camels.'

Brett's eyebrows shot up. 'Camels? In Tahiti? How come?'

'Not, naturally, Tahiti,' Holly denied regally. 'But I have a fondness for some out-of-the-way places you cannot get to by *other* means.' She gave the word "other" a tremendous French twist.

'So do I,' he murmured and frowned again as his masked gaze roamed over her.

Holly waited with some trepidation. Would he recognize her beneath the Holly Golightly outfit, the wide, downturned hat-brim and the French accent? She'd recognized him almost immediately, but that deep, mesmerizing voice would be hard to disguise. For that matter, so were those wide shoulders and lean hips.

Then it occurred to her that she was once again being summed up in that inimitable way of his.

The slender line of her neck, the outline of her figure beneath the little black dress, the smooth skin of her arms above her gloves, her trim ankles—they all received his critical assessment. And they all traitorously reacted accordingly, which was to say he might as well have been running his hands over her body.

'Actually,' she said airily—not a true reflection of her emotions as she was battling to stay cool and striving to take a humorous view of proceedings, 'You make a *trés* arrogant Spaniard.'

'I do?'

'*Oui.* Summing up perfectly strange women with a view to ownership is what I would call arrogant. Could it be that there is little difference between you and the pirate with the parrot, *monsieur*?'

'Ownership?' he queried.

'Of their bodies,' she explained. 'Tell me this was not so a moment ago?' She tilted her chin at him.

He pushed his hands into his pockets and shrugged. 'It's a failing most men succumb to. But unlike the pirate I would never attempt to maul you, Miss Golightly.'

He paused and allowed his dark, masked gaze to travel over her again. 'On the contrary, I would make your skin feel like warm silk and I would celebrate your lovely, slim body in a way that would be entirely satisfactory—for both of us.'

Holly stifled a tremor of utmost sensuousness that threatened to engulf her down the length of her body—at least stifled the outward appearance of it, by the narrowest of margins.

All the same, she went hot and cold and had to wonder how he did it. How did he engender a state of mind that could even have her wondering what it would be like to be Brett Wyndham's woman. How dared he?

Despite his arrogance, did that dark, swashbuckling presence do it to most women he came in contact with?

Her mind swooped on this point. Would it be a relief to think she was just one of a crowd when it came to Brett Wyndham? Or would it make it worse?

She came to her senses abruptly to find him studying her intently now and rather differently. 'You have a problem, *señor*?'

'No. Well, I just have the feeling I've met you before, Miss Golightly.'

Holly took the bit between her teeth and contrived a quizzical little smile. 'Many men have that problem. It is a very—how do you say it?—unoriginal approach.'

'You feel I'm making a pass at you?' he enquired lazily.

'I am convinced of it.' She presented him her half empty champagne glass. 'Thus, I will return to my party. *Au revoir.*'

But he said, 'Were you riding a camel when your sheikh propositioned you?'

Holly, in the act of sweeping inside, stopped as if shot.

'Or a donkey, when the Mexican approached you?' he added softly.

'You knew!' she accused.

'The accent and the outfit threw me for a while, but I'm not blind or deaf. Is it *all* made up? And, if so, why?'

Holly walked back to him and retrieved her champagne. 'I've got the feeling I might need this,' she said darkly and took a good sip. 'No, well, Tahiti was true—a bit. I've just come back so it seemed like a good idea to—' she gestured airily '—to...' But she couldn't think of a suitable way to cloak it.

'Help pull the wool over my eyes?' he suggested.

Holly choked slightly on a second sip of champagne but made a swift recovery. 'Why would I want to be recognized by you? All you ever do is query my motives, accuse me of appalling posturing and make passes at me!'

'You have to admit it all sounds highly unlikely,' he drawled. 'Are you here with your mother?'

Holly opened her mouth but closed it and stamped her foot. 'Don't you dare make fun of my mother! She—'

A flash of pale colour registered in her peripheral vision and she turned to see her mother coming out onto the balcony. Her mother was dressed as Eliza Doolittle at the races, complete with huge hat and parasol. 'We might as well both reprise Audrey Hepburn roles,' Sylvia had said upon presenting the idea to her daughter.

'Mum!' Holly said. 'What—'

But her mother interrupted her. 'There you are, darling! And I see you've met Mr Wyndham.' Sylvia turned to Brett. 'How do you do? I'm Sylvia Harding, Holly's mother—yes, her real name is Holly, that's why we thought of Holly Golightly!' Sylvia paused and took a very deep breath. 'But I feel sure there was some misunderstanding at the shelter lunch, and she didn't have the opportunity to tell you that she's a journalist and would love to interview you.'

There was dead silence on the balcony but Sylvia went on, apparently oblivious to the undercurrents. 'I also know she'd do a great job; she's not her father's daughter for nothing. He was Richard Harding, incidentally—perhaps you've heard of him?'

'Yes, I have. How do you do, Mrs Harding?' Brett said courteously.

'I'm fine, thank you. You may be wondering how I recognized you, but as soon as I saw you with Sue it clicked. She's such a lovely person, your sister. Well, I'll leave you two together.' She hesitated then walked back inside.

Holly let out a long breath then finished the champagne with a gulp. 'Don't say a word,' she warned Brett, once again presented him with her glass. 'I did not arrange that, and anyway I don't believe leopards change their spots, so I have no desire to interview you.'

'Leopards?' he queried gravely but she could see he was struggling not to laugh. 'On top of camels, asses, Mexicans and sheikhs?'

'Yes,' she said through her teeth. 'I believe they can be cunning, highly dangerous and thoroughly bad-minded into the bargain. If anyone should know that, you should.'

'I do,' he agreed. 'Uh—where is this analogy leading?'

'I have no faith in you *not* making any more passes at me, that's where.'

'I'd be demolished,' he said. 'But I'm pretty sure it isn't all one-sided.'

Another deadly little silence enveloped the balcony.

Holly opened her mouth but had to close it as no inspiration came to her. In all honesty, how could she deny the claim? On the other hand, every bit of good sense she possessed told her that to acknowledge it would be foolhardy in the extreme.

So, in the end, she did the only thing available to her: she swung on her heel and walked away from him.

'How was the ball?' Mike Rafferty enquired of his boss the next morning.

Brett lay back in his chair and appeared to meditate for a moment. 'Interesting,' he said at last.

'Well, that's got to be better than you expected,' Mike

replied and placed some papers on the desk. 'The lead up to the wedding,' he said simply.

Brett grimaced and pulled the details of Mark's pre-wedding festivities towards him. 'I just hope it's not a three-ring circus. Oh hell, another ball!'

'But this one's just a normal ball,' Mike pointed out.

Brett did not look mollified as he read on. 'A soirée, a beach barbecue, a trip to the reef—da-da, da-da.' Brett waved a hand. 'All right. I presume they've got someone in to organize it all properly?'

Mike hesitated and then coughed nervously.

Brett stared narrowly at him. 'Who? Not…? Not Natasha?'

'I'm afraid so.'

Brett swore.

'She is the best—at this kind of thing,' Mike offered.

'But I believe they had someone else to start with who made a real hash of things, so they called on Ms Hewson and she saved the day, apparently. She and Aria are friends,' he added.

'I see.' Brett drummed his fingers on the desk then looked to have made a decision. 'Mike, find out all you can about a girl called Holly Harding. She's Richard Harding's daughter—the well-known writer—and I believe she's a journalist herself. Do it now, please.'

Mike stared at his boss for a moment as he tried to tie this in with Mark Wyndham's wedding.

'What?' Brett queried.

'Nothing,' Mike said hastily. 'Just going.'

* * *

On Monday afternoon Glenn Shepherd called Holly into his office, and hugged her. 'You're such a clever girl,' he enthused. 'I might have known I was laying down the gauntlet to you when I mentioned his name, but how on earth did you pull it off? And why keep it such a secret?' He released her and went back behind his desk.

Holly, looking dazed and confused, sank into a chair across the desk. 'What are you talking about, Glenn?'

'Getting an interview with Brett Wyndham, of course. What else?'

Holly stared at him, transfixed, then she cleared her throat. 'I—wasn't aware that I had.'

Glenn gestured. 'Well, there are a few details he wants to sort out with you before he gives his final consent, so I made an appointment for you with him for five-thirty this afternoon.' He passed a slip of paper to her over the desk. 'If you've got anything on, cancel it. This could be your big break, Holly, and it won't do *us* any harm, either. Uh— there may be some travel involved.'

'Travel?'

'I'll let him tell you about it but of course we'd foot the bill where necessary.'

'Glenn…' Holly said.

But he interrupted her and stood up. 'Go get it, girl! And now I've got to run.'

At five-twenty that afternoon, Holly glanced at the piece of paper Glenn had given her and frowned. Southbank was a lovely precinct on the Brisbane river, opposite the tall towers of the CBD. It was made up of restaurants, a swimming lagoon and gardens set around the civic theatre and the art gallery. It was not exactly where she would have expected to conduct a business meeting with Brett Wyndham.

Then again, that was the last thing she'd expected to be doing this Monday afternoon, or any afternoon, so why quibble at the venue?

She parked her car, gathered her tote bag and for a moment wished she was dressed more formally. But that would have involved rushing home to change, and anyway, she didn't want him to think she'd gone to any trouble with her appearance on his behalf, did she?

No, she answered herself, *so why even think it*?

Because she might have felt more mature, or something like that, if she wasn't dressed as she usually was for work.

She looked down at her jeans, the pink singlet top she wore under a rather beloved jacket and her brown, short boots. This was the kind of clothes she felt comfortable in when she was traveling, as well as at work.

As for her hair, she'd left it to its own devices that morning and the result was a mass of untamed curls.

There could be little or no resemblance to the girl at the shelter lunch or Holly Golightly, she reasoned, which should be a good thing.

But, she also reasoned, really her clothes and hair were nothing compared to her absolute shock and disbelief at this move Brett Wyndham had made. What was behind it?

She shook her head, locked her car and went to find him.

It took a moment for Brett Wyndham to recognize Holly Harding. He noticed a tall girl in denims and a pink singlet with a leather tote hanging from her shoulder, wandering down the path from the car park. He noted that she looked completely natural, with no make-up, from her wild, fair curls to her boots, as well as looking young and leggy. Then it suddenly dawned on him who she was.

He saw her look around the restaurant terrace—their designated meeting place—and he raised a hand. He thought she hesitated briefly, then she came over.

He stood up and offered her a chair. 'Good day,' he murmured as they both sat down. 'Yet another incarnation of Holly Harding?'

'This is the real me,' Holly said dryly, and studied him briefly. He wore a black sweater, olive-canvas trousers and thick-soled black-leather shoes. His short, dark hair was ruffled; while he might have made a perfect Spanish aristocrat a few nights ago, today he looked tough, inscrutable and potentially dangerous.

'Would you like a drink?'

'Just a soft one, thank you. I never mix business with pleasure,' Holly replied.

He ordered a fruit juice for her and beer for himself, ignoring her rather pointed comment. 'If this is the real you,' he said, 'What makes you moonlight as a social butterfly?'

'My mother. Please don't make any smart remarks,' she warned, and explained the situation to him in a nutshell.

'Very commendable.' He paused as his beer was served, along with a silver dish of olives and a fruit-laden glass of juice topped by a pink parasol for Holly.

'But a bit trying at times,' Holly revealed, allowing

her hostilities to lapse for a moment. 'I think I would have preferred standing on a street corner with a collection box rather than that lunch, but perhaps I shouldn't say that in deference to your sister.' She eyed him curiously then stared out over the gardens towards the river. The sun was setting and the quality of light was warm and vivid.

He watched her thoughtfully. 'Each to his own method, but we seem to have a few things in common.'

'Not really,' Holly disagreed, going back to clearly hostile, and turned to look straight at him. 'Why have you done this?'

He countered with a question, 'Did you or did you not tell your mother you would love to interview me?'

'I...' Holly paused. 'I told her an interview with you could provide the boost my career needed. I told her that I'd had no idea who you were, but if there'd ever been any chance of an interview I'd blown it.'

'Only, being a mother, she didn't believe you,' he said wryly. 'Well, it *is* on, on certain conditions.'

'So I hear.' She glanced at him coolly, as if she was highly suspicious of his conditions—which she was. 'What are they?'

'I'm a bit pressed for time. I need to be in Cairns—Palm Cove, precisely. I have an important meeting. And I need to be out at Haywire the following day for a few days. It's the only free time I have before my brother gets married, and anyway—' he looked at her over the rim of his glass '—it will set the scene for you.'

'You—want me to come to Palm Cove and then on to this Haywire place with you?' she queried a little jaggedly.

He nodded. 'Not only am I pressed for time, but logistically it makes sense. The best way to get you to Haywire is for you to fly out there with me from Cairns.'

'Do I,' Holly gestured, 'actually have to see this Haywire place?'

'Yes.'

'Why?'

He sat back and shoved his hands into his pockets with a slight frown. 'That doesn't sound like a dedicated journalist. Why wouldn't you want to see it?'

'Mr Wyndham,' she said carefully, 'You have not only accused me of being a serial socialite and a gold-digger, you've mentally undressed me often enough to make me *seriously* wary of being stuck somewhere out beyond the black stump with you!'

Like lightning, a crooked grin creased his face which didn't impress Holly at all.

'I apologize,' he said then. 'I was—' he paused to consider '—not in a very good mood—not at the lunch, anyway. However, you'd be quite safe at Haywire. There's staff up there, and I'm not in the habit of forcing myself on unwilling women.'

Holly chewed her lip then said finally, 'What are the other conditions?'

'I mainly want to talk about the work I do—so nothing personal, unless it's ancient history. And I want to vet it before it gets published.'

Holly blinked several times, then she said frustratedly, 'Why me?'

He shrugged. 'Why not? Not only are you a journalist, but you're interesting.' He looked amused. 'I've never been walked-out on before, as you did at the lunch. I've never been told I was making a pass in a French accent. And I've *never* been accused of being as bad-minded as a leopard.'

Holly realized she'd been staring at him open-mouthed. She shut it hastily and watched him twirl his beer bottle in his long fingers before pouring the last of it into his glass.

'But what really decided me,' he continued, 'was your mother.'

'My mother?' Holly repeated in dazed tones. 'How come?'

'I thought what she did was quite brave. Maybe it's mistaken maternal faith—we'll see, I guess—but I liked her for it.'

Holly was seized by strong emotion and had to turn away to hide it as her eyes blazed. If it killed her, she would dearly love to prove to Brett Wyndham that her mother's faith in her was not *mistakenly maternal*, even if it meant spending some days with him at Palm Cove and beyond the black stump…

After all, there was bound to be staff at the station, and Palm Cove was highly civilized, wasn't it? It was not as if she'd be stranded in some jungle with him. It would actually be quite difficult to be stalked by him up there, as predator and prey, and she was no silly girl to be seduced by palm trees and mango daiquiris.

Was that all there was to it, however? Was simply to be in his company seductive? Was he just that kind of man? She couldn't deny he'd had a powerful effect on her a couple of times—without even trying too hard, she thought a little bitterly. But surely that was in *her* power to control? Well, if not control, ignore.

After all, was she not getting gold in return for a little self-discipline?

She opened her mouth, looked frustrated and said, 'You never give interviews. So I'm having a little difficulty with that.'

'I'm branching out in a new direction that I was going to publicize anyway. I've read some of your pieces, you have your father's touch and I thought you could do justice to it.'

Holly's lips parted and he could see the quickening of interest drowning the doubt and suspicion in her eyes. 'Am I allowed to know what it is?'

He shook his head. 'Not yet. But it's the very good reason for you to see Haywire.'

Holly looked unamused. 'I find you extremely— annoying at times,' she told him.

Brett Wyndham's lips twisted; he wondered what she'd say if he told her how annoyed he'd been when they'd first met. He'd been annoyed at the lunch; he'd arrived annoyed, then got further annoyed at finding himself feeling a niggle of attraction towards the kind of girl he'd castigated to himself so thoroughly. When she'd walked out, the niggle had become tinged with a grudging kind of admiration—that had also annoyed him.

Then her Holly Golightly hauteur had claimed his attention, and on discovering it was the same girl his annoyance had turned to intrigue. He was still intrigued by this version of Holly Harding—even more intrigued because he was quite sure he'd stirred some response in her...

Still, he reflected, these were improbable lengths to go to over a smattering of intrigue to do with a woman, particularly for him. But he had liked her fresh, slightly zany style in the pieces he'd read, he reminded himself, and he had even considered the possibility of offering her some publicity work for his new venture.

'So?' He lifted an eyebrow at her.

Holly meditated for a moment then replied quite candidly. 'I'd love to say no, because you've pressed a few wrong buttons with me, Mr Wyndham. But—' she flipped her hand '—you've also pressed a few right ones. My mother was an inspired one, in more ways than one.' She cast him a strange little look from beneath her lashes. 'Then there's my editor. How I would explain to him I've knocked back this opportunity, I can't even begin to think.'

She paused to take several breaths.

'There's more?' he queried with some irony.

'A bit more. You've got to be interesting—you've certainly captured the public's imagination—so, on a purely professional level, I can't turn it down.'

'Am I expected to be flattered?'

Holly searched his eyes and could just detect the wicked amusement in their dark depths. 'Yes,' she said baldly. 'I'm usually no pushover.'

'OK, take it as read that I'm flattered.' He stopped, flagged a passing waiter and ordered a bottle of champagne.

'Oh. No!' Holly protested. 'I didn't mean...'

'You don't think we should celebrate?' He looked

offended. 'I do. It's not every day I score a coup like this. Besides, I thought you liked champagne.'

'You're making fun of me,' she accused.

'Yes,' he agreed. 'Well, yes and no. You can be quite an impressive twenty-four-year-old. Thanks,' he said to the waiter who delivered the champagne and carefully poured two glasses.

He handed one to Holly and held up his own. 'Cheers!'

Holly reluctantly raised her glass to his. 'Cheers,' she echoed. 'But I'm only having one glass. On top of everything else, I'm driving.'

'That's fine,' he said idly.

'Isn't that a waste of champagne? Or are you going to drink it all?'

'No. I'm meeting someone else here shortly. She also likes champagne.'

Holly took a hurried gulp. 'Well, the sooner I get going the better.'

'No need to rush; she's my sister.'

Holly looked embarrassed. 'Oh. I thought...' She tailed off.

'You thought she was a girlfriend?'

'Yes. Sorry. Not that it matters to me one way or the other.'

'Naturally not,' he murmured.

She eyed him over her glass. 'You know, I can't quite make you out.'

He allowed his dark gaze to drift over her in a way that caused her skin to shiver of its own accord. She'd been inwardly congratulating herself on *not* having this happen to her during this encounter—an involuntary physical response to this man—but now it had.

'The same goes for me,' he said quietly. 'Can't quite make you out.'

Holly made an effort to rescue herself, to stop the flow of messages bombarding her senses. How could it happen like this? she wondered a little wildly. Out of the blue across a little glass-topped table on a terrace in the fading light of day.

But her rather tortured reflections were broken by a canine yelp, a squeal then howls of pain as, limping badly, a dog skittered across the terrace and disappeared into the shrubbery.

CHAPTER THREE

HOLLY jumped to her feet but Brett Wyndham was even quicker.

He plunged into the shrubbery, issuing a terse warning to her over his shoulder to be careful because the dog, in its pain, could bite.

The next few minutes were chaotic as Brett captured then subdued the terrified dog, a black-and-white border collie. How, Holly had no idea, but he did, and a lot of people milled around. None of them was its owner, or had any idea where it had come from, other than it must have got loose from somewhere and possibly got run over as it had crossed the road.

'OK.' Brett pulled his phone out and tossed it to Holly. 'Find the nearest vet surgery.' He pulled out his car keys and tossed them to her. 'And drive my car down here as close as you can get. It's the silver BMW.'

Holly grabbed her tote and did so, and ended up driving the four-wheel-drive so Brett could attend to the dog on the way to the surgery. He was staunching a deep cut on its leg with his handkerchief and she heard him say, 'You're going to be all right, mate.'

She found the surgery with the aid of the GPS and

helped carry the dog in. 'Is he really going to be all right?' she asked fearfully as they handed it over.

'I reckon so.' He scanned her briefly then looked more closely. 'You better sit down; you look a bit pale. I'm going in for a few minutes.' He turned to the receptionist, who was hovering. 'Could you get her a glass of water?'

'Of course. Sit down, ma'am.'

Holly was only too glad to do so. A mobile phone with an unfamiliar ring sounded in her tote. She blinked, remembered it must be Brett's phone and after a moment's hesitation answered it.

'Brett Wyndham's phone.'

'Where is he and who are you?' an irate female voice said down the line.

Holly explained and added, 'Can I give him a message?'

'Oh.' The voice sounded mollified. 'Yes, if you wouldn't mind. It's his sister, Sue. I'm waiting for him at Southbank, but I'm going out to dinner so I won't wait any longer. Could you tell him I'll catch up with him tomorrow?'

Ten minutes later Brett reappeared and held his hand out to Holly. 'Let's go. He's got a broken leg, as well as the cut, but he'll be fine. He's in good hands, and he's got a microchip so they'll be able to track down his owner.'

'Thank heavens.' She got to her feet.

'How are you?' he queried.

'OK.'

He studied her narrowly. 'You don't altogether look it.'

'I...I once lost a dog in an accident. He was also a border collie. I called him Oliver, because as a puppy he was always looking for more food. He was run over, but he died. It just took me back a bit.'

Brett released her hand and put an arm around her shoulder. He didn't say anything, but Holly discovered herself to be comforted. Comforted and then something else—acutely conscious of Brett Wyndham.

She breathed in his essence—pure man—and she felt the long, strong lines of his body. She was reminded of how quick and light on his feet he'd been, how he'd used the power of his personality and expertise to calm the dog—but above all how he'd impressed her on a mental level, and now on a physical one.

'Better?' he queried.

'Yes, thanks.'

They stepped out onto the pavement, but he stopped. It was almost dark. 'My sister,' he said with a grimace and reached for his phone, but it wasn't there.

Holly retrieved it from her bag and gave him the message.

'OK.' He steered her towards his car.

'If you drop me off at the parking lot...' Holly began.

He shook his head. 'You still look as if you could do with a drink.'

'No. Thanks, but no. Anyway, we left the restaurant without paying!'

He shrugged and opened the car door. 'They know me. In you get—and don't argue, Holly Golightly.'

Holly had no choice but to do as she was told, although she did say, '*My* car?'

'Mike will collect it.' He fired the engine.

'Who's Mike?'

'The miracle worker in my life.' He swung out into the traffic. 'The PA *par excellence*.'

Not much later, Holly was sitting on a mocha-colored leather settee in what was obviously a den. The walls were *café au lait*, priceless-looking scatter rugs dotted the parquet floor and wooden louvres framed the view of a dark sky but a tinsel-town view of the city lights.

Brett had poured her a brandy then she'd washed her face and hands and handed her car keys over to his PA. Brett had gone to take a shower.

She'd only taken a couple of sips but she was thinking deeply when he strolled back into the room. He'd changed into jeans and a shirt; his hair was towelled dry and spiky.

'Will you stay for dinner?' he queried as he poured his own brandy.

'No thank you,' Holly said automatically. 'You know, it's just struck me—this could look strange.'

'What could?' He sat down opposite her.

'Me flitting around with you.'

'In what respect?'

She glanced at him then looked away a little awkwardly. 'People might wonder if I've joined the long list of, well, perhaps not beautiful—I mean *they* were all probably stunning—but the long list of women you've squired around.'

'What long list is that?' he enquired in a deadpan kind of way that alerted her to the fact he was secretly laughing at her.

Holly went slightly pink but said airily, 'Just something I read somewhere. But, believe me, I have no ambition to do that. Unless...' she stopped, struck by a thought, and relaxed a bit. 'I'm not stunning enough or upmarket-looking enough to qualify? Don't answer that,' she said with a lightning smile. 'I'm just thinking aloud.' She sobered and contemplated her drink with a frown.

Does she have no idea of how unusually attractive she is? Brett Wyndham found himself wondering. *Maybe not*, he conceded. She certainly didn't appear to expect him to counter her claim that she wasn't stunning enough to qualify as someone he would "squire around".

On the other hand, she'd had to fight off a bandit and a sheikh, if she was to be believed, so...

He shrugged. 'I never bother with what people think.'

'You may be in a position not to bother—your reputation is already set,' she retorted. 'Mine is not.' Then she took a very deep breath. 'Please tell me why you're doing this.'

He rolled his glass in his hands then looked directly into her eyes. 'I'm intrigued. I can't believe you're not.' He paused. 'And I guess that's brought out the hunter instinct in me. At the same time, I *don't* ever force myself on unwilling women, if that's what's worrying you.'

Holly looked away. She paused and pressed her palms together tightly. 'And if I told you I don't have any interest in... Well, the thing is, I got my fingers pretty badly burnt once due to "chemistry". It's—it hasn't left me yet. I don't know if it ever will.'

He narrowed his eyes. 'Not the bandit or the sheikh, I gather?'

Holly waved her hand. 'Oh, no,' she said dismissively.

'I think you better tell me.'

She glanced at him from under her lashes, then smiled briefly. 'I don't think I should. It's supposed to be the other way round—you telling me stuff. And *you* have no intention of going into your private life.' She looked at him with some irony.

A silence lingered between them.

'So, should we just leave it there?' she suggested at last.

He stared at her pensively. 'Don't you want the interview now?'

'I thought you might have changed your mind.'

His lips twisted. 'Because I got my wrist slapped metaphorically? No, I haven't changed my mind.'

'But you won't—I mean—bring this up again?' she queried, her eyes dark and serious.

'Tell you what,' he drawled. '*I* won't say a word on the subject.'

Holly frowned. 'That sounds as if there's a trap there somewhere.'

'Sorry, it's the best I can come up with. So, are we on or off?'

She hesitated then put down her glass, stood up and walked over to the louvres that framed the city view. She was in two minds, she realized. She sensed an element of danger between her and Brett Wyndham, but she had to admit he'd been honest, whereas she hadn't—not entirely, anyway.

On the other hand, her career was vitally important to her. It had been her mainstay through some dark days.

She turned back to him. 'On. My journalistic instincts seem to have won the day,' she said ruefully. 'Can I go home now?'

'Of course.' He stood up, called for Mike Rafferty, and when he came asked him if he'd found Holly's car.

'Sure did,' Mike replied, and handed Holly the keys. 'It's parked downstairs, Miss Harding.'

'Thank you,' She hesitated then turned back to Brett Wyndham. 'Well, goodnight.'

'Goodnight, Holly,' he said casually, and turned away.

After he'd dined alone, Brett took his coffee to his study, where he intended to work on his next trip to Africa, only to find himself unable to concentrate.

The fact that it was a girl coming between him and his plans was unusual.

He swirled his coffee and lay back in his chair, Well, a change of direction in his life was on the cards; whilst he knew it was one he needed to make, would he ever be able to resist the call of the wild? Was that why he was unsettled?

It was a juggling act holding the reins of all the Wyndham enterprises based here and being away so frequently. Also, there was something niggling at him that he couldn't quite put his finger on, but he suspected it was the need to establish some roots.

In the meantime—in the short term, more accurately—a girl had come to his attention. A girl he wasn't at all sure about.

A girl who continued to hold him at arm's length, now with the claim that she'd had her fingers burnt due to "chemistry". How true was that? he wondered.

Could it all be part of a plan to hold his interest? He'd come across many a plan to hold his interest, he reflected dryly.

None of that changed the fact that she was attractive in a different kind of way—when did it ever? Good skin, beautiful eyes, clean, very slim lines; at times, sparkling intelligence and a cutting way with her repartee...

He smiled suddenly as he thought of her 'Holly Golightly from Tahiti' act.

He finished his coffee and contemplated another possibility. It was so long since any woman had said no to him he couldn't help but be intrigued. Especially as he could have sworn there'd been that edgy, sensual pull between them almost from the moment they'd first crossed swords.

Why, though, he wondered, had he gone to the lengths of dangling an interview before her?

Because she was likeable, kissable, different?

He drummed his fingers on the desk suddenly; or did he have in mind using her to deflect his ex-fiancée?

'I'm off to Cairns—well, Palm Cove—then the bush for a few days tomorrow,' Holly said to her mother that evening over a late dinner. She pushed away the remains of a tasty chicken casserole. 'You're not going to believe this, but I got the Brett Wyndham interview after all.'

Sylvia uttered a little cry of delight. 'Holly! That's

marvellous. I wasn't sure I did the right thing. I know you tried to gloss over it, but I wasn't sure whether you really approved.' Sylvia paused and frowned. 'But why do you have to go to Cairns?'

Holly made the swift decision to gloss over that bit and murmured something about Brett being short of time.

Sylvia mulled over this for a moment, then she said, 'He's very good-looking, isn't he? I mean he has a real presence, doesn't he?'

'I guess he does.'

'Holly,' Sylvia began, 'I know that awful thing that happened to you is not going to be easy to get over. Actually, you've been simply marvellous with the way—'

'Mum, don't,' Holly interrupted quietly.

'But there has to be the right man for you out there, darling,' Sylvia said passionately.

'There probably is, but it's not Brett Wyndham.'

'How can you be so sure?'

Holly moved the salt cellar to a different spot and sighed. 'It's just a feeling I have, Mum. For one thing, he's a billionaire, so he could have anyone and there's nothing so special about me. And, for me, I suppose it started with the way he behaved that day of the lunch. Then I read that he'd broken off his engagement to a girl who would have thought she was the last in a *long* line of women he'd escorted. And it seems,' she said bitterly, 'He's a master at getting his own way.'

'In view of all that,' Sylvia replied a shade tartly, 'I'm surprised you're going to Palm Cove and the bush.'

Holly shrugged. 'I once made the decision I wouldn't

be a victim, and what really helped me was my career.
I can't knock back this opportunity to further it.'

Glenn Shepherd said to Holly the next morning, 'So
it's all set up?'

'Yes. But there's no personal side to it, Glenn, other
than "ancient history"—I guess that means how he grew
up—and he wants to have final say. It's his work he
wants to talk about, and some new project.'

'Even that's a scoop. So, you're off to Palm Cove and
points west?'

Holly nodded then looked questioningly at her editor.
'How did you know that? I mean, so soon?'

'His PA has just been on the phone. They offered to
pay for your flights; I knocked that back, but they will
provide accommodation in Palm Cove—they own the
resort, after all.'

Holly grimaced. 'I'd rather stay in a mud hut.'

'Holly, is there anything you're not telling me?'
Glenn stared at her interrogatively.

'What do you mean?'

'I don't know.'

'No,' Holly replied. '*No.*'

'Enjoy yourself, then.'

Cairns, in Far North Queensland, was always a pleasure
to visit, Holly reflected as she landed on a commercial
flight and took the courtesy bus out of town to Palm
Cove. With its mountainous backdrop, its beaches, its
lush flora, bougainvillea, hibiscus in many colours,
yellow allamanda everywhere and its warm, humid air,
you got a delightful sense of the tropics.

It was also a touristy place—it was a stepping-off point for all the marvels of the Great Barrier Reef—but it wasn't brash. It was relaxed, yet still retained its solid country-town air.

Palm Cove, half an hour's drive north of Cairns, was exclusive.

Lovely resorts lined the road opposite the beach and there was a cosmopolitan air with open-air cafés and marvellous old melaleucas, or paper-bark trees, growing out of the pavements. There were upmarket restaurants and boutiques that would have made her mother's mouth water. The beach itself was a delight. Lined with cotton-woods, casuarinas and palms, it curved around a bay and overlooked Double Island and a smaller island she didn't know the name of. On a hot, still, autumn day, the water looked placid and immensely inviting. Whilst summer in the region might be a trial, autumn and winter—if you could call them that in the far north—were lovely.

The resort owned by the Wyndhams was built on colonial lines. It was spacious and cool and was right on the beach.

Holly unpacked her luggage in a pleasant room. It didn't take her long; she was used to travelling light and had evolved a simple wardrobe that nevertheless saw her through most eventualities. She'd resisted her mother's attempts to add to it.

She was contemplating going for a walk when she got a phone message: Mr Wyndham presented his compliments to Ms Harding; he had some time free and would like to see her in his suite in half an hour.

Ms Harding hesitated for a moment then agreed.

As she put the phone down, she felt a little trill of

annoyance at this high-handed invitation but immediately took herself to task. This was business, wasn't it?

She had a quick shower and put on jeans and a cotton blouse. But the humidity played havoc with her hair, so she decided to clip it back in order to control it.

That was when she found a surprise in her bag. Her mother had been unable to let her come to Palm Cove without some maternal input: she'd tucked in a little box of jewellery. Amongst the necklaces and bangles was a pair of very long, dangly bead-and-gilt earrings.

Holly stared at them then put them on.

Not bad, she decided, and tied her hair back.

Finally, with her feet in ballet pumps and her tote bag on her shoulder, she went to find Brett Wyndham's suite.

It was on the top floor of the resort with sweeping views of Palm Cove. Although the sun was setting in the west behind the resort, the waters of the cove reflected the time of day in a spectrum of lovely colours, apricot, lavender and lilac.

It was a moment before she took her eyes off the panorama after a waiter admitted her and ushered her into the lounge. Then she turned to the man himself, and got a surprise.

No casual clothes this time. Today he wore a grey suit and a blue-and-white-striped shirt. Today he looked extremely formal as he talked into his mobile phone.

Merely talking? Holly wondered. Or in the process of delivering an extremely cutting dressing-down as he stood half-turned away from her and fired words rather like bullets into the phone? Then he cut the connection, threw the phone down on a sofa in disgust and turned to her with his dark eyes blazing.

Holly swallowed in sudden fright and took a step backwards. 'Uh—hi!' she said uncertainly. 'Sorry, I didn't mean to interrupt. Maybe I'll just go until your temper has cooled a bit.' She turned away hurriedly.

He reached her in two strides and spun her back with his hands on her shoulders. 'Don't think you can walk out on me, Holly Harding.'

Holly stared up at him, going rigid and quite pale with anger. 'Let me *go*!'

Brett Wyndham paused, frowned down at her then let his hands drop to his side. 'I'm sorry,' he said quietly and went over to a drinks trolley. 'Here.' He brought her back a brandy.

'I don't—'

'Holly...' he warned.

'All I ever seem to do is drink either champagne or brandy in your presence,' she said frustratedly.

A faint smile twisted his lips. 'Sit down,' he said, and when she hesitated he added 'Let me explain. In certain circumstances I have a very short fuse.'

'So it would appear,' she agreed wholeheartedly.

He pulled off his jacket. 'Yes, well.' He gestured towards the phone. 'That was news that a breeding pair of black rhino—highly endangered now in Africa—has been injured in transit. I bought them from a zoo where they were patently *not* breeding due to stress, too small a habitat and so on.'

'Oh,' Holly said and sank into a chair, her imagination captured—so much so, she forgot her fright of a few minutes ago. 'Badly injured? In a road accident or what? A road accident,' she answered herself. 'That's why you were informing the person on the other end of the phone—' she glanced over at his mobile phone lying on the sofa opposite '—that he must have got his driving licence out of a cornflake packet. Amongst everything else you said.'

Brett Wyndham grinned fleetingly. 'Yes. But no, not badly injured. All the same, their numbers are shrinking at such an alarming rate, it's a terrifying thought, losing even two. And it only adds to their stress.'

'I see.' She frowned. 'Not that I see where I come into it. Are you trying to tell me that when your short fuse explodes anyone within range is liable to cop it?'

'It's been known to happen,' he agreed. 'However, there was a grain of truth in what I said. By the way, your hair looks nice. But I have an aversion to long, dangly earrings.'

Holly raised her eyebrows. 'Why?'

He said, 'A girl invited me home for dinner once. I arrived on time with a bunch of flowers and a bottle of wine. She opened the door. She had her hair all pulled back and all she wore were long dangly earrings, high heels and a G-string.'

Holly gasped.

'Exactly how I reacted,' he said gravely. 'Only I dropped the flowers as well.'

'What did you do then?' Holly was now laughing helplessly.

'I was younger,' he said reflectively. 'What did I do? I suggested to her that maybe she was putting the cart before the horse.'

'Oh no! What did she do?'

'She said that if all she'd achieved was to bring to mind a cart horse—not what I'd meant at all—she was wasting her time, and she slammed the door in my face. Of course, I've often wondered whether it didn't fall more into a "looking a gift horse in the mouth" scenario or "horses for courses".'

'Don't go on!' Holly held a hand to her side. 'You're making me laugh too much.'

'The worst part about it is I often find myself undressing women with long, dangly earrings to this day—only mentally, of course.'

'Oh, no!' Holly was still laughing as she removed her earrings. 'There. Am I safe?'

He took his tie off and unbuttoned his collar as he studied her—rather acutely—and nodded. 'Yes.' He paused and seemed to change his mind about something. 'OK. Shall we begin?'

Holly felt her heart jolt. 'The interview?'

'What else?' he queried a little dryly.

'Nothing! I mean, um, I didn't realize you wanted to start tonight—but I've made some notes that I brought with me,' she hastened to assure him and reached for her bag.

He sat down. 'Where do you want to start?'

She drew a notebook from her tote and a pen. She nibbled the end of the pen for a moment and a subtle change came over her.

She looked at Brett Wyndham meditatively, as if sizing him up, then said, 'Would you like to give me a brief background-history of the family? I have researched it, but you would have a much more personal view, and you may be able to pinpoint where the seeds of this passion you have for saving endangered-species came from.'

'Animals always fascinated me,' he said slowly. 'And growing up on a station gave me plenty of experience with domestic ones, as well as the more exotic wild ones—echidnas, wombats and so on. I also remember my grandmother; she was renowned as a bush vet, although she wasn't qualified as one. But she always had—' he paused to grin '—a houseful of baby wallabies she'd rescued, or so it seemed to me anyway. She used to hang them up in pillow slips as if they were still in their mother's pouch.'

'So how far back does the Wyndham association with Far North Queensland go…?'

An hour later, Brett glanced at his watch and Holly took the hint. She put her pen and notebook back into her tote, but she was satisfied with their progress. Brett had given her an insight into how the Wyndham fortune had been built, as well as a fascinating insight into life on cattle stations in the Cape York area in the early part of the twentieth century—gleaned, he told her, from his grandmother's stories and diaries. And he'd included a few immediate-family anecdotes.

'Thank you,' she said warmly. 'That was a really good beginning. It's always important to be able to set the scene.' She drained her brandy. 'And I'll try not to require any more medicinal brandy for our next session.'

He stood up and reached for his jacket. 'I'm sorry; I have a dinner to attend, but you're welcome to use the resort dining-room on us.'

Holly slung her bag on her shoulder. 'Oh no, but thank you. I was planning to wander down the waterfront and indulge in a thoroughly decadent hamburger at one of the cafés, then an early night. We are still flying to Haywire early tomorrow, I take it?'

'Yes. I plan to leave here at nine sharp. I'll pick you up at Reception.' He hesitated and frowned.

Holly studied him. 'Are you having second thoughts?' she queried.

'No. But you're good,' he said slowly. 'Especially for one so young.'

'Good?' She looked puzzled.

'You seem to have the art of putting a person at ease down to a fine art.'

'Thank you,' Holly murmured. 'Why do I get the feeling you don't altogether approve, though?' she added.

'Could you be imagining it?' he suggested with a sudden grin, and went on immediately, 'I am running late now; I'm sorry...'

'Going; I'm going!' Holly assured him and turned towards the door. 'See you tomorrow.'

But, even though he *was* running late, Brett Wyndham watched her retreating back until she disappeared. Then he walked out on to the terrace and stared at the moon and the river of silver light it was pouring onto the waters of the cove.

She'd been right, he reflected. He wasn't entirely approving of her skills as an interviewer. She did have an engaging, relaxing way with her. She did also have an undoubted enthusiasm for, and a lively curiosity about, his story and that of his family and its history. Not that he'd told her anything he hadn't wanted to tell her, nor did he have any intention of exposing the dark secret that lay behind him.

But was she capable of digging it out somehow?

Or, in other words, had he unwittingly put himself into a rather vulnerable situation because he'd underestimated a leggy twenty-four-year old who intrigued him?

For some reason his thoughts moved on to the little scene that had played out when she'd first arrived in his suite, and how she'd reacted when he'd stopped her walking out. She'd been genuinely frightened and angry at the same time. She *had* told him she'd got her fingers burnt once and it was still with her. He had to believe that now. He also had to believe it had pulled him up short, the fact that he'd frightened her.

All the same—call it all off and send her home? Or deliberately shift the focus to the project he really wanted to publicize, as had been his original intention?

He shrugged and went out to dinner with his brother, his sister, his sister-in-law-to-be and several others. He was unaware that his ex-fiancée would be one of the party.

Holly had her hamburger, and was strolling along the beach side of the road opposite the fabulous restaurants of Palm Cove, when she stopped as Brett Wyndham caught her attention.

He was with a party of diners at an upmarket restaurant that opened onto the pavement and had an amazing old melaleuca tree growing in the middle of it. It was not only an upmarket restaurant, it was a pretty upmarket party of diners, she decided. One of the women was his sister, Sue Murray, looking lovely in turquoise silk with pearls in her ears and around her neck. Two of the other women were exceptionally sleek and gorgeously dressed, one a stunning redhead, the other with a river of smooth, straight blonde hair that Holly would have given her eye teeth for.

It looked to be a lively party as wine glasses glinted beneath the lights and a small army of waiters delivered a course.

After her initial summing-up of the party, Holly turned her attention back to Brett and felt that not so unexpected frisson run through her. She frowned. Was she getting used to the effect his dark good looks and tall physique had on her? She certainly wasn't as annoyed about it as she'd been only a few days ago.

But there was something else to worry about now, she acknowledged. Ever since she'd left his suite she'd been conscious of a sense of unease. *Was* she imagining it, or had he rather suddenly developed reservations about the interview?

No, it wasn't her imagination, she decided. Something had changed. Had she asked too many questions?

She shook her head and went back to watching Brett Wyndham, only to be troubled by yet another set of thoughts. How would she feel if he pulled out of the interview? How would she feel if she never saw him again?

Her eyes widened at the chill little pang that ran through her at the thought, leaving her in no doubt she would suffer a sense of loss, a sense of regret. If that was the case for her now, after only a few brief encounters, how dangerous could it be to get to know Brett Wyndham better?

CHAPTER FOUR

HOLLY decided to go for a swim as dawn broke over Palm Cove the next morning.

She put on her swimsuit, a pretty peasant blouse and a skimpy pair of shorts. She laid out the clothes she would wear after her swim and looked at her luggage, all neatly packed. The only thing that wasn't quite neat and tidy in her mind was, which way would she go when she left Palm Cove? Out to Haywire, or back to Brisbane?

She collected a towel from the pool area and walked through the quiet resort to the beach.

There was a sprinkling of early-morning walkers and swimmers and, even so early, a feel of the coming heat of the day on the air.

She hesitated then opted to go for a walk first.

Palm Cove—most of Far North Queensland, for that matter—didn't offer blinding white sand on its beaches, although its off-shore islands might. What you got instead was sand that resembled raw sugar but it was clean, and towards the waterline, firm.

What also impressed her was that from further down the beach you would not have known Palm Cove was there, thanks to the height limitations put on the buildings and the trees that lined the beach.

She strode out and reviewed her dilemma as she did so. If she did go back to Brisbane off her own bat—assuming she wasn't sent back, and she had the feeling it wasn't impossible for that to be on the cards—how would she handle it? She would have to confess to Glenn and her mother that she'd been unable to handle the Wyndham interview, and she would go back to travel reporting with a sense of relief.

If she did get sent back, though, she'd have to confess that she must have pressed some wrong buttons with Brett Wyndham.

In either case, she would not even contemplate the fact that at times Brett Wyndham fascinated her mentally and stirred her physically, probably more than any man had done. Well, she could tell herself that, anyway.

It would be true to say she was still on the horns of a dilemma when she got back to her towel. She shrugged frustratedly, dropped her top and shorts on it and waded into the water. It was heavenly, refreshing but not cold, calm, buoyant; when it was up to her knees, she dived in and swam out energetically.

After about ten minutes, she swam back to where she could stand and floated on her back, feeling rejuvenated—cleansed, even—as if she'd experienced a catharsis and could put the whole sorry business behind her one way or another.

'Morning, Holly.'

She sank, swallowed some water and came up spluttering. Brett Wyndham, with his dark hair plastered to his head, was standing a few feet away from her, his tanned shoulders smooth and wet.

'What are you doing here?' she demanded, somewhat indistinctly, through a fit of coughing.

He looked around. 'I thought it was a public beach.'

'Of course it is!' She felt for the bottom with her toes. 'I mean—it doesn't matter.'

'Have I done something to annoy you?' he queried gravely.

Holly lay back in the water and rippled it with her fingers. Then she sat up and flicked her gaze from the strong brown column of his throat, from his sleek outline, and eyed a line of opal-pale clouds above, then their reflection on the glassy surface of the sea. 'I thought it might be the other way round.'

He raised an eyebrow. 'Why?'

'I thought—I thought you were having second thoughts last night.'

She moved a few steps towards the beach, then something swirled in the water next to her; she jerked away and fell over with a cry of fright.

'Holly!' Brett plunged to her side and lifted her into his arms. 'What was it? Are you hurt?'

'I don't know what it was. I don't think I'm hurt, though. I just got a fright!'

'OK.' He carried her up the beach and put her down on her towel. 'Let's have a look.'

He could find no wound on her feet or legs and he looked patently relieved.

Holly sat up. 'What could it have been?'

'It could have been a stingray.'

She stared at him round-eyed. 'That could have been fatal!'

He smiled. 'Not necessarily, not in your feet and legs, but it can take a long time to heal.'

Holly allowed a long breath to escape. 'So, a serpent in paradise, you could say.'

'Mmm... Have you had breakfast?'

'No. Uh, no, but—'

'Come and have it with me.' He stood up.

Holly stared up at him. He wore a colourful pair of board shorts; as she'd always suspected, his physique was outstanding: not an ounce of excess weight and whipcord muscles. There was only one way to describe it: he was beautifully proportioned. Tall, lean, strong as well as dark, and pirate-like—altogether enough to set her pulses fluttering.

She swallowed and realized she was on the receiving end of his scrutiny. His dark gaze lingered on her legs, her waist and the curve of her breasts beneath the fine lycra of her costume, as well as the pulse beating at the base of her throat. She found herself feeling hot and cold as her nipples peaked visibly.

She jumped up. 'Thanks, but no thanks. I really...' She picked up her towel and flapped it vigorously. 'I really got the feeling last night that things had gone sour somehow, and it might be best if I just go back to Brisbane, so—'

'Holly.' He wrested the towel from her. 'Before you cover us completely with sand, if you still want to go after breakfast, fine. But I haven't told you about my new project yet—my plans to open a zoo.'

Holly went still and blinked at him. 'A zoo?' she repeated.

'Yes, I'm planning one along the lines of the Western

Plains zoo outside Dubbo, but up here on Haywire—
that's why I wanted you to see it. I'm thinking of an
adopt-an-animal scheme as a means of publicizing it,
as well as the whole endangered-species issue.'

Her eyes widened. 'What a great idea! Tell me
more.'

He shook his head. 'You have to come to breakfast
if you want any more details.'

She clicked her tongue. 'You're extremely domineer-
ing, aren't you?'

He shrugged and handed her back her towel.

He ordered breakfast to be served on the terrace of his
suite.

Holly sat outside waiting for it while he made and
received some phone calls to do with the welfare of his
rhinos, and she tried to work out a plan of action.

Nothing had occurred to her by the time breakfast
arrived. It was a ceremonial delivery. There was champagne and orange juice; there was a gorgeous fruit-plat-
ter with some of the unusual fruits found in the area, like
rambutans and star-fruit; there was yoghurt and cereal,
a mushroom omelette for her and eggs and bacon for
him.

The toast was wrapped in a linen napkin and there
was a silver flask of coffee.

'Thank you, we'll help ourselves,' Brett murmured,
and the team of waiters withdrew discreetly.

'I'll never eat all this,' Holly said ruefully.

'Eat as much or as little as you like. I usually start
with the main course then work my way backwards,

with the fruit topped with a little yoghurt—as dessert, you might say.'

'Really?' Holly eyed him with some intrigue. 'That's a novel approach.'

'Try it.'

'I will. By the way, how long would we stay at Haywire, assuming we go?'

He glanced at her. 'Two or three days.'

'You did mention your brother's wedding.'

He glanced at his watch to check the date. 'That's a week from today, here.'

'Here?'

'Uh-huh, but there are a few preliminaries in the form of balls, soirées, a reef trip et cetera.'

Holly had to smile. 'You don't sound impressed.'

'I'm not.' He shrugged. 'But he is my brother. OK—the zoo.' He started on his eggs and bacon, and gave her the broad outline of his plans for the zoo—the size of the paddocks he intended to create, the animals he wanted and some of the difficulties involved.

'Impressive,' she said. 'I think it's a marvellous idea. But…' She pushed away her plate and picked up a prickly purple rambutan, wondering at the same time how you were supposed to eat it. 'But I'm not sure I'm the right person to do this. What I mean is, I'm not sure *you* think I am.' She watched him keenly for a long moment.

He reached for the coffee pot, poured two cups and pushed one towards her. 'I do think you're right for it. I think you have fresh, innovative views.'

'But something changed last night,' she persisted quietly.

He looked out over the water and was silent for a time. *Yes, Holly Golightly*, he thought with an inward grimace, *some things did change last night—one you're not even aware of—but it's the reason I'm* not *putting you on the next plane down south.*

He clenched his fist as he thought of the dinner last night. His sister-in-law-to-be had decided she might be able to mend some fences, so she'd produced Natasha Hewson at the dinner with the disclaimer that the wedding next weekend was going to be all Nat's work of art, and they'd be bound to run into each other anyway.

So I'm back in the bloody position, he thought, gritting his teeth, *of using you, Ms Harding, to deflect my ex-fiancée.* Not that he had any expectations that the two would ever meet, because he intended to whisk her off to Haywire as planned this morning before she went back to Brisbane. But as soon as Nat knew he was travelling with a girl—and he had no doubt she would know it!—she might get the message.

Not exactly admirable behaviour, he mused rather grimly, *but needs must when the devil drives.*

'It occurred to me last night,' he said, switching his gaze suddenly back to Holly, 'That I might be going into areas I don't really want to go into—not any further, anyway.'

Holly looked puzzled for a moment and she opened her mouth to say that it had all been pretty harmless, surely? But she changed her mind at the last moment. It was, of course, his prerogative, but it raised a question mark in her mind.

'Um...' She hesitated and put the rambutan down.

'That's up to you. I'm happy to go along with whatever you want to talk about.'

'So.' His lips twisted. 'Are we on again?'

Holly looked down and felt a strong pull towards taking the safe path—the one that would get her away from the dangerous elements of this man. From the undoubted attraction she felt towards him—her fascination with the mystique behind him. But at the same time her feeling was that Brett Wyndham could not be a long=term prospect for her.

She thought briefly of the dinner party she'd witnessed last night and it struck her that, while the man himself embodied the kind of life she found fascinating, there had to be a dimension to his life that occupied another stratum—one she did not belong to—that of ultra-glamorous, gorgeously groomed, sleek and glossy women. Last night they'd all looked like models or film stars.

Should that not make her feel safe with him, however? The fact that she patently didn't look like a model or a film star...?

She shrugged at last. 'On. Again.'

They exchanged a long, probing glance until finally he said, 'I see. We're still in the same boat.'

She looked perplexed. 'Boat?'

'We can't quite make each other out.' He smiled, but a shade dryly. 'All right. Are you ready to fly out shortly?'

Holly hesitated momentarily, then nodded. She went away to change and collect her things.

As she changed into her jeans, a sunshine-yellow singlet top, her denim jacket and her boots, she stared at her image in the mirror a couple of times and realized she looked and felt tense, and didn't know how to deal with it.

Here she was about to step out into the wide blue yonder with a man she hardly knew—a man she'd clashed with but at the same time felt attracted to—and her emotions were, accordingly, in a bit of a tangle.

How was she going to revert to Holly Harding, journalist, on a very important mission?

She was still preoccupied with this question as she drove down the Bruce Highway with Brett Wyndham, between sugar cane fields, towards the city of Cairns in its circle of hills and the airport.

Brett piloted his own plane, she discovered later, still not quite able to believe what was happening to her. The plane was a trim little six-seater with a W on the tail.

She was still pinching herself metaphorically as the nose of the plane rose and the speeding runway fell away. She was also trying to decide how to handle things between them. Common sense told her a matter-of-fact approach was the only way to go, but even that wasn't going to be easy.

She waited until they reached their cruising altitude then asked him how long the flight would be.

He told her briefly.

'Can you talk?'

'Of course,' he replied.

'Could you give me a run-down on the country we're flying over and our destination?'

He did so. They were flying west over the old mining towns of the Tablelands towards volcanic country famous for its lava tubes; then the great, grassy lands of the savannah/gulf country, as in the Gulf of Carpentaria, where their destination lay.

'Haywire?' she repeated with a grin. 'Where did it get its name?

He grimaced. 'No-one seems to know.'

Holly glanced across at him. He looked thoroughly professional in a khaki bush-shirt and jeans, with his headphones on and his beautiful hands checking instruments.

Professional and withdrawn from her, she contemplated as her gaze was drawn to her own hands clasped rather forlornly in her lap.

Who was she to quibble about 'professional and withdrawn' being the order of the day? It was what she'd almost stipulated, wasn't it? The only problem was she needed to get him to open up if she was going to get full value out of this trip. But—big but—there was a fine line between getting him to talk easily and naturally from a professional point of view and not finding herself loving his company at the same time.

She shook her head and realized he was watching her.

She coloured a little.

'Some internal debate?' he suggested.

'You could say so. Where are we now?' She looked out at the panorama of red sandy earth below them, with its sage-green vegetation, at the undulations and the space.

'About halfway between Georgetown and Croydon. If you follow the Savannah Way it takes you on to Normanton and Karumba, on the gulf. Over that way,' he pointed, 'is Forsayth and Cobbold Gorge; it's quite amazing. And those are the Newcastle Ranges to the east, and the sandstone escarpment to the west.'

'It's very remote,' she said in awe. 'And empty.'

'Remote,' he agreed. 'Hot as hell in summer, but with quite a history, not only of cattle but gold rushes and gem fields. Georgetown has a gem museum and Croydon has a recreation of the life and times of the gold rush there.'

'They look so small, though—Georgetown and Croydon,' she ventured.

He shrugged. 'They are now. Last count, Georgetown had under three-hundred residents, but it's the heart of a huge shire, and they're both on the road to Karumba and the gulf, renowned for its fishing. With the army of grey nomads out and about these days, they get a lot of passing traffic.'

Holly grinned. 'Grey nomads' was the term given to retired Australians who travelled the continent in caravans or camper vans or just with tents. It could almost be said it was the national retiree-pastime.

Half an hour later they started to lose altitude and Brett pointed out the Haywire homestead. All Holly could see was a huddle of roofs and a grassy airstrip between white-painted wooden fences in a sea of scrub.

Then he spoke into his VHF radio, and over some static a female voice said she'd walked the strip and it was in good order.

'Romeo, coming in,' he responded.

Ten minutes later they made a slightly bumpy landing and rolled to a stop adjacent to the huddle of roofs Holly had seen from the air.

A girl and a dog came through the gate in the airstrip fence to meet them.

'Holly,' Brett said, 'This is Sarah. And this—' he bent down to pat the red cattle-dog who accepted his ministrations with every sign of ecstasy '—is Bella.'

'Welcome to Haywire, Holly,' Sarah said in a very English accent.

Holly blinked in surprise, and Brett and Sarah exchanged grins. 'Sarah is backpacking her way around the world,' Brett said. 'How long have you been with us now?' he asked the English girl.

'Three months. I can't seem to tear myself away!' Sarah said ruefully. 'Brett, since you're here, I'm a bit worried about one of the mares in the holding paddock— she's lame. Would you mind having a look at her? I could show Holly around a bit in the meantime.'

'Sure. I'll leave you to it.'

Haywire homestead was a revelation to Holly in as much as it wasn't a homestead at all in the accepted sense of the word. All the accommodation was in separate cabins set out on green lawns and inside a fence designed to keep wallabies, emus and other wildlife out, according to Sarah.

All the other facilities were under one huge roof: lounge area, dining area, a small library-cum-games room et cetera. But the unique thing was, there were no outside walls.

The floor was slate; there was a central stone-fireplace, and at intervals there were tubs of potted plants and artistically arranged pieces of dead wood, often draped with ferns.

There was a long refectory table, comfortable cane-loungers and steamer chairs; beyond the fence and lawn, looking away from the rest of the compound, there was a lake alive with birds, reeds and water lilies.

The whole area reminded Holly of a safari lodge, and she was most impressed.

'Just one thing, what do you do when it rains or blows a gale?' she asked Sarah ruefully.

'Hasn't happened to me yet,' Sarah replied. 'But there are roll-down blinds.' She pointed them out. 'And I believe they put up shutters if they get a cyclone. Otherwise it lets the air flow through when it's really hot. Here's the kitchen.'

The kitchen was not visible from the rest of the area; it was also open on one side, yet had all mod cons. There were, Holly learnt, several sources of power on Haywire: a generator for electricity and gas for the hot-water system. There were still some old-fashioned combustion stoves for heating water in case other means failed. And there was a satellite phone as well as a VHF radio for communications.

There was an above-ground swimming pool surrounded by emerald lawn and shaded by trees.

Sarah explained that she was actually a nurse, but she enjoyed cooking, she loved the outback and she loved horses, so a stint as a housekeeper at Haywire suited her down to the ground.

'Mind you, most often there's only me, Bella, the horses and a few stockmen here. We don't get to see the family that often. Actually, I'm surprised to see Brett. I thought he'd be down at Palm Cove with the rest of them.'

'We were—he was,' Holly said, and intercepted a curious little glance from Sarah. She found herself thinking, *I knew this would happen! Probably no passable woman is safe in Brett Wyndham's company without being thought of as his lover.* 'I'm actually working with him,' she added.

'So she is,' the man in question agreed as he strolled up to them.

They both turned.

'The mare has a stone bruise in her off-fore. I've relieved the pressure, but keep an eye on her or get Kane to,' he added to Sarah. 'Are they coming in tonight? Kane,' he said for Holly's benefit, 'Is station foreman, and he has two offsiders.'

Sarah shook her head. 'They've got a problem with a fence on the northern boundary. That's miles away, so they decided to camp out overnight.'

'OK, then it's just us. I'm going to take Holly for a drive; we'll be back before dark. Incidentally, what's for dinner?'

Sarah grinned her infectious grin. 'Would you believe? Roast beef!'

'Standard cattle-station joke—roast beef for dinner,' Brett said to Holly as they climbed into a sturdy, high-chassis four-wheel-drive utility vehicle. Holly had brought her camera.

She laughed, but said, 'Look, I'm really surprised at how few people you have working here. From memory you run ten-thousand head of cattle; that sounds like a huge herd to me, and Haywire covers thousands of square kilometers.' Holly said.

'That's because you probably don't know much about Brahman and Droughtmaster cattle.'

'I know nothing,' Holly confessed.

'Well—' he swung the wheel to avoid an anthill '—Brahmans come down from four Indian breeds; they were first imported here from the USA in 1933. Droughtmasters are a Brahman cross, developed here. They've all adapted particularly to this part of the world for a variety of reasons. They're heat-and-parasite resistant, they're mobile, good foragers and they can survive on poor grass in droughts. They have a highly developed digestive system that provides efficient feed-conversion.'

'They sound amazing.'

'There's more,' he said with a grin. 'The fact that they're resistant to or tolerant of parasites means they don't require chemical intervention, so they're clean and green,' he said humorously. 'The cows are good mothers; they produce plenty of milk and they have small calves, so birthing is usually easy, and they're renowned for protecting their calves. All of that—' he waved a hand '—means they require minimum management. In answer to your question, that's why we don't need an army of staff.'

Holly looked around at the now undulating countryside they were driving through. It was quite rocky, she noticed, and dotted with anthills as well as spindly trees and scrub. The grass was long and spiky.

'But this is only one of your stations, isn't it?' she said.

'Yes, we have two more, roughly in this area, and

one in the Northern Territory.' He drew up and pointed. 'There you are—Brahmans.'

Holly stared at the cream and mainly brown cattle with black points. They were gathered around a dam. They had big droopy ears, sloe eyes, dewlaps and medium humps. 'They look so neat and smooth.'

'It's that smooth coat and their highly developed sweat glands that help them cope with the heat.'

'Do they come in any other colours?'

'Yes, grey with black points, but we don't have any greys here on Haywire.'

'It's so interesting!' She took some pictures then folded her arms and watched the cattle intently.

Brett Wyndham watched her for a long moment.

In her yellow singlet top, her jeans and no-nonsense shoes, she didn't look at all out of place in the landscape. In her enthusiasm, she looked even more apt for the setting; with her pale skin, that cloud of fair curls and no make-up, she was different and rather uniquely attractive.

He thought of her in her swimming costume only this morning: very slender, yes, but leggy with a kind of coltish grace that he'd found quite fascinating. Then again, in all her incarnations he'd found her fascinating...

He stirred and glanced at his watch. 'Seen enough?'

Holly turned her head and their gazes clashed for a moment. She felt her skin prickle as an unspoken communication seemed to flow between them, one of mutual awareness.

Then he looked away and switched on the engine, and the moment was broken, but the awareness of Brett

Wyndham didn't leave her as they bounced over the uneven terrain back to the compound.

Quite unaware that her thoughts echoed his thoughts, she remembered him all sleek and tall in the waters of Palm Cove that morning. She recalled how easily he'd picked her up in his arms and carried her up the beach. She shivered inwardly as she remembered the feel of her skin on his skin.

Brett parked the ute outside the compound fence and pointed out of his window. Holly followed the line of his finger and saw three emus treading with stately precision down the fenceline.

She breathed excitedly—not only in genuine interest, but because she was grateful to be relieved of her memories of the morning...

'It's already like a zoo here,' she told him.

They watched for a while, then got out, and he led the way to the cabin she'd been allotted.

'You've got half an hour before pre-dinner drinks. Would you like to freshen up?' he asked.

'Thanks,' she said gratefully.

'This is a guest cabin. By the way, there's plenty of hot water.'

'Lovely,' Holly murmured,

He turned away, but turned back. 'Oh, there should be a functioning torch in there—use it when you're walking around the compound at night. There could be frogs. Or snakes.'

'Frogs I can handle,' Holly said. 'Snakes I'm not too keen on, but I guess usual practice—make a bit of a noise as you move about so the ground vibrates and otherwise beat a hasty retreat?'

'Good thinking; they're not common,' he agreed.

'That's nice to hear,' Holly said with some humour.

'We *are*—almost—beyond the black stump.'

'Now you tell me,' she quipped, and closed herself into the cabin.

She immediately discovered that Haywire might be remote, and might resemble a safari camp in some respects, but its cabins were sturdy, beautifully appointed and had very modern bathrooms.

The double bed had a sumptuous thick-looking but light-as-air doona covered in an intricately embroidered cream-linen cover, with four matching pillows. It was also a four-poster bed. There were paintings on the dark-green walls and the carpet was the kind your feet sank into in a soft sea-green. There was a beautiful cedar chest, two armchairs and a delicate writing-desk with cabriole legs. The bedside lamps had porcelain bases and coral-pink linen shades.

The bathroom was a symphony of white tiles, black floor and shiny chrome taps. Lime-green and lemon-yellow was echoed not only in the towels and the robes that hung behind the door but in the cakes of soap and toiletries all provided in glass bottles, with an ornamental 'H' for Haywire entwined with a 'W' for Wyndham.

She took a hot shower and changed into a pair of clean jeans and a long-sleeved blue blouse that matched her eyes. She thought about wearing her heavy shoes as protection against any snakes on the loose, but decided her feet needed a change, and slipped them into her ballet pumps.

As usual she spent a few minutes grappling with her hair; she'd washed it, but in the end merely pushed her fingers through it and left it to its own devices. She'd discovered that very few people with curly hair actually appreciated it, whilst many who did not have it thought it would be marvellous to do so. She grimaced at her reflection as she recalled the agonies in her teens when she would have given her eye teeth to have straight smooth hair.

That Brett Wyndham didn't seem averse to it occurred to her—and, since she had five minutes to play with, she sat down in one of the armchairs and thought about him.

In particular she thought about that charged little moment out in the ute when their gazes had locked and she'd been so aware of everything about him. Not only that, but she'd sensed it was mutual. Where could it ever lead? she wondered. There was something about him she couldn't put her finger on. Yes, she'd decided he was a loner—it was pretty obvious he lived the kind of life that didn't go well with domestic ties—but was there something even more remote about him?

If so, did it come from his broken engagement to Natasha Hewson or did it go deeper than that?

She frowned as she suddenly remembered what he'd said this morning about going into areas he didn't want to go to. What could that be about? she wondered as she cast her mind over all the material she'd collected from him the previous evening. None of it had been especially riveting, mostly family history, history of the area and some anecdotes... *Hang on!*

She paused her thoughts as it struck her that those

few anecdotes from his formative years had included his brother Mark, his sister Sue, his mother, who was a doctor, and his grandparents but not one word about his father. Wasn't that a little strange?

She shook her head, more than ever conscious that Brett Wyndham was an enigma. She also had to concede that there was a spark of chemistry between them— more than a spark. She couldn't deny there were times when she loved his company, even though he'd so incensed her at the beginning, but she also couldn't deny her wariness.

Of course, some of that was to do with what had once happened to her, but who would wittingly fall in love with an enigmatic loner? She posed the question to herself.

CHAPTER FIVE

SHE didn't encounter any snakes or frogs on the way to dinner. In fact, Bella came to meet her as she opened her door and escorted her.

'You are a lovely dog,' she said to Bella as they arrived, then, 'Wow—this looks amazing!'

Oil lamps hung from the rafters, shedding soft light. The table was set with colourful, linen place mats, pewter and crystal, and a bowl of swamp lilies. There was a bottle of champagne in an ice bucket, and there was the tantalizing smell of roast beef in the air.

Brett had obviously showered too; his hair was damp and spiky and he'd changed into khaki trousers and a checked shirt. He looked devastatingly attractive, Holly thought privately.

'Champagne?' he invited, lifting the bottle by its neck and starting to ease the foil off.

'Yes, please.' Holly looked around. 'I must say this is amazingly civilized for beyond the black stump.'

'We do our best. Champagne, Sarah?' he called.

'No, thanks,' Sarah called back. 'I'm in the midst of dishing up; I'll have one later.'

'Has it always been like this—Haywire?' Holly

asked, and lifted her glass in a response to Brett's silent toast.

'More or less,' he replied and shrugged. 'Ever since I can remember, although the cabins have been renovated and more mod cons put in. But I never wanted to change *this*.' He gestured comprehensively.

'I'm so glad; it's magic,' Holly said enthusiastically.

Not a great deal later Holly said to Sarah, 'That was fantastic,' as she put her knife and fork together and pushed her plate away. 'Not only roast beef but Yorkshire pudding.'

'I am a Yorkshire lass,' Sarah revealed as she stood up and began clearing plates. 'There's fruit and cheese to come, and coffee.'

'Please, let me help,' Holly offered.

'No way! I am being paid to do this. You and Brett relax,' Sarah ordered.

Holly breathed a little frustratedly. She didn't really want to be left alone with Brett—well, she did and she didn't, she decided. But she felt tense about it; she felt jittery.

On the other hand, she didn't want to force herself on Sarah in the kitchen. Some cooks hated having their space invaded with offers of help.

She got up, but stood undecided beside her chair, and it seemed to show in her face.

She saw Brett watching her rather narrowly and wondered what he was thinking. Then she realized, as his dark gaze flicked up and down her figure, that he was thinking of her in a particular context—the awareness that continued to spring up between them—and she felt herself colour; she turned away, biting her lip.

He was the one who solved the problem. He said, 'I've got a few things to do, a few calls to make. Why don't you look through the albums? It might give you more background material.'

She turned back. 'Albums?'

He indicated the library area and some thick albums arranged on a teak table. A comfortable armchair stood beside the table and a lamp above it shed light.

'There are photos going way back; there are visitors' comments and press cuttings.'

'Oh, thank you! I will,' she said eagerly, but didn't miss the ironic little glance he cast her. In fact, it caused her to bridle as she stared back.

But he only shrugged and drew her attention to a drawer in the table that contained pens and paper, if she wanted to make notes.

'Thank you,' she said stiffly. Feeling foolish, which didn't sit well with her, she waved her hands and recommended that he go away and leave her alone.

'By all means, Miss Harding,' he said with soft sarcasm. 'By all means.'

Holly ground her teeth.

An hour later she looked up as he came back into the library area, then put her pen down and stretched.

'Finished?' he enquired.

'No. They're fascinating—I could go on for hours, but I won't. Thanks very much.' She closed the album she'd been working on and stood up. 'I think bed might be a good idea. I seem to have done an awful lot today,' she said with evident humour.

'I'll walk you to your cabin,' he murmured.

'I can walk myself.' But she paused, feeling recalcitrant and juvenile. What could happen between here and her cabin? 'OK. Thanks.'

They called goodnight to Sarah, who was watching a DVD, and set off. In the event, there were no snakes, but there was a flying fox. As Brett opened her cabin door and reached in to switch on the light, it swooped down on Holly.

It startled her so much she dropped her torch, gave a yelp and with an almighty shudder sought refuge in Brett's arms.

The creature flew into the cabin, then straight out again.

'It's only a flying fox,' he said, holding her close, though, and flipping off the light. 'It was the light.'

'Only a flying fox!' she repeated incredulously. 'Aren't they responsible for the Lyssa virus or the Hendra virus—or both?'

'It didn't actually touch you, Holly.' He passed a hand over her hair then closed the cabin door.

She shuddered again. 'Can you imagine it getting caught in my hair? Yuck!'

'Some people love them.'

'Not in their hair, I bet they don't. Look, I'm not keen on them; snakes, spiders, rats and frogs I can manage to stay sane about—flying foxes, not!'

He laughed down at her then bent his head to kiss her.

Holly was taken completely by surprise, but it felt

so good, she was immediately riveted and all her fears seemed to melt away.

Then some common sense prevailed and she drew away a little.

'We shouldn't be doing this,' she whispered.

'We've been wanting to do it all day,' he countered.

'I...' She swallowed. 'The thing is, I'm here to do a job and I really need to concentrate on that. So.' She managed to look up at him humorously. 'Thanks for being here, otherwise I could have really freaked out! But now I'll say goodnight.'

He released her promptly, although with a crooked little smile. 'All right. Don't switch the light on until you're closed in.' He turned away and left her.

Holly closed herself into the cabin and stood in the dark for a long moment with her hand to her mouth.

The next morning, after breakfast, he had a surprise for her.

She'd greeted him cautiously, but he'd been casual and friendly and they'd eaten breakfast companionably.

Then he recommended that she bring a hat and sun-screen, along with her camera, and meet him at the holding-paddock gate.

When she got there, there were two saddled horses tied to the fence.

'I'm sorry,' he said. 'I couldn't rustle up a camel or a donkey.'

Holly groaned. 'Thank heavens! But I have to tell you that, although I have ridden horses before, I'm not much of a rider—I usually get led.'

'No problem.' He produced a long rein out of his

saddle bag and attached it to one of the horses' bridles. 'Up you get.' He put his hands around her waist and lifted her into the saddle.

'Where are we going?'

He mounted his horse with ease and clicked his tongue. As they set off, he said, 'We're putting in a new dam; I want to see the progress. It's a pleasant ride.'

'You're not going to gallop or do anything that'll contribute to me falling off?' she queried as she clutched her reins and tried to adjust herself to the motion as they broke into a trot.

'Nope. Just relax. Are you always this nervous when you're on a job?'

'Often with good cause, believe me,' she said a shade tartly. 'I've even been known to get off and walk, but I do always get there in the end.'

Brett Wyndham grimaced.

'What?' she asked with conspicuous hauteur.

He laughed softly. 'I believe you. You're a stubborn one, Holly Golightly; that I don't doubt. OK. Let's see if we can enjoy this ride.'

An hour later they reached the dam sight, and to Holly's surprise she had enjoyed the ride. They'd stopped a couple of times, once on a rocky crest that had afforded them a sweeping view of the countryside, and once beside a salt lick.

Both times she'd dismounted and asked a lot of questions. By the time they reached the dam, she was confident enough of her horse not to need the leading rein, and she was genuinely charmed when Brett lit a small fire and boiled the billy he had in his saddle bag.

She reached into hers as instructed and withdrew some damper Sarah had baked to go with their tea.

'A real bush picnic,' she enthused as she sat on a rock and fanned herself with her hat. 'Oh—I can see a bulldozer over there. And a camp—but not a soul in sight!'

'Yes.' Brett squatted beside the fire and put a few more sticks on it. 'They usually work two weeks on, one week off. I wanted to check it all out on their off-week. Ready for your tea?' He poured boiling water onto a teabag in an enamel mug and handed it to her.

'Mmm...I'm looking forward to this. Thank you. But I don't see any cattle.'

'We rotate paddocks; this one's resting.'

'I see. How long...?'

But he interrupted her to give her all the information she was about to ask for about the paddocks, and more besides.

Holly had to laugh, although a little self-consciously, when he'd finished. 'Sorry, I'm asking too many questions, but it is interesting.'

He sent her a thoughtful look. She seemed to be completely unfazed by the heat and the flies; she seemed quite unaware that she had a dirty smudge on her face, or that her hands were grimy, that her hair was plastered to her head or that her shirt was streaked with sweat.

'You'd make a good countrywoman,' he said at last.

Holly tried the damper and pronounced it delicious. 'I'm insatiably curious,' she said. 'That's my problem.'

He looked thoughtful, but he didn't comment. When

they'd finished their tea, he put the fire out carefully, they mounted again and went to explore the dam workings.

Two hours later they cantered back into the holding paddock and Brett suggested a swim in the pool.

'Sounds heavenly,' Holly said in a heartfelt way, and went to change into her togs. She was on her way to the pool when it occurred to her that Sarah wasn't around, and that she hadn't been quite her cheerful self at breakfast. She hesitated then went to knock on her cabin door.

Sarah opened it eventually and was full of apologies. 'I'm sorry, I'll get stuck into lunch—I've just got a touch of sinus, but I've taken something. Makes me feel a bit sleepy, though.'

Holly studied the other girl's pale face and the dark rings under her eyes. 'Oh, no,' she said. 'You go back to bed. I can handle lunch!'

'I wouldn't dream of it,' Sarah replied, but her gaze fastened on something over Holly's shoulder. Holly turned round to see that Brett was standing behind her. Before Sarah got a chance to say anything, she explained the situation to him and finished by saying, 'I could make lunch easily.'

'Done,' Brett said with authority. 'You do as you're told, Sarah.'

'I should be better in time to make dinner,' Sarah said anxiously.

'We'll see about that,' her boss replied, and reached out to rumple Sarah's hair. 'Take it easy,' he advised her.

Sarah sighed and looked relieved.

* * *

In the event Holly made both lunch and dinner. They had a swim in the pool before lunch, then Brett poured them a gin and tonic each—a fitting aperitif for the middle of a hot day, he told her—while she made open cold roast beef sandwiches with hot English mustard and salad.

They took their drinks and lunch to a table beside the pool beneath a shady tree.

Holly had put her peasant blouse on over her togs but Brett had added nothing to his board shorts. Bella lay beside them, gently indicating that she'd be happy to clean up any scraps. The bush beyond the fence was shimmering in the heat and vibrating with insect life.

'How do you manage to leave this place so often?' Holly asked.

'Don't kid yourself,' Brett responded. 'You can feel isolated up here.'

'But you can drive out, can't you?'

'Sure, but it's a long way on a rough road.'

Holly sipped her drink. 'Do your sister and brother like it up here?'

'From time to time, but they don't really have cattle in their blood. Neither does Aria. She doesn't really enjoy roughing it.' He grimaced then elaborated. 'She's the girl Mark's marrying.'

'What's she like?'

Brett considered and gave Bella the last bit of his sandwich. 'Very beautiful. She has long blonde hair, a striking figure. She and Natasha make a good pair, come to think of it, although Nat's a redhead.' He paused. 'My ex-fiancée.'

Holly's mind fled back to the dinner party she'd

witnessed at Palm Cove. Unless there were two stunning redheads in his life, had the one she'd seen been his ex-fiancée? If so, did that mean they were still friends?

'No curiosity on that subject, Miss Harding?' he queried, a shade dryly.

Holly shrugged and looked away. 'I'm sure it's out of bounds, and besides, its none of my business.'

'True.' He looked reflective. 'Anyway, Aria is a biochemist and actually very nice, although something of a meddler.' He looked briefly heavenwards. 'But since Mark's a computer genius they have similar lifestyles in common.'

Holly looked around. 'So all this falls to you? I mean all the responsibility, the planning and so on.'

'Yes.' He sat back and crossed his hands behind his head.

'It must be quite a handful, combining it with your other work.'

'More or less what I've been thinking for a while now,' he agreed with a wry little smile. He sobered. 'But it's in my blood. Just as you inherited your father's writing gene, I must have inherited my f—' He stopped abruptly.

Holly waited but found she was holding her breath.

'Much as I don't care to admit it,' he said finally, 'I must have inherited my father's gene for cattle and the land.'

Holly released her breath slowly. Although the thought chased through her mind that she'd been right—there had been something between Brett and his father—she was mindful of his warning about going into things he didn't want go into.

'So it's something you really love,' she said instead. 'I can understand that.'

He looked at her penetratingly. 'You can?'

'I think so. It's probably unfair to say there are more challenges out here than in suburban life, but to me anyway these open spaces are not only exciting—' she looked up at the wide arc of blue, blue sky above '—they're liberating. I guess that's what motivated my father and may have come down to me.'

'You really mean that, don't you?' He sat up.

Holly nodded, then grimaced. 'Probably easy enough to say. So. What's on this afternoon?'

He eyed her, sitting so relaxed in her chair in her peasant blouse with its pretty embroidery, her legs long and bare and her hair curling madly.

What's on this afternoon? he repeated to himself. *What would you say, Miss Harding, if I told you I'd very much like to take you to bed? I'd love to strip your togs from your body and explore those slender lines and delicate curves. I'd like to touch you and make those pink lips part in surprise and pleasure, those blue eyes widen in wonder...*

It was a disturbance over the fence in the holding paddock that drew his attention away from Holly—saved by the bell, he thought dryly. He saw that his foreman, Kane, had arrived back from the fencing trip with his two offsiders.

But as his gaze came back to Holly, he saw that she was staring at him with her lips parted, her eyes wide— all in some perplexity.

His lips twisted. 'Why don't you relax? I've got some things to discuss with Kane. I may take him back to the dam to show him what I want done, so I could be tied up all afternoon.'

'Uh, all right,' Holly responded after a moment. 'I can do some work anyway.' She hesitated. 'If Sarah's still not well would you like me to cook dinner?'

'Thanks.' He stood up. 'That would be great.'

Holly withdrew her gaze from the physical splendour of Brett Wyndham in his board shorts. 'Um, do I cook for Kane and the others?'

'No. They'll cater for themselves in their quarters. See you later.' And he walked away.

Holly cleared up their lunch and retreated to her cabin, where she admitted to herself that she was somewhat bothered and bewildered. Or bewitched.

She lay down on the bed and stared at the ceiling, feeling like a star-struck teenager, she admitted as she pulled a pillow into her arms. So, what to do about it?

No answer presented itself and she fell asleep.

It was starting to cool down when she re-emerged, showered and once again changed in her blouse and jeans.

She checked on Sarah first and took her a pot of tea and a snack—all she wanted. She persuaded her to stay where she was, assuring her she was quite able to handle dinner.

A couple of hours later, with the oil lamps lit and the table set attractively again, Brett put down his knife and fork and said, 'You can cook. Another gene from your father?'

Holly's face dimpled into a smile as she glanced at the remains of the golden-brown lasagne she'd prepared, along with a fresh green salad and some warm rolls.

'No. The cooking gene comes from my mother, in case you thought I was all my father's doing.'

Brett lay back in his chair and studied her. He had also showered and had changed into a clean khaki shirt and beige chinos. 'What does come to mind...' He twirled his wine glass. 'Is the fact that you'd make someone a really handy wife.'

Holly looked put out, although there was glint of laughter in her eyes. 'That's not exactly a compliment, Mr Wyndham,' she said gravely.

'Sorry,' He grimaced. 'As well as a very attractive wife, of course.'

'That's a bit better!' Holly approved. 'But I don't think I'd make a good wife, actually.'

'Why not?'

She gathered their plates. 'Oh, I don't know.' She shrugged and stood up.

He rose too and told her to sit down. 'I'll do this.'

Holly sank back and watched him clear the table. He came back and topped up their wine glasses. 'Why not?' he asked again.

She looked at him and looked away. She stroked Bella's head. Somehow the dog must have gauged her inner distress with the subject, because Bella had risen and put her head on Holly's lap. Despite her inner distress, there was something else, something new. For the first time she wanted to explain why she was the way she was.

It was to do with this man, she thought. Because he moved her, whether she liked it or not...

She took a deep breath. 'A couple of years ago I fell madly in love,' she said quietly. 'What I didn't know was that he was a married man. And I only got to know it when his wife started stalking me.'

Brett stopped with his wine glass poised in his hand, then he slowly put it down. 'I'm sorry. *Seriously* stalking you?'

'I thought so. She wrote threatening letters, she threatened me over the phone, she turned up at work, she harassed my mother—she threw a brick through my car window once. It got to the stage where I was looking over my shoulder all the time, even scared to go out.'

'She sounds crazy,' he said.

Holly shrugged. 'I'll probably never know whether it was the cause or the effect of her husband's philandering, but it left me with several complexes. Strangely, although she scared me silly at times, I felt a streak of sympathy for *her*, whereas I could have killed her husband for putting me in that position. You could say I fell off cloud nine with a huge bump.'

She looked away and for a moment tears glittered in her eyes.

'Go on,' he murmured eventually.

'I couldn't believe I'd been so thoroughly taken in by him. I can only—I'd just lost my father, who meant the world to me, so I was depressed and so on when I met him.'

'He was still living with her?'

'No, he'd moved out, so I had no reason to suspect he was married. But I guess that's my number-one complex—a terrible lack of judgement on my part. Funnily enough, I'd never believed I was the kind of girl to be swept off her feet by a man.'

'Or vice versa—who does?'

Holly smiled bleakly. 'It doesn't help. Anyway, I'm very much on guard against that kind of thing happening to me again. And I'm terribly, terribly wary now of the maelstrom of emotions that can go with love and marriage.'

'Maybe she was a unhinged. Perhaps you struck a one-in-a-million situation?' he suggested.

'Or maybe she just felt herself to be a woman scorned. Maybe she felt she couldn't live without him; they had two children. Maybe she just felt desperate; I don't know,' Holly said.

'What happened to them?'

'He went back to her and they moved overseas.' Holly fiddled with her napkin then looked straight into his eyes.

'But for a few months I was in serious trouble. I felt so guilty, even though I hadn't known about her. I was a nervous wreck—I still sometimes break out into a sweat and think I'm being followed. But my mother finally persuaded me to get some counselling and that's when I realized only I could get myself out of it. So I plunged into my work and the harder, even the more dangerous it was, the better.'

'And now?'

Holly rubbed her hands together. 'For the most part, fine, but still terribly wary of men and love and marriage—and my own lack of judgement.'

'I see.' He finished his wine. 'I guess that explains your aversion to *chemistry*.'

Holly bit her lip. Of course, he was quite right. The only thing was, she hadn't had any problems with "chemistry" after that disastrous affair until *he* had come into her life. Well, she'd been perfectly capable of stonewalling it without feeling it herself, but that was not the case now.

She looked across at him. 'My mistrust of it, yes. But I can't say it hasn't happened.'

'Between us?'

'Yes,' she whispered. She gestured a little helplessly. 'But you—you're… This is business, *serious* business for me anyway. I need to get this interview right. If I don't, you'll can it or my editor will.' She said with sudden passion, 'I need to make it vibrant and compelling. I can't do that if I'm—distracted.'

He stared at her with his lips twitching.

'What?' she asked huskily.

'You are on the horns of a dilemma.'

'If you're going to laugh at me…'

'I'm not,' he interrupted. 'Although that did strike me as, well, probably the least of our problems.'

Holly felt herself blush. She said honestly, 'You're right. I don't know where that bit came from.'

'Come and see the moon.' He stood up, came round to her and held out his hand.

She looked up at him. 'Where did *that* come from?'

He smiled. 'The moon? It just struck me, it's full tonight. See?' He pointed out towards the east.

Holly gasped at the orange globe rising above the tree line. 'Oh! How beautiful.' She got up.

'Mmm…' He took her hand and led her out onto the lawn.

Holly was transfixed as the moon rose, and in the process lost some of its orange radiance and shrunk a bit. She shivered. Days out in the savannah might be hot, but the nights were very cold, and she hadn't put on her jumper.

Brett put his arms around her. She couldn't help herself, and she snuggled up to him.

'Maybe this says it all,' he murmured, and started to kiss her.

Her lips quivered, but it seemed to her that her senses would no longer be dictated by her mind. They clamoured for his touch; they were lit by the feel of him, tall and hard against her, and tantalized by the pure essence of man she was breathing in.

She loved the press of his fingers against her skin; she loved the way they explored the nape of her neck and behind her ears while he kept his other hand around her waist.

But a skerrick of common sense claimed her and she raised her hands to put them on his chest. 'We ought to stop and think,' she breathed. 'This could be very dangerous.'

He lifted his head. 'Why? It has nothing to do with anyone but us, and we couldn't be in more agreement at the moment if we tried.'

Holly made a strange little sound in her throat. He stared down at her mouth in the moonlight and started to kiss her again.

She was almost carried away with delight when he stopped and raised his head to listen.

She came out of her enchanted trance with a start as she too heard footsteps. 'Sarah,' she breathed. 'I'd forgotten about her. She must be feeling a bit better— hungry, maybe!'

'We'll go to your…'

'No! I need to go and see if she's OK.' Holly stood on tiptoe and kissed him swiftly. 'Thanks for listening.' She sped off back towards the house.

Brett said something unrepeatable under his breath then looked down to see Bella sitting beside him. 'Come to sympathize, old girl? Well, what would you say if I told you that Holly Harding could be the right one for me? She's taken to Haywire as if she was born to it; she could be running the place, but of course it's not only that. She's becoming more and more desirable. But do I want a wife? It's hard to put down roots without one. How good would I be with a wife, though?

CHAPTER SIX

THERE was a triple knock on Holly's door before sunrise the next morning.

She'd been hovering on the edge of wakefulness for a while and she jerked upright, scrambled out of bed and went to open the door. 'What? Who? Why?' she breathed. 'Has something happened?'

'No.' It was Brett dressed in jeans and a jacket. 'Come and see the sunrise.'

'But I'm not even dressed!'

'Throw some warm clothes on, then; we haven't got much time.'

She hesitated then shrugged. 'OK.'

Ten minutes later she joined him in the ute.

She'd thrown on some slouchy trousers and a jacket and she was finger-plaiting her hair. They bumped over some rough ground for a few minutes then came to a lip in the ground, as far as she could see in the headlights.

Brett pulled up and switched the ute off. 'Won't be long now. Come and sit on the bonnet.'

Holly did as she was bid, and slowly the rim of the horizon started to lighten. As it did the chill breeze that had seen her wrap her arms around herself dropped.

With gathering speed, the darkness faded and she was looking down a long valley; all the colours of the landscape—the burnt umber and olive greens, the forest greens and splashes of amber—started to come alive as the sun reached the horizon.

It was so beautiful in the crystal-clear cool air, and alive in every little detail. She found she was holding her breath as she watched a wedge-tail eagle planing the thermals. Then as the sun climbed higher, that particular vividness of early dawn faded a little, and she sighed wistfully.

'Thank you for that,' she whispered, as if she was afraid of breaking the spell by talking aloud.

He merely nodded and got off the bonnet, but only to reach into the ute for a thermos flask and two cups.

The coffee he poured from the flask was full-bodied and aromatic. 'I thought you might be cross with me for dragging you out of bed.'

'No. Well…' Holly grinned. 'That may have been my first tiny reaction.' She sipped her coffee and sniffed appreciatively. 'Smells so good!'

He climbed back onto the bonnet. 'So you slept well?'

'I did. I…' She hesitated and thought of the tussle she'd had with herself before she'd been able to fall asleep. 'I did decide I needed to apologize.'

He raised an eyebrow at her. 'What for?'

Holly chewed her lip. 'This is not that easy to say but I seem to have developed the habit of—kissing you—and, uh, sloping off.'

'You have,' he agreed after a moment.

Holly looked slightly put out.

'What did you expect me to say?' He drained his coffee and put his cup down.

'I didn't expect you to agree quite so readily. And there are reasons for it, of course.'

'Of course,' he echoed. 'Such as, we just can't seem to help ourselves? That's what promotes it in the first place, at least.'

Holly wrapped her hands around her mug and was considering her reply when he went on, 'Then you get cold feet.'

'Well, I do! Why wouldn't I?'

He tilted her chin, observed the indignation in her eyes and smiled slightly. 'I could be going too fast. Should we just be friends for today?' He released her chin and put his arm around her shoulders.

Holly opened her mouth to ask him *what* he was going too fast towards, but she decided against it. She diagnosed one good reason for that: it felt so good to have his arm around her, and to contemplate a friendly day ahead, she didn't feel like debating anything.

'What else will we do today?' she enquired.

'I'm flying to Croydon for a meeting, cattle stuff. If you'd like to come, you could visit the old gold-rush museum and we could fly onto Karumba for lunch. Karumba is on the Gulf of Carpentaria.'

'Sounds great. I think I'd like that very much.'

She did.

She pottered around Croydon while he was in his meeting, she marvelled at the size of the Norman River from the air and she enjoyed a seafood basket on a thick, green lawn beneath shady trees. The Sunset Tavern at

Karumba Point sat on the mouth of the Norman River and overlooked the shimmering waters of the gulf.

'It must be magic at sunset,' she said idly.

'It is. Pity we can't stay, but I've got another meeting this afternoon at Haywire.' He stretched his legs out and clasped his hands behind his head.

'Never mind. It's been beautiful.'

He looked across at her. 'You're easy to please.'

'I don't think it's that. It *has* been great.' She pushed away her empty seafood-basket. 'So were the prawns.'

He laughed. 'Karumba is the headquarters of the gulf prawning-industry—they should be!'

Holly patted her stomach and sat back. That was when she noticed a couple of young women seated at a table nearby and how they were watching Brett with obvious fascination.

She grimaced mentally and felt some sympathy for them. Whether they knew who he was or not, *she* did. Thinking about him in his cargo pants and black sweat-shirt, with his ruffled dark hair and that eagle intensity at times in his dark eyes, and with his tall, streamlined physique, she had no difficulty picturing him engaging in dangerous exploits like shooting tranquilizer darts out of helicopters or parachuting into jungles.

Worse than that, she herself had not been immune from the effect of Brett Wyndham, although it had been designated a 'friendly' day. His hands on her waist when he'd lifted her down from the plane had sent shivers through her. Walking side by side with him had done the same.

Even doing those mundane things—not to mention laughing, chatting and sometimes being teased by him, channelled an awareness of him through her pores, both physical and mental.

I love him, she thought suddenly. *I love being with him. I love his height and his strength, his hands; I love breathing in his essence. But how can that be? It's only been a few days...*

She looked up suddenly to see him eyeing her with a question in his eyes.

'Sorry,' she murmured, going faintly pink. 'Did you say something?'

'Only—ready to go?'

'Oh. Yes. Whenever you are.'

'Something wrong?' His dark eyes scanned her intently.

'No,' she said slowly—but thought, *I don't know; I just don't know...*

Back at Haywire that afternoon, she took herself to task and forbade any more deep thinking on the subject of Brett Wyndham—in relation to her personally, that was. She went to work on her notes while Brett had his next meeting. She didn't ask what his business was, but two planes landed on the strip and he was closeted with the passengers for several hours.

She worked in her cabin, going over all the material she'd gathered, including the zoo details, and putting it into order.

She paused once; she was conscious of a lack, a hole in her story about Brett Wyndham, and realized it was the lack of any detail about his father. But there was another lack, she felt, brought on by her vision of him out at Karumba performing dangerous deeds. So far she had no details about his life as a vet in far-off exotic lands, and she would need that.

She made some notes then paused again and frowned. It occurred to her that if she were asked whether she could capture the essence of Brett Wyndham she would have to say no. There *was* something missing. But what made her think that? Some invisible barrier in him, drawn fairly and squarely so you couldn't cross it. The way just occasionally, when he was talking about his life, she sensed that he retreated and you knew without doubt you'd come to a no-go zone.

She realized she'd put it down to him being a genuine loner, but now she couldn't help wondering if there was more to it.

She shook her head as she wondered if it was her imagination. Then she put her pen down as she heard the noise of aircraft engines, and the two visiting planes taking off. Bella scratched on her door. She let her in and noticed a note attached to her collar with her name on it.

'Why, Bella,' she murmured. 'You clever girl!'

She smoothed the note open and digested the gist of it: a couple of the visitors had decided to stay overnight and would be picked up the following morning. Would Holly care to have dinner with them in about an hour?

Holly sent Bella back with an acceptance penned to the note. Then she went to find Sarah and offer her help, but Sarah was quite restored and wouldn't hear of it. So Holly showered and changed, this time into slim burgundy trousers and a pale-grey jumper over a white blouse.

* * *

It was a pleasant evening.

The two visitors were a couple from a neighbouring station and they proved to be good, lively company. It wasn't until ten-thirty that Holly excused herself and Brett walked her to her cabin.

'Had a nice day?' he enquired when they got there.

Holly turned to him impulsively. 'I've had a *lovely* day!'

'That's good. Ready to fly back to Cairns tomorrow?'

Holly grimaced. 'Yes, if not willing. But thanks for everything.' She glanced back towards the homestead where his guests were still sitting. 'You better get back. Goodnight.'

'Goodnight,' he echoed, but with an ironic little smile.

'I know what you're thinking,' she said, then could have shot herself.

'You do?' He raised an eyebrow at her.

She clicked her tongue in some exasperation and soldiered on. 'You're thinking *I'm* thinking that I've been saved by the bell!'

'Something like that,' he agreed. 'That the presence of visitors will prevent me from kissing you goodnight? But, since I've been on my best behaviour all day, and since it really has nothing to do with anyone else, you're wrong.'

And he put his hands around her waist, drew her into him and kissed her deeply.

Holly came up for air with her pulses hammering and her whole body thrilling to his touch, to the feel of him against her.

He put her away from him gently and smoothed the collar of her blouse. 'Don't put the light on until you're closed inside,' he advised. 'Goodnight.' And he turned away.

It took ages for Holly to fall asleep that night as she examined and re-examined her feelings; as she wondered about his, was conscious of a thrilling little sense of excitement. How could she have grown so close to him in such a short time? she asked herself. It was like a miracle, for her. But it wasn't only the physical attraction—although that was overwhelming enough—it was the powerful pull of his personality. It was as if he'd taken centre-stage in her life and she had no idea how to go on with that lynchpin removed...

Where would it all lead?

There was no opportunity for any personal interaction the next morning. The two guests were picked up after breakfast and then Brett and Kane were called to the home paddock for a colt with colic.

Holly watched the proceedings from the paddock fence as Brett worked to keep the horse on its feet whilst Kane prepared a drench. Once again she could see how good Brett was with animals as he soothed and walked the stricken horse and then administered the drench.

He came out of the paddock wearing khaki overalls, with sweat running down his face, and asked her if she was ready to leave. She nodded, said her goodbyes to Sarah and Bella and looked around. 'Bye, Haywire,' she murmured. 'You're quite a place.'

She hadn't realized that Brett was watching her thoughtfully while she'd said her goodbyes.

When they were alone, finally in the air, they didn't have much to say to each other at all, at first—until Brett made a detour and flew low over the ground to point out to her where he planned to locate the zoo.

'There's water.' He indicated several dams. 'There's good ground cover, but of course we'll have to feed by hand, so we'll establish several feed-stations.'

'There are no roads,' she said slowly.

'Not yet, and no fences, but that'll all come.'

'Are you planning to make it a tourist attraction?' she queried. 'I don't know if it's what you have in mind, but I read somewhere about a zoo that offered a camping ground as well. If you're thinking of an adopt-an-animal scheme, people might be interested in seeing their animals in the flesh, so to speak.'

He glanced at her. 'Good thinking.'

'It's a huge project.'

'Yes,' he agreed. 'But it needs to be done—I feel, anyway. OK.' The little plane lifted its nose and climbed. 'Back to the mundane—well, back to Cairns, anyway, and the wedding.'

But fate had other ideas for them. Not long after they reached their cruising altitude, the plane seemed to stutter, and Brett swore.

'What?' Holly asked with her heart in her mouth.

'I don't know,' he replied tersely as he scanned gauges and checked instruments. 'But it could be a blocked fuel-line. Listen, I'm going to bring her down.' He scanned the horizon now. 'Over there, as best I can.'

Her eyes nearly fell out on stalks. 'Over there'

appeared to be a dry river-bed. 'But we're in the middle of nowhere!'

'Better than what might be the alternative. I'm also going to put out all the appropriate distress signals and hope to get a response before we go down. Holly, just do exactly as I say and buckle in tightly. If anything happens to me, once we're on the ground get out as fast as you can in case the fuel tanks go up.'

She swallowed convulsively several times as he spoke into his radio and the plane lost altitude and stuttered again.

Expecting to nose-dive out of the sky any moment— not that she knew anything about the mechanics of flying—she had to admire his absolute concentration and the way he nursed the little plane down.

'All right, now duck your head and hold on tight,' he ordered. 'I'm bringing her in.'

Holly did just that as well as send up some urgent prayers for help, through the next terrifying, never-ending minutes.

They landed and hopped over the uneven sandy ground, slewing and skidding madly until they finally came to a halt with the nose about a metre from a huge gum-tree on the bank. A cloud of birds rose from the tree.

It had been like being in a dry washing-machine, for Holly. She'd been buffeted and bruised even within the confine of her seat belt. Her limbs had reacted like she'd been a rag doll being shaken, but all of a sudden everything was still and there was an unearthly quiet. Even the birds had stopped squawking.

She stared at the gum tree, so close, so solid, and

swallowed. Then she switched her gaze to Brett. He was slumped over the half steering-wheel with a bleeding gash on his forehead. After a frozen moment of panic for Holly, he lifted his head, shook it groggily and was galvanized into action.

'Out,' he ordered. 'It only takes some fuel to drip onto a hot pipe and we'll be incinerated.'

With an almost Herculean effort, he managed to open his door and climb out. He turned immediately and reached for Holly, manhandled her out of her seat and down onto the ground, where he took her hand and dragged her away from the plane.

They were both panting with exertion by the time he judged them far enough away to be safe; running through the sand of the riverbed had been almost impossible. Holly sank to her knees, then her bottom, her face scarlet, her chest heaving. Brett did the same.

They waited for a good half-hour in the shimmering heat of the river bed but the plane didn't explode. He told her he was going back to it to salvage whatever he could. He also told her to stay put.

'No,' she said raggedly. 'I can help.'

'Holly.' He looked down at her with blood running down his face. 'Please do as you're told, damn it!'

'No.' She reared up on her knees. 'I can help,' she repeated. 'And you can't stop me. Besides, you're bleeding—you could have concussion—'

'It's nothing,' he broke in impatiently.

'I'm coming. In fact, I'm going.' She got painfully to her feet and started staggering through the sand.

He swore quite viciously, then followed her.

Between them they managed to get their bags and two

blankets out of the plane. Brett also found a spare water-bottle strapped to a small drinking-fountain with a tube of plastic cups. He took out not only the spare bottle but the fountain itself. Then he discovered a few cardboard cartons with Haywire stencilled on their sides.

'I was probably meant to deliver these, but no-one mentioned it.'

'What's in them?' Holly breathed.

'No idea. Maybe soap powder—maybe not. We'll take them,' he said.

He also checked the radio, but it was dead, and the satellite phone was smashed. Just as he left the plane for the last time, the starboard wheel-strut collapsed suddenly, tilting it to an unnatural angle and crumpling the starboard wing into the ground.

They froze and waited with bated breath but nothing more happened.

'When is it completely safe?' she asked shakily.

He put an arm round her shoulder. 'If it was going to happen, it would probably have happened by now.' He put his other arm around her. 'Holly.' He stopped and put his other arm round her. 'How are you?'

She tried to break free but he held her closer, and it was only then that she realized she was shaking like a leaf and not quite in control of herself. 'I—I'm sorry,' she stammered. 'It's reaction, I guess. But I'll be fine; just give a me a few moments.'

'Of course.' He held her very close and stroked her hair until she stopped shaking.

'How do you feel now?'

It was a few hours later and the sun was starting to slip

away. The constraint that had had them in its grip earlier in the day had melted away under the circumstances.

'Oh, fine,' Holly responded. 'Thank you. You?'

They'd made themselves as comfortable as possible in the creek bed not far from the plane. Brett was leaning back against a smooth rock. There was a tree growing out from the bank, giving them shade. They'd pegged out in the sand a bright-orange plastic sheet with a V on it, which they'd got from the plane, where it would be most visible from the air.

He grimaced. 'I've got a headache that would kill a cow.' He touched his fingers gingerly to the cut on his forehead that Holly had cleaned as well as she'd been able to.

The packages for Haywire had proved a godsend. They contained packets of biscuits, some self-opening tins of luncheon ham, packets of dates and raisins, six tins of sardines, six tubes of condensed milk and one cardboard carton of white wine.

An odd mixture, he'd commented when they'd broken them out, but at least it was not soap powder, so they wouldn't starve.

She'd agreed ruefully.

They'd also found a small axe and a gas firelighter.

Now, as she watched the sun slipping away, she said, 'It looks as if we'll have to spend the night here.'

'Yes.' He shrugged. 'I doubt if it will be more than a night. But it takes time to co-ordinate a search and hard to do in the dark.'

She looked around and shivered. 'It's a big country.'

He studied her dirty, rather tense face. 'Come here.'

She hesitated then crawled over and leant back beside him. He put an arm round her.

'I'm really worried about my mother,' she said. 'She'll be devastated when she hears this news.'

'Yes.' He said nothing more for a long moment, then, 'You do realize you have me at your mercy, don't you, Holly?' He brushed his lips against her hair.

'Well, I certainly wouldn't take advantage of you with a headache, if that's what you mean,' she returned with some humour.

'Pity about that,' he drawled, then relented as she looked at him incredulously. 'What I meant was, we could talk—fill in the gaps, go on with the interview.'

'Now? But I'm not at all organized.'

'I wouldn't have thought it would take a girl who handled a crash-landing in the middle of nowhere with aplomb long to organize herself.'

'It wasn't all aplomb.'

'Believe me, one little attack of the shakes is very close to aplomb.'

She considered. 'Well, I've got a good memory, so I'll rely on that. Oh!' She put a hand to her mouth. 'My laptop. I didn't even think to check if it got smashed. But hang on…' She fumbled in one of her pockets and with a cry of triumph produced a flash key. 'Safe and sound.'

'You back everything up on that and keep it on your person at all times?' he guessed.

She nodded vigorously. 'Bitter, if not to say heart-breaking experience has taught me that. OK. Uh, I was thinking only yesterday that we haven't touched on any of your exploits to do with saving endangered species. I'm sure readers would find that riveting. And do you have a favourite animal?'

He thought for a while. 'Yes—giraffe. There's nothing like seeing them cross a plain with that rocking-horse rhythm, or staring down at you from above the crown of a tree. I'm very keen on giraffe—or Twiga, which is their Swahili name.'

She chuckled and led him on to talk about some of the successes he'd had as an endangered-species expert. Then their talk turned general until he asked her about her childhood.

She told him about her adventures with her father and couldn't prevent the love and admiration she'd felt for her father shining through. 'I miss him every day of my life. Is your father alive—?' She stopped and bit her lip.

'No.'

'Your mother?'

'No.'

'I'm sorry,' she said.

'You don't need to be sorry on my father's account,' he said dryly.

Holly took an unexpected breath and wondered if he would enlarge on what she was pretty sure was the thorny subject of his father. But he said no more, and she regretted the fact that they had somehow lost their sense of easy camaraderie, so she took another tack.

'How *do* you combine your lifestyle—travelling the world and so on—with running a grazing empire? And it's more than that, isn't it? You've branched out into mining, transport, even a shipping line for live-cattle exports amongst other things. Or does it all run itself?'

She felt a jolt of laughter run through him and breathed a secret little sigh of relief.

'No, it doesn't.'

'They say you're a billionaire,' she observed. 'They say you're responsible for tripling the family fortune.'

He shrugged. 'I told you, in some ways I'm a quintessential cattle man. It's in my blood, so some of it comes naturally. I'm also very attached to this country.' He looked around. 'And I did set out to prove something to myself—that when I took over I'd never allow the empire to go backwards.' He paused, pushed himself upright and looked down at her. 'Do you realize you have a dirty face?' He touched the tip of her nose.

Holly grimaced as she thought, *subject closed*. She said, 'If you had any idea how battered as well as dirty I *feel*.' She looked around. 'There wouldn't be any pools in this river bed, do you think?'

'There could be. There could be tributaries with some water in them, it was a fairly good wet season, but there'll also be crocs.'

'Croc… Crocodiles?' she stammered.

'Uh-huh. Mostly fresh-water ones, usually safe, but enough to give you a fright. And it's not completely unknown for the odd salt-water croc to find its way up here. They are not safe.'

'I see. OK,' she said judiciously. 'I'm happy to stay dirty.'

He frowned. 'You also said battered, but you told me you were fine earlier. Where…?'

She held up a hand. 'I am fine. Just a bit shook up. It's

also starting to get cold—that might be making me feel my age,' she said humorously. 'Don't old cowboys feel every mended bone when there's a chill in the air?'

'I don't know.' He looked rueful. 'But we should make some preparations. I don't want to light a fire— the breeze is blowing towards the plane now—so our best bet is to wear as much of our clothing as we can.'

Holly had inspected their bags earlier. Hers had mostly contained clothes, his had yielded a few useful items other than clothes: a serious penknife with all sorts of attachments, a small but powerful pair of binoculars, a compass and a torch. And they both had wind cheaters fortunately, for later when the temperature dropped.

'All right.' She got up. 'But I do have to go on a little walkabout. I'll add some clothes at the same time. I presume if I'm not close to water I'm safe?'

'Relatively,' he replied. 'But don't go far, and stamp around a bit. There could be snakes.'

Holly swore under her breath.

When she returned, he'd laid out a meal. He'd cut up one of the tinned hams and, together with biscuits, dates and raisins, he'd set it all out on two pieces of cardboard roughly shaped as plates. And he'd poured two plastic cups of wine.

He handed her his pocket knife and said he was happy to use his fingers.

They ate companionably in the last of the daylight, then the dark. He told her about some of the safaris he'd been on and the electronic-tagging system he'd been involved with that tracked animals.

She got so involved in his stories, she might have

been in Africa or Asia with him, experiencing the triumphs and the disasters he'd encountered.

He also poured them a second, then a third, cup of wine.

'This will send me to sleep,' she murmured. 'Or make me drunk, as well as give me a hangover.'

She didn't see the acute little glance he beamed her way.

'I doubt the hangover bit,' he said. 'It's very light, but it might be an idea to get settled now. How about we scoop some sand about to make a bit of a hollow and something to rest our heads on?'

'OK. You hold the torch and I'll—'

'No. *You* hold the torch and I'll—'

'But I can—'

'For once in your life, just do as you're told, Holly Harding!'

She subsided, then chuckled suddenly.

'I probably look quite amusing,' he said as he scooped sand. 'But you don't have to laugh.'

'I'm not laughing at you,' she told him.

'Who, then?'

She waved a hand. 'It just seems a very long way from society weddings, balls and so on— Oh!' She put a hand to her mouth. 'When was your first pre-wedding party?'

'Tomorrow. Nothing we can do about it,' he said with a grimace.

'Perhaps they'll cancel it because you haven't turned up?'

'Perhaps. Not that I would wish it on them—having

to cancel it—but the more concerned people are about us, the sooner they'll start organizing a search.'

'Of course,' she said eagerly, then sat back again. 'What was I saying? Yes, it's actually rather lovely. Look at the stars,' she marveled, and hiccupped. 'Told you,' she added.

'Listen, take the torch if you need another bathroom call—don't go too far—and then let's go to bed, Miss Harding.'

'Roger wilco, Mr Wyndham!'

When she came back, he'd lined the hollow that he'd scooped with the cardboard of the cartons and the paper the foodstuffs had been wrapped in. As they settled themselves, he draped the rest of their clothes over them, then the two blankets.

She slept for about three hours, curled up beside him with his arm protectively over her.

Then she woke, and it wasn't so lovely any more. It was freezing. At first she had no idea where she was, then there was something large moving around on the edge of the creek bed.

She moved convulsively and backed into Brett's arms with a squeak of fear.

'Shh,' he murmured and flicked on the torch. 'It's only a kangaroo. I've been watching it for a bit. It's just curious. Kangaroos aren't renowned for attacking and eating people.'

'I k-know that,' Holly stammered. 'It must have been all the tales of Africa you told me. I feel terrible.' She added.

'What's wrong?' he queried with a hint of surprise.

'Stiff and sore. Everything's aching. How about you?'

'I'm too damn cold to feel a thing. Come closer,' he ordered, and as she turned around with difficulty he gathered her into his arms. 'It's all the result of bouncing around in the plane, performing heavy tasks and sleeping on a river bed.'

'I suppose so. Mmm…at least that's a bit warmer. Do you mind if I really burrow in?'

'Why should I mind?' He stroked her back. 'In the light of hypothermia, it's the only thing to do. Just relax if you can.' He pulled the thin blankets from the plane more securely over her.

She was too grateful to protest, and gradually the protection of both blankets plus his body brought her some warmth, and her aching muscles unknotted a little.

She wasn't aware of the moment things changed—the moment when it wasn't only warmth and comfort she was seeking, or receiving, but something different. It came about so subtly it seemed entirely natural, a natural progression towards a greater closeness that claimed them both at the same time.

His hands slipped beneath her clothes as their mouths touched and he teased her lips apart. She moved her hands and slid them beneath his windcheater, responding to his kiss as she hugged him. From then on she forgot the cold and the discomfort of the river bed; she was lost to all good sense, she was to think later.

But, at the time, it was magic. She remembered something he'd said to her at the masked ball about celebrating her lovely, slim body to both their satisfactions. It wasn't quite like that—they were too hampered by clothes, covers and freezing night-air for that—but he gave her an intimation of what it would be like if they were together on a bed, or anywhere smooth and soft.

He transported her mentally to an oasis of delight where her skin would feel like warm silk—as he'd also promised. Even in the rough environment of a dry river-bed he managed to ignite her senses to a fever pitch as he kissed and caressed her, as he touched her intimately and made her tremble with longing, need and rapture.

She had her own sensory perceptions. She drew her fingers through the rough dark hair on his chest; she laid her cheek then her lips on the smooth skin of his shoulder, before returning her mouth to his to be kissed deeply again. And again.

She cupped her hand down the side of his face; she moved against the hard planes of his body. She was provocative, pressing her breasts against him and tracing the long, strong muscles of his back.

She was alight with desire for Brett Wyndham, she thought, when she could think. Alight, moving like a warm silken flame he couldn't resist in his arms.

How much further things would have got out of hand between them, she was never to know as a belligerent bellow split the chilly air.

They both jumped convulsively then scrambled to their feet, rearranging their clothes as best they could as Brett also searched for the torch. When he found it, it was to illuminate a mob of wild-looking cattle, some with huge horns, advancing down the creek bed towards them.

'Bloody hell!' Brett swore. 'Stay behind me,' he ordered. He reached up and tore a spindly limb from a tree growing out of the bank. 'They're probably as surprised as we are.'

With threatening moves, and a lot of yelling and whistling, he dispersed the mob eventually—but only after they'd got uncomfortably close. Then they took to their heels as if of one mind and thundered back the way they'd come, causing a minor sandstorm and leaving them both coughing and spluttering, sweating and covered in sand.

'Just goes to show, you don't have to go to Africa for wildlife excitement,' he said wryly.

'You have quite a way with cattle!'

'That was more luck than anything.'

Holly frowned. 'They didn't look like Brahmans.'

'They weren't, that's why I was a bit lucky. They were cleanskins, in case you didn't notice.'

'Cleanskins?'

'Yes. Rogue cattle that have evaded mustering and branding and therefore are not trained to it. Independent thinkers, in other words. Throwbacks to earlier breeds.'

'Oh.'

'Yep.' He dragged a hand through his hair and put the torch on the ground. 'Where were we?'

CHAPTER SEVEN

THEY stared at each in the torchlight then started to laugh.

In fact, Holly almost cried, she laughed so hard; he put his arms around her.

'I know, I know, but one day I will make love to you with no interruptions,' he said into her hair.

Holly sobered and rested against him.

'Look,' he added. 'You can just see the horizon. A new day.'

'How long will it take them to come?' she asked.

'No idea, but just in case we have to spend another night we'll need to get organized.'

Holly sat up. 'Another night?'

'That's the worst-case scenario,' he said. 'The best is that they know we're missing and they know roughly the area. So they'll keep looking until they find us.'

But full daylight brought another challenge: rain and low cloud.

'I thought this was supposed to be the dry season,' Holly quipped as a shower swept up the river bed.

They'd moved all their gear under tree-cover on the bank as best they could as soon as the clouds had rolled over. They were sitting under the cover of the plastic V-sheet Brett had hooked up from some branches.

'It is. Doesn't mean to say we can't get the odd shower. You know…' He stared out at the rain drumming down on the river bed, then looked at her. 'If you cared to take your clothes off, it might be quite refreshing.'

Holly looked startled. 'Do you mean skinny-dip?'

He shrugged. 'Why not? It's our only chance of getting clean for a while.'

Holly drew a deep breath and closed her eyes. 'Clean,' she repeated with deep longing. Her eyes flew open and she jumped up and started shedding clothes.

Brett blinked, not only at the fact that she did it but at the speed she did it. A rueful little smile twisted his lips as she stopped short at her underwear—a lacy peach-pink bra with matching bikini briefs.

'That's as far as I'm going to go,' she told him, and climbed down the bank to run out into the rain with something like a war cry.

He had to laugh as he watched her prancing around for a moment, then he stood up to shed his clothes down to his boxer shorts and climbed down the bank to join her.

It was a heavy, soaking shower but it didn't last that long. As it petered out, Holly—now more subdued—said in a heartfelt way as her wet hair clung to her head and face, her body pale and sleek with moisture, 'That was divine!'

She ran her hands up and down her arms and licked the raindrops from her lips.

'Yes, although I didn't expect you to do this.' He

grinned down at her and flicked some strands of wet hair off her face.

'I suspect most girls would have done the same if they'd been through what we have. Now, if only I had a towel...'

As she spoke, thunder rumbled overhead and a fork of lightning appeared to spear into the river bed not far from them.

Holly jumped convulsively and flew into Brett's arms. He picked her up and carried her swiftly to their makeshift shelter.

'Th-that was so close,' she stammered.

'Mmm...I don't think it'll last long; it's just a freak storm.' But he held her very close as more thunder rumbled.

'Lightning,' she said huskily, 'Is right up there with flying foxes for me. It's funny; there are a whole heap of things I can be quite cool about.'

'Mexican bandits and sheikhs?'

'Yep—well, relatively cool. But lightning—' she shivered '—I don't like.'

'Just as well I'm here, then,' he murmured and bent his head to kiss her.

'This—this is terrible,' Holly gasped, many lovely minutes later.

'What's so terrible?' He drew his hands down her body and skimmed her hips beneath the elastic of her briefs.

They were lying together beneath the protection of the plastic sheet in each other's arms on one of the blankets. They were damp but not cold—definitely not cold...

'How did I get to the stage of not being able to keep my hands off you?'

He laughed softly. 'For the record, I'm in the same boat.'

'But it's been so *fast*. There's got to be so much we don't know about each other.'

'It's *how* you get to know people that matters.'

'Maybe,' she conceded. 'I guess it helps, but there's an awful lot I don't know about you.'

He opened his mouth, appeared to change his mind and then said, 'Such as?'

Holly went to sit up but he pulled her back into his arms.

'In fact, you know more about me than most people,' he growled into her ear.

'But, for example—' She hesitated suddenly aware that she was about to tread on sacred ground, from an interviewer's perspective. But surely she was more than that now? 'I know you were engaged and that it didn't work out, but I don't know why. And I sense some—I don't know—darkness.'

She felt him go still for a moment, then his arms fell away and he sat up and stared through the dripping view to the river bed.

Holly sat up too after a couple of minutes, during which he was quite silent.

'Have I offended you?' she ventured hesitantly. 'I didn't mean to.'

He turned his head and looked down at her. Her pink bra had a smudge of mud on it, but he could see the outline of her high, pointed breasts clearly. Her waist was tiny, tiny enough to span with his hands, but her hips were delicately curved and positively peachy.

He rubbed his jaw. 'No.' He smiled suddenly and ironically. 'Are you open to a suggestion?'

'What is it?' she asked uncertainly.

'That we put some clothes on? Just in case a rescuer arrives.'

Holly stared at him, convinced she'd crossed a forbidden barrier, then she looked down at herself and took a sharp little breath. She scrambled up. 'Definitely!'

The thunder storm moved away pretty quickly as Brett had predicted, and there was no more rain, but the low cloud-cover remained.

'That's got to make it harder for them to find us,' she said as they ate a very light lunch, with a view to preserving their limited supplies. They'd also rationed the water, but Brett had found some shallow rock pools with fresh water in them for future use.

By mid-afternoon the cloud cover had cleared and they heard two planes fly over—not directly overhead, but fairly close.

They said nothing during the tense wait both times, just exchanged wry little looks when the bush around them returned to silence.

Brett returned to the plane and, after crawling in with some difficulty, spent some time working on the radios but to no avail.

By four o'clock they were sitting back against their rock in the shade when he put his arm around her. Without any conscious thought, she leant her cheek against his shoulder.

'There is an option to consider now,' he said. 'We could walk out.'

'Is that a viable option?' she queried.

'It's not what I'd prefer to do. At least we're visible here—the plane is, anyway. I do have a rough idea of where we are, though, and where this river leads. But it's a long walk—maybe a couple of days.'

'What's at the end of it?'

'A cattle station near the head waters. We'd have to travel light, more or less food and water only. We'd really have to eke out the food, but it could be done.'

'What if someone spots the plane but we're not there?'

'We'd leave a note, but anyway they'd automatically assume we've followed the river bed. You see—' He paused and glanced at her, as if he wasn't quite sure whether to go on, then said, 'I didn't mention this yesterday but there's the possibility that none of our signals or radio calls were picked up. That means our position won't be known except very roughly, and we did make a detour.'

'Ah,' she said on a long-drawn-out breath. 'Well, then, I guess it makes sense to take things into our own hands. At least,' she added rather intensely, 'We'd be doing something!'

'My thoughts entirely.'

'And if we take the V-sheet with us we can always wave it if anyone flies overhead.'

'Good thinking,' he said, and kissed her on the top of her head. 'But listen, it could mean a very cold night. He sat up. 'Unless I make a sled of some kind so we could take a bit more with us—a blanket, at least. Come to that,' he said as if he was thinking aloud, 'once we're well away from the plane, we could make a fire. I had thought of doing that this afternoon, but well away from the plane.'

'Send up smoke signals, you mean?' she asked humorously.

'Something like that,' he replied with a grin. 'But everything's still damp. Tomorrow it may have dried out if we get no more rain. Uh, I have to warn you, though—this river bed could have rapids in it that would mean rock climbing, now its mostly dry, so it could be a very arduous walk.'

'And there could be wild cattle, there could be dingoes, heaven alone knows what,' she said with a delicious little shiver of anticipation of adventure.

His eyebrows shot up, then he laughed down at her. 'You're a real character—you're actually looking forward to it.'

'I was never one for sitting around! Perhaps we should have gone today,' she added seriously.

'No. It'll have done us the world of good to have a lay day after all the trauma of yesterday. But an early night'll be a good idea. Should we put it to the vote?'

'Aye aye, skipper—I vote yes.'

'OK. We'll get to work before the light runs out so we can leave at the crack of dawn tomorrow morning.'

It was just that, barely light, when they set off the next morning.

They'd finished all their preparations the afternoon before and spent a companionable night. Holly was at least buoyed up by the prospect of some action rather than sitting around waiting for what might not come. The more she thought about the vast, empty terrain surrounding them, the more she realized it could be like looking for a needle in a haystack.

Brett used the axe to make two long poles from tree branches and, using a variety of clothes, they constructed a light but sturdy sled for carrying stuff. Holly wrought two back-packs out of long-sleeved shirts.

Between them they smoothed an area of sand in the middle of the creek bed, helped by its dampness, and in big letters they wrote WALKED UPSTREAM, with several arrows pointing in the direction they would take. Then they lined the scores the letters had made in the sand with small rocks to make them more lasting and visible.

Brett also wrote a note and left it in the plane. He pointed out that the heavy shower of earlier had been a blessing for another reason, apart from allowing them to clean up a bit—it would also provide rock pools of fresh water along the way.

Not surprisingly—after a light supper of sardines on biscuits, and half a tube each of condensed milk for energy plus one cup of water each—they had little trouble falling asleep. Even the cold hadn't bothered Holly as much as it had the night before. Being curled up in Brett's arms gave her a lovely feeling of security.

She did wonder, briefly, where all the passion that had consumed them last night had gone, and concluded that either she had touched a nerve he hadn't wanted to be touched although he'd been perfectly normal during the day—or the physical exertion they'd expended had simply worn them out too much even to think of it.

She was to discover soon enough that being tired was no guard against anything...

It was a long, arduous day.

They walked in the cool of the morning, they slept beneath some leafy cover through the midday heat and they walked again in the afternoon.

It was fairly easy going, as far as sand could be easy, and they encountered no rocks they had to climb over.

They did see some pools of water and a couple of times they saw freshwater crocodiles slither into them.

She marvelled at Brett's strength and tirelessness as he towed the sled with a belt around his waist, as well as carrying a backpack.

As for herself, she sang songs to keep herself going when she would have loved to lie down and die. And she thought a lot as she trudged along, thoughts she'd never entertained before, about mortality and how, when you least expected it, swiftly, you could be snuffed out. It was delayed reaction to the plane crash, probably, but nonetheless to be taken seriously. It was about seizing the day or, instead of looking for perfection in every thing you undertook, letting the way life panned out have some say in the matter.

Brett took a lot of the credit for keeping her going. Every now and then he made her stop and he massaged her shoulders and back, or he told her jokes to make her laugh. He'd insisted on adding her backpack to the sled when she was battling.

Fortunately they both had hats in their luggage and Holly had a tube of factor thirty-plus sunscreen with which they'd liberally anointed themselves. This proved to be a mixed blessing, causing the sand to stick to them.

But there were some marvels to observe along the way: some black cockatoos with red tail feathers sailed overhead, with their signature lazy flight and far-away calls. They also saw a huge flock of pink-and-grey galahs and a family of rock wallabies.

Otherwise, the hot, still bush all around them was untenanted, even by wild cattle. Again they heard plane engines a couple of times but, the same as the day before, the planes were nowhere near enough to see them.

Then, just as they were about to call it a day, they got a wonderful surprise: the river bed wound round a corner and opened into a lagoon, a lovely body of water full of reeds, water lilies and bird life and edged with spiky, fruit-laden pandanus palms.

'Is it a mirage?' Holly gasped.

Brett took her hand. 'No, it's real.'

'Thank heavens! But is it full of crocodiles?'

'We'll see. Look.' He pointed. 'There's a little bay and a rock ledge with a beach above it. There's even a bit of a shelter. Good spot to spend the night.'

Holly burst into tears, but also into speech. 'These are tears of joy,' she wept, and laughed at the same time. 'This is just so—so beautiful!'

He hugged her. 'I know. I know. Incidentally, you've been fantastic.'

The shelter was rough-hewn out of logs, closed on three sides with a bark roof. There was evidence of occupation, a burnt ring of sand within a circle of rocks outside, and a couple of empty cans that had obviously been used to boil water over a fire.

'We can't be too far away from somewhere!' Holly enthused as she slipped her backpack off with a sigh of relief. Then she sat down, and took her boots off and wiggled her toes with another huge sigh, this time pure pleasure.

'No,' Brett agreed as he cast around, looking at the ground inside and outside the shelter. 'But there's no sign of— Ah, yes, there is.' He squatted down and outlined something in the sand with his fingers. 'A hoof print. Who ever uses this place comes by horse.'

'A horse, a horse, my kingdom for a horse!' Holly carolled. 'Or a camel. Or a donkey!'

Brett laughed.

'So who do you think uses it?' she enquired.

'A boundary rider—a mustering team, maybe.' He stood up. 'Whoever, we could be closer to the homestead than I thought.'

'That is music to my ears. Now, if only I wasn't covered in a repulsive mixture of sweat, sand and sunscreen, I'd be happy.'

'There's an easy remedy for that.' As he spoke Brett pulled off his shirt. 'I'm going for a swim.' He stripped off to his boxer shorts again and jogged down to the beach.

'But...' Holly temporized, thinking inevitably of crocodiles.

'This is fresh water,' he called back to her after he'd scooped a handful up and tasted it. 'And this,' he added as he waded in up to his waist, sending a variety of birds flying, 'is an old Aboriginal remedy for crocs.'

He started to beat the water with his palms. 'Frightens them off. Come in, Holly. I'm here anyway.'

She hesitated only a moment longer, then started shedding her clothes down to her underwear. Today she was wearing a denim-blue bra and matching briefs. She went into the water at a run in case her courage gave out to find it was divine, cool and refreshing, cleansing, incredibly therapeutic.

They played around in it for over half an hour then came out to the chilly air; it was close to sunset.

'Use whatever you can to dry off properly,' he recommended. 'We can always dry clothes tomorrow in the sun.' They'd only brought one change of clothes each.

'What if it rains again?'

'I doubt it will.' He towelled himself vigorously with a T-shirt and looked around. 'You know what they say— red sky at night, shepherd's delight.'

'Oh.' She looked around; the feathery clouds in the sky, a bit like a huge ostrich-feather fan or a group of foxtails, turned to orange as she watched.

'Anyway, I'm going to build a fire, so we can dry things beside it as well as keep warm. But get dressed and warm in the meantime.' He hung his shirt on a nail in the shelter wall and pulled on jeans and his second T-shirt. He was just about to turn away when he kicked his toe on something sharp protruding from the sandy floor.

He knelt down and, using his long fingers, unearthed a metal box. It wasn't locked, and what it contained made him say with absolute reverence, 'Holy mackerel! Look at this.'

Holly was now dressed in a pair of long cotton

trousers and her long-sleeved blue blouse. She bent down and looked over his shoulder. 'Oh my,' she breathed. 'Coffee! Tea! And a plate and a cup. I could kill for a cup of tea or coffee; don't mind which. But what's the other thing?' She frowned.

'This.' He lifted the red plastic spool out of the box. 'Is like gold. It's a fishing reel, complete with lure.' He showed her the curved silvery metal plate with a three-pronged hook on it. 'And sinker. I wondered if there'd be fish in the lagoon; there usually are.' He stood up. 'I was thinking I could kill for a beef steak, but a grilled fish would do nicely. All right, I'm going to collect firewood, you're going to fish.'

'Uno problemo—I have never used one of those things.'

'I'll show you how. Just watch.' He walked to the rocky ledge above the lagoon and unwound about a metre of the fishing line from the reel with the lure on the end. Holding the reel facing outward in one hand, he swung the lure on the line round several times then released it towards the water. The fishing line on the reel sang out as it followed suit, and she heard the lure plop into the water.

'Now what?' she asked keenly.

'Hold the line—you can put the reel down—and when you feel a tug on the line give it a jerk and pull the line in. Try.' He wound the line back onto the reel and handed it to her.

It took Holly several goes—the first time she hooked the lure into a tree—but finally she got it right and was left in charge in the last of the daylight as Brett went to collect firewood.

Her ecstatic shout when she felt the first tug on the line and pulled in a fish set all the water birds squawking in protest. Getting it off the line was her next test. Brett had to show her how to wrap one of her socks around the fish so she could hold it with one hand and wiggle the hook out of its mouth with the other. By the time he'd collected a big pile of wood and was setting the fire, she'd caught six very edible fish.

Brett had a go but caught none.

The first thing they did when the fire was going was boil water in one of the tins and make a cup of coffee, which they shared. Then, using a grid he'd found under one of the rocks around the fire area, Brett grilled the fish, which he'd cleaned with his penknife.

They shared the plate and ate the fish with their fingers.

'I don't know why,' Holly said, 'But this is the best fish I've ever tasted.'

'Could be a couple of reasons.' He glanced at her in the light of the blazing fire, but she didn't see the wicked little glint in his eye. 'After two days of ham and sardines on biscuits, anything would taste good.'

Holly pouted. 'That's one, what's the other?'

'I'm a good, inventive cook.'

'All you did was put them on a grid.'

'That's *not* all,' he countered. 'I had that part of the fire going to perfection so it wouldn't burn them, dry them out or leave them raw.'

'But I caught them!'

'So that makes them very superior fish?'

'Yes,' she said with hauteur, then giggled. 'You wouldn't be a little miffed because you *didn't* catch any?'

He looked offended. 'No. What makes you say that?'

She shrugged, still smiling. 'Just that I can't help feeling very proud of the achievement.' She paused and sobered. 'If I wasn't so worried about my mother, I'd really be enjoying all this.'

'We may be able to end her suspense sooner than we thought—end everyone's.'

'I hope so,' Holly said fervently. 'And she is an eternal optimist.'

She was sitting with her knees drawn up and her arms around them. He was stretched on the sand with his head on his elbow. Because of the fire they were not rugged up to the nines, and Holly had arranged the V sheet in the shelter for them to lie on, with the one blanket they'd brought covering them.

Brett thought to himself, as he watched her in her light trousers and blue shirt, with her bare feet and the fire gilding her riotous hair, that she had never looked more desirable.

Was it because she'd coped so well? he wondered. Had that added to his attraction to her? But was he going to be able to overcome her wariness? She might tell him she couldn't keep her hands off him, but he knew that deep down she was still wary, still burnt by her previous experience.

And he thought about *his* wariness—about the discovery he'd made about himself that he hated and feared, and made him wonder if he was a fit mate for any woman.

It was, of course, the thing Holly had sensed in him, the thing she couldn't put her finger on—the thing he had never wanted to admit to himself. But what was between them wasn't the same thing that had happened to him before, was it?

This was a powerful attraction, yes, but it was also affection. Yes, it was sweet, but it was also sane and sensible because she would fit into his lifestyle so completely...

Then he realized she was returning his regard, her deep-blue eyes very serious, as were the young, lovely curves of her face.

A slight frown came to his face, because he had no idea what she was thinking. Was she thinking about her mother? He got the feeling she was not.

'Holly?'

She looked around, as if unwilling for him to see what was in her eyes. She looked at the fire, at the darkened lagoon beyond, at the moon rising above them and the pale smoke of the fire wreathing against the dark blue of the sky. 'I think I'm running out of steam,' she said at last. 'I feel terribly weary.'

'I'm not surprised,' he said after a moment, and stood up. 'Come to bed. But have a cup of water first; I don't want you to dehydrate.'

'Are you coming to bed?' she asked.

'Shortly. I'm going to get more wood so we can keep the fire going as long as possible. Goodnight.' He held his hand out to her.

She took it and got to her feet. 'I— Thank you.'

'What for?'

'All you've done today, and tonight. The swim, the fish, the fire; that's all been magic.'

He frowned. 'You're not afraid we won't get out of this, are you?'

She shrugged. 'No. What will be, will be.'

He stared down at her intently for a moment then kissed her lightly. 'Sweet dreams, Holly Harding.' He turned away.

Holly woke from a deep, dreamless sleep at two o'clock. There was just enough light from the glowing embers of the fire for her to see her watch, but her movement woke Brett. She was resting in his arms.

'Sorry,' she whispered.

'Doesn't matter,' he mumbled.

It was nowhere near as cold as it had been the two previous nights, even though the fire had died down. The heat of it must be trapped within the shelter, she thought.

She went still as Brett pulled her closer into his arms and his mouth rested on her cheek. Her senses started to stir, started to clamour for his touch, for his kiss. But had he gone back to sleep?

Her lips parted and his mouth covered hers; no, he hadn't. But he hesitated, and Holly suddenly knew she couldn't bear it if he withdrew.

She put her hand on his cheek and arched her body against him, and found herself kissing his strong, tanned throat. He made a husky sound and then his hands moved on her body and she rejoiced inwardly, knowing they were claimed by the same need and desire.

Once again they fumbled with their clothes as best they could, but the rhythm of rapture made light work of it. She put her arms above her head and let his hands travel all the way down her, then gasped as they came back to her breasts.

She lay quietly, quivering in his arms, and allowed him to tantalize her almost unbearably as those fingers sought her most secret places. Then she wound her arms around him and kissed him as if her life depended on it.

He accepted the invitation to claim her completely in a way that brought them both intense and exquisite pleasure.

They were still moving to that pleasure as they slowly came back to earth, then they separated at last but stayed within each other's arms.

'We didn't say a word,' he murmured, and kissed her.

'It didn't seem necessary,' she answered. 'Did it?'

'No, but—' He broke off and lifted a hand to stroke her hair.

'I wanted to say something earlier,' she told him. 'When we were sitting by the fire—I wanted to say I didn't think I could do it.'

He raised his head and frowned down at her. 'Holly...'

'No.' She touched her fingers to his lips. 'Let me finish. I wanted to say I didn't think I could lie on this V-sheet without wanting to be held, kissed and made love to.'

He sat up abruptly.

'Not after everything,' she went on. 'Because you

were incredible—not only in all you did today, but in the way you kept me going.'

'Holly…'

She broke in again. 'I'm just happy to be with you tonight. It—it just seemed to be so fitting and right for the moment, and sometimes I think you need to *live* for the moment. But you don't have to worry about the future.'

He sank back beside her and pulled her into his arms again. 'I'm not worried about it. I'm looking forward to it. When will you marry me?'

CHAPTER EIGHT

HOLLY gasped, then evaded his arms and sat up urgently. 'That's exactly what I *don't* want you to feel you have to do!'

He propped his head on his elbow and looked up at her with a glint in his eyes she couldn't decipher. 'You've had time to work that out?' he queried.

She bit her lip. 'Obviously, otherwise it wouldn't have come to mind.'

He grimaced. 'But why not?' He lifted a hand and touched his fingers to her nipples.

Holly shivered but forced herself to concentrate. 'How could you suddenly want to marry me? I'm sure you don't ask every girl you sleep with to do that.'

He looked briefly amused. 'No. But it's not so sudden. It's been on my mind since you came to Haywire. Look, you asked me how I juggled things earlier: the truth is I'm at a bit of a crossroads. I'm getting tired of all the juggling I have to do. I'm thinking of coming home on a fairly permanent basis. That's what prompted the zoo idea—it's a way I can carry on my work and be here at the same time.'

Holly turned her head. 'Won't that be an awful wrench for you?'

'Sometimes,' he said slowly and pulled her back against him. 'And I'll probably always take off now and then; I won't be able to help myself. But it's time to put down some roots. The thing is—' He paused. 'I've had trouble really coming to grips with the idea—not the zoo, but putting down roots. Because I've had no-one to do it with. But now there's you.'

Holly tried to think. 'I'm—I don't know what to say. Please tell me, are you serious?'

'Deadly serious.'

She stirred against him. 'Brett, could I be—and I ask *this* seriously—a bit of a novelty for you?'

She felt him shrug. 'A wonderful novelty,' he agreed. 'But we also have a lot in common. You fitted into Haywire almost as if you'd been born to it.' He threaded his fingers through hers. 'Could you see yourself living there? Us living there?'

It occurred to Holly that she could. It was a lifestyle that encompassed all the things she loved: far away, exciting, different and still a challenge at times. And with a huge challenge coming up, if he went ahead with his plans for the zoo.

What about her career, though?

She could always freelance, she thought.

She even found herself contemplating a serious journalistic career focusing on the cause that was so dear to his heart and was becoming more and more fascinating to her.

Of course, there was the other factor: she was conscious of his body against hers and the sheer delight, the strength and warmth, it could bring her. Not only that, it was as if she'd found the centre of her universe in him.

She moved abruptly. 'I… Brett, could this not be love but something more—convenient?'

'It didn't feel convenient a little while ago. Did it for you?'

She shivered again as she relived their passion. 'No,' she whispered, shaken to her core.

'And there's this,' he went on very quietly. 'How easy would it be for you to get up and walk away from me?' He smiled ironically. 'Assuming it was possible anyway and we weren't marooned in an oasis in a bloody river-bed.'

She had to smile but it faded swiftly as she battled with how to answer him. 'I…' She stopped as tears suddenly beaded her lashes.

'Don't cry,' he said very quietly. 'It would be hell for me too.'

'The last thing I would want to feel is that you're sorry for me.' She sniffed.

'I'm not. But I do feel as if I want to look out for you.'

'That could be the same thing,' she objected.

'No. It means I care about you.'

Holly sniffed again. 'Do I have to make a decision right now?'

'Why not? We're never going to get as good an opportunity to think clearly.'

She frowned. 'What—how do you mean?'

'No outside influences at all.'

She swallowed in sudden fear. 'What if we don't get rescued or we don't find the station?'

His lips twisted. 'Perhaps the perfect solution. We could do a "me Tarzan, you Jane" routine. No, only joking. We will get rescued.' He pushed aside the layer of cover and took her in his arms. 'Believe me,' he added, and kissed her gently.

Holly felt herself melting within, and when he lifted his head she laid her cheek on his shoulder.

'Is that a yes?' he queried.

She hesitated. 'I don't know yet. I just don't know.'

He grimaced but said, 'Never mind. I'll ask you again every hour on the hour until our rescuers arrive or we arrive somewhere. Go back to sleep.' He looked at his watch over her head. 'We've got a couple of hours before dawn. Comfy?'

'Yes,' she breathed. 'Oh, yes.'

Five minutes later she was fast asleep, although Brett stayed awake for a while and contemplated this turn of events. Surely she wasn't planning to walk away from him now? he theorized.

It wasn't dawn that woke them; they slept well past it, in fact.

It was the sound of a man clearing his throat and saying, 'Excuse me, but were you two in a airplane crash?'

CHAPTER NINE

THEY both shot up. Holly immediately grabbed the blanket and pulled it up as she realized what a state of disarray she was in.

Not only was there a tanned, wiry little man with bowed legs and a big hat looking in on them, but two horses were looking over his shoulders with pricked ears and what appeared to be deep interest.

Even Brett was lost for words.

The man said, 'Don't mean to disturb anything, but if you are from the plane there's a hell of a hue and cry going on over you. Tell you what, I'll just take a little walk while you get—organized.' He wheeled his horses around and walked away.

Holly and Brett turned to each other simultaneously and went into each other's arms.

'I told you we'd get out of this,' he said as he hugged and kissed her.

'You did, you did!' she said ecstatically. 'And I offered my kingdom for a horse—I can't believe this! Where on earth did he come from?'

In the event, their saviour was a boundary rider for the station they were making for, and he was quite happy to wait while they had a swim. Fully clothed and decorous, they changed into their other set of clothing. He even made them a cup of coffee while he waited.

While they drank coffee, he explained how he'd heard the news of the loss of the plane just before setting out from the homestead on a routine inspection, and how he'd promised to keep his eyes open.

'Didn't see nothing, though,' he added. 'But last night I smelt smoke on the breeze and the breeze was coming from this direction, so I thought I'd take a look and see.'

'Is this your camp?' Brett asked.

'Sure is,' the man, Tommy, replied proudly. 'I put the shelter up, and they call it Tommy's Hut.'

'Well, your fishing gear was a lifesaver, Tommy. So was the rest of it. How far are we from the homestead?'

Tommy chewed a stalk of grass reflectively. 'Bout a three-hour ride, considering there's three of us and only two horses. Won't be able to make much time. You and the missus can share a horse.'

'Any family in residence at the homestead?' Brett enquired.

'Nope, just a manager. The place has gone up for sale, actually—family quarrels over money, I hear, so they need to cash it in. But they got radios and phones to get word out you're OK, and to rustle up a plane to get you back to Cairns.'

'Great.'

'Goodbye,' Holly said softly half an hour later when the camp had been tidied up and most of their gear stowed in the shelter.

She was perched in front of Brett on a tall brown horse.

'Talking to me?' he enquired.

'No. I'm farewelling a lovely spot, a place that was a bit of a lifesaver and a bit of a revelation.' She turned for a last look at the lagoon, the water lilies, the birds and the palms. 'An oasis.'

'Yes,' he agreed. 'And more.' But he didn't elaborate.

It was late that afternoon when they flew back into Cairns. A plane similar to the one they'd crashed in had retrieved them from the cattle station, where they'd taken fond farewells of their rescuer and his horses.

They hadn't had any time alone together at all.

What Holly hadn't expected, or even thought about, was that there would be an army of press waiting behind a barrier to greet them. She blinked somewhat dazedly into the flashlights as she stepped down onto the runway in the general-aviation section of the airport. Then she made out a face she knew in the crowd and, with a little cry, she ran forward and into her mother's arms.

A day later, Holly was still at Palm Cove.

Her mother had gone home and Holly had been in two minds as to whether she should go back to Brisbane too. She'd seen little of Brett, who'd been tied up with air-crash investigators and all sorts of authorities. She herself had kept a very low profile.

In fact, after she'd said farewell to her mother, she'd gone for a walk along the beach and felt like pinching herself. Had she dreamt that Brett Wyndham had asked her to marry him? Had she dreamt up a magic oasis that had become a place of even greater pleasure? No, she knew she hadn't dreamt that. She still had some marks on her body to prove it.

But was she a journalist with an interview to complete, or what?

'Remember me?'

She jumped as Brett ranged up alongside her. 'Oh. Hi! Yes, although I was wondering if I'd ever see you again.'

He took her hand and swung her to face him. He wore a loose, blue cotton shirt and khaki shorts; his feet were bare.

'I'm sorry.' He bent his head and kissed her lightly. 'Can you remind me the next time I'm tempted to crash-land a plane that the amount of paperwork involved is just not worth it? And it's not finished yet!'

Holly giggled. 'All right.'

'Incidentally, I sent a helicopter out to the crash site and Tommy's Hut. They brought all our stuff back.'

'Good. Although my mother brought me some clothes.' She looked down at the long floral skirt she wore with a lime T-shirt.

'Would she have brought anything appropriate for a ball?'

Holly stiffened.

'It's tonight,' he said. 'Please come as my partner. And to the wedding tomorrow evening.'

'No. Thank you, but no. I—'

'Holly, sit down. Look, there's a handy palm-tree here.'

'Brett' She tried to pull away, but he wouldn't let

her, and finally they sank down and leant back against the tree.

'You're looking a little dazed,' he said. 'And I can't blame you—'

'Yes, well, if I didn't dream it,' she interrupted, 'please don't ask me to marry you again, because at the moment I am— I don't know if I'm on my head or my heels.'

He stared down at her. 'You didn't dream it,' he said with a glimmer of a smile in his eyes. 'Although I won't ask—not immediately, anyway.' He sobered. 'But this ball is a way for us to be together tonight, because I can't get out of it and I'm having withdrawal symptoms. How about you?'

Holly drew her knees up, put her arms around them and rested her chin on them in a bid to hide the powerful tremor that had run through her.

'Holly?' He said her name very quietly.

She turned her head and laid her cheek on her knees. 'Yes. Yes, I am. I'm missing you.'

'Then?'

She sighed and looked out to sea. 'All right. Do you have to go off somewhere now?'

'Not for at least half an hour,' he said. 'What would you like to do?'

'In half an hour?' She smiled. 'Well, talk, I guess.'

He stretched out his legs as she sat up, and he put his arm around her. 'Did I tell you how fantastic you were?'

Holly made her preparations for the ball in a state of mind that could have been termed 'a quandary'.

On one hand, she wanted to be with Brett rather desperately but, on the other, did she want to be with him under the scrutiny of his family and doubtless a whole host of people?

Not only a host but probably a high-profile host.

It was in line with this thought that she followed an impulse and booked into a beauty parlour when she normally wouldn't have. The impulse was not only prompted by a need to hold her own in an upmarket throng; her nails were broken and ragged and her hair resembled a dry bird's-nest despite having washed it.

So she had a manicure and a deep-conditioning hair treatment, as well as a mini-facial. She came out of the parlour feeling a bit better about the ball and definitely better about her hair and nails.

Next decision was what to wear. For once in her life she was tempted to shop, then she remembered that her mother had brought one of her favourite dresses, one that was the essence of simplicity but which she always felt good in.

It was black, a simple long shift in a clinging silk jersey with a scoop neck and no sleeves. With it she wore a necklace made of many strands of fine black silk threaded with loops and whorls of seed pearls and tiny shells. It was the necklace that really made the dress, and the shoes. They were not strappy sandals but a pair of low court-shoes in silver patent with diagonal fine black stripes. Her mother had even packed the bag that went with the outfit, a small patent-leather purse that matched the shoes.

How had her mother known she would need these items? Holly wondered suddenly. Then she recalled with a smile that Sylvia never went anywhere without being fully prepared for any eventuality. It struck her suddenly—had her mother guessed that there was something between her only daughter and Brett Wyndham?

It probably was not such an unusual conclusion to come to since they'd been forced into each other's company for the last three days, not to mention the days that had gone before, and Sylvia could be pretty intuitive.

She shrugged and started to put on a light make-up.

Brett came to collect her from her room an hour early, and took her breath away in a dinner suit.

'You look lovely,' he said and took her hand.

'So do you,' she answered with a glint of mischief in her deep-blue eyes.

'Lovely?'

'In your own way.' She studied his tall figure in the beautifully tailored black suit. 'Distinguished. Dangerous.'

His eyebrows shot up 'Dangerous?'

'Dangerously attractive. Did I ever tell you that you were rather stunning as a Spanish nobleman?'

'No.' He grinned down at her. 'You were far too busy impersonating a French Holly Golightly and spinning me yarns about asses and camels.'

Holly gurgled with laughter. Somehow the ice was broken between them, which was to say, somehow she felt a lot better about going to this ball with him.

'I'm early,' he said as they walked away from her room, 'Because Sue is having pre-ball drinks in her suite. I'll be able to introduce you to her, as well as

Mark and Aria. Incidentally.' He paused. 'My ex-fiancée will be at the ball, and she could be at Sue's drinks. I don't think I told you she's in charge of all the wedding festivities.'

Holly missed a step.

He stopped beside her. 'She's a friend of Aria's, and she's the best at this kind of thing. It's been over between us for some time now.'

Nine months; it shot through Holly's mind. *It's not that long, is it?*

But she said nothing, although some of her feel-good mood about the ball ebbed a little as she thought of being confronted by Natasha Hewson.

She need not have worried, she soon discovered. Her presence both at Sue's drinks and the ball was that of a celebrity—the girl who'd survived the plane crash with Brett but kept a very low profile since.

Mark and Aria were warmly friendly, so was Sue Murray. And so was Natasha Hewson. She *was* the same redhead Holly had seen dining the night before they'd flown to Haywire.

She was also extremely beautiful, tall and exotic in a bouffant shocking-pink gown.

Holly did have a momentary vision of Natasha and Brett as a couple and thought they would have been absolutely eye-catching. But Natasha appeared to be happily in the tow of a handsome man, and Holly could detect no barely hidden undercurrents between her and Brett. Which was probably why what did eventuate later in the evening came as such a shock to Holly.

In the meantime, she started to enjoy herself.

The resort ballroom faced the beach and the cove

through wide glass windows, so the view was almost unimpeded. Due to a trick of the evening light, you felt as if you could lean across the cove and touch Double Island and its little brother.

Dinner was superb, a celebration of "reef and beef" that included the wonderful seafood found in the waters off the coast. Not only was dinner superb but the company beneath the chandeliers and around the exquisitely set tables was too.

Cooktown orchids decorated the tables, and the women's gowns, in contrast to the men in dark dinner-suits, brought almost every colour of the spectrum to the scene: primrose, topaz, camellia pink, sapphire, violet, oyster, claret and many more. Not only the colour, but there was every style and texture: there were silks, satins, taffetas, there were diaphanous voiles encrusted with sequins that flashed under the lights. There were skin-tight gowns, strapless ones, ruched and frilled ones. As it happened, there was only one plain-black one...

She and Brett dined at a table for eight that included his sister Sue as well as the bridal couple, Mark and Aria. Natasha Hewson was on the other side of the room.

After dinner, Brett invited her to dance.

'You know,' he said as she moved into his arms, 'You've done it again.'

She shot a startled look at him.

'You stole the show as Holly Golightly; you've done it here.'

Holly blinked, then shook her head. 'Oh, no.'

'Believe me, yes.' He pulled her close. 'Do you dance as well as you do everything else, Miss Golightly?'

She lowered her voice a notch. 'Possibly better than I ride, monsieur.'

He laughed and dropped a kiss on her hair.

Neither of them noticed that Natasha Hewson was watching them as Brett swung Holly extravagantly to the music. When they came back together, lightly and expertly, they danced in silence for a few minutes.

They really were well matched, but it wasn't only a rhythmic experience, Holly thought. It was a sensuous one too. She was aware not only of her steps but that she felt slim, vital and willowy.

As his dark gaze ran down her body, a frisson ran through her because she knew he was visualizing her breasts and hips beneath the black material. Nor could she help the same thing happening to her, being aware of his grace and strength beneath his dinner suit.

But as the moment threatened to engulf her in more specific fantasizing, the music came to an end. They came together but he didn't lead her off the floor.

He said instead with his arms loosely around her, no sign of humour in his dark eyes, 'Have you made up your mind, Holly?'

She took a breath. 'I— Brett, this isn't the time or place—'

'All right.' He broke in and took her hand. 'Let's do something about that.' And he led her off the floor, through a set of glass doors, out onto the lawn and behind a row of trees. There was no-one around. 'How about this?'

She took a frustrated little breath. Not only was there no-one for them to see, there was no-one to see them. 'Brett.' She paused, then took hold. 'All right, I've been thinking really seriously about it. It seems to make good sense.'

'There has to be more to it than that now.'

'Well, yes,' she conceded. 'I don't know how reliable that is, though.' She paused, then she said urgently, 'Please, could you give me a little longer? It's a huge step for me…' She trailed off a little desperately.

He said after a long moment, 'Only if I'm allowed to do this?' He took her into his arms.

'Do what?' she breathed.

'Kiss you.'

'Well…'

But he did the deed anyway. As she stood in the protective circle of his arms afterwards, she was trembling with desire and conscious of the need to say *yes, I'll marry you, I'll marry you…*

Some tiny molecule of resistance held her back. Something along the lines of *he always gets his own way* managed to slip above her other feelings. 'Will you?' she whispered. 'Give me a little more time?'

Something she couldn't decipher passed through his eyes, then his lips twisted. 'All right. So long as you stay by my side. The wedding's tomorrow evening—will you come?'

Holly hesitated.

'Or do I have to make all the concessions?' he asked rather dryly.

Holly shook her head. 'I'll come. But in the meantime perhaps we should get back in case people imagine all sorts of things?'

'Such as, I've made off with you and seduced you?'

He looked briefly amused. 'If it wasn't for Mark and Aria that's just what I'd like to do.'

Holly gazed at him and thought for a moment that, despite his dinner suit, he looked dark and pirate-like and quite capable of spiriting her off to a place of seduction. She shivered slightly.

'Cold?' He looked surprised.

'No. But I do need to visit the bathroom. I don't want to look...' She stopped.

'Thoroughly kissed,' he suggested with a definitely pirate-like smile. 'Believe me, it suits you.'

He took her hand and led her back inside.

Holly went to find the facilities. The only person she encountered as she crossed the foyer, other than staff, was Natasha Hewson in her beautiful bouffant shocking-pink gown that should have clashed with her hair but didn't. They stopped, facing each other.

'The bathroom is that a-way,' Natasha said, indicating the direction she'd come from.

'Thank you,' Holly replied, then paused a little helplessly.

'Do you think you'll hold him?' Natasha asked. 'Do you think you'll be the one he'll give up his jungles and his endangered species for? Or were you planning to join him? Don't,' she warned, 'be fooled by *this* Brett Wyndham.'

Holly couldn't help herself. 'What do you mean?'

'Not many of us are immune from that charisma—the good company, the man who makes you tremble, makes you laugh and want to die for him. But he's really a loner. He reminds me of one of the tigers he's trying to save: secretive, thrives on isolation and challenges, clever, dangerous.'

Holly blinked several times. 'Natasha,' she said then, 'Do you have any hopes of getting him back?'

Natasha Hewson shrugged her sleek, bare, beautiful shoulders. 'One day he'll realize that even tigers need a tigress. And that will be *me*.' She blew Holly an insolent kiss as she walked past her.

Fortunately, Holly found herself alone in the bathroom. Fortunately, because as she stared at herself in the mirror she could see how shell shocked she looked as she rinsed her hands.

It was printed in her eyes; it came from the fact that, whether wittingly or not, Natasha had pinpointed the core of her concerns about Brett.

Was he a loner who would never change? He himself had told her he'd probably always take off for the call of the wild. Would she ever get to know what that darkness she sensed in him was about? Would she be a convenient, handy wife who would give him roots, a family perhaps, but never be a soul mate?

She took a painful breath; that wasn't the only cause of her shell shock, intensely disturbing as it was. No, there was also the fact that it wasn't over between Brett and Natasha—it certainly wasn't over for Natasha—and that brought back terrible memories for Holly. Memories of being stalked by a bitter woman pushed almost over the edge.

I can't do it, she thought, and felt suddenly panic-stricken. *I have to get away—but how?*

She finally gathered enough composure to leave the

bathroom to find Brett waiting for her in the foyer. A rather grim, serious-looking Brett.

'Holly,' he said immediately. 'I've just had a call redirected to my phone because they couldn't raise you. Your mother—' he hesitated '—has been taken to hospital. She's going to be all right; it could be an angina attack, but they feel they have it under control. She's asking for you.' He put his arms around her. 'I'm sorry.'

'Oh!' Holly's eyes dilated. 'I've got to get down to her. Oh, it's late—there may not be flights. What will I do?' She stared up at him, agonized.

'Relax. It's all organized?'

'Organized? How?'

'The company jet is here in Cairns on standby. It's picking up some special wedding-guests in Brisbane tomorrow. It was due to fly out early tomorrow morning, but there's no reason for it not to leave now.'

'Thank you,' Holly breathed. 'I don't know how to thank you enough.'

'You don't have to. Look, I'd come with you—'

'No,' she interrupted. 'It's the wedding tomorrow. You need to be here for them.'

'I'll be down the day after. Promise me one thing.' He cupped her face. 'Don't go away from me, Holly Harding.'

She made a gesture to indicate that she wouldn't, but she did.

She wrote him a note while she was winging her way through the dark sky back to Brisbane and her mother. She told him she believed she'd never get to know him well enough to marry him. She told him she'd come to know that Natasha hadn't got over him, and maybe never would, and how that would always make her feel uneasy.

She bit the end of her pen and wondered how to point out that, if things hadn't been resolved completely for Natasha, perhaps they hadn't been for him either. But she decided against it. She asked him to please not seek her out because she wouldn't be changing her mind.

Then she wondered how to end her note so he wouldn't guess that her heart was breaking. Finally she wrote, *thanks for some wonderful experiences, and so long! It's been good to know you...*

She sealed it in an envelope and asked the stewardess to make sure it was delivered to Brett when the plane returned to Cairns.

Then she sat with tears rolling down her cheeks, feeling colder and lonelier than she'd ever felt in her life. How could she have grown so close to him in such a short time? she wondered. It was as if he'd taken centre-stage in her life and she had no idea how to go on with that lynchpin removed.

But it wouldn't have worked, she told herself; it couldn't have worked.

CHAPTER TEN

SEVERAL weeks later, Holly brushed another set of tears from her cheeks and wondered when she'd stop crying whenever she thought of Brett Wyndham.

What brought him to mind this early morning was the fact that she was walking down a beach on North Stradbroke island when she came across a fisherman casting into the surf.

North Stradbroke, along with South Stradbroke and Moreton islands, formed a protective barrier that created Moreton Bay. On the other side of the bay lay the waterside suburbs of Brisbane and the mouth of the Brisbane River. It was a big bay littered with sandbanks and studded with islands, and huge container ships threaded their way through the marked channels to the port of Brisbane. Holly was on the ocean side of North Stradbroke, affectionately known as 'Straddie' to the locals, where the surf pounded the beaches and where there was always salty spray in the air, and the call of seagulls. It was where her mother owned a holiday house, at Point Lookout.

Sylvia had recovered from what had turned out to be a chest infection rather than angina.

Holly had been coming to Point Lookout ever since

she could remember for school holidays, long weekends and annual vacations. Her father had loved it. The house was perched on a hillside with wonderful views of the ocean, Flat Rock and Moreton Island across the narrow South Passage bar.

She'd come over on the vehicle ferry in her car and some mornings she drove back to Dunwich on the bay side of the island. She had a fondness for Dunwich and for a particular coffee shop that served marvellous cakes and pastries, as well as selling fruit and vegetables.

There was also a second-hand shop, an Aladdin's cave of room after room of 'tat,' from jewellery to clothes, china to books and everything in between. Outside there were bird baths, garden gnomes and logs of treated woods. You could lose yourself for hours in it.

She loved wandering through the Dunwich cemetery, beneath huge old tress with the thick turf beneath her feet, reading the inscriptions on the graves that went back to the first settlers to come to Brisbane in the eighteen hundreds. She loved wandering down to the One Mile Anchorage where the passenger ferries came in and all sorts of boats rode at anchor.

Point Lookout might be upmarket these days, but Dunwich was actually an old mining town—although the only evidence of that was the huge trucks that rumbled through the little town laden with mineral sands mined on uninhabited parts of the island.

This overcast, chilly morning she'd decided not to drive across the island but take herself for a long, long walk along the beach. Her thoughts had been preoccupied with how she'd managed to persuade her mother that she needed some time on her own, although Sylvia rang her daily.

Of course, the reason she'd declared a need for peace and privacy and an inspirational setting was so she could write the Brett Wyndham interview.

Although she herself had heard nothing from Brett, to her amazement her editor Glenn had let her know that he'd been in touch and had given the go-ahead for her to write the piece, although he would still have the final say.

Why had he done that? she'd asked herself a hundred times. She could only assume he'd decided not to go back on his word in the interests of her career.

The magazine had given her two weeks' leave after the plane crash and she'd tacked on to that the two weeks' leave she was overdue. She had a week to go before she was due back at work, but she hadn't written a word. A fog seemed to descend on her brain every time she thought about it. She'd spoken to Glenn and explained the difficulty she was having.

'So if you're holding a slot for it, Glenn, I may not be able to reach the deadline—I'm sorry.'

'Holly.' Glenn had said down the line to her. 'You don't walk away from a plane crash and three days of wondering if you're going to survive without some mental repercussions. Don't force it; I'm not holding any slot for it. If it comes, when it comes, we'll see.'

Holly had opened her mouth to ask him if he'd heard from Brett again, but she'd shut it resolutely. Brett Wyndham needed to be a closed book for her now, but she'd clicked her tongue exasperatedly as soon as the thought had crossed her mind. How could he be a closed book when she had this interview to write?

Why hadn't she just admitted to Glenn she couldn't do it? Perhaps she could hand her notes to someone else—but so much of it was still in her head...

On the other hand, why couldn't she grit her teeth and get herself over him?

You did it once before, she reminded herself. *Yes, but I came to hate and despise* that *person,* she answered herself. *I could never hate Brett...*

If she'd had any doubts about that, they were quashed as she walked down the beach and saw a man fishing. She stopped to watch. She saw the tug on his line and the way he jerked the rod back to set the hook in the fish's mouth, just as Brett had shown her, although she'd only had a reel. She watched him wind the line in and saw the silver tailor with a forked tail on the end of it.

She took a distressed breath and turned away as she was transported back to the lagoon in the savannah country, with its reeds, water lilies and all its birds, where she'd swum and caught fish; where she'd sat over a fire; where she and Brett Wyndham had made love without saying a word.

Wave after wave of desolation crashed through her like the surf on the beach as she acknowledged what she'd been trying to deny to herself: that he would always be with her. He would always be on the back roads of her mind. There would always be a part of her that would be cold and lonely without him.

How it had happened to her in such a short time, she still didn't fully understand. She knew there were things about him she didn't know, areas perhaps no-one, no woman, would ever know. But it changed not one whit the fact that she loved him.

She knew that somehow he'd helped her overcome her fear of men and relationships. And she knew something else—that it wasn't her old fears that had affected her so badly that evening at Palm Cove when confronted by Natasha, it was her dreadful sense of loss because she'd come to know that it could never work for them.

She didn't notice that it had started to rain and that the fisherman had packed up and gone home after glancing uncertainly in her direction a couple of times. She ignored the fact that she was soaking wet, so consumed was she by a sea of sadness.

Then, at last, she turned towards the road and started to trudge home.

There was a strange car parked outside the house.

Well, not so strange, she realized as her eyes widened. It was a car she'd actually driven—a silver BMW X5—and as she came to a dead stop Brett got out of it. Brett, looking impossibly tall in charcoal jeans and a black rain-jacket.

They simply stared at each other, then he cleared his throat. 'Holly, you're soaked. Can we go in?'

She came to life, reached into her pocket for her key then stopped. 'Why… Why have you come?'

'I need to talk to you. You didn't think I'd leave it all up in the air like that, did you?'

'I don't think there's any more to say.'

'Yes, there is.' He closed the gap between them and took the key from her. 'And you need to get warm and dry before you get pneumonia. What have you been doing?'

'Walking. Just walking.'

He took her hand and propelled her down the path to the front door, where he fitted the key and opened the door. With gentle pressure on her shoulders, he manoeuvred her inside.

The front door opened straight into an open-plan living, dining and kitchen area. The floors were polished boards, the furnishings comfortable but kept to a minimum. The view was spectacular even on a day like today as showers scudded across the land and seascapes.

'Holly.' He turned her round to face him. 'Holly, go and have a shower. I'll make us a hot drink in the meantime.'

She licked her lips.

He frowned. 'Are you all right?'

She swallowed and made a huge effort to recover from the shell shock of his presence. 'Yes. Fine. Oh.' She looked down at herself. 'I'm dripping! I'll go.' And she fled away from him towards the bedroom end of the house.

He followed her progress with another frown, then turned away and walked into the kitchen area.

Twenty-minutes later Holly reappeared, wearing a silky dressing gown tied at the waist.

She'd hastily dried her hair and, because it looked extremely wild, she'd woven it into a thick, loose plait.

'I hope you don't have anything against plaits,' she said brightly as she reappeared. 'There was *nothing* else to do with it. Ah.' She looked at the steaming mugs on the kitchen counter and inhaled. 'Coffee. Thank you.

Just what I need. Do bring yours into the lounge; we might as well be comfortable.' She took her mug over to an armchair.

He followed suit and sat down opposite. 'You seem to have made a bit of a recovery.'

She grimaced. 'I wasn't expecting you, although I had been thinking of you. I guess I got a bit of a surprise. How did you find me?'

'I persuaded your mother to tell me where you were.'

Holly's lips parted in surprise, which he noted with a faint, dry little smile.

Holly sat back. 'I'm surprised she didn't ring me.'

'You have been out for quite a while,' he pointed out.

Holly sipped some coffee. 'So, why have you come?' she asked quietly. 'You don't have to explain to me why you've gone back to Natasha. I understand.'

'I haven't.'

'Then you should.'

'No.' He put his mug down on a side table. 'And I need to tell you why.'

'Shouldn't you be telling her?'

'I have. Holly, will you just listen to me?' he said with a bleak sort of weariness that was quite uncharacteristic.

'Sorry,' she said on a breath of surprise. 'I'm sorry.'

He beat a little tattoo on the arm of his chair with his fingers. 'This is not generally known outside the family, but my father had a very violent temper.'

Her lips parted. 'I wondered—I mean, I sensed

there was something about your father...' She couldn't go on.

'You were right. I hated him. I hit him once when he and my mother were arguing. She, and I, were usually the ones he took his temper out on. I can't say she was blameless.' He stopped and sighed. 'She should have got out, but it was as if there was this life-long feud going on between them that neither of them could let go of.'

'Why you, though?' Holly whispered. 'I mean you, as opposed to your brother and sister?'

He shrugged. 'Oldest son—maybe he saw me as a threat. I don't know. I do know he never stopped putting me down and I swore that when I took over I would never look back.

'I haven't. Things are in far better shape than they ever were when he was at the helm. But I guess I have to credit him with my interest in animals.'

Holly blinked. 'How so?'

'It was a world I could retreat into when things got impossible—my dogs, my horse and more and more anything on four legs. But the real irony is, much as I hated him, I'm not so unlike him.'

Holly stared at him, struck speechless.

'I also have a temper at times. I also got into a relationship that was—explosive.'

'Natasha,' Holly breathed, her eyes huge.

He nodded and rubbed his jaw. 'Once the first gloss wore off, we argued over the little things, we fought over the big things. We drove each other crazy, but she didn't see it that way. Every grand reunion we had seemed to reassure her that while it might be tempestuous between us—perhaps that even added a little spice to it for her—it was going to endure.

'I don't think she had any idea that I was really alarmed at the way I felt at times. I couldn't tell her. I couldn't put it into words, but I knew I had to get out. Whereas she thought that the fact we were so good in bed was going to compensate for the rest of it. But I could see myself looking down a tunnel at something that closely resembled my parents' marriage.'

'So—so you walked away?'

'Yes, I walked away. I broke it off. I told her— All I told her was that I wasn't cut out for marriage; I was a loner.' He shook his head. 'It was what I preferred to believe rather than admit the truth to myself. I hated the thought that there was any way I could resemble my father. Now, looking back, I can see it was always there. That's why I prided myself on being on the outside in my affairs with women, never deeply, crucially involved. Until Nat managed to break through.'

Holly put a hand to her mouth. 'Have you told her now?'

'Yes.'

'What happened?'

'She didn't believe me at first, but I had some other insights that I tried to explain. Such as—' he paused '—how egos get involved in these matters. How we were two naturally competitive people with a penchant for getting our own way, and we always would be. But that real hole in the gut and the heart, that sense of loss for someone who is not there for you, hadn't touched us. Not that kind of love.'

He got up and walked over to the windows.

Holly stared at his back and the lines of tension in his body.

'She understood that?' she queried huskily.

'I don't know. It made her stop and think. But it clarified things for me. We were never right for each other.' He said it sombrely but intensely.

'How can you be sure?'

He turned at last. 'Because that hole in the gut and heart slammed into me when I got your note.'

Holly's mouth fell open.

'That sense of loss and love almost crippled me, because I knew you were right to go away from me.'

'Brett,' Holly whispered. 'In light of all this, and the fact that you did ask me to marry you...'

'Let me finish,' he broke in. 'I asked you to marry me out of respect, affection, admiration—the way you seemed to fit into my life. But I told myself it wasn't a grand passion. I told myself I was safe from that, *you* were safe from that. Now I know I was wrong.

'I feel more passionate about you than I've ever felt in my life. It wasn't until you left I realized I'd got my grand passions mixed up. But the problem is that whilst how we are—you and I—is different from anything that went before, I keep wondering if my father will come out somehow and that scares me. Scares me far more than it did with Nat.'

She found it hard to speak as her heart beat heavily somewhere up near her throat. 'What—what are you saying?' she asked jaggedly.

His shoulders slumped and he took an uneven breath. Then he said harshly, 'It's best if we say goodbye now, but I had to explain.'

Holly stumbled to her feet with her thoughts flying in all directions. Then, out of nowhere, her epiphany from the plane crash came back to her: her conviction that she should really put her past behind her and live for the future. Plus the belief that had come to her this morning—that this man meant more than anything in the world to her.

She clenched her fists. 'Brett, she *was* the wrong one for you. Just as your parents were probably wrong for each other. But you've dug into your psyche and exposed the roots of it all—that means you *can* cope with it. It also means you could never be a carbon copy of your father. Anyway, you aren't. I know.'

'Holly.' He walked over to her and touched his fingers lightly to her face. 'You're very sweet, but you don't know what can happen—although you should have an inkling of it. I did lose my temper with you once, and frightened you into the bargain.'

Holly looked backwards in her mind's eye and shrugged. 'It wasn't at me, in the first place. It was at some driver who got his licence out of a cornflake packet. And you made amends almost immediately. Right from then you've always protected me,' she said tremulously.

He looked away from her and a nerve beat in his jaw.

'And there's something I do know,' she continued barely audibly. 'I'd trust you with my life, Brett Wyndham. I believe in you with all my heart. You can walk away from me now, but I'll always believe in you, and I'll always carry you in my heart.' Tears slid down her cheeks but she didn't notice them.

He hesitated, then brushed her cheeks with his thumbs. 'It'll go; it'll pass.'

'No, it won't.'

'We haven't known each other that long.'

'That was my line,' she said huskily, and smiled faintly through her tears. 'Yours was, "it's how you get to know people that matters".'

'Holly,' he said on a tortured breath, then swept her into his arms.   He held her closely, not speaking, and little by little she began to feel the terrible tension in him receding. He said, 'I had to warn you.'

'I'm glad you did because I always knew there was something buried really deep within you that I didn't understand. Now we both know we can cope with it together.' She hesitated. Although it was no longer a primary concern for her, she had some sympathy and had to ask the question: 'How is Natasha?'

'She's decided to open a branch of her agency in London. She told me it was over for her, whatever the rights and the wrongs of it were.' He smiled slightly. 'Whatever else, she's not one to wallow.'

Holly rested against him and sniffed.

He tilted her chin so he could look into her eyes. 'Tears? For Nat?' he queried.

Holly considered denying it, but found she couldn't. 'I've held some not altogether complimentary opinions of Natasha Hewson,' she confessed. 'But I'd like to wish her well.'

'Me too,' he murmured. 'You know, you don't have to worry about her—in any other context.'

Holly nodded. 'I've got over that. It was silly to go

through life waiting for it to happen again. Anyway, compared to losing you, it just seemed to fade away.'

'Do you really mean that?'

She looked deep into his eyes and breathed. 'Yes.'

'Sure?' A glint of humour suddenly lurked in his dark eyes and she felt her heart starting to beat faster.

'Yes. Why?'

'You were the one who accused me of being thoroughly bad-minded. Like a leopard,' he added for complete clarification.

'Ah.' She controlled the smile that wanted to curve her lips. 'You were the one who kept making verbal passes at me, not to mention mentally undressing me in the most awkward circumstances!'

'In that respect, I have to warn you I'm unlikely to change my spots—and definitely not in the immediate future,' he told her gravely.

She relented and laughed softly. 'I actually like the sound of that. And there's something I can bring to it that'll be unique for us.'

He raised his eyebrows questioningly.

'A bed.' Her eyes danced. 'A real bed. Not a river bed. No sand, no plastic V-sheet or cardboard bedding, no wild cattle to frighten the life out of me...'

He stopped her quite simply by kissing her. Then he lifted his head and looked into her eyes. 'Since you were the one to bring it up, could you lead me to it before I expire with desire?'

She took his hand. 'Come.'

It was not only a bed, it was a double bed, with a beautiful silk coverlet in the colours of the sea and sky on a clear day. Beneath the cover, the linen was starched and white.

'This is almost too much luxury,' he remarked as he pulled the cover down and laid her on the sheets.

'I know. Despite the sand and everything, I have some wonderful memories of a certain lagoon and Tommy's Hut, as well as—'

'I bought it,' he interrupted.

'As well as— You *what*?' Holly sat up, wide-eyed and incredulous.

'I bought the station.'

'Brett,' she breathed. 'Why?'

'Why do you think?' He looked down at her. 'Because of its memories of us, and you.'

'I— I…' There were tears in her eyes as she slipped her arms around his neck. 'I had no idea you were so romantic.'

'Neither did I. Would you like it as a wedding present?'

'I—I'm speechless. Are you serious?'

He nodded and kissed her. He laid her back against the sheets again and leant over her. 'We can go back on our anniversaries.'

'That would be lovely; thank you,' she whispered. 'Oh, Brett, I don't know what more to say.'

He smiled into her eyes and started to unzip her tracksuit top. 'We don't have to say anything. I seem to recall it working pretty well for us like that.'

'So do I. OK; my lips are sealed…'

But of course they weren't, as he took his time about undressing her. Then, when they were naked and celebrating each other's bodies, he took her to the edge several times, only to retreat and sculpt her breasts and hips with his lips and hands. She had to open her lips, not only to kiss him and his body, but to tell him that—much as she'd loved their love-making in Tommy's Hut—the freedom from clothes and the comfort they were experiencing now were adding a dimension to it that was mind-blowing; it drew a joyous response from her.

She moved in a way that obviously tantalized him. She grew bolder and touched him in a way that drew a growling little response from him.

Desire snaked through her from head to toe, but at times she felt as light as air and more wonderful than she'd ever felt in her life.

Then the rhythm changed and what he did to her was so intense, she was wracked with pleasure and begging for the only release she wanted.

'Now?' he breathed.

'Please, now,' she gasped, and they moved on together as one until he brought her to the shuddering peak of sensation he shared.

She was breathless and speechless as those waves of climax subsided slowly and they clung to each other. Finally they were still and he loosened his arms around her.

She took his hand and put it against her cheek. 'I love you,' she said huskily.

'I love you,' he answered. 'I always will.'

Later, when they were snuggled up together on the sofa sipping champagne and watching the afternoon sky clear up, she said rather ruefully, 'How is my mother? Did you see her or speak to her on the phone?'

'I went to see her. We have one thing in common, your mother and I.'

'What's that?'

'We'd both probably die for you.'

'You don't have to do that, either of you.' Holly wiped a couple of tears from her eyes. 'Just be friends.'

'We will. If you can convince her you're happy. You see, she told me that, if I hurt you again, I'd have her to contend with.'

Holly gasped. 'I didn't know she knew. She never said a word.'

'I actually always admired your mother,' he informed her.

Holly chuckled, then was struck by a thought. 'How did the wedding go?' she asked.

'The wedding was very nice—had I been in the mood to appreciate it.' He looked rueful.

'You...?' She hesitated.

'I felt like cutting my throat.' He played with a strand of her hair. 'But there was a positive note. Sue met someone at the wedding. She's very taken with him, and I get the feeling he could be the right one for her. Uh, talking of weddings...?'

'Yes. Let's,' Holly said contentedly, but hid the sudden sparkle of mischief in her eyes. 'I'm not into balls and barbecues, but I did think perhaps we could hire an island in the South Pacific? We'd need one with accommodation for, say, at least a hundred guests—and we could have fire walkers and luaus—'

'There's not much difference,' he broke in ominously, 'Between a beach barbecue and a luau.'

'Well, there is. Roast suckling-pigs on spits. We could all wear leis and dance those fabulous Polynesian dances to drums.'

'Holly, stop!' he commanded.

But she'd stopped anyway, because she couldn't stop laughing. 'If you could see your face,' she teased. 'Look, I'd be happy to marry you in a mud hut with a herd of giraffe as guests.'

He kissed her. 'You're a witch, you know. But we won't go to those lengths. Something small and simple?'

'Done! When?'

'A month from today?'

She looked at him innocently. 'Why do we have to wait so long?'

'Just in case you want to change your mind.'

'Brett.' All laughter fled. 'I won't,' she promised. 'I won't.'

'Darling,' Sylvia said a month later, 'Are you very sure about this?'

'Mum.' Holly put her bouquet down and pulled her mother to sit down beside her on her bed.

Sylvia looked beautiful in a cornflower-blue silk suit with a cartwheel hat and lilies of the valley pinned to her bodice.

Holly, on the other hand, was all in white, an exqui-site lace dress over a taffeta slip with a heart-shaped bodice, long-sleeves and slim skirt.

Her hair was loose, although suggestions had been

made that it should be put up or pulled back—suggestions she declined with a secret little smile in her eyes.

Her full veil fell from a sparkling coronet and her bouquet was made up of six just-unfurled roses, each a different subtle colour from cream through to salmon.

'Mum,' she said again. 'I know you're—I know you've got reservations about Brett. But you did send him to me because, you told me, you thought only I could decide what to do.'

'I know. And I did think that; I still do.' Sylvia heaved a sigh. 'It's just that sometimes people don't change, however much they want to.'

'That was what Brett was afraid of,' Holly said quietly. 'And he may never have, if he didn't have someone who really believed in him as I do. And you know what Dad always used to say?' Holly went on. 'If you really believe in something, you have to go for it, otherwise you're denying that belief.'

'That's true. Well, my darling, I hope you'll be as happy as I was with your father, even though we were like chalk and cheese,' Sylvia said.

They both laughed. 'I will, I will.' Holly kissed her mother.

The wedding was small but very beautiful.

The homestead without walls at Haywire was decorated with greenery and magnificent flowers, all flown in that morning along with the bouquets.

A small altar had been contrived at the library desk, where Holly had made notes on her first visit to Haywire, and a red carpet led to it.

A feast was laid out on tables covered in heirloom damask cloths that Sue had inherited from her grandmother; each table was decorated with orchids in silver pots.

Mark and Aria were there, looking bronzed and exuberant after their prolonged and exotic honeymoon. Sue Murray was there with her new man, looking like a new person.

Glenn Shepherd was there, quite resigned to the fact that he'd lost the Brett Wyndham interview, as well as his travel writer extraordinaire, although the magazine would be the first to break the news of the zoo. He and Holly had also discussed the possibility of her freelancing for the magazine.

Sarah was still in residence, so she was there as well as well as Kane, the station foreman, and some of the staff from the other stations. And there were friends of both Holly and Brett as well as Sylvia, of course.

Even Bella had been invited, and she wore a silver horseshoe attached to her collar.

There was a covey of small planes on the airstrip and they'd stay there for the night.

The ceremony itself was short but moving—mainly, as many noted after the event, because of the palpable emotion between the bride and groom.

They all sat down to the luncheon; the champagne flowed, and it moved on to become a party.

In fact the only ones to leave were Brett and Holly. They took off on their honeymoon to a destination so secret, not even Holly knew where she was going— although she soon had an inkling.

It was a short flight and one that still brought back

some hair-raising memories, despite her having flown it with Brett several times since their plane had crashed. But, by the time they landed at the station Brett had bought for her as a wedding present, she'd long since been in no doubt as to where they were going.

This time they didn't ride the distance between the homestead and Tommy's Hut on a horse, they drove in a powerful, tough four-wheel-drive and reached their destination before sunset.

And there were other changes. Someone had been there before them. Someone had chopped the firewood and piled it up handily. Someone had provided camp chairs and a blow-up mattress. Someone had left an esky with champagne and foodstuffs in it.

All the same, Holly looked around with tears in her eyes, at the water lilies, the birds and the palms. 'I never, never thought I'd come back. Thank you.' She went into his arms.

'Did you like your wedding?' he enquired, holding her close.

'I loved it. How about you?'

'Same. Well,' he said after kissing her thoroughly, with a sudden little wicked glint in his eye, 'how about a swim, then a fish? We have two reels now, and I'm determined to out-fish you.'

Holly lifted her head from his shoulder. 'Oh! We'll see about that!'

But later, much later, when the fire had died down and they were lying in each other's arms, all forms of competitiveness had left them and they were awash with a lovely form of contentment.

'By the way,' he said, 'I thought two nights here, then

a trip to Africa. Or anywhere on earth you'd like to go, Mrs Wyndham.'

Holly breathed happily. 'I wondered when the mud hut and a herd of giraffe were going to make an appearance in my life!'

CHAPTER ELEVEN

Two years later they were sitting on a beach watching the moon rise and holding hands.

But this beach wasn't in the middle of nowhere; it was Palm Cove, and they'd come down from Haywire for a very important appointment.

It was a magic evening. The moon hung in the sky like a silver Christmas bauble. The sea was a slightly darker blue than the sky, apart from its ribbon of reflected moonlight, and you felt as if you could reach out and touch Double Island again.

It had been a magic two years since she'd married Brett Wyndham, Holly thought. Busy, productive and fulfilling.

His zoo was no longer a dream, it was a reality, and she'd taken part in a lot of the planning and the doing of it. Haywire was now very much home to her, although they spent time in Brisbane and they travelled extensively.

Yes, she conceded, there'd been some ups and downs—and she'd decided it was not possible to go through a marriage without them—but if anything they were growing ever closer.

And she felt confident that Brett had got over his fears that he was going down the path his father had trod.

Curiously, or perhaps not so curiously, it was her mother who'd put it into words only a few days ago.

When Holly had rung her full of delighted suspicions, Sylvia had said, 'You were right, darling—about Brett and believing in him.'

'You can tell now?' Holly had queried.

'Of course. Would you be so happy otherwise?'

'No.'

Now on the beach at Palm Cove, after an appointment in Cairns with a gynaecologist that had confirmed her pregnancy, Holly patted her stomach and said a little anxiously, 'Are you really thrilled at this news?'

'Of course.' He released her hand and put his arm round her shoulders. 'Why wouldn't I be? I like kids, and our kids will be special.'

She smiled, but it faded. 'But it means—it does mean we'll be tied down a bit. You see, I've got the feeling I'm going to be a pretty hands-on mother, and that will cut down on travelling and so on.'

'Holly.' Brett put his hands on her shoulders and turned her to face him. 'When will you accept that it's where *you* are that counts for me? Nothing else.'

And he stared down into the deep blue of her eyes with complete concentration in his own.

'Still? I mean, it hasn't worn off a bit or…?'

'Still. Always,' he said very quietly. 'Don't doubt it, Holly.'

She breathed deeply and went into his arms.

PUPPY LOVE FOR THE VETERINARIAN

AMY WOODS

This one is for the animal rescuers;
thank you for the wonderful lives you save.

And for my Maggie dog, who has my heart.

Chapter One

"June, hon, why don't you go on home now? I can finish closing up here myself, and it looks like things may get worse than they originally predicted."

June Leavy looked up from her mop bucket and followed the owner of Peach Leaf Pizza's eyes to the small television behind the counter, tuned in to the evening weather segment. January in west Texas could be unpredictable, but the idea of the twelve to eighteen inches of snow the meteorologist called for actually covering the ground and sticking was just surreal.

She studied her boss's face, not missing the lines around Margaret's mouth and the shadowy thumb-prints beneath the older woman's usually lively eyes. It had been a busy day, amid a busy week; they were both exhausted, but the work would be completed much faster with two pairs of hands.

June shook her head, causing a few more strands of hair to escape her ponytail. "Nonsense. I'm almost finished with the floor, and then all that's left is taking out the garbage."

Margaret offered a weary smile as her thanks, but June could see the relief in her boss's face. She would never admit it, but Margaret Daw was getting older. It was time for her to retire and June could feel that the day was coming when her boss would ask her to take over. Margaret had all but asked her about it on more than one occasion—who could blame a new grandma for wanting to spend more time with the adorable twin babies recently born to her pediatrician son and daughter-in-law?—and besides, June was her only full-time employee and comanager. In many ways, it just made sense.

June sighed and sloshed the mop back into the gray water, wondering again how she would respond if and when the day arrived. She could see the pros and cons list she'd pored over so many times in her mind's eye, her options jotted out clear as day on the yellow pad sitting next to the remote control on her coffee table. But no matter how many times she mulled over the bullet points, the decision wouldn't be easy.

Margaret was a wonderful boss—kind and fair— and the job provided steady income. There was something comforting in the daily tasks, in kneading the dough each morning, chopping fresh vegetables and taking orders, in the warm, familiar faces of Peach Leaf Pizza's many regular customers. She would miss the banter, catching up with people she'd known her whole life and the excitement in kids' faces when they piled into the red leather booths after winning baseball games or performing well in dance recitals.

But she had dreams of her own, too.

And until recently, June had been so close to turning them into reality. So close, in fact, that the bruises from losing everything hadn't yet healed.

Now her choice was between picking up the pieces and starting over—letting herself believe that she could somehow regain what was lost—or sticking with the safe option, taking over the pizza parlor and borrowing her neighbors' joy as they lived their lives.

Put that way, it didn't seem like much of a choice at all, but she reminded herself that starting over wouldn't exactly guarantee a happy ending, either.

"Back to square one," she said aloud without meaning to.

"What's that?" Margaret called from the counter.

"Oh… I was just wondering if it's really going to get as bad as they're saying."

She tilted her chin at the television, where the Austin meteorologist gesticulated animatedly, her arms waving in circles and lines to indicate high and low pressure points across a multicolored map of Texas.

"Beats me." Margaret shrugged, her shoulders tapping the pizza-slice painted earrings she wore so that they swirled around beneath her silvery curls. "Wouldn't be the first time, though, you know."

June finished cleaning a blotch of spilled marinara and pushed the wheeled bucket toward the back of the shop, doing a once-over of the black-and-white checked tiles in case she missed a spot.

Margaret wiped the last bit of counter and stood on her tiptoes to turn off the TV before removing her apron. "When I was a girl, we got a couple of feet out at our house, and I'll tell you, it is no easy time getting around town in that much powder." She put a hand on one hip and pointed at June with the other. "Especially when nobody around here knows how to drive in that stuff."

Nodding her agreement, June crossed the kitchen and emptied the mop bucket into the designated sink, then shoved the cleaning supplies into a broom closet. She supposed it was possible that the weather might take a turn for the worse—it had been snowing steadily for a few days, so there was already a little covering the ground—but the thought of that much more coming down in the span of just a few hours in their neck of Texas still somehow didn't seem realistic. Sure, they got a few inches most years, and there was always the danger of ice, especially on the country roads outside of town, but she didn't think there was too much to worry about. She was certain she had plenty of time to get home before anything major hit.

But when she closed the supply closet door and turned around, June found Margaret looking up at her from all of nearly five feet, her boss's clear blue eyes fully of worry beneath a forehead creased with concern.

"Just promise me you'll be extra careful, and if it gets bad, we won't open tomorrow. Just stay home. I don't want you getting hurt trying to make it into work, you hear?"

June gave a reassuring smile, promised that she'd be safe and patted Margaret's shoulder. Over the years, their relationship had deepened into more than just a typical owner/employee situation. Her boss treated her more like a daughter than a paid worker, which only made things harder when thinking about the next chapter of her life. She knew Margaret would hate the idea of June factoring her needs into future plans, but they *were* a factor. A big one. If she ever got back on her feet, if she ever found a way to get back all the money she'd spent years carefully saving to open her own bakery, she would have to leave someone she cared about, someone who'd helped see her through the lowest point of her life. That mattered. Deeply.

She shook her head. There was no use thinking about it now.

The money was gone. In all likelihood, that meant her dreams were gone with it. She'd worked herself to the bone for over a decade earning it and had gone without quite a few comforts to save until it amounted to enough to buy her own bakeshop. Her shoulders sunk as the weight of loss settled once again. It would take years before she could build her former financial stability and credit back up, and even more to get her savings back.

Six months had passed since Clayton left, taking everything with him. Their money. Hers, really, if she were being honest, and she was now—too much had happened for anything less. Her dreams.

And, last but not least, her heart.

Even after all he'd done, taking the cash from their joint account and running off to gamble it away in Vegas, June thought there might be a place inside of her that still missed that stupid man. It wasn't that she loved him still—no, he'd broken her trust and hurt her far too much for that to be the case—but the loss of him and all they'd shared, and the deep chasm of loneliness in his wake, the death of the life they'd built together... June thought maybe those were the things she truly mourned. And it wasn't that she needed him, either, or any man, for that matter. She'd been single for most of her life until Clayton came along and had been happy and fulfilled before his presence.

But that was just it. Until he left, she would have sworn to anyone that he was the one she'd spend the rest of her life with, and when he'd gone, all those promises of a family and a life with him vanished, and she was back where she'd been before—only this time, it wasn't the same. This time, she knew what it was like to share her home with someone she loved, to talk about having kids one day and to dream together, staring off into the future, side by side. This time, she felt the absence.

Shoulders up, chin up, she told herself, remembering Margaret's wise words in the aftermath of that mess. Better to make peace with the present, than to dwell on the past, right?

Of course.

Starting with her small, albeit cozy, apartment, June forced herself to make a list of all of the things she had to be grateful for. When she finished, she headed back to the storefront and kitchen to fetch the two large trash bags, hefting them over her shoulders to carry through the restaurant to the Dumpster in the loading area out back.

Things weren't so very bad. She had her job, her friends and a warm place to live, and for that she was thankful. It was a good thing right now to be single and free, to have time and space to decide what to do next, what path to take in putting her life back together. No strings, no one else to care for, no one to put before her own needs. She planned on staying that way for a good while; it would take someone very special to convince her to put her trust in a relationship again, and she was fairly convinced that person might not be anywhere in her future, near or far. It was a…difficult thought to swallow, but one she was doing her best to accept.

June dropped the trash bags near the back door and went to get her coat. Margaret was doing the same. "Bundle up, now."

"Yes, ma'am," she teased, holding her fingers to her forehead in a salute.

Margaret put both hands on her hips, a foreboding

figure. "I'm not joking around, Junie. You forget I'm from upstate New York, where it gets dangerously cold in the winter. You Texans don't know from cold, and you're always caught unawares when it hits. Don't let it get the best of you."

"Okay, I promise."

Both women pulled on gloves, hats and purses, and Margaret opened the back door for June when she picked up the garbage bags. A blast of frigid air slapped her across the face and briefly challenged her footing until she steadied herself against its force.

"I'm good here, Marg. I'll drop these off and lock up. See you in the morning," she shouted over her shoulder as she stepped onto the loading dock and into what felt like gale-force winds.

"I'm not so sure about that."

June chuckled to herself. "Okay, then, see you soon."

"All right, hon. Don't forget what I said about not coming in if it's bad," Margaret called, her voice fading as the back door slammed behind her and she headed for her car in the front parking lot, which she always parked next to June's fifteen-year-old jalopy.

June shook her head at the older woman's cosseting, then heaved the bags into the giant metal bin, starting at the loud clanging sound that erupted.

Something else must have heard it, too, and re-acted the same way, because June caught motion in her peripheral vision as she turned back to lock up the door. Her heart jumped into her throat, and it fluttered there like so many trapped butterflies as she spun quickly to take in her surroundings.

"Hello?"

She listened carefully and heard…nothing, except maybe her own pulse pounding at her temples.

"Is anyone out here?" she called again, reaching into her purse for her pocketknife and cell phone. There was probably nothing to worry about. This was Peach Leaf, after all, where the running crime rate was pretty much zilch. All the same, she was a woman alone in an alley after dark, so it was only smart to be cautious.

Scanning the view once more to make certain she wasn't about to be attacked, June decided that instead of locking the back door and walking around front to her little car as she usually did, she'd just go through the store.

That was when she heard something again. A quiet rustling, followed by what sounded like a series of soft squeaks. She closed her eyes for just a few seconds, trying to decide whether or not to ignore the sound, knowing the wise thing to do was to walk away. Whatever it was, it was not her problem, and Lord knew she did not need any of those in her life just then.

But then she heard it again, and this time, the soft, sad little cries were like warm fingers squeezing her heart. As the snow began to fall harder, flakes catching in her eyelashes and forming a thin, shawl-like layer on the red fabric of her coat, June released a great sigh and made the decision to investigate.

Whatever was making that noise—*please don't let it be a baby of any kind*, she thought—did not belong out there in a lonely alley on a freezing winter's night.

With the garbage bags out of her hands, June now pulled her coat closer around her and closed all four toggles before carefully descending the loading dock steps. A thin layer of ice had already formed, and she had no intention of tumbling down and breaking a bone or two. She pulled her purse strap up from her shoulder and over her head to secure it tightly, then dug out her cell phone, turning on the flashlight app. Its slim, bright beam shot out into the dark, and June crept slowly behind the pizza shop's garbage bin, the light illuminating nothing but a coating of grimy snow. She stopped and waited a moment, listening for the sound again so she could follow it to its source. Just as she was about to restart her search, she heard it again; this time, it was more distinct.

Placing a palm behind her ear, June tried to zero in on what it was—a kitten, maybe? Something small and helpless and lost? Again, she pleaded that it wouldn't be a baby. The thought of someone leaving a little one behind their restaurant, especially in this weather, was just…unthinkable.

There it was again, and now she was certain it was some sort of cry. Rolling her eyes upward in a silent prayer, she braced herself and started off in the direction of the noise, continuing as it became louder and louder, which meant she must be close. She was halfway down the alley, almost to the street, when she reached it, hidden in a dark corner behind another garbage bin.

Shining her flashlight into the shadows, June gasped, cold air filling her lungs and what felt like the rest of her body. The hand that wasn't holding her phone flew to her mouth as she looked into two pairs of big, brown eyes.

Big, brown…puppy eyes.

The squeaking, she now realized, was the heart-wrenching sound of tiny little canine yips, probably calling for their mother.

There, cuddled together in a heap of trash behind another store's Dumpster, were two itty-bitty bodies coated in black fur, with eight little white, black-spotted boots. But their tiny faces were the clincher. June's eyes filled with moisture, not from the biting air, as she stared at two pairs of fuzzy black ears, each separated down the middle by a thin line of white fur that traced down into identical white muzzles.

For a full minute, June remained frozen in place, her instinct telling her to rush forward and gather the pups in her arms to warm them up, but she wasn't yet positive on what was the right thing to do.

On the one hand, the temperatures had probably dropped to below freezing when the sun had disappeared—at least, it sure felt that way—but on the other, well, what if the puppies' mother returned, looking for them? What if she was around there somewhere and returned to find them gone? But the more pressing question was, of course—what if she didn't? The little ones couldn't have been out there for too long; otherwise they'd be…

No, she didn't want to think about that. Yet… that would certainly be the outcome if she didn't get the little dogs out of the cold, and quick. She could always check the alley the next day and put up flyers to find out if anyone had seen a female dog wandering around the strip mall or a suspicious person dropping off a little bundle. But for now, if she didn't get them out of the increasingly cold night air—and the snow that seemed to be falling faster and thicker each minute—they would surely freeze to death. Not much of a choice there.

Having made up her mind, June hurried forward and opened her coat, then picked up the puppies very gently and with extreme care, and tucked them into the front pouch of her Peach Leaf Pizza sweatshirt. She wrapped her coat across her middle, leaving it unfastened so they could breathe, and, head down, turned the corner out of the alley.

The wind was much fiercer without the protection of the buildings, and the several yards to her car seemed more like miles as June trudged through the now-blinding wind and snow in the direction of the front parking lot. Finally, she reached her car and pulled her keys from her purse to unlock the doors. Opening the trunk, she retrieved her gym bag and slammed down the lid, sliding into the backseat as quickly as possible. She pulled the door shut—no easy feat against the wind—and took a deep breath before unzipping the bag. She took out her jogging clothes and shoes, leaving her towel to make a sort of nest. Opening her coat, she removed the little balls of fluff and placed them carefully inside, close against each other for warmth.

"There," she said. "You guys hang on tight. We're going for help."

Satisfied with the answering squeaks, June pulled a seat belt around the bag and fastened it, hoping it would do, and then crawled into the front seat. Thankfully, her old car started after just a couple of tries, and she was able to pull out of the parking lot.

Snow fell in sheets as she made her way onto the main road with her blinkers on full blast, sifting through her memory for any winter-weather driving advice Margaret might have offered over the years, sorry that she hadn't listened more closely.

Wrapping the fore- and middle fingers of her left hand together for luck as she gripped the wheel with white knuckles, June set off to the only place she could think of that might be able to help her with two very fresh puppies.

Chapter Two

Ethan Singh cursed before his father's absurdly messy monster of a desk. One of these days, he promised himself for the hundredth time, he would have to suck it up and organize the damn thing. One of these days.

But not today. Or tonight, he supposed, strolling from the office and past the empty receptionist's desk to glance out the front window of his father's veterinary clinic, only mildly surprised to find a dark sky staring back. It was almost a relief to know that, as soon as he arrived at his parents' home and ate a quick dinner, it would be past time to head straight to bed.

Straight to bed meant no time to think about what he was doing in Peach Leaf, Texas, for the winter, and more importantly, what he would do when the season was over and it was time to head back to campus in Colorado, where he was scheduled to teach several veterinary classes over the spring semester.

Ethan gave his head a little shake and turned back from the window. It wouldn't do to ruminate on that now. The whole point in coming here, agreeing to run Dad's clinic while his parents took a one-month, long-overdue vacation to visit his father's brother in Washington, DC, was to *not* think about what happened in Alaska. Ethan sat down in the receptionist's seat and put his head in his hands. How could he not think about it? How could he not think about *her*—about what she'd done to break his heart into a thousand tiny shreds?

It was impossible.

He had looked forward to that research trip with great enthusiasm, knowing he'd get to spend every day with Jessica Fields, the incredibly intelligent and physically stunning colleague he'd been dating for a couple of weeks, following her recent arrival at his department at the university. And he'd gotten everything he wanted. Their time in northernmost Alaska, a place he'd learned both to love and respect for its extreme beauty and danger, had been absolutely perfect. The team's research on the impact of climate change and infectious disease in polar bears advanced far beyond what they'd initially anticipated, and so had his relationship with Jessica.

It wasn't until their final day that she'd begun to show signs of unease that any scientist worth his salt would have noticed. When he'd leaned in to kiss her on the flight back to Colorado, an action that at that point in their time together had become commonplace, Jessica had pulled away, and he confronted her.

She wasn't single, she said, her eyes full of regret but not, he'd noted sadly, remorse. She was engaged to marry her college sweetheart and had no plans to break it off on account of what she called a "fling." She had led him on, she said.

Well, on that point he certainly would not argue. Sleeping with him, telling him she loved him, making plans with him...yes, he'd say she was damn right that she'd led him on. Ethan had immediately requested an alternative seat on the airplane, enduring the remainder of the flight with a clenched jaw, knotted stomach and the blinding urge to scream at the woman who had, in the space of a few months, turned his life upside down, and then quickly and heartlessly destroyed him.

The department head, though confused at his hasty, fictional explanation, had granted Ethan's request for a short sabbatical, a semester off. Ethan hadn't taken a vacation since accepting the position five years before, and he supposed he was due a break. Though it hurt, not to get started right away on compiling and writing up the Alaskan data for conference presentations. He would never forget the way his breath had caught and his heartbeat raced as he'd knelt next to one of those regal bears to take a blood sample before the tranquilizer wore off. They were the most beautiful creatures he'd ever seen; they deserved saving and he would spend the rest of his life working to do just that.

He pushed out a breath, lifting his head to stare out the window once more as he listened to wind that had begun to swirl and howl. For now, he needed time—even just a few months—to figure out how to go back to the university and face Jessica, who had made it clear she had no plans to leave the team, despite what she'd done to him. He needed to come to terms with the fact that the only woman he'd ever fallen for was getting married to someone else and, worst of all, didn't seem to give a single damn what it would do to him.

In the meantime, he had the clinic, and over the past two weeks, he had to admit, he'd become fond of the locals and their beloved pets, and even of his house calls to care for a few horses and cattle on nearby ranches. He'd always loved the research part of being a veterinary pathologist, but this…this change of pace and reminder of where his career had begun, was nice, too, at least for now.

Ethan's head jerked up at the sound of raucous banging. It took him a minute to realize that it was coming from the front door, which he'd locked an hour ago after closing. Who on earth could be knocking— no, pounding—on the door now? Ethan knew that his father occasionally extended his workday beyond its normal twelve hours when a special circumstance arose, but no one had called to say they'd be coming in late or anything of the like.

He got up from the chair quickly, leaving it swiveling as he paced to the door. Whoever stood on the front stoop wasn't visible from the window he'd been looking out before, and the blinds were pulled down on the other side to cover the spot where the sun hit in late afternoon; he'd have to get much closer and peer through them to identify his visitor.

Ethan rolled his eyes. Yes, it was his duty to help out the local animal population in any way he could, but the day had already been particularly trying—several regular exams on top of two challenging, back-to-back house calls—and he practically ached to warm up a frozen meal, shower away the fur and jump into the cozy bed in his parents' guest room.

When he got to the door, he slid a finger between two blinds and peered out, but the snow was quite thick now, surprisingly so, and the visitor so bundled up that he couldn't make out anything other than the bright crimson of a coat and matching hat. He didn't even see any animals. But the wind was so fierce, and the snow falling in such a thick blanket, that he was compelled to open the door and let the poor person in, reminding himself that this was Peach Leaf, therefore generally void of a large city's potential threats.

Bracing himself, Ethan unlocked and pulled open the door, breath rushing from his lungs as the icy air hit. A tall figure rushed forward, nearly pummeling him to get inside the building, and for a second he regretted his decision to be kind.

"Oh, thank you," came a voice, definitely a woman's,

from somewhere in the depths of the coat and beanie. Ethan closed the door behind her.

"Thank you so, so much for letting me in. I thought there might not be anyone here this late and I was about to turn around and go back to my car, but…"

"Whoa, there. Hang on just a minute. Let's start at the beginning. How does that sound?" He clasped his hands in front of his abdomen and gave her some space.

The woman stopped speaking and pulled up her hat, which had fallen down into her face, nearly covering what he now saw were large, green—a very lovely green, in fact—eyes. "I'm sorry," she said, pushing out a puff of air. She reached out a gloved hand in Ethan's direction and he took it, startled to discover how cold it was.

She must be absolutely frozen from head to toe. He'd checked the thermometer that afternoon and, even before the sun had gone down, the temperature was below freezing. If he hadn't let her in, she might have been in real trouble. His semester in Alaska had taught him plenty about the dangers of extreme cold, and even though they were in Texas, which was generally mild, the hazards were the same if one wasn't careful. It didn't matter that the weather was out of the norm; it simply was, and therefore caution would need to be observed.

He hadn't anticipated things getting so bad, and hadn't much of a chance to pay attention to the forecast other than his brief check on the internet as he'd scarfed down a sandwich earlier, but now he could see plainly that the winter storm the meteorologists predicted had escalated quickly.

The woman pumped his hand up and down a few times before letting it go. "I'm June. June Leavy. I came by on the slim chance that Dr. Singh might still be here this late, and, well, I didn't really know what else to do."

"I'm Dr. Singh," Ethan said, doing his best to offer a warm smile despite feeling anything but.

The woman—June—narrowed her eyes and tilted her head to study him, chuckling softly. "Wow, Dr. Singh, I have to say, you look like you've stumbled upon the elusive fountain of youth."

Ethan had to laugh at that. Most folks, unless their pets were ill or aging, only came in for annual check-ups and vaccinations. It made sense that the senior Dr. Singh would not have had a chance to inform all clients of his winter vacation plans.

"No, I mean, I am Dr. Singh, but perhaps not the one you'd hoped to find. I'm his son Ethan."

June's face visibly relaxed as realization hit and she nodded, then proceeded to remove her gloves and hat. As she grasped her lapels and moved to take off her coat, Ethan noticed the bit of roundness at her middle and the thought crossed his mind that she might be pregnant. "Here, let me help you with that," he said, taking her coat.

He couldn't help but catch the subtle, sweet scent of her hair as he pulled the red fabric from her shoulders. Like melon, he thought. Odd that he should even notice. Odder still he should notice that it tumbled down her shoulders in soft, auburn waves, framing a face, he could see after he'd turned back from hanging her coat on an iron rack near the door, that was rosy from the cold and, well, quite lovely.

·June smiled, and it occurred to Ethan that she was aptly named. Her skin was as bright as sunshine and the curve of her wide mouth heated his insides, head to toe. Her eyes were lively and warm like summer, although…her smile didn't quite reach them.

Not that he cared, though. Pure observation—like you'd get from any good scientist.

"Thank you," she said. "Now, as I was saying, I drove here on my way home from work and my car broke down about, well, I don't really know how far away, but it sure seemed like a long distance." She took a deep breath and closed her eyes as if willing calm. "Anyway, I'm here now and you're here, thank goodness."

Ethan must have looked confused, and that would make sense because he definitely was. He was glad to help if she was stranded. Perhaps he could call a tow truck for her and let her stay to wait out the storm, but other than that, he wasn't at all sure why she'd been headed this way in the first place.

When she stopped speaking, he took the chance to ask, "Is there something I can do to help you, Miss Leavy?"

"Actually, yes, there is. At least, I hope so."

His heart seemed to speed up as she bit her bottom lip and reached into the pocket of her sweatshirt with

both hands. Not that he thought she would pull out
a weapon, per se, but because he knew instinctively
that nothing she might reveal would be easy to deal
with. And what he wanted at that moment, and more
than that, for his life in general right then, was just
that—simplicity.

But that was simply not in the cards.

So when June Leavy pulled two shivering black-
and-white puppies out of her pocket and held them
out to show him why she'd driven to his office,
walked an unknown distance in a freak snowstorm
and nearly pounded down the door, all Ethan Singh
could do was sigh.

Chapter Three

As June stared at the junior Dr. Singh awaiting a response, the skin between his brows bunched into a frown over eyes that were cool and impassable, despite what she'd just revealed, making it impossible to determine what he thought of her unannounced arrival on his doorstep. Or rather, *their* arrival.

She knew it was late, that it would be an inconvenience to stop in without even a phone call when the veterinary office had closed over an hour before, but she didn't know what else to do with the two little bundles. She didn't know this man—Ethan, he'd said—but she knew his father, a kind, attentive doctor whose smiles could soothe even the saddest of children when their pets were sick, and for now, that was enough to give her hope that maybe that man's son wouldn't turn her, or her little charges, away on such an awful night.

June hadn't realized she'd been holding her breath until he reached out both hands to take the puppies from her. Letting the air slowly from her lungs, she watched as he tucked them under his arms the same way she had when she'd discovered them in the alley.

"We need to get them warmed up," he said, getting right to business. Ethan turned from where they still stood near the door and lifted a shoulder to motion for her to follow as he headed toward the examination rooms.

June had been in this office many times when her beloved cat reached his twilight years. Being there again caused memories to resurface that she hadn't prepared for when she'd made the impulsive decision to stop in, hoping someone would be there to save two little lives. Trailing behind the doctor, she focused instead on the waves of dark hair that just brushed the collar of his white coat and the broad span of his shoulders. Something about the look of him—the stormy but not unkind dark eyes, the beautiful shade of his skin, like black tea with a bit of milk stirred in, and his height, which had to be considerable to reach well over her own six feet— worked to unravel the tight ball that had formed in her belly.

Driving there in what now seemed to be a full-blast snowstorm was one of the scariest things June had ever done. It was lucky that she knew the roads as well as she did, having lived in Peach Leaf her whole life; otherwise, she wasn't sure there would have been much of a chance of making it this far, not to mention the likelihood that she and the puppies would not have survived if they'd stayed in the car. And until the extreme weather passed, it was impossible to tell what had caused her old lemon to die. Terror had struck when the engine coughed and gave up, the snow coming down so hard as the wind blew fiercely that she could barely see a foot in front of her. She'd followed the road as best she could and somehow, thankfully, had made it to the office.

What was probably only half a mile or so had become a nearly impossible journey until the glass door of the clinic came into view. And now there she was. There hadn't been time to mull over the next step— how she would get home with no working vehicle, especially with the weather throwing such a fit.

At least now she wasn't alone. Even though he didn't seem too happy to see the three of them—and really, who could blame him?—June knew somehow that he would do his best to help. Then they would just have to go from there.

Dr. Singh stopped in front of one of the exam rooms and lifted his chin toward the door, presumably asking June to open it, which she did quickly. When they were all in the room, he held the puppies out to her. "Okay, I need you to hold them for a moment. I'll be right back."

The apprehension she felt must have been poorly hidden because when he saw the look on her face Ethan's stoicism seemed to evaporate briefly; his eyes softened and the thin, serious line of his lips was replaced by a curve at one corner of his mouth that could almost pass for a grin.

"It's okay, Miss Leavy. I'll be right back, I promise. I just need to get some supplies, and it would help if you'd keep the puppies warm for just a moment longer. Can you do that for me?"

June nodded. She'd gotten the babies that far, but the thought of being responsible for them any longer seemed more daunting now as the stress of the day compounded and the idea hit her suddenly that they might not make it. Even now, in the safety of the clinic, with a trained veterinarian to help, the chance remained that the little ones might not pull through.

"Good," he responded, nodding. "You had a great idea earlier, keeping them close together in your pocket. That way, they had each other's warmth, plus that coming from your body."

A little flutter passed through her chest at the mention of her body coming from Dr. Singh's mouth, but she just shook her head and took back the little bundles of fur, tucking them into her sweatshirt once more.

"All set?" he asked.

"Yes, I think so."

At that, he left the room and June concentrated on snuggling the little pups close, willing her warmth to be enough to keep them alive. She couldn't tell how they were doing, other than that the tiny heartbeats she'd felt for before were still thumping softly, and their sweet brown eyes were open. With any luck, that meant they were okay, but a part of her warned that there could be any number of things wrong on the inside.

She swallowed and closed her eyes, and a moment later Dr. Singh returned with what looked like a pile of fluffy towels. He placed the bundle on the exam table and moved to the bench where June sat, wrapping one around her shoulders and gently settling the warm terry cloth in place, a gesture that was completely logical considering that she still shivered from the cold, but also surprisingly intimate. She couldn't recall the last time a man had done something so simple and caring for her, and before she could think about it, she found herself gazing up at him with a warm smile.

"Thank you," she said. "That feels…wonderful."

"You're quite welcome. We've got a small washer and dryer in the staff room, so I warmed these up for a minute or two."

As he spoke, though he didn't exactly return her smile, soft crinkles formed at the outer corners of those deep brown eyes and it struck her just how exceptionally attractive this man was. She hadn't even known that the older Dr. Singh had a son, but then, they'd only shared a doctor/patient-parent relationship, so it made sense that he wouldn't have gone into detail about his family.

Strangely, now, June very much wished he had.

Ethan went back to the table and returned with another towel, kneeling to spread it on the floor at her feet. He sat cross-legged in front of it. "Here, let's put the pups in this while I take a look at them. Safer than having them up on the table for now."

June nodded and retrieved them from her pocket one at a time, cringing as they squeaked in protest at the brief separation. "Do you think…" She swallowed. "Will they be all right?"

"It's hard to know until I can look them over," he said, wrapping the towel around the puppies. "But I will say this." He looked up at her. "You've done a great job here, keeping them warm and bringing them in. From what I can see so far, I think they have a good chance, all because of you."

June's insides melted a little at his compliments, but she wouldn't feel better until she knew the puppies would be okay.

After a few moments, Dr. Singh pulled the towel to one side and very gently moved one puppy closer to him, stroking it softly behind the ears with one hand as he ran his fingers over each tiny limb, probably feeling for broken bones. He then felt the pup's adorable pink tummy, almost grinning when the little guy—she could see plainly now that the term was accurate—closed his eyes.

June placed her nervous hands into the pouch of her hoodie, crossing her fingers.

"It's a good sign that they don't mind being held," Ethan said, using a thumb to gently pry the animal's mouth open, examining its tiny teeth before listening to its heart with the stethoscope that circled his neck. "Their friendliness toward humans will certainly make it easier to place them in homes when the time comes," he pointed out matter-of-factly. "Where did you say you found them?"

June cleared her throat, surprised at how much she disliked talk of giving the puppies away, even though she had no intention of keeping them for herself. "Behind the pizza shop, where I work."

The doctor winced, then looked up and met her eyes, listening intently as she spoke.

"We were done for the day, and I went out to toss the garbage. That's when I found them behind a Dumpster." Her throat threatened to close up as she thought again of someone leaving two little dogs in the icy alley.

"Any idea how long they were there?"

June shook her head. "No. I wish I had more to tell you, but unfortunately, that's it. I didn't know what else to do."

"Well, you did precisely the right thing, though it would appear you endangered yourself attempting to make it here. These are quite the lucky little guys, having been discovered by someone like you. Their fate might have been much worse, as I'm sure I don't have to tell you." An unmistakable wave of sadness crossed over the veterinarian's face.

"I wasn't thinking about that. I just wanted them to be okay...still do."

Ethan nodded and set down the first pup, picking up the other—a girl—to go through the same exam. "There's a good chance they will, thanks to you." Finished, he tucked the brother and sister back into their towel and folded his hands together in his lap.

"So, how's it look?" she asked, nails digging into her palms.

Ethan stared at her, his eyes warmer now, perhaps resigned to the outcome of his evening. She hadn't even considered that he might have plans...perhaps a wife at home waiting for him. Then again, he wasn't wearing a ring and he hadn't texted or called anyone upon her arrival, or once he'd realized that he would be at work for a bit longer.

"Well, I'll have to do some blood work within the next few days to get a full picture, but from what I can tell at this point, it seems they'll be okay."

Relief flooded through her at the optimistic statement.

"They're about three and a half weeks old, give or take. No broken bones, healthy lungs and hearts, and their teeth are coming in, which is great news."

"So they can eat solid food? We won't have to feed them with a bottle?" June had to admit she was a little disappointed. The idea of holding the tiny puppies and feeding them sounded...nice. She had always wanted children, anyway, but after her experience with Clayton, she wasn't sure she could trust anyone enough ever again to even think about building a life with another person. Another person who had the potential to break her heart. Maybe someday, if she ever had the time and energy to spare, she could have a little puppy just like these to care for. Maybe she could try letting herself love something again... one day...but it would take time, far more than she could spare with her life the way it was, working sixty-hour weeks at the pizza parlor just to pay her rent and keep her car in working shape. She hoped things wouldn't be that way forever; it was a sobering thought.

"Yes, they can eat solid food, but we'll need to mix it with some canine milk replacer that's specially formulated for puppies. Cow's or any other kind of milk would upset their tummies."

For some reason, June grinned at the word, so much more fatherly and sweet than the more technical *stomachs*.

"Do you have that here?"

"Sure do. We've got plenty, and I can have my receptionist, Sadie, order more in the morning if need be." He lifted a corner of the towel and glanced in at the puppies. "For now, we need to get them some water and get a little food in them. We won't give them too much yet, as I don't know what or how much they've been eating and I don't want them to get bloated."

June nodded as he stood and held out a hand to help her do the same, then knelt to pick up the squeaky bundle. He led her to the back area and into a room lined with shelves of food and medicine, handing over the puppies so he could scan the stock for what they needed.

"Ah, here we are," he said, lifting a small bag from a top shelf.

He opened a cabinet and pulled out two shallow bowls, then headed to the back room, stopping at a sink to fill one with water. Into the other, he poured a small amount of pebble-size kibble. He grabbed a bottle from a nearby refrigerator and poured thin, white liquid on top, like milk on cereal. Placing the bowls on the floor in a corner, Ethan motioned for June to set down the towel. At the scent of the food, two little black noses began to wriggle and both humans laughed quietly.

"The little stinkers are cute, aren't they?"

Ethan looked up at her as he spoke and this time his smile reached those gorgeous, mahogany eyes. She felt his gaze all the way down into her middle, as warm and comforting as the towel he'd so recently wrapped around her shoulders.

"Very," she replied, her voice little more than the squeaky sound the puppies made.

Dr. Singh helped her to guide the puppies over to the bowls, and they watched with bated breath, waiting to see if the little ones would eat. Finally, both pups sniffed at the bowl of food and buried their faces in the kibble, and the sound of Ethan's and June's sighs of relief were audible.

As the dogs worked on their dinner, Ethan disappeared into the supply closet and returned holding what looked like a baby gate and paper towels. He set to work in the corner of the room, spreading out what June now saw were puppy pads, which he surrounded with the gate, creating a little pen. "All right. We'll settle them in here for a bit, give them a little time and see if they'll do their business, then we can put them to bed."

He looked up at June. "If I'm correct on their

age, they should be able to go to the bathroom on their own."

"What do you mean?"

"Well, if they're too young, they'll need a little help to go, but I'm hoping they're old enough." He winked at her. "Time will tell."

"Ah." June had never been around such young animals before; once again, she was thankful to have an ally who knew far more than she about this unexpected development in her evening.

"In the meantime, is there anything I can get you?"

Her stomach grumbled, reminding her that she hadn't yet eaten and it was almost nine o'clock, but she doubted there was much in the way of people food in a veterinary clinic. "I'd love something hot to drink. That is, if you have anything."

"Come," Dr. Singh said, holding out an arm. June walked through the door in front of him and he left it open, leading her to what had to be the staff break room, where he pulled a chair from a small, round table, motioning for her to sit.

She watched as he took a measuring cup from a cabinet and placed it on a hot plate before pulling milk from the fridge and what appeared to be a few spice bottles from a drawer.

"So tell me, Miss Leavy…"

"Please, call me June."

He set to work, mixing ingredients in the glass cup as though he were a chef in an upscale kitchen, rather than a very patient veterinarian in a small-town clinic. "June, then. Have you ever had chai?"

It was only one of her favorite drinks. "Oh, I love chai tea."

The doctor let out a chuckle as he stirred the mixture with a spoon.

"What's so funny?"

"Just chai. When you say *chai tea*, what you're really saying is *tea tea*. The word *chai* means *tea* in Hindi."

"Oh, goodness," she said, feeling like a doofus. "I'm sorry."

"Not at all," Ethan said, laughing.

June found she very much liked the deep, warm sound of it tickling her ears. He seemed much more relaxed now than he had when she'd first arrived, almost certainly ruining his night.

"Is your family from India?" she asked, surprising herself. She supposed it wouldn't hurt to find something to talk about to pass the time until the storm let up and she could go on home.

"My father was born in Delhi and came here as a child."

"And your mother?"

"She's American, from New York. They've lived in Texas for most of my life, since my father opened this clinic."

It was quiet for a few moments as Ethan continued to stir the tea and June took a couple of deep breaths, allowing herself to calm down for the first time since she'd found the puppies over two hours ago. Her shoulders ached with tension and her tiredness reached all the way down to her bones; she longed for a hot shower and her bed. For once, she would be happy to go home to her lonely, closet-size apartment, where she hoped to get at least a couple hours of sleep before her alarm clock sent her back to work.

When she opened her eyes, Ethan set two steaming mugs on the table and June lifted hers to take a sip. The hot liquid soaked all the way down into her veins, warming her through and through, the sweet, yet spicy, flavors tingling her throat in an incredibly pleasant way. "Oh, my gosh," she said, rolling her eyes toward the roof, "this is amazing."

Ethan grinned, then took a sip from his own mug. "Better than Starbucks, huh?"

"Um, yeah. Way better. Apples and oranges better."

"I'm glad you like it," he said, taking a few more sips. He got up and went back to the counter, turning on a small television set to the same local weather she'd watched earlier with Margaret. She made a mental note to text her boss soon to make sure she'd made it home.

"We'd better see what's going on out there," he said, returning to the table. "It looked much worse than I thought it was when I opened the door and you brought an arctic blast in with you and those puppies."

"It's pretty bad. I'm hoping it will clear so I can get home soon."

Ethan looked skeptical but didn't say anything as they both turned to watch the screen. It only took a few minutes for them to learn that the weather had gotten worse as they'd been taking care of the dogs. According to the meteorologist, a mass of cold, dry Canadian air had moved south into their area to intersect with a warm, moist air mass moving north from the Gulf of Mexico. Evidently, the cold air had advanced and pushed away the warm air, orchestrating the crazy mess outside. Over a foot of snow had fallen on already-icy roads and the whole of Peach Leaf was now under a winter weather warning.

June put her elbows on the table and lowered her head into her arms. It would be hours before it would be safe to drive home...for a person who had a working ride.

"Well, June," Ethan said, getting up to turn off the steady stream of impending doom on the television. "Looks like you're stuck with me for a while."

"I... I can't stay here. I've got to get home."

Ethan tilted his head. "Not going to happen, at least not tonight. It's really nasty out there—not anywhere close to safe for driving." He finished the last of his tea and picked up both of their cups, carrying them to the sink.

"My car's broken down, anyway. Surely I can at least get a tow truck out here. Maybe they can take me home."

Ethan came back and sat down across from her at the table. "It's not likely we'd be able to get a tow truck out here in this weather. I would drive you if I felt it was safe, but I've spent some time in Alaska and I've seen firsthand what can happen when people don't heed weather warnings." He paused, perhaps not wishing to sound overly concerned. "Of course, I'm not going to stop you from leaving, June, but I have to tell you, I don't think it's safe, and I'd really rather you not put yourself into any more danger than you already have today."

Ignoring the fact that this man shouldn't care about her well-being so much, June ran through all of her options in her head—all zero of them. She sighed. He was right. She was stuck there for the foreseeable future. She'd never in her life experienced such a dangerous storm and she definitely didn't know how to safely travel in one. Besides, she had the puppies to think of now. The minute she'd picked them up, they'd become her responsibility, and she couldn't just abandon them with a doctor who had other patients to care for, especially one who was only temporarily managing his father's clinic.

She looked up at Dr. Singh, who appeared almost as uneasy as she.

"I hate to break it to you, June, but under the circumstances, the smartest thing for you to do is to spend the night here with me."

Chapter Four

It took June longer than it should have to register what Dr. Singh—Ethan—had said. Mostly because, somehow, she'd gotten momentarily lost in those cinnamon eyes of his. The man was handsome in a way that could almost be described as beautiful, but his looks were also sort of unnerving at the same time, as though they had the potential power to unravel her completely.

It occurred to her that looks like his didn't really fit in with the men she was used to seeing in Peach Leaf, almost as though she'd woken up still inside a dream involving a movie set. Men who looked like Ethan Singh were generally employed as actors or male models...not small-town veterinarians. And they usually associated with other exceptionally attractive or powerful people, or in his case, highly educated people…people nothing like her.

Staring at him made her think of all the ways she couldn't quite measure up. Though she wasn't sure where that notion had even originated from. After all, why would she need to measure up at all?

It wasn't like he was interested in her, at least aside from his medical duty to assist her in getting the puppies healthy. He certainly wasn't interested in her as a woman, as well he shouldn't be, because she was not interested in him as a man.

Really, she was not.

She shouldn't be, at any rate, not after what she'd been through the past several months. No woman in her right mind would seek to get back out there after the burn she'd suffered. And even though she might not be thinking clearly, what with her only real possession stuck out in the snow enduring God only knew what horrors, which might prevent it from ever working again—and with this man staring at her with unmistakable amusement as she waited for appropriate words to arrive—she could at least be certain that she was, in fact, in her right mind.

With that, she cleared the cobwebs from her throat and finally spoke, hoping her voice wouldn't come out too rusty from lack of use.

"Um, okay. I guess that makes sense." She swiped a hand across her forehead, suddenly warm despite the weather outside and the room's cool temperature.

"Of course it does," Ethan answered, his tone final as if the issue had been decided and there was nothing more to be discussed. But June thought there was plenty in need of discussion. Like, for example, the fact that she was suddenly starving.

And not, it would seem as she found herself in danger of falling deep into those eyes again, just for food.

The thought rushed in unbidden and was stuck there in her mind before she could stop it, meaning that the mature thing now would be to address where it had come from and what it meant. At some point. For now, feeling more ragged than she did after a double shift at work and hungrier than she could ever recall having been before, maturity was the last thing on her mind.

"Is something wrong?" the devastatingly handsome doctor asked, his voice even sexier thanks to its thick note of concern.

June shook her head. "No, it's fine. Or in any case, I suppose it has to be." She looked away from him and, not surprisingly, her mind was instantly clearer.

She would have to be careful around those eyes from now on, especially if she was meant to endure an entire night—possibly more, if the weather didn't clear up—with a man who looked like he'd just walked out of the latest glossy issue of *GQ*.

He made her want things she shouldn't want, things she couldn't have.

"What is it, then?"

When she didn't answer, he tilted his head like a curious puppy—like a ridiculously adorable, curious puppy.

"Come on now, I can tell you were thinking about something."

Like a tickle of wind against her cheek, she sensed him staring at her, willing her to speak.

"It's just that, well—" a hand flew to her stomach involuntarily "—I'm starving."

Ethan threw his head back and laughed, the sound low and sultry and full of mischief, leaving June almost frustrated with his level of physical perfection. Couldn't he at least have an absurd-sounding, high-pitched laugh or something? Was there nothing about this guy that wouldn't make her want to kiss him?

It was just her luck—she should be used to this by now—to be stuck overnight with the most distractingly attractive guy she'd ever met, right after the absolute worst breakup she'd ever endured.

Come on, Junie, she chastised herself. *That's about enough negativity for two lifetimes, don't you think?*

Best to push on. Besides, with the cards she'd been dealt, what choice did she have?

"All right. What's so darn funny?" she asked.

"Nothing, really. It's just that here you are looking so incredibly serious and come to find out you're just hungry."

"Hilarious," she responded, this time allowing a hint of playfulness to escape. "But seriously, I haven't had anything to eat since lunch, which now seems like years ago. I know it might be useless to ask, but is there anything to eat around here? That is, anything we can get to without risking our lives."

Ethan grinned, his full lips setting in motion a series of thoughts that she wasn't entirely certain were legal.

"Actually, this might be one problem we can solve."

"Don't tease me now. I'm this close to sneaking some of that puppy kibble from the storage room."

He laughed. "I wouldn't dare. There's a bakery a few doors down. It might be a rough trip, but I think if we stay right next to the building and, well, right next to each other, we can probably make it with only minimal danger."

"Stay—" June swallowed "—next to each other?"

"Of course. For warmth."

June felt her cheeks heat, hoping they weren't turning as ghastly pink as they were in the habit of doing—the eternal curse of redheads like herself. "Yes, right. Warmth. Of course."

It made perfect sense under the circumstances; it really did. But the mere thought of being near Ethan for the duration it might take them to reach sustenance raised her temperature enough that she was fairly certain she could comfortably walk all the way to her apartment in the wind that had begun to howl outside the clinic like a wild animal.

Without a coat.

"Let's check on the puppies, get you bundled back up and see if we can't get some food," Ethan said, tossing his new companion a sweet smile. "I could go for some dinner myself."

While that was definitely true—his stomach had been protesting against its emptiness since he'd seen his last patient, and that had been hours ago—there was another reason, equal in weight to the first, that he'd suggested leaving the office and grabbing something to eat.

That reason was June Leavy.

A few hours before, his life in Peach Leaf had been simple and clear, intentionally so.

This morning, he'd woken with a relatively muddled head for the first time since leaving Colorado.

Since he'd left *her*.

Sure, he still thought about his ex a few times a day still; that was perfectly normal following the demise of a serious relationship. But aside from those few painful moments, things had actually started to look up, and he'd gotten into a comfortable groove. Wake up and go for an early run, shower and eat breakfast, arrive at the clinic before sunrise to relieve the night technician and check on the overnight patients, work through his father's back-to-back appointments, breaking only for a quick lunch, and then go home after he'd completed evening rounds and closed up. He'd say goodbye to the staff and head home, too tired to think. Working from dark sky to dark sky suited him at this odd juncture in his life. The routine kept him busy and, most importantly, left little time for ruminating over all he'd left behind.

At least it had, until that evening, when June Leavy had burst through the door, literally bringing with her a blast of fresh air.

The image made him smile. As cold as it had been when she'd walked in, June was about as different from his frosty ex as she could be—a truth he didn't really want to examine closely.

But as beautiful as June was, as sweet and warm as he could clearly see she was even in the limited time they'd spent together, the truth remained that her presence was simply not welcome.

She filled the room in a way that, while extremely pleasant—intoxicating, even—made him uncomfortable. Tall, bright in color and in mood and lively, June was impossible to ignore. Sharing a cup of tea with her had been difficult enough, but offering to let her stay the night—something he'd had no choice but to do on account of the growing danger outside—was going to take an iron will.

He didn't want her in his clinic, didn't want her on his mind. Being in the same room with her for the past while, as warm as she made him feel, he'd almost forgotten about the blizzard wailing away outside.

All of which was dangerous. What he needed was space, and a clear head.

Taking June for a bite to eat was the perfect solution. They were both hungry, and it would give him a chance to get a grip on whatever spark she'd ignited within him. Plus, he'd like to check on his father's business neighbors—the couple who owned the German bakery next door had been there for years and were close with his dad. They were elderly, and it would be good to make sure they were holding up through the freak snowstorm.

A blast of frigid air would do him good, and then he could figure out how to handle himself around June for the rest of the evening.

Things came to mind. So many things.

None of them realistic, or even appropriate for that matter.

A guy like him was in no position to be picturing those endless legs curled up next to his on the office sofa, for example, or better yet, wrapped around his middle as he kissed the daylights out of those undoubtedly soft lips and…

No. He couldn't let himself go there. Not again. It was stupid enough that he'd allowed his thoughts to wander this far. It seemed any time he ventured away from work for five minutes, he landed in trouble. He didn't want to be the sort of man who was so easily distracted by a pretty face and a pair of killer legs.

He looked up to find the object of his musings worrying her bottom lip as she studied him.

It wasn't sexy, the way she did that. Not at all.

The resultant swelling of those soft pink clouds did not affect him. Not in the least.

Also, he needed to check the thermostat—had it gotten warmer inside the clinic?

"So, what kind of place is it?" June asked, her cheeks slightly more flushed than they'd been when she first came in from the wind. Surely she wasn't… she couldn't possibly be having similar thoughts to the ones he'd been entertaining. The idea was absurd.

He'd been radiating a cool demeanor and a general *leave me alone, I'm busy* attitude for weeks now that would put off any woman. More likely, she was just in a hurry to get out of there as much as he was.

"I mean what kind of food do they have?"

"Oh, well, there's the rub," he answered, trying not to get distracted again by those wicked lips, which had reddened to a pretty ruby shade—from the cold or from her nibbling, he no longer cared.

And what difference did it make, anyway?

It certainly didn't matter that they looked good enough to feast on himself, like fresh cherries ripe for the picking.

Dammit!

What the hell had they been talking about again?

"The rub?"

Ah, yes.

"It's just a little German bakery, you see. So we won't be able to get any real dinner. We'll have to skip straight to dessert. Hopefully it'll do until the weather lets up and you have a chance to head on your way." A thought that disturbed him far more than he cared to acknowledge.

Something crossed her features very briefly—a shadowy hint of darkness, perhaps—and then disappeared.

Was it something he'd said that had so quickly stolen the light from her eyes?

He didn't have time to figure it out before she spoke again.

"Oh, that's right. How silly of me to forget. I've

been working such weird hours the past few years that I haven't been to Bauer's in ages—I'd forgotten about the place until now." Her features softened into wistfulness. "My mom used to take me there as a kid, on special occasions. They have the best pastry and…"

She blushed again and he wished to touch the crimson apples on her cheeks. He enjoyed her rambling—quite a lot actually. But what good would it do to say so? After that night, she would be gone and he would go back to his temporary, if somewhat lonely, life.

Still, it was nice to see her talk about something so obviously important to her; it was nice to see inside her just a little.

"Anyway, I'm rambling, but that will be just fine. I'm so hungry I really don't care what we eat, as long as it passes for food."

"And is preferably intended for human consumption," he teased, recalling her earlier comment about kibble, and wanting to restore her brightness.

"That would be great," she said, beaming.

Pleased, he gestured for her to follow him to the back room and she did so. When they stepped through the door, the puppies were curled so tightly together that he and June had to check to make sure the little ones were both accounted for. After changing out the potty pad, they watched the critters sleep for a few moments, Ethan checking their breathing before he gently touched June's elbow, whispered that the pups would be okay with only each other as company for a short while longer and led her out to the front of the clinic.

"I feel like I'm leaving my kids alone at home," June said, shrugging into her coat, which he held open for her.

"I completely understand, and sadly, I don't think this is their first time on their own," Ethan said, wanting to reassure her, "but we won't be long and I promise they'll be fine until we return."

What was he thinking, making a promise like that? Yes, the animals appeared relatively healthy and strong, considering their situation, and yes, he was confident in his ability to usher them back to full health, but he had no history of clairvoyance and therefore no business making guarantees regarding things he couldn't fully control.

What had gotten into him? Would he say anything to make this woman smile?

Catching the worried crease between her brows as she glanced once more over her shoulder in the direction of the pups, Ethan tucked his hand beneath her elbow. "Trust me, June. They'll be all right. Their bellies are full, they've had fresh water and have done their business, they're safe inside the pen and they're not alone."

The answer was yes, apparently, he would say anything.

At his words, her expression softened, and though he didn't want to examine why it mattered to him at all, he found himself relieved at the idea of having provided some comfort. "Also, I would not leave them if I believed them to be unsafe, okay?"

She nodded.

"So then, do you trust me?"

She wasn't quick to answer, a fact that made him like her even more. After all—though he wasn't entirely sure any longer whether he believed time to be a reliable factor in the decision to invest trust in someone—they'd only known each other for little over an hour.

"Yes," she finally said. "I do trust you."

He smiled, more pleased than wisdom should allow.

"Good." He squeezed her elbow, then let go. "I figure the best thing to do now is grab something to go and come back here. That way, we won't risk getting stuck at the bakery. Even though it's only a few yards away, we could end up unable to get back, and I don't want to leave the puppies alone for a full night."

"Sounds like a plan," June agreed.

Ethan pulled on his coat and wrapped a scarf around his neck and face before donning his hat. By the time he'd finished, June had done the same and looked adorable, a description that, despite being worlds apart from characterizing the women he was typically attracted to, seemed somehow more enticing.

June looked like someone he could curl up and have hot chocolate with after a long day at work, someone who would be joyful when a guy walked in the door, happy to spend an evening at home with him just relaxing, doing nothing in particular.

That was just it—the sight of her evoked *home* to him, something he could never ascribe to the women he'd dated before, women who preferred nights out on the town on the arm of a successful professor. It didn't escape him that, over the past few years, being a "nerd" had become an asset, one he'd not hesitated to take full advantage of, and there had been plenty of young women, even a few former students, who had been eager to date an up-and-coming scientist who'd begun, much to his dismay, to attract media attention.

But June was part of a different world than the one he'd become accustomed to. For reasons he couldn't explain, she brought to mind everything he missed about living in a small town, being close to family and so much more. He'd spent a good portion of the last decade thinking only of his career, dedicating all of his time to furthering his research and, if he was honest, to impressing his department at the university.

June made him think of other things. Things he used to want but truly thought he didn't need any longer—things like home, and family, and someone to share it with. Someone to love.

None of which he would entertain, because that word—*love*—was no longer part of his vocabulary when it came to women.

Of course he loved his parents, his siblings and his nieces and nephews, but that was the safe kind of love. Loving a woman, which would inevitably lead to a broken heart again—well, that was an experience he'd rather not repeat. Especially not when his heart hadn't quite healed from the last.

What kind of scientist would he be if he didn't learn from failed experiments?

"Remind me again why we're doing this?" June asked as he opened the door and snow crashed through with the force of a speeding train.

He reached for her hand and, when she grabbed it with her own, pulled her close to his body, tucking an arm over her shoulders. He chose to ignore the way she stiffened as their figures came together, not caring to assess whether it was aversion or pleasure at the contact that made her react in such a way.

"Because we're starving, remember?"

"Oh, right," she said. "Somehow the idea of having my face frozen off made me forget how hungry I am."

He started to laugh but stopped when icy air hit his lungs, and set his focus on moving ahead instead. As they made their way in the direction of the bakery, Ethan was careful to keep his free hand against the wall of the building as the wind's forceful blasts threatened to send them flying into the white abyss that used to be a parking lot. June's head was down, her chin tucked into the top of her coat as he led the way. Despite the circumstances, Ethan couldn't help but enjoy the way her tall, slim figure nestled against his own, her body's warmth seeping through the layers of his clothing, strong enough to set off a flame in his lower abdomen.

Astounding, the lack of discipline he'd allowed in letting himself get carried away over June. Having her huddle against his skin for warmth was one thing; that just made practical, biological sense.

Letting her under it, though, was another matter entirely.

"Looks like there's a note on the door," Ethan shouted to June, who was still tucked under his arm. It was virtually impossible to hear himself think, let alone to communicate with each other with the high-speed wind whipping around them. They were only a couple of yards from Bauer's Bakery and, Ethan hoped, his stomach growling like an angry dog, something hot to eat.

He felt June nod beneath his shoulder as it occurred to him for the first time, stupidly, that the Bauers might have closed up early and hit the road once the weather started to get worse. He certainly couldn't blame them; it's exactly what he would have done if he didn't have so many little furry creatures depending on him. Even if he'd been able to earlier before June showed up, after he'd told the overnight tech not to risk the trip in, he would never have left the babies alone on a night like this.

As soon as they made it to the door of the bakeshop, June emerged from his side and reached for it, only to find it locked. He wasn't surprised, but he sure as hell was disappointed. The note on the door had been taped at all four corners, three of which were now torn. Peeling off the last, he read it only to confirm his earlier assumption that the Bauers had gone home, and he was glad for their safety.

"Well, crap," June said, turning to face him. "Guess we'll have to head back to the clinic. Maybe we can find a granola bar to split or something. Or... doggy biscuits are basically flour and water, right? So, maybe if we use our imaginations, it would be like eating cookies."

He'd have to be a little more desperate to try a canine treat, but if they did find a granola bar, Ethan would let June have the whole thing. However, it was too early in the game to consider giving up just yet.

"Hang on a minute."

June's face was bright pink from the well-below-freezing temperature and the wind's icy fingers slapping at her cheeks. He needed to get her inside that building, needed to get her warm.

"I've got a key." He took off one mitten and, reaching under his coat, pulled his wallet out of his back pocket and dug through the compartments until he found what he was looking for. "My dad gave it to me in case the Bauers had an emergency."

June didn't look too relieved; probably she was holding out to make sure it worked. That made two of them. He hadn't paid much attention when Dad went through all the important numbers and files and such that Ethan might need while caring for the clinic, and it hadn't occurred to him to check and see if the key worked. Who would have guessed that the worst storm in Texas history would hit during his stay?

"Well, what are you waiting for?" she yelled so he could hear, her eyes squinting against the brutal air.

With fingers on the brink of frostbite, he gripped the key and shoved it into the lock, releasing an audible sigh when it fit and the knob turned.

"Oh, thank God," June said, her eyes shooting toward the sky.

Ethan opened the door and ushered her inside, pulling it closed against a turbulent gust.

Once inside, Ethan leaned his back against the door, then they looked at each other and both started laughing as relief and the possibility of getting their hands on some food settled in. The moment of relaxation didn't last long, though, and suddenly Ethan heard a sharp, incessant beeping.

"Oh, crap!" he shouted, echoing June's words from when she'd thought they were locked out in the cold. This could be worse.

When she met his eyes, hers were wide as salad plates. "Is that what I think it is?"

"Uh, yeah. 'Fraid so."

"Oh, no. No, no, no." Her hands flew to her cheeks and she stared at him with obvious fear. "We are going to be in so much trouble when the police…"

He held up a hand in an attempt to prevent her panic from gaining momentum.

"Hang on. It would take them ages to get here if they were coming at all, but I've got a strong feeling that's not going to happen. Luckily, I also have a plan." He reached into his pocket once more, praying his phone was still in there; he hadn't checked before they left the clinic, a distraction he could justifiably blame on June. He pressed his thumb against a button, unlocking the cell, and dialed as quickly as his icicle fingers would allow.

"What are you doing?"

"Just trust me, okay?"

She nodded at the same time his father picked up.

"Dad, hey, I'm glad you answered. I need you to listen carefully. I don't have much time."

"Ethan, is that you?" his father asked.

He rolled his eyes.

"Yes, Dad, of course it's me. Look, do you have the alarm code to the Bauers' place?"

He waved at June to get her attention and motioned for her to open the keypad near the door where the alarm continued to blare its warning.

"Just a minute, son, I think I have it here somewhere." Ethan could picture the older man digging through the kitchen junk drawer of his uncle's apartment in DC.

Ethan groaned—getting his father to hurry up was about as futile as trying to force a cat to walk on a leash—but thankfully, he'd set to work without an argument.

"Time is of the essence here, Dad."

"All right, all right. I've got it right in front of me now. Just let me put on my reading glasses." More shuffling ensued. "Are you ready?"

"Of course I am. Go ahead."

He listened as his dad recited the code, repeating it to June, who promptly punched the numbers into the keypad. When the inane beeping stopped, Ethan dropped the phone to his side and they both let out the breaths they'd been holding since the noise began.

"Is everything okay now?" his father's voice chimed from the cell.

"Yes, Dad, it's fine. Thanks a bunch. It's a long story and I can't talk now, but I needed to get into the Bauers' and I've got the key you gave me. I just hadn't considered the alarm system."

"Tell Dr. Singh thank you for me," June called out.

He nodded that he would.

"Is that a girl?" his dad asked.

Ethan rolled his eyes. "Yes, Dad. And she said to tell you she's thankful for the help, as well. But like I said, I'll have to explain later. I have to go…"

"What girl?" came his mother's voice in the background.

Grumbling rose up from his throat when he heard her snatch the phone from his father's hand.

Here we go.

"Ethan Singh, do you have a girlfriend you haven't told us about? Are you on a date? You should not be on the phone while on a date. I raised you better than that and…"

"Mom, Mom! I'm not on a date." He shook his head at the curious, teasing smile that sprung up on June's face. She crossed her arms, clearly enjoying his misery just a little too much.

"Look, like I told Dad, I've got to go. I'll talk to you guys later."

"You'd better not be out with a woman and keeping it a secret from us, Ethan. I'm your mother and I deserve to know if your heart isn't broken anymore and you're back out there. Are you back out there, Ethan? I certainly hope so. I never liked that last girl and I know you can do so much better."

"Jessica, Mom. Her name was Jessica. All right, thanks for the lecture. I really do have to go, though."

"Bring her by the house so we can meet her, son," his dad interjected from the background. "I don't know if your mother has told you yet but we're coming back down for Neena's birthday party in a few days. We will see your new friend then."

"Yes, do so," Melanie Singh agreed. "And sooner rather than later. I don't like to see you so down all the time."

He could practically see the maternal finger shaking in his face.

"You're not getting any younger, Ethan," she continued, "and I want to see you settled before you're old and gray."

He gazed heavenward, hoping maybe the guy upstairs would throw him a bone. As if getting stuck in a blizzard without dinner wasn't bad enough, now he had to endure an inquisition from his overinvolved parents while a woman he'd been attracted to the moment he laid eyes on her looked on with thinly veiled amusement.

June could at least have the courtesy not to look so thoroughly entertained.

"Yes, Mom. Tell Dad I said bye. I will talk to you later."

"Not so fast. First, promise you'll bring this young lady by for Neena's birthday party. The more, the merrier, I always say."

He'd never heard her use that expression before in his life, but this was a time for picking battles.

"I can't do that."

"And why ever not?"

His jaw clenched and he withheld choice words. "Because as I said, we are not dating. If you'd been listening you would know that we've only just met, June and I. Now I really do have to go."

"Oh, June is such a pretty name, but, Ethan, if you're not dating this young woman, then what are you doing with her in the middle of this weather? After the clinic is closed?"

"She's not...we're not..." He closed his eyes, drawing in a slow breath and hopefully a hefty dose of patience, too. "I will explain later."

"I know you, Ethan," his mother said, her voice stern now. "The party. Next weekend. You'll call me later for the details."

"I..." Oh, what was the point in fighting her? When Melanie Singh got an idea in her head, there was simply no talking her out of it. "All right, Mom. I promise."

"Good boy," she said, the sound of victory clear as a bell in her falsely innocent voice.

He knew when to admit defeat. "Okay, Mom. Goodbye."

He pushed the end call button with a bit more ferocity than was necessary. June was standing there staring at him, arms still crossed, a pleased grin curling her lips up at the corners.

"You don't have to look so smug, you know."

June's eyebrows shot up. "Smug?" she asked, pointing at her chest. "Who, me?"

She batted her eyelashes, a gesture that was meant to be silly but instead ticked up his pulse a notch.

"Yes, smug. I can see you got a kick out of watching me get dominated by my overbearing family, and you're enjoying it far too much." He shoved his cell back into his pocket and took a few steps nearer to the woman who'd turned his evening upside down—whether in a good way or bad still remained to be seen.

Something in her eyes darkened, but she quickly brushed aside whatever had bothered her for half a second. "Not at all. I mean, I did enjoy listening in on your conversation, I admit, but probably not in the way you think."

"I'm intrigued. Go on." It was his turn to cross his arms, and he did so with a smile on his face, enjoying the easy banter with her. It had been a long time since he'd felt so tranquil in a woman's presence, and even though he wasn't willing to invest his heart in one again, what harm could there be in having a bit of fun? They were stuck in each other's company for the night, after all. Maybe it wouldn't hurt to enjoy the short time they had.

He expected June's next words to be playful, flirty even, but instead they were serious.

"It's just that...well, it sounds like your parents are very sweet. You're a lucky guy."

"Oh, June, you have no idea," he said softly, trying to set the tone to light again. "My parents are many things, but sweet is not one of them."

Her eyes crinkled at the corners and registered disbelief. "You're bluffing. They sound incredibly sweet."

"They are kind people, I'll allow that. But—" he made a clicking sound with his tongue "—meddlesome to an unholy degree."

He stood only inches away from her now, and the heat radiating in that small space was enough to warm the entire cold bakery.

"At any rate, I'm in debt to them for that alarm code, so I'm in no position to complain."

"Goodness, me, too," June added. "I think my butt was literally about to freeze off."

"Wouldn't that be a shame?" he quipped, the words popping out before he could reconsider.

June would have been justified in socking him a good one, but the thing was, he didn't for a second regret the comment. It was true—the woman had a great ass—and he wasn't afraid to admit it.

For a second, her pretty mouth hung open in surprise, and then it did something rather unexpected.

She smiled—a gorgeous, sexy smile—even a little naughty, he would say, and he couldn't help but grin back.

They stood there like two teenage idiots on a first

date until finally June gave a little cough. "Right. Food," he said, more than a little sorry to see the moment pass.

Chapter Five

"Obviously no one's here, so what are we going to do?"

Ethan pulled off his outerwear and made a motion for June to let him help with her coat. He plucked the garment from her shoulders and she was instantly grateful for the air that slid over her skin like cool water.

He'd gone and done it again—made her uncomfortably warm with that silky voice and those delicious brown eyes. Not to mention she was certain her heart would melt as she'd listened to his humorous but charming conversation with his folks.

June swallowed, willing the lump in her throat to dissolve.

She loved her own mom fiercely, but that had

never stopped her from wanting more as a kid, from wanting a real family. A whole family. It was easy to admit that she wasn't a kid anymore, that she should grow up and accept reality, but some wishes did not go away.

When her ex had deceived her, stolen every cent of the money she'd saved to start her own bakery, then topped that off by leaving her in the dust with a shattered heart, she'd thought more than once how comforting it would have been to have a sister. And yeah, she had good friends—not many that she kept in touch with, considering the long hours her job required, but a few close ones nonetheless. Her best friend, Katie, was always there for her, when she and her husband, Ryan, weren't too busy with their kids' many activities. It was just that sometimes she couldn't help thinking how wonderful it would be to have someone she'd grown up with, someone who knew her history—who loved her deeply and unconditionally—to have her back when things got really tough. Really, really tough. Like you're-on-your-back-and-someone-kicks-you-in-the-face kind of tough. That's certainly how she'd felt when Clayton had taken everything she'd ever invested into the bakery.

And, it sometimes seemed, much more.

On the loneliest nights in her tiny apartment, without even a cat to keep her company anymore, June sometimes felt like he'd taken her very future from her. To her name, she had a rented apartment, a car she didn't yet own and a job that paid only slightly over minimum wage. Nothing that really, truly, belonged to her.

Sometimes her whole life felt borrowed, as if someone could come collect at any time and she would have nothing left but the clothes on her back.

Of course, she would never admit that to anyone— not ever. She was June Leavy, the positive girl who'd grown up poor with a single mom who broke her back at multiple jobs to put food on the table but could never scrape together enough for a much-deserved vacation—all with a smile on her face.

Because if she didn't smile, there was only one alternative. And even on her lowest days, feeling sorry for herself was not an option.

And then there was Ethan Singh, saving puppies and rocking her world during the biggest storm of her life.

If she didn't watch herself, he might convince her that she was not a woman who no longer trusted men. Or, at least, he might make her want to try.

She gave herself a mental shake.

No way. She wasn't going there again. She knew to stay away from a face like that when she saw one. Her ex had been a good-looking guy and she'd been the envy of all her friends, until he'd broken her heart into a thousand little pieces.

She was a much stronger woman now, and would not fall victim to a handsome face, liquid-gold voice and a knock-your-pants-off body.

"We're going to do what we came to do—get something to eat."

His comment brought her back to the present situation. She was starving, yes, but she wasn't about to steal food from a sweet old couple who'd pinched her cheeks as a child. Perhaps they could leave a note and pay later.

"We can't just take food when no one's here."

"Of course we can. These are dire circumstances, June, on the off chance you haven't noticed."

Something about the way he said her name turned her insides into custard.

"I've known the Bauers since my dad opened the clinic, and they won't mind one bit."

She was skeptical and it must have shown in her expression.

"Look, there's nothing to worry about. I'll leave a note and some cash and drop by to explain when the storm is over. No worries. Besides, I'm pretty sure Mrs. Bauer would hate to see us leave here empty-handed. She's always bringing the clinic staff cookies and trying to fatten us up. If anything, she'll be happy we helped ourselves."

He had a point there. The Bauers were childless and seemed to take immense joy in spoiling other peoples' kids with their stellar baked goods. The bakery was their passion and the older couple loved nothing more than watching people savor their home-made desserts.

She wasn't exactly keen on the idea, but desperate times and all…

"If you're sure."

Ethan pulled a large bill out of his wallet and left

it on the counter, promising to find a pen and paper before they left.

"I'm sure."

She raised her hands in surrender. "I suppose we don't really have a choice, now do we?"

"That's my girl."

The words hit her harder than the wind outside. Why did she like them so much? And why, when she'd only been around him for a few hours, did this guy have the power to unravel her with a couple of words?

Yep, she definitely needed to watch out.

As if to remind her that biology had a say in things, June's stomach let out a lion-worthy roar, making Ethan laugh and lightening the mood.

She covered her mouth to stifle a grin. "Sorry about that."

"Nonsense. Let's just get something in there already."

"Deal."

With that, they made their way behind the glass cases, which had been emptied for the night, and into the kitchen. June didn't see any pastries, but the scent of fresh dough tickled her nose and made her even hungrier, if such a thing was possible at that point. And yet there was absolutely no food in sight. Which made perfect sense—under normal circumstances, the Bauers would be there early in the morning to make everything from scratch for the day. Unfortunately, there were two ravenous people in need of immediate sustenance, and baked goods weren't exactly known for being made quickly.

Ethan appeared as disappointed as she felt.

"Okay, so I don't see anything to eat, and now's probably as good a time as any to admit that I know less than nothing about baking."

June chuckled, scanning the shelves stocked with flour, sugar and other products. She had an idea that just might work if she could drum up the right stuff. "You're in luck. I do happen to know a thing or two."

"Oh, really?" Ethan asked, his dark brows lifting in hope.

"Really." She rubbed her hands together. "I just need the proper ingredients, so let's see what we can find."

"By all means, then. Put me to work."

"I'd really rather not use the Bauers' electricity by turning on the industrial-size ovens, and I'm anxious to get back to the clinic and see how the puppies are doing, but I think I know just the thing to make back at the clinic." Now it was her turn to ask. "Do you trust me?"

He grinned, giving her a full view of his perfect white teeth between chestnut-colored lips that looked good enough to bite.

"I do."

"Okay, then. If you can grab a sack of sugar and one of flour from those shelves—" she pointed behind him "—I'll see if I can't manage to scare up some cocoa powder."

He clapped his hands together and headed toward

the rows of neatly organized baking supplies. "I don't know what you're up to, Miss Leavy, but if it includes cocoa, I'm in."

There were lots of things she'd like to do with him that included various forms of chocolate, but she supposed she'd have to settle with baking. Especially since, she reminded herself, no matter how sexy he was and no matter how many unwanted but delicious images he brought to mind every time he graced her with that smile, she wasn't looking for a relationship. Her stay in Singlesville was meant to be permanent.

Having given him an assignment, she made her way to the walk-in refrigerator and, shivering at the climate that matched the one she'd just escaped from, grabbed a carton of eggs.

She opened the door and ran smack into Ethan.

The eggs were safe as she had instinctively pulled their carton against her chest to shield the contents from impact, but when he grasped her shoulders and stared into her eyes, she was very, very far from safe.

"I'm so sorry, June. Are you all right?"

His lips were too close to hers, but yes, technically she was okay. She looked away, fighting to slow the sudden surge in her heart rate.

"Yes, I'm fine," she lied, averting her eyes. "What were you doing here, anyway?"

Perhaps he wasn't immune to her, after all. She caught a tiny jump in the muscle of his jaw, and he was definitely breathing more heavily than the situation warranted. And his pulse was tap-tap-tapping against the velvety skin of his throat, almost in time with her own.

"I was just... I came to check on you. I got the flour and sugar like you said, and, well, you were in there for longer than I liked."

Oh, God, she needed to get away from him. Now. She pulled back and he let his hands drop.

"Great. I just need to get some vegetable oil and we'll be set."

If she just kept busy, the awkward moment would pass and they could both forget about it.

Ethan cleared his throat but didn't have the decency to stop looking at her. If she hadn't been mistaken, for a second there, it seemed like he might have been on the verge of kissing her.

Far worse, she could not guarantee that she wouldn't have stopped him.

She watched as he moistened his lips, reassuring herself that this was reality and he could not, in fact, read her mind. He could see that, in spite of herself, she would have allowed him to press those lips against hers, just to see what it would be like to have that sensual-beyond-words mouth covering her own.

But the moment was gone forever, and that was a good thing.

It was.

She pushed her shoulders back, remembering where she was and what she was doing there.

"Right," he said. "We'd better get back and check on the puppies."

Her head bobbed rapidly up and down.

"I couldn't agree more."

"You're making what in a what now?" Ethan asked when they were back at the clinic.

June rolled her eyes in exasperation.

"Brownies. In a cup. Like I said."

"I'm not following. I have had brownies a time or two and I really do not see how you could successfully make such things in a coffee mug."

"Well, you'll just have to wait and see, then, ye of little faith."

Having traipsed back through the weather carrying zippered bags of flour, sugar and cocoa, the little bit of oil she'd poured into a mason jar, along with the couple of eggs she'd stuffed in her pockets, they were both dying to eat.

While she'd set out the ingredients on the limited counter space of the tiny break room, Ethan had checked on the pups, returning to say that he'd freshened their water, changed out their potty pad and given them a little more food to eat, and they were snuggled back up for additional, much-needed rest.

The poor little ones were doubtless exhausted from the sheer effort of staying warm in below-freezing temperatures, not to mention having fended for themselves for who knew how long. She knew they would need homes soon, but she didn't want to think yet about giving them away. There was no way she could keep a puppy—not with hours like hers at the pizza place—but their little faces made her heart ache.

So much had been lost to her over the past several months that, even though she knew the tiny creatures did not belong to her, the idea of losing them might threaten to push her over some invisible edge of grief.

"All right," she said, winking at her companion and focusing on the task at hand, trying to block those little brown puppy eyes from her mind, "prepare to be awed and amazed."

Ethan smiled at her, looking ridiculously adorable with his elbows on the counter, chin in hands, watching her like an eager little boy.

She pulled their tea mugs from earlier out of the dish drying rack and mixed ingredients into each one. As Ethan stared, intrigued, she then put the mugs into the microwave. Only a minute and a half later, out popped deliciousness.

She presented him with a mug and stood back, ready to watch him take a bite. When he did, he closed his eyes and remained still long enough to worry her.

"Oh. My. God," he said, barely in time to take another mouthful. "This is amazing."

She shrugged and picked up her own serving. "It's not that exciting, but it's the best I can do with limited time and materials."

"You're being too modest, June. I'm not kidding— this is possibly the best brownie I've ever tasted."

She covered her mouth and a laugh escaped as she swallowed a large bite of moist chocolate. "That's just the starvation talking."

It was true. Microwave brownies were no secret—

they had been trending all over the internet for a while—and she was absolutely not the first one to make them. But in a pinch, they'd have to do.

Out of nowhere, something hit her in the gut, and this time, it wasn't hunger.

It was longing, deep and pure.

She couldn't recall the last time she'd baked anything. Not microwave brownies, not her favorite apple caramel pie or any of her secret cookie recipes that were famous among her friends.

It had been…months.

And she missed it. So, so much.

She had a sudden, desperate urge to bake something for Ethan. Something far better than the stupid brownie he was digging into so hard and clearly enjoying, if the periodic moans he emitted between bites were anything to go on.

While it was absolute bliss to see him loving something she'd made for him, it would be a thousand times more satisfying to see him dive into something really special, something that was truly an original creation of her own.

Baking had been her passion, the one constant in her life. Despite working a full-time job, June's mom had always made time for her when she'd had the chance, time they usually spent in the kitchen mixing up delightful things to eat.

June disagreed with the common conception that baking was a science, not an art. On the contrary, she and her mom had thrown caution to the wind when it came to treats; they played with ingredients and measurements to their hearts' content, never afraid to risk disaster for the possibility of unearthing new greatness.

June released a soft sigh. Those were some of her very favorite memories.

She made a mental note to give her mother a call as soon as she got home, and not another of the short Sunday night check-ins they usually shared, but a real, long, catch-up call. And as soon as she had a break from work, she would visit, and they would bake something fun, something new that neither had tried before.

She could use a little adventure in her life, at least of the safe variety.

Closing her eyes, she poked her spoon around in the last bits of gooey chocolate at the bottom of her mug, the best part in her opinion, and took her final bite of the impromptu dessert. When she slid the clean spoon out of her mouth, June found Ethan studying her, his expression a strangely pleasant blend of curiosity and...joy, as though he'd happened across an interesting painting.

"Something on your mind?" he asked, resting his spoon in his own mug and setting it on the counter.

The way he did that—put down the dish to focus all of his attention on her—was simultaneously intoxicating and unsettling. He gazed at her as though what she might say next was the most fascinating thing in the world, before he'd even heard it. She wasn't entirely sure she liked being examined so intently; there was great potential to make a fool of herself in front of someone she was slowly coming to respect and even like.

She decided to be honest, to be brave.

"The truth?"

He nodded affirmation.

"I was just thinking about my mother."

Ethan's features softened. "Ah, mothers. A complicated bunch, aren't they?"

It was alarming, how much she enjoyed the sound
of his voice, that singular mix of accents she'd never
heard all in one place before and couldn't quite identify. His words were more carefully formed than
the looser, more drawn-out cadence of the locals
she'd grown up around; they were tighter but also
smoother—not better, of course, just different. And
his vocabulary, his way of putting sentences together,
was more formal than any man she'd ever spoken
to before.

Ethan Singh was a rare, increasingly fascinating
gem. He was cool and direct, almost hard, at first
meeting, but like a fine baklava, she had the sense
he would be infinitely more complex inside, lovelier.
Hearing the way he'd talked with his parents on the
phone—his tone warm and indulgent, the opposite
of his annoyed words that didn't fool anyone—she
knew already that he cared deeply for his parents
and he placed great value on family.

As did she.

It seemed as the evening progressed, she and the
doctor had more and more in common.

"It's true," she conceded. "They are complicated,
but I can tell you adore yours."

His cheeks shaded to a slightly darker almond.

"Guilty as charged," he answered, raising up his palms.

June giggled. "An admirable quality in a guy."

"I try." He winked at her and took another bite, not at all shy about how much he relished the experience.

You're doing very well, she wanted to say, but didn't.

"Is she the one who taught you to bake?" he asked. "Your mother, I mean."

June moved to wash out her cup so as to have something to do with her hands. She was used to being in perpetual motion, on her feet all day at work, then crashing into her bed at night. It had been a while since she had been in one-on-one company with someone else for this length of time. To tell the truth, she was nervous she'd run out of things to say—not that she'd said much, as it were—and Dr. Singh, highly educated, was way out of her league.

She rinsed the last bubbles of soap from her cup and set it to dry. "Yes. Or…at least at first."

"Ah. Did you then go to culinary or pastry school before you started at the pizza shop?"

She knew the question wasn't judgmental, but the subject of school was a sore spot for her; her features must have registered as much because Ethan looked suddenly worried.

"Did I say something wrong?" he asked.

"No, not at all." She stopped fidgeting and did her best to show him the same courtesy as he had her, by slowing down to really listen. She knew that must not be easy for a man as busy as he must be—the sole doctor in a clinic that served an entire small town full of furry clientele—so she could at least try to do the same.

She raised and then lowered her eyebrows. "I wish I could have gone to pastry school." She heard the dreaminess in her own words. "In Paris or someplace far off and amazing like that."

She didn't know what else to say, so she simply stopped there. She'd wanted so many things, but the money had not been available, and though she'd worked her butt off to ace her high school classes while keeping up with part-time jobs, her grades just hadn't cut it; they were good, but not exceptional. Not enough for scholarships. And her mom's income had been on that fine line that partially determined the future of so many hopeful kids. According to the government, her mom's finances were healthy enough to put a roof over their heads, to feed and clothe the both of them, and they were too high for her to qualify for aid. But, alas, not enough to help her pay for school. She'd tried combining community college with a full-time job for a few months, but the long days and nights of fighting desperately to keep juggling all those plates had gotten to her, and she'd felt like a failure.

Her mom had wanted June's life to be better than her own, and June wanted to make her proud. She'd let them both down.

"So, why didn't you? Go to school like you wanted, I mean?"

"Lots of reasons." The last thing she wanted was to talk openly about education and money with a man like Ethan Singh, who had likely excelled in school and who, she knew from small-town gossip, was blessed with wealthy parents.

"June," he prodded, his eyes as soft and warm as melted caramel. "I'm sorry to have to tell you this, but that is a pathetic excuse for an answer."

"No, it isn't."

"Yes." He laughed softly. "Indeed it is."

She almost asked what difference it made, but she didn't want to know the answer to that question. The only logical solution was to change the subject.

"Why do I have to talk about my education?" Or lack thereof. "I'd be willing to bet that yours was much more interesting."

His eyes bore into hers for several long seconds and she wondered what he was thinking, what picture he was forming of her in his mind.

It's better this way, she thought.

If he didn't know the truth—that despite her heavy and eclectic reading habit, her attempt to give herself the knowledge she hadn't been able to formally obtain, she'd never be as smart as he was.

She would never fit into his world, even if she had reason to.

At one point, she'd had a chance to be as successful, but that had been stolen from her.

She would get it back—oh, yes, she would—but each time her car broke down or she made another rent payment, she gained fresh understanding that it might well take the rest of her life to do so.

Ethan Singh did not want to hear about that. Heck,

she didn't, either. She'd much rather go back to the beginning of the evening when their only subject of discussion was a pair of precious fur babies.

"Really?" he asked, skepticism written all over his face. "You seriously want to hear about my time at a boys' boarding school and then my grueling years as an intern in the biology department of a university that spent the bulk of students' tuition hiring new football coaches?" He moved his face closer to hers. "I think not."

"Oh, come on. You've lived all over the world, while I've been digging my heels in good ol' Peach Leaf, Texas." She injected an exaggeratedly thick drawl into her words. "So, tell this country girl what it's like in them big, fancy cities."

She was teasing, but when he gave a short laugh in response, it wasn't the full, loose sound it had been before. Was it possible that, in making fun of herself, she'd unintentionally offended him?

How could that be? Wouldn't he have to care for her to be affronted by something she'd meant to be self-deprecating?

"So you really want to know about my past, huh?" Ethan asked.

She nodded, a tad too vigorously.

"All right, then, but this is a two-way street, you know."

"Fair enough," June said, biting her lip. There was something mischievous in his tone.

"So let's make a deal, then, shall we?"

Chapter Six

June forgot everything around her except being there with him, listening to that accent that melted over his words like butter and, of course, sinking deep into those decadent eyes.

It shouldn't have surprised her by then that his charm came with a generous side of cunning. The rules he'd proposed were simple on the surface; she was allowed to ask one question at a time, which he would answer truthfully, but then it was his turn. The problem was, every time he started to speak, follow-up questions popped up in her mind like whack-a-moles, and she was forced to wait until it was her chance to ask another.

It was just that his life had been so starkly different from hers. His father had come to the US to live with family while attending veterinary college and met his mother, who'd been working as an intern at the Library of Congress. Despite their cultural differences—he was from India and she was American—it was classic love at first sight. The couple married quickly, and a son, Harry, and daughter, Sani, had followed before they finally had Ethan.

Because the senior Dr. Singh had become renowned in the field of veterinary science, specializing in the prevention of infectious disease, he was frequently asked to speak at conferences and even to work on long-term research projects abroad, always opting to bring along his family.

"Sounds like a dream childhood," June said, her voice sounding wistful even to her own ears.

"It was certainly interesting, I'll give you that." There was a hint of sadness in his tone.

Her eyes narrowed as she studied him. "You didn't like it?" Such a thing was hard for her to imagine. It wasn't until adulthood that June had even set foot outside of Peach Leaf. She'd never had reason to complain, and she knew she was fortunate for the blessings in her life. But one thing had always bothered her: her world had always been very small, and she wasn't sure why, but for some reason that fact made her self-conscious and overly careful, as though she feared saying something that would reveal a deficit in her intelligence.

He pondered the question for a bit before answering. "I suppose I did like it sometimes, but like anything else, it wasn't always perfect."

"What do you mean?" To June, endless opportunity for travel sounded like a dream come true.

"Well, it was lonely, for one thing, moving around so much. Seeing the world was a lovely gift my father gave me and my siblings, but it's not exactly easy to make and keep friends if your address changes frequently."

"That makes sense," she said, not about to remind him that he seemed to have forgotten his own rules and she'd sneakily asked more than one question in a row.

"I suppose there are two sides to every coin." She paused. "I guess I am lucky in that I've always lived in the same place, so I'd have to really make an effort to get away from my friends," she said, chuckling. "Small-town life has its ups and downs. You can't exactly run away from your mistakes, and if you try to forget them, someone else will inevitably be there to fill in the gaps, whether you want them to or not. It's almost like the whole town has a collective memory. Everybody knows everything about everybody else, including all the bad stuff."

He watched her carefully. "You don't seem like someone who would have any bad stuff you'd like to forget, June."

How wrong he was there.

"In fact, you're one of the most thoughtful people I've ever had the pleasure of meeting."

His words came out slow and with intention, as though he'd been planning them for some time, a thought that made her knees a little weak.

She swallowed, careful not to meet his eyes. "You can't possibly know that about me. We've only just met."

"You have a point," he said, "but I don't know many people who would have driven to this office in such a terrible storm to try to save a couple of puppies. Not to mention your reluctance to take food from the Bauers, even though it was compensated fairly."

He was grinning, only teasing her; nevertheless, her cheeks went suddenly warm.

"In fact, I don't need to see much more to believe that the world would be a much better place if there were more like you in it, Miss Leavy."

The next few seconds seemed like an eternity, as the absolute last thing she'd ever expected to happen, happened.

Ethan leaned forward and kissed her—the softest brush of his lips against hers. It was so sudden and so surreal, and over so quickly, she couldn't swear it had even actually occurred. That is, until she opened her eyes and found his face still very near her own, the pleasing scents of sandalwood and lemon blended with something male and uniquely Ethan, tickling her nose. She couldn't keep her eyes from those lips as the corners kicked up in a sultry smile.

Finally, he pulled them away. This was a good thing because June was pretty sure that if he'd left them lingering much longer, achingly close to hers, she would have wrapped her hands around his neck and devoured that mouth, and possibly anything else she could get her hands on.

It had been such an innocent kiss in its softness, yet somehow it had sparked a flame that had rapidly caused her to burn for more.

"You've cheated me, June."

"Hmm?" Apparently he'd rendered her unable to form words, much less full sentences.

"I said you cheated."

"What do you mean?"

"And there you've done it again. Asking questions of me without letting me have a go."

Ah, so he *had* noticed. Evidently she wasn't as sneaky as she'd assumed.

"All right, then. Go ahead." Great, now her voice was embarrassingly creaky.

Way to keep it cool around the hot guy, June.

If she kept this up, he'd regret having kissed her at all, a thought she couldn't bear because now she wanted more, more, more of him.

She glanced up into dark, soulful eyes.

"Here's my question, then. What is it that you'd like to forget?"

"Way to keep it light, Dr. Singh," she joked, but he wasn't having it.

"You know the rules," he said.

She licked her lips, the chocolaty taste of his kiss still lingering there; it took a concentrated effort to refrain from touching them, just to see if the buzz she felt would spark against her fingers.

She focused on the question, organizing her response carefully. Since Clayton had left with everything she had, June had not talked to anyone about how painful that experience was, how badly it had broken her. Her friends pressed from time to time, but she knew her role among them. She was the positive one, the upbeat girl. Letting herself be vulnerable might change how they saw her, and she worried it might scare them away.

She wasn't the one who let her tears show, who wore her heart on her sleeve. She was the one who'd always been the romantic—who'd truly believed that love was out there in some form for everyone, and they just had to find it. She couldn't let anyone see how wrong she'd been, how naive.

"Come on, June. What is it?"

She hesitated. Why did he want to know? And what about that kiss?

Part of her wanted to force the subject, to make him talk about why he'd done it, but the other part was content to just let it be. It would go down in her history as one of the best kisses of her life, possibly *the* best, as it had been completely unexpected, sweet and without any strings attached.

Couldn't she just leave it at that?

No, she could not, and she knew the reason as well as she knew, from an evening of charting them like stars, the pattern of gold flecks in Ethan's brown eyes.

"All right, then. Fair enough." She glanced up at him again, as much to make sure he wasn't something she'd dreamed up as to see if he really did want to know.

"It's a really short story," she started. "There was

a guy. I loved him. I gave him everything I had and planned to spend the rest of my life with him. He broke my heart. The end." She waved a hand, emphasizing the relationship's finality.

Ethan's eyes narrowed and appeared to be full of pain, which was impossible. They were not friends; they certainly weren't lovers. So why did he look so sad? Further, why did he appear as if he knew exactly how she felt?

"I'm very sorry to hear that, June. I truly am. And trust me when I say I've been there myself."

Somehow, she didn't find that the least bit comforting.

"You have?"

"I have. Same song, as they say, different tune."

"Why would anyone...?" She stopped, placing a hand over her mouth. She'd been so caught up in the moment, so enraptured by the feel of those eyes on her, that she'd almost said too much. Her bruised heart needed protection, not more exposure to potential harm, so it was good she hadn't blurted out her confusion over how any woman in her right mind could possibly ruin a chance to be with a guy who, she was quickly learning, was kindhearted, gentle, attentive and thoughtful.

And whose kisses came straight from a fantasy.

"Why would anyone what?" There was a tinge of hopefulness in his expression that she could not have explained for the life of her. So when she heard a low, buzzing sound that startled them both and interrupted their conversation, she almost shouted with relief.

"That's me," she said. "I'd better get it."

Pushing away from the counter where they'd been standing so long her legs were a little wobbly with use, she began following the sound. Finally, she reached her purse, discarded earlier in the reception area, and grabbed it on the last ring.

"Hello?"

"Oh, June, thank goodness." Margaret sounded relieved to hear her voice. "I was worried when you didn't pick up. It's getting late and I hated to call, but I've got some news."

"It's okay. I'm glad to hear from you. It's a long story, but I found some puppies behind the restaurant and ended up bringing them to the veterinary clinic. I've been stuck here with Dr. Singh's son—" she gave Ethan a little wave as he joined her "—for the past few hours. Looks like I might have to spend the night."

"Do you mean Ethan? I haven't seen that boy in years, but last time he was home from college I ran into him at the market. Lord, he's a handsome one."

"That's the one," June blurted. "I mean, not handsome, just that, you know, you've got the right person."

Margaret gave a low whistle. "Sweetie, you are one lucky girl. I'm telling you if I was still young, stuck overnight with a good-looking man like that, I'd make the most of it."

"Margaret!"

"Oh, hush, Junie," she said, but when she spoke

again, her words had softened. "You've been hung up far too long on that damn jerk that broke your heart. It's time you moved on, so if this guy is single…is he single?"

"Yes," she reluctantly admitted, knowing the mess she'd walked into.

"Good, then take my advice—get back on the horse, kid."

June refrained from pointing out the fact that, being in her late twenties, she was hardly a kid, but she knew all the same that her well-meaning boss had her best interest at heart.

"What was it you wanted to tell me?"

"Oh, yes. Hank called a few minutes ago," she said, referring to an elderly restaurant regular that lived in the neighborhood, across the street from Peach Leaf Pizza. "He told me that the power lines are out. Several people nearby have called the electric company and it looks like it could take several days to a week to get things up and running again."

"A week?" June's hand went to her forehead as a series of figures flashed across her mind's eye. A week of no work meant…it meant she likely would not be able to pay her rent the next month without cutting into the miniscule amount of savings she'd managed to scrape together after Clayton had wiped her out.

"That's right." The older woman's voice sagged. "I'm so sorry, honey, but listen, we'll work some-thing out. I did some math before I called you and I'd like to pay you three-quarters of what you'd make if you worked the week. I know it's not the same, and you know I'd give you all of it if I could manage, but without the business coming in…"

"Margaret, stop. It's okay. That's more than generous, but I'll manage."

"Nonsense, June. I…"

"I mean it. I can't take money from you without earning it. I'll be fine."

"I don't like this at all, dear."

"Well, neither do I, but I'm not changing my mind."

Her boss made a dissatisfied noise. "You're allowed to change your mind, hon. Anytime. You know I consider you like my own daughter and it won't do you any good to be proud among family, you hear?"

"I know," June said, emotion welling up in her throat at her boss's kindness. She desperately needed the money, so much so that with an ounce more prodding, any pride she had left would fly out the window. But she wasn't about to take payment without working for it. "But this is final."

"Well, I know stubborn when I see it, and you're a gal after my own heart, but don't you forget that I'm here if you need me. And I want to hear more about those puppies when we're back at the shop. And more about you-know-who, of course."

"All right, that's it. I'm hanging up."

"Details. I mean it."

"Talk to you later, boss," June said, forcing back laughter. "Call me when I can come back to work."

"Hint taken."

"And, Margaret?"

"Yeah, sweetie?"

"Are you going to be okay? With all of this going on, I mean."

"I'll manage. I've got Vince's little Social Security check every month for when the pizza business is slow. Besides, I'm as hardheaded as you are and I've been around a hell of a lot longer, so don't you worry about me."

When she hung up and tucked the phone back into her purse, Ethan's hypnotic gaze was on her again. Her cheeks warmed, remembering that kiss.

"Everything okay?" he asked.

"It has to be." She sighed as the long hours caught up with her, knotting something awful in her shoulders. She'd been going full-force all evening and into the night—first with the puppy emergency, then braving the crazy weather to get something to eat, and finally enduring the shock of that world-rocking kiss. Intense longing for a hot shower and her lonely, albeit warm, bed was almost enough to send her into tears.

"It doesn't sound okay," he said, coming to her side. "And you look tense enough to crack in two." He stood behind her and placed his hands on her shoulders, the touch of them shooting electric warmth all the way down her arms. "Mind if I help?"

Did she mind? Did the man even have to ask?

"No, um, that sounds nice actually."

When he began to rub her muscles, she had to

bite her tongue to avoid moaning. Evidently, his skill wasn't limited to healing members of the animal kingdom; he had expert hands when it came to humans, too. She closed her eyes as the knots loosened and her bones turned to jelly.

Maybe Margaret had a point. Maybe she should take advantage of her limited time with this sexy, tender, animal-loving wonder-god she'd accidentally stumbled upon. With his hands on her like that, did it really matter that he looked like he'd walked off the set of a magazine shoot, whereas her hair had probably frizzed into a puffball and she hadn't set foot in a gym since college?

She didn't like the answer. *Yes*, it did matter.

In case she'd forgotten, the last guy who had wooed her with a fit physique and slick words had broken her heart. She didn't want to be that girl—no, she refused to be that girl—who slipped right into one bad relationship after another.

Ethan Singh might be handsome, and he might even be kind and all the other things she'd seen that night. None of that mattered. She simply wasn't ready to start over, to risk putting all of herself into someone new, only to have it blow up in her face.

Even if he proved to be a good guy, even if he was interested in her, she needed things only she could give herself: time, self-respect and space in which to put her life back together.

Grabbing his hands, she removed them from her shoulders and let them drop as she pulled away and turned to face him.

"Thank you. That was…wonderful, but I—" she hated that hurt expression on his face she'd caused "—I just need a minute. Excuse me."

With that, she left him standing there as she walked quickly away from emotions that threatened to undo her.

Ethan followed, still confused about what had happened.

He hadn't meant to be so forward. Hell, in the space of half an hour he'd not only kissed the woman, but had pulled the most cliché move ever known to man by offering to rub her shoulders.

Dammit, could he be any more of an ass?

What had come over him?

All he knew for sure was that when he saw June hang up from what had obviously been a difficult conversation with exhaustion practically crumpling her body, he'd have done anything he could to make her feel better.

He stopped abruptly in the hallway.

His instinct had been to go after her, to fix the awkwardness that hung in the room after she'd gone, but she had asked for a moment alone. And as his head began to clear, sifting through that spontaneous, intoxicating kiss from earlier, and the way his hands felt digging into her muscles, he realized he needed to give her what she'd asked for.

He needed to back off.

But that kiss.

It made him want to do anything but.

That kiss had wrecked everything he'd been so certain about. Up until it happened, his lips moving toward hers, propelled by a will of their own, he'd been so sure he didn't want a woman in his life. Not when he'd come to Peach Leaf for the sole purpose of getting over the last one.

But with June…it was like he wasn't even in control. Every minute he spent with her made him want another to follow.

Which was ridiculous, considering she'd told him her own heart had been broken recently. What kind of guy forced himself on a woman who clearly didn't want that kind of attention?

What he needed was some air, and for the storm to be over so that he could get her out of his space and off his mind.

When he stepped out the front door, the wind was still blowing with greater than normal force, but it had calmed down significantly since he and June had returned from the bakery. It was a pleasant break from the heat that had developed back in the office between the two of them.

He hadn't expected to feel that way again for a very long time, if not ever. It disturbed him, how much this sensation, this primal drive to be with a woman, resembled those first few days with Jessica.

The two women didn't abide comparison. Jessica had been cool, cosmopolitan, gorgeous in a cold, almost untouchable way, like a model from the cover of a magazine, and fiercely competitive—things he'd admired at first, until he'd discovered the heartlessness she was capable of.

June, on the other hand, was girl-next-door-beautiful, soft and curvy in all the right places and sweet. Sweetness was an underrated quality in a woman, he now believed.

A gust of wind swiped at his face and he had to go back inside. The storm had subsided, but it clearly was not over yet.

Being in the cold made him briefly miss Colorado, and he wondered what June would think of the place he called home, the place he'd lived the longest now and where he'd begun to put down roots. She'd said she had always wanted to travel, and before he stopped the train of thought, it crossed his mind that he might like to take her there one day. Her eyes had sparkled when she talked about wanting to see the world, and that would be a good place to start.

He imagined her face lighting up when she saw the Rocky Mountains for the first time—how drastically more majestic they were in real life than in photos. He would take her to Estes Park to visit the haunted Stanley Hotel, and to Aspen to ski, and the list went on and on, nearly bursting out of him.

Unlike Jessica, who had been near-impossible to impress no matter how hard he tried, somehow he knew June would relish every minute of it, and he longed to feel that way again about a place he loved so much.

As it were, returning would be painful. Those ugly memories would be waiting for him at the university, and even in his home, and he didn't want to face them alone.

"Ethan?"

June had stuck her head out the door to call after him. He turned to follow her inside.

She looked at him like he'd lost his mind.

"What the hell, Ethan?" She gasped, hugging herself against the cold. "You're not wearing a coat." She slammed the door behind them. "What were you thinking?"

He didn't answer the question, ignoring the concern etched in the crease of her forehead. "I'm fine. Just got a little too warm."

The response in her features told him she knew how he felt, but it passed quickly and she forged ahead.

"Ethan, something's wrong with one of the puppies."

His heart lurched into his throat. He'd promised her he wouldn't let harm come to them.

Without speaking further, she grabbed his hand and led him to the back room. When he saw both puppies still inside their little pen, each of them wiggly and energetic, his breathing slowed a little.

"I think one of them threw up," June said, her voice catching in a way that made him ache. "But I can't tell which one."

He crouched down onto his knees and lifted one puppy at a time, palpating their stomachs and checking the rest of their warm, squirmy bodies. When he realized that the pups were completely okay, he almost laughed, but caught himself.

June would be hurt if she thought he was making fun of her for worrying. It wasn't overreacting for her, he reminded himself, because she wasn't used to looking for symptoms like he was. She just followed her heart, an admirable quality.

He put the puppy he'd been holding back into the pen and spent the next several minutes cleaning up and replacing their soiled towels with fresh, warm ones. Then he set his hands on June's shoulders, urging her to meet his eyes. When she did, he noticed glistening at the corners.

"Hey," he said, giving her shoulders a little squeeze. "Hey, it's okay. They're fine." As soon as he'd said the words, a tear slipped down her cheek and, without thinking at all, he reached up to wipe it away before pulling her shaking body against his chest.

He let her cry for a few moments, hating it but wanting to give her a chance to release some of her pent-up emotions. When she pulled back, she wiped her eyes and leaned back on her heels, looking embarrassed.

"I'm so sorry, Ethan. I have no idea what's gotten into me."

He shook his head. "Please do not apologize to me when you didn't do anything wrong."

She grinned, her eyes shimmering with dampness, greener than any emerald he'd ever seen.

"You must think I'm a complete idiot," she said with an unsteady voice.

"Absolutely not. Look, it's been a crazy, long day, and I think we both might be on the verge of simultaneous nervous breakdowns, but don't you ever say you're sorry for being concerned about something you care for."

As she finished wiping her face once more, her eyebrows rose in surprise. "Thank you for that. That's incredibly sweet of you." She was quiet for a moment, and he wondered what was running through her mind.

"I just saw the…" She pointed at the place where one of the little ones had regurgitated its supper, clearly a tad bit grossed out. "And I just lost it. I don't really know why." She tossed up her hands.

"It's okay, June. I'll run some tests again in the morning, but from what I can tell now, they are still holding up really well. It would probably be safest to put them in a crate for the night, but I'd rather not, and this pen is fine."

She nodded and he tucked a strand of auburn hair behind her ear, taking his time in letting his finger slide along her soft cheek before pulling it back. "My educated guess is that they just ate a little too much. Sadly, if they've been without food for a while, it might take some time for their stomachs to get back to normal so they can eat the portions they'll need to gain weight."

June looked as relieved as he felt.

"In the meantime, they'll just need for us to be patient."

He met her eyes as a surge of emotion threatened to overwhelm him.

"After all, this will take some time. What they've suffered simply cannot be healed in one night."

Chapter Seven

The rich scent of coffee brewing pulled June from the short nap she'd finally managed to sink into. Her eyes slowly opening, she glanced around at the unfamiliar room, realizing, as the fuzzy edges of sleep slipped away, that she was in Dr. Singh's office.

The black leather couch squeaked as she pushed up to lean against its back. Chilly, she decided not to give up the blanket that Ethan must have draped over her as she'd snoozed. As the smell of delicious caffeine beckoned her further into wakefulness, her mind drifted back to the night before—and that kiss—the oh-so-delicious kiss that had seared her lips and sent sparks zipping through her veins.

That kiss—spontaneous, incredible, though highly unexpected—made her feel like a woman again.

It was the first time she'd been that close to anyone since Clayton and, she thought with more sadness than she wanted to admit, probably the last.

After she'd had that slightly humiliating breakdown over one of the puppies' mild tummy ache, which she'd replayed over and over until deciding to chalk up her emotions to lack of sleep or an adequate meal, Ethan had dried her tears and sent her to bed, promising to take care of the dogs while she got some rest.

There hadn't been the slightest hint of judgment in his tone or expression, but what had been there instead scared her a little.

She'd looked up into those intense, mahogany eyes of his and found only concern.

He'd been sweet, nurturing even, and had shown her a softness she wasn't used to in men, but she got the feeling that wasn't really Ethan's usual style.

Perhaps the strange magic of a Texas night covered in snow had affected them both. She'd resisted him at first, had not wanted to like him so easily, so much; she hadn't wanted to enjoy his company, but her attempts to not care had been futile, and now her heart had jumped into the game, forcing her to admit that she didn't want their time together to be over.

That sentiment had even kept her from sleep for a while, as she'd tried desperately not to let her eyelids slam shut. But they'd been so heavy from exhaustion, Ethan's voice so soothing as he'd sat in his father's desk chair telling her stories of his Alaskan research trips.

Like a desperate Cinderella, she hadn't wanted it to end.

But in real life, pumpkins weren't carriages and tattered shoes weren't glass slippers...and Prince Charming did not exist.

She needed the reminder; Ethan could have fooled her last night.

But finally she'd succumbed to rest, and it was over. For better or worse, her normal life would resume.

She stretched her arms behind her head before taking a moment to rub a charley horse out of her neck. Wrapping the blanket around her shoulders, she made a quick trip to the bathroom, careful to avoid the mirror, adamantly not wanting to know what she'd be met with following a full shift and a night without a shower. She splashed water on her face and headed to the front of the clinic to check the weather.

"Morning, June," Ethan said, turning as she entered the room. Dark stubble covered his jaw and chin and, instead of looking like hell, which would be perfectly appropriate after being awake for over twenty-four hours, he was even sexier than he'd been the day and night before. And when he graced her with a sleepy smile, she almost threw herself across the room and kissed him. It took effort to remind herself that she'd only stumbled into this situation through a weird turn of events—it didn't truly belong to her. He had not chosen to spend the night with her; it was forced, and he'd been kind to let her stay, as she knew he would have anyone else.

"How'd you sleep?" he asked. "Considering, I mean. I know my father's office couch isn't exactly like a king-size bed in a five-star hotel."

Beds, hotels, unkempt but perfect Ethan with a shadowy beard following a night of...

June shook her head. That wasn't real. The reality was that she'd stumbled upon him due to a freak snow-storm. Reality was, that if the snow had melted enough and the roads were moderately safe, she'd be back at her car and home to her empty apartment in a matter of a couple of hours at best.

The fantasy would be over.

As it should be.

Clayton, with his smooth talking, his well-toned body and those promises he'd made with a straight face while looking right into her eyes—it had all been a fantasy, too. And June needed no reminders of how that turned out.

She may not be highly educated like Ethan, but she was smart enough not to make the same mistake twice. A woman who couldn't trust herself, who couldn't protect her own heart from destruction, was better off alone.

Ethan was staring at her, waiting for her to respond.

"The couch was fine." She smiled. "I can't thank you enough for letting me get a little rest."

He waved a hand, brushing her gratitude aside. "It's nothing. Not my first twenty-four-hour shift, and probably not my last. You get used to it after a few times."

"All the same."

"Don't mention it." He beckoned her to join him at the window. "Looks like we're in luck. I watched the weather on the news a little bit ago and it seems the snow is starting to melt. Also, half the town lost power last night and some won't get it back for a few days. We were pretty fortunate here, with the heater running and all. Would have been a cold night otherwise."

Not if they'd snuggled together, she mused.

He took a sip from the mug in his hand. "The pups were doing great when I checked in and fed them a few minutes ago, and in an hour or so, we'll be able to head out and check on your car."

The news should have been welcome, but for some reason her heart sank. She plastered a smile on her face and crossed her fingers it was convincing. She didn't think she could bear any more of Ethan's insightful kindness or another second of those dark eyes boring into hers, seemingly capable of unearthing her most private thoughts.

"That's excellent news. I can't wait to get back to my place and take a shower."

"I'm with you there. I probably smell like my furry clients," he said, laughing as he turned back to the window.

Outside was a veritable winter wonderland. Snow had blanketed the parking lot, glittering like sugar in the sunlight.

"It's beautiful, isn't it?" he asked.

"Very."

"Have you ever seen snow like this before, June?"

She nibbled her lower lip, stopping, suddenly self-conscious when his eyes followed. "I've seen snow, yes, but never like this. It usually melts so quickly that it doesn't cover anything."

"So you've never really gotten to enjoy it, then? Never built a snowman? Gone sledding?"

She shook her head. His eyes lit up when he'd spoken, and he made all those activities sound so fun.

He tsked. "Well, that is a shame. We get plenty of snow in Colorado, and of course we did during my time in Alaska, too. Most people don't like the weather in the more remote areas, but for some reason, I took to it during my research there."

"Do you miss it?" she asked, instantly regretting the question when a muscle in his jaw jumped, betraying some reaction he probably hadn't meant to reveal.

"I miss the place, not the memories." He was far away somewhere for a moment, but then quickly returned to ask if she'd like a cup of coffee.

"How selfish of me, standing here drinking mine without checking if you want one of your own." He turned, surprising her by tucking a finger under her chin, lifting it to look into her face. "It's been a long time since there's been anyone to ask. Too long."

She licked her lips and his eyes snapped to her tongue. In a matter of seconds, he moved as if to kiss her again and alarms went off inside her, louder even than the one at Bauer's had been.

June pulled her face away from his with effort, disappointment spreading through her body like a virus. If she thought she could let him kiss her again without strings, without involuntarily building an attachment that she knew would be one-sided, she would have allowed it. But that was the thing about mistakes; if you were smart, you learned from them. She supposed she could thank Clayton for that— she knew herself better now, knew she couldn't go in halfway.

It was all or nothing from then on, and nothing was by far the safer route.

Safer, maybe, but a hell of a lot less fun, a little voice chided in her mind.

Unmistakable hurt clouded his features the second she made that decision, but he quickly, expertly erased it.

"I'd love a cup," she said, the air thick with static between them. "It smells amazing."

He nodded, giving her a soft grin. "Stay here. I'll be right back with it."

Ethan was halfway to the break room before he realized he hadn't even asked how June took her coffee. The oversight was just another testament to the trouble he'd gotten into.

She was intoxicating, mesmerizing like a siren, and like a fool, he couldn't stay away from her song.

And if he didn't watch out, he'd be back in the same place, drowning once again as he had with Jessica.

Even though everything in him wanted to do the exact opposite, he would have to be more careful.

He pressed his fingers into his tired eyes, then pulled a clean mug from the dish dryer, a reminder of the night before. Those delicious brownies and those even more delicious lips. The taste of her was almost gone, and he'd stupidly attempted to get it back, only to have June turn away from him.

He should be grateful—at least one of them was thinking clearly.

Grabbing the carafe, he poured her a cup of the expensive, delicious brew his father indulged in and shared with everyone at the office, adding a splash of half-and-half from the fridge and just a little sugar, feeling like an idiot for wanting to get it right. He stopped himself from adding a sprinkle of cinnamon. It would just have to do.

And with any luck, he'd have her back in her car and out of his life soon enough.

He gave the coffee a quick stir and headed back down the hallway, taking a deep breath to steady his nerves.

It had just been a long night; that was all. June was a beautiful, sweet girl, and he enjoyed her company, but that didn't mean it had to turn into anything more.

If only someone could tell his stupid-ass heart the same.

June was still standing at the window when he entered the reception area, the blanket he'd draped over her the night before wrapped around her shoulders.

Her red hair draped across the soft white material, and she looked like an angel.

Which gave him an idea. Snow angels, snow-men—June had never experienced a real chance to enjoy this kind of weather.

"Here you are." She turned and reached for the coffee, closing her eyes as she drew in her first long sip.

"Oh, my God, this is *sooo* good. How'd you know how to fix it just the way I like it?"

"Wild guess. Speaking of wild, finish that coffee and put your coat on."

She raised an eyebrow.

"I'm going to give the pups their breakfast and I'll meet you out front in ten minutes." She opened her mouth to ask questions or to argue, but he held up a finger, stopping her.

"Out front. Ten minutes. See you there."

Ethan's pulse raced and his heart felt lighter than it had in months. He didn't want to believe that it was June making his body behave that way, so he gave credit to the snow. The problem with that theory was that he'd seen a hundred snowfalls, most of them even more magical than this one. Paris, London, New York—the small-town Texas weather couldn't even begin to compare. He loved the idea of sharing this one with someone he barely knew but who'd reminded him that life could go on after heartbreak. He knew there was no future with June for lots of reasons, the most basic being that the two lived in different cities and probably had different goals, but right then, none of that mattered. The only thing he wanted that morning was to show her a great time in his favorite weather.

After checking and feeding the puppies, he threw on his coat and dashed outdoors, regretting that his father didn't keep a sled in his office. The temperature was perfect when he opened the back door and stepped into several feet of powder that reminded him of fresh whipped cream. There was not a hint of the previous day's harsh wind, just cold, crisp air on an occasional whispery breeze. The snow stung his hands as it seeped through his mittens, but Ethan didn't care.

He worked as if in a trance, determined to make June share one of those beautiful smiles with him again, the kind she'd tried to hide after he'd kissed her berry lips. What harm could there be in making a woman smile? It didn't have to mean forever, and it wouldn't. But didn't he deserve a moment's happiness after the way the past year had gone? Didn't June?

Just as he'd thought her name, the woman stepped outside, glancing around before she caught his eye.

"Ethan, what are you up to out here?"

He watched her as she paced nearer, enjoying the way the sun's bright rays danced over her hair, causing it to glisten like a crown adorned with rubies. Her eyes were impossibly green in the dreamlike morning light.

"What's that behind you?" she asked, veering right so she could get a glimpse of what he'd hidden.

He couldn't stop himself smiling like a little boy as he stepped out of her way, waving his arms like a magician's assistant.

June's hands flew to cover her mouth, and those emerald eyes lit up, glistening in the sunshine that reflected off the snow.

Then he heard the best music ever as she threw her head back and laughed, before her feet did a little dance. She squealed. "Is that a snowman?"

"Just for you," he answered, taking far too much delight in her reaction to his simple gift, the only thing he could think to give her for making him feel like the frost inside him had begun to melt a little.

"He's perfect." She held out her arms and spun in a little circle before running toward him. Ethan opened his arms just in time to catch her, but lost his footing as she threw her body into his, plunging them both into the snow.

His laughter mingled with hers, and he didn't at all mind the wetness starting to soak into his back. All he knew was her weight on top of him as she raised up on her elbows and stared down into his face, and the curtain of auburn that came down to tickle his cheeks as she bent to kiss him, her mouth warm and eager, pressing hard into his. When their lips parted, he pulled her close into his chest and held her there for a long moment, unwilling to let her go just yet.

Finally, only when he began to freeze and thus worried that June would be vulnerable to the same, he twisted his body to the side and rose, holding out his hands to help her up.

Her smile disappeared as they stood face-to-face, and all he heard was their matched heavy breathing.

"Ethan, I…"

He covered her lips with a finger. "Shh, don't say anything. Just…just enjoy this with me, will you?"

She was right, of course.

"I get where you're coming from," he said, the words pouring out of him before he could measure them to make sure they conveyed what he wanted them to, not necessarily exactly what he was thinking. "But that's just it, June. I don't want to talk about it, at all. I don't want to try to figure out what's going on between us."

Her eyes had narrowed and there was a crease between her brows.

"Wouldn't you rather just let this be what it is?"

She looked down at her hands.

"That's my point, though, Ethan. We just met. I don't know what this is, and I don't think you do, either."

He rubbed a soggy mitten over his forehead. "I know, I know. But why do we need to understand it at all? Why can't we just enjoy it while it lasts?"

Her expression changed, and as she took time to think of what to say next, he thought he saw something new register.

"I'm not sure where this is going, but I think I see what you're saying."

He waited.

"And, well, the more I think about it, and even though it sounds crazy, you might be on to something."

He took her hand.

"All I mean is that, we both know this thing won't last—it can't, anyway—because I'm leaving in a few weeks and you've got a life here."

She cringed at that last part, but he didn't want to stop and examine that. He needed to convince her to let him spend more time with her, before it was all over. He wanted to soak up her sweetness, to let it seep under his skin so he could take it with him. It didn't need to mean anything more. Maybe not everything happened for a reason. Weren't some things in life just pleasant coincidences?

"We seem to get along, you and I, and if I'm not mistaken, we both had some fun last night, despite the evening not going the way either of us had planned. So while I'm here, and while you've got those puppies for the next few days and they'll need some medical care, let's just enjoy each other."

She bit her lip again, that sexy little gesture that let him know she was considering it.

"But, Ethan, is that wise? You've had your heart broken recently, as have I, and we both need time to mend. Does it really make sense to start something up right now?"

"That's just it, though. We wouldn't be starting anything. Look at it like this. We'll just be having a little fun before we both go our separate ways and get back out there. You're right that we're both unprepared to get into relationships again any time soon, so let's…use each other as practice…for lack of a better term."

He grabbed her hand and pulled her into his

chest, pushing past her resistance. "Let's enjoy each other's company, make each other better and have a few laughs, before we go back to real life. What do you say?"

A look of sadness whispered across her features, but was gone instantly. She smiled up at him, making his heart flutter a little.

"All right, Dr. Singh," she said. "You have yourself a deal."

He placed his hands on each side of her face and brushed her chilly nose with his lips.

He didn't care what kind of fire he might have been walking into, as long as he got to see her again after that morning.

"Deal?" she asked.

"Deal."

With that, he picked her up and swirled her around and around until they were both dizzy, from the spinning, yes, but also probably from something else. When he set her down, June headed over to examine the snowman, giggling with joy over the jerky treat nose, kibble mouth and doggy biscuit eyes he'd scrambled together. As she studied his creation, Ethan knelt to form a snowball, gasping in surprise when one of June's own smacked him right in the middle of his back.

"I don't know why, but it surprises me a little that you like country music so much."

Ethan grinned, the corner of his eye crinkling

behind aviator glasses. Of course they made him look even more stunning.

"Is it because I'm half-Indian?"

She considered his question; she hadn't really thought much about his ethnicity, other than the fact that his father's heritage had obviously given him the most gorgeous, terra-cotta skin she'd ever seen in her life.

"Nope, not that," she said, drawing out her answer to make him sweat a little. He tried to pretend he didn't care, but the longer she spent with him, the more she could see how much he wanted her to like him.

Even though they'd discussed their intention earlier that morning, that whatever their odd little relationship was would not turn into anything serious, it was still a refreshing quality in a man, to be able to see that he wanted to please her.

"I've got it," she said. "I think it's just that country music doesn't mesh with your worldliness or something." She poked his side, making him laugh. "Seems like you'd be more of a classical music type." She eyed him up and down. "I can totally see you fake-conducting an orchestra as you drive to work or something."

"Ah, but that's why I like it so much." He turned and flashed a smile full of perfect white teeth against incredible copper skin. "Reminds me of the simple things in life."

They were in Ethan's large black SUV, headed in the direction where June had left her car. The weather couldn't have been more different than it was the day before; not a cloud in the blue sky, thick mounds of snow gradually beginning to melt as the sun reclaimed her throne. It would take time for the powder to turn back into liquid, and then Peach Leaf would face the possible threat of flooding.

They weren't out of the dark just yet, but things were beginning to look up. She said a silent little prayer that they would find her car in decent shape, but it wouldn't do much good to hold her breath. The old thing wasn't in great health to begin with; it would be a small miracle of it survived the beating it had taken the night before.

Loosening her seat belt a little, June turned toward the backseat to check on the pups. Ethan had nestled blankets into one of the crates from the clinic, then wrapped the little guys inside so they'd be safe on the way to her apartment, where June was thrilled she'd get to watch them until Margaret called her back into work. Ethan had said they'd figure things out from there, but she'd made him promise he wouldn't let anyone adopt them until they were one hundred percent healthy. She wouldn't say it out loud, but the idea of never seeing them again made her stomach churn.

Gently, she poked a finger between the bars, squealing when the male pup bounced over and began to nibble on it. She took that as a sign that he was having a good morning.

That made two of them, she thought, reminiscing about the impromptu snowball fight with Ethan and the adorable snowman he'd built for her, completely out of the blue. She tried not to overanalyze how good it made her feel to be with him, to play, and to have the freedom to kiss him with such abandon without expecting anything serious in return.

She knew it wouldn't last, but maybe he had a point. It was a hell of a lot of fun to be spoiled, to be enjoyed, and even though she hadn't agreed with him at first, she was beginning to come around to his way of thinking. Perhaps their plan would work out fine, after all. No strings, no attachments and, most important, no promises.

Just pure, unbridled fun between two people on the mend. Surely, everything would be fine.

"Okay, that's starting to hurt, mister," she said, taking back her nibbled finger.

"I wouldn't let him do that too much, June. He might start to think it's okay."

"I won't," she promised. "I just like seeing him up and full of energy."

"Well, you'll get plenty of it over the next few days." He tossed a glance her way before refocusing his attention on the road. "Are you sure you want to do this?"

"What? Take care of a few puppies? How hard can it be?"

He coughed out a laugh. "I'd love to hear you say that again in a few days."

She started to retort, but paused as Ethan slowed the SUV.

"Is that it?" he asked. "Your car."

She turned back to the front and caught sight of the old hunk of metal out the front window, barely recognizable underneath a mountain of snow. "Yep, has to be."

He turned off the road, getting as close to her vehicle as he could manage without pummeling into a bank of powder. When the SUV stopped, June reached into her purse and pulled out her keys. Without lifting her head, she grabbed at the door handle only to find Ethan had gotten out, come around and opened the door for her. Such a gentleman. She accepted his offered hand and stepped out of the warm vehicle, which he'd left running to keep the puppies from getting too cold.

By the time they reached her car, moisture had soaked the bottoms of her jeans, but that problem took a backseat to a bigger one pretty darn fast.

She shouldn't have been surprised, but that didn't make it any less annoying when she stuck the key in the ignition, only to find the engine wouldn't turn over after a dozen tries.

Someone in control, someone who had her life together, would have bought a new battery before the weather turned so cold and sapped the last dredges of energy from the nearly four-year-old one. But June had not been so responsible. Between her full work schedule and not wanting to part with the hundred or so bucks a new one would cost, this was what she deserved.

She looked up to find Ethan staring at her, his long body blocking out the sun as he leaned over her driver's side door.

"Thought you were getting rid of me that fast, did you?"

She tossed her shoulders back and tilted her head, debating whether to punch him in those toned abs or straight on the nose.

"What the hell do you look so happy about?" Her question was genuine; shouldn't he be getting tired of her just about now? Shouldn't he be dying to get back to his parents' house so he could get cleaned up and take a much-needed nap?

"Nothing," he said, but the grin didn't fade. He offered her his hand. "Come on, then. No use beating a dead horse."

"I've never liked that expression," she said.

"Neither have I actually, but it suits the situation. There's no point in trying that key again."

She did just that as he rolled his eyes, then shook his outstretched hand.

They tried jumping her car a few times, but it wouldn't take the juice. The old thing had simply given up.

"Come on. Let's get you home. Once you've had something to eat and we get the puppies settled in, we'll call a tow truck."

She hated to admit it, but she liked the sound of that *we*. Exhausted, hungry and craving a near-boiling bath, it was nice to have someone with her, someone who still managed to drum up energy after the long night, someone who put her needs first. It was a good quality in a man…a good quality in a boyfriend…or even a husband.

She almost gasped when the word entered her

mind, but the more she tried to shoo it away, the stickier it got.

Once they got back at her apartment, Ethan was relentlessly sweet, making oatmeal for them both while June took the puppies out of their crate and onto her small back patio. She cheered them on and gave them treats when they went to the bathroom on the least snowy patch of grass she could find, which seemed to come naturally to them since they'd likely been living outside. Her heart ached at the thought of their mother, and she promised then and there that she would take good care of them until she found them good homes. She knew it might not be possible, but she hoped she could find a way to keep them together.

When she went back inside, Ethan had made himself at home in her kitchen, and she couldn't help but think he looked good there. They ate together and he sent her off to take a hot shower while he fed the puppies some of the kibble he'd packed up for her from the clinic's supply closet and texted his vet techs to find out if either of them would be able to drive in and take over that morning while he went home to take a nap.

By the time she finished relishing the steamy water as it thawed her cold skin and wrapped herself in comfy sweats and socks, Ethan had fallen asleep on the couch. The puppies had done the same, snuggled together, safe inside their shared crate with full bellies.

She stood in the doorway for a long time, just enjoying the view. The stunning, kindhearted doctor passed out on her couch after a night spent caring for the two most adorable little fur balls she'd ever seen, all nestled into her small living room.

If she'd been certain it wouldn't wake them all, she would have dug out her phone and taken a photo.

It was an image she didn't want to forget as long as she lived. Instead, she went with her very next impulse. For once, she allowed herself to do exactly what she wanted, without thinking.

Ethan sighed as she lay down next to him on the couch, eyes remaining closed as he drew her against his chest and tucked an arm around her. She looked up just in time to see him smile before drifting back to sleep.

Chapter Eight

"Over here!" June called when she caught sight of her mother's strawberry-blond head passing through the front door a few days later. The coffeehouse, which had the unique luxury of being the only such place in their small town, did not belong to any competitive chains and was especially crowded.

"My goodness," Abigail Leavy said, joining June at the long counter by the window. She set her purse on the bar stool June had saved for her. "Looks like folks got a little case of cabin fever in the storm."

"I think you're absolutely right," June said, standing to give her mother a big hug. "Hi, Mom. I'm glad to see you're okay."

"Hi, sweetheart," the older woman answered, squeezing June in response.

Her mom was tiny and resembled a pixie with her short, stylish haircut, sparkling blue eyes and cheeks that always looked as though they'd been recently pinched. At sixty-five, Abigail looked a decade younger. Despite having worked since she was fourteen, June's mother had not slowed down after retiring from the grocery store, where, over the years, she'd climbed from bagger to manager; the woman made a point of spending time regularly with her numerous friends, walked several miles per day and took pride in her commitment to a healthy diet. June always teased her that she put her daughter to shame.

"Let me go get a cup of joe and I'll be right back." She pulled out her wallet and pointed a finger at June. "Don't you run off now, girl. I haven't seen you in ages and it's getting harder and harder to track you down."

June waved her away and took a sip of her peppermint hot chocolate, a foray from her usual Americano. For some reason, since that first cup of coffee Ethan Singh had made for her a few days ago, nothing she prepared for herself or purchased tasted anywhere near as good.

She smiled, whipped cream tickling her nose as she let her mind circle around and around that man.

Though, at the time, she'd thought that night with him would go down as the longest of her life, it had been nothing compared to the past few days.

He'd gone back to his regular shifts at the clinic, of course, and she'd been happily soaking up her lazy days at home as the power company worked to restore electricity at the pizza place. Only the challenge of training the puppies occupied her time, and she was loving every minute of it.

Despite being busy with the clinic, Ethan called every day on his lunch break to check on her and see how the little ones were doing, and they'd met for coffee once.

But *dammit*, she missed him.

And nothing she tried could make that fact go away. He'd gotten under her skin.

"All right, sweetheart," her mother said, setting a ginormous cup of black coffee on the counter. "Let me just get some of this stuff into my veins and I'm all yours."

"It's certainly no mystery where I got my coffee addiction," June said, giggling.

Abigail took a long sip before putting down her extra large cup. "Come on, girl. You ain't foolin' nobody." She gave June's frothy beverage the stink eye. "That is not coffee."

June looked down into her delicious but admittedly oversweet drink. "You've got me there."

"What's up with that, anyway? Why aren't you having your normal Americano with cream and sugar? What's on your mind?"

"Nothing's on my mind, Mom. I just wanted to try something different."

Her mother glared at her, without a word, and that's all it took for June to break.

"Okay," she said. "Maybe there is a little something on my mind."

Abigail looked a little too satisfied.

"But that's not why I'm here. I really just wanted to spend a little time with you while I've got a few precious days off work."

"That's more like it. I knew something was up. You're usually so chipper, and today you look like you've got a bug in your biscuit."

June snorted at her mom's goofy expression, one of many in the woman's vast collection of odd colloquialisms. Even after hearing it all her life, that particular one still made her laugh.

"It's just the puppies, Mom. Nothing more."

Her mom smiled. "How are those little squirts? Have you given them names yet?"

"No, not yet. I want to, but Ethan—Dr. Singh—keeps discouraging it for some reason."

Abigail was silent for far too long before speaking again. "Ah, so that's what this is about."

June kept her features as neutral as possible, determined not to give in. If her mom caught a glimpse inside her head and managed to figure out how stupidly smitten June was with the doctor, she would never let it go.

She cleared her throat and glanced out the window with as much nonchalance as she could muster.

"That's what *what* is about?" she asked awkwardly. "I have no idea what you mean."

The statement rang false even to her own ears.

Her mom set aside the massive coffee and June knew she was in for it.

"It's this Dr. Singh, isn't it? You've got a thing for him?"

"Mother, I do not…"

"Don't give me that." She held up a palm. "I know my daughter, and I know when she's been bitten by the love monster."

June chuckled in spite of her good intentions. "Mom, you're so silly sometimes."

"Don't you try to change the subject on me. You've got a thing for this guy and I want details."

"Mom," she said, injecting seriousness into her tone as she tried to conjure up sad images to keep from grinning like an idiot at the mere mention of the man's name. "It's nothing. Really, it's not."

"Like you'd tell me if it was." Her words were teasing on the surface, but underneath June detected the hint of hurt feelings.

"Mom." June rested a hand over her mother's and squeezed. "Why would you say that?"

Abigail shrugged. "I didn't mean it, sweetheart. Really, I didn't." Her eyes settled on something out the window, but June could see they weren't focused and her mother's mind was far away.

"I guess what I mean is that, well, I don't see you much anymore."

"I'm sorry, Mom." June cringed. "I had no idea you were feeling neglected lately."

"It's okay. I know you can't help it and I did not mean to guilt-trip you."

"No, really, I'll make more of an effort to see you." June's shoulders sagged. "It's just that I work so much, and when I'm not at the pizza parlor, I'm resting up to *be* at the pizza parlor."

Her mother nodded. "I understand what you mean, June Bug. It was like that for me after your father left."

Her mom didn't talk about her father much, and June had never met the man; all she knew were bits and pieces she'd picked up over the years. He and her mother had never had a real relationship and June had essentially been, as her mom put it, "a happy accident," but she'd always felt loved. Not once had her mom ever made her feel unwanted.

"I've probably never said this before, Mom, but I know how hard you worked to give me the things I needed growing up, and I've always been thankful for it."

Abigail's eyes filled with moisture. "Oh, honey, I did it because I loved you, and I wanted you to have the best I could give you, but all the same, that means a great deal to me."

June's mom wrapped her in a big hug, then pulled her torso back to study her daughter, a hand on each of June's arms. "I just don't want you to make the same mistakes I did."

"What do you mean?" She sipped her lukewarm hot chocolate.

Abigail released her and then did the same with her own drink. "Well, you work so hard, and you've always been so independent, like I was. I certainly

can't blame you for that, because you got it from me."
She winked a pretty blue eye. "At the same time, I
don't want to see you miss out on the same things
I did, honey."

"What mistakes, Mom?" she asked. "When I look
at you, all I see is a strong woman who worked hard
her whole life, who has a daughter and lots of friends
who love her."

"Oh, sweetheart, thank you."

"I mean it—I don't see any mistakes."

Abigail's forehead creased as she studied her fresh
manicure.

"Surely there were times when you were a kid that
you wished your father was around or that I didn't
work so much."

June nodded. "That's true. I did wish those things
sometimes, but if my father didn't make you happy,
and if you wouldn't have been happy with him in our
lives, then I trust that you made the right decision."

"He wasn't a bad guy, but he didn't want to be a
dad, and no kid needs that kind of burden. Plus—"
she gently touched June's cheek with her palm "—I
was so excited to have you, and you were such a
sweet little thing, always smiling and happy to see
everybody."

Though there had been times when she'd wished
for a brother or sister, it was true that she'd enjoyed
a happy childhood, and she knew that some kids
didn't have any parents; she was always just glad to
have one that loved her so dearly.

"I'd love to see you back to your old sunny self,

Junie. I know you're working hard and you probably won't let me, stubborn girl, but is there anything I can do to help?"

June shook her head. "I'll be fine, Mom. Just need to keep working and save up again so I can change things." She swallowed, wishing she could believe it would be that simple to start over. "I'll find a way."

"I know you will, sweetheart." Abigail paused. "I swear, if I could find that Clayton Miller, I'd kick his ass into next year."

June laughed so hard she almost snorted hot chocolate out of her nose. "I know you would, Mom. I know you would."

"Seriously, though, don't work yourself too hard and forget to live your life. You're too young for that." Abigail's voice quieted, her tone softening. "I dated a guy once, back when you were little—a good one— and I should have let him in more. He wanted to build a life with us, and he was so wonderful with you, which mattered to me more than anything else, but for some reason—I guess because I was too afraid to let any man near us again because he might disappoint you like your father did—I let a very good person go. Now I can't tell if that was the right or wrong choice, and life's too damn short to dwell on such things. But I'm telling you this because, if it happens to you, I don't want you to miss out on love by being afraid that what happened with Clayton might happen again."

June's eyes were tearing up, and she dabbed at them discreetly with a napkin, not wanting to attract attention.

"The point is, I don't want you to stop living life to the fullest. No one can promise that your heart won't get broken again, but if something good comes along, don't be afraid to take it, June Bug."

"Mom, I can't…"

"Just promise me you won't be too scared to try flying again."

She pulled in a breath, then released it slowly. "I promise."

"June?" Her ears picked up the low, smooth voice in the distance and she turned.

"Ethan. Hi," she said, standing up from the stool, righting her cup after nearly tipping it over. *Very smooth indeed.*

He waved over the crowd, so tall she had no trouble seeing him. His hair was still damp from a shower and he'd shaved all that sexy stubble off, which would be a pity if he didn't still paint a gorgeous picture. He wore a deep silver button-down shirt the color of storm clouds, the sleeves rolled up, revealing toned forearms with a coating of dark, silky hair.

The thundering in her heart increased as he neared, women looking up from their tables to catch a glimpse of him as he passed. The thing that really set off her pulse, though, was that he didn't notice a single one of them; he had eyes only for her. She wondered if it was possible that he'd gotten more handsome since she'd last seen him a few days ago.

When he stood only a foot or so away, the intoxicating scent of his skin caused all rational thought to fly out the window.

"June, it's so great to see you here," he said, seemingly unsure of what to do with his arms. For a man who had previously exuded confidence, seeing him a little flustered was just plain cute.

Her little heart completely ignored her and went to town—the traitor.

"It's good to see you, too," she said, helplessly grinning from ear to ear. "The puppies are doing really well. My neighbor—who is supertrustworthy, by the way, and has a rescue dog of her own—practically jumped at the chance to spend a couple of hours with them."

"That's wonderful to hear," he said, reaching out to touch her forearm, a gesture that was both unexpected and incredibly intimate. His touch tingled all the way up her arm, making the fine hairs stand at attention.

Good Lord, the things he could do to her with such simple, innocent contact.

She wondered if he had any idea what kind of effect his presence had on her. On her body, her mind, deep inside her most intimate places.

"But how are you doing?" he asked, lowering his head to make up for their difference in height so he could stare straight into her eyes. Heat blossomed in her belly and spread all over.

"Me? Oh, I'm… I'm good," she stammered. "Thanks for asking."

"Ahem." The sound of June's mom clearing her throat startled her and Ethan.

"Ethan," she said, turning to include her mom,

"this is my mother, Abigail Leavy. Mom, this is Ethan Singh, the veterinarian I told you about."

His eyebrows rose in response to that last part. "Ms. Leavy," he said, and June reminded herself to thank him later for not assuming she was a *Mrs.* "It's so very nice to meet you."

"Likewise," Abigail said, flashing those baby blues at him. "I hear you were quite the hero the other night, saving those puppies."

June was tickled to see his cheeks darken. Suave, classy, worldly Ethan Singh, blushing over a simple compliment? She hadn't thought she'd live to see the day and, of course, she made a quick mental note to tease him relentlessly about it later.

"I was just doing my job. It was nothing out of the ordinary."

June's mother practically burst out, "Oh, I'm sure June would disagree."

"Mom," she said through clenched teeth. "I'm sure Dr. Singh has to get back to work."

"It's true," he said, those illegally sexy lips curving upward. "But I was hoping I could borrow you for a moment first, June. There's something I'd like to talk to you about, if you can spare the time."

"Oh, she absolutely can. Can't you, sweetheart?"

"Yes, Mother." She turned and shot daggers at her mom. "I think I can take it from here."

"I certainly hope so. Remember earlier when I advised you ought to say yes to a good thing, should one come along? Well, this is exactly what I was talking about, so do yourself a favor," she whispered quickly to June, then turned and offered Ethan a million-dollar smile. "I'll leave you two alone," she said. "Call me later, June Bug."

Abigail picked up her purse and remaining coffee and hurried off, blowing her daughter a kiss over her red acrylic fingernails.

June rolled her eyes, but was unable to help grinning at her mother's tenacity.

Ethan watched the older woman go, then turned to June. "She's a firecracker, that one, isn't she?"

June chuckled. "That's one way of putting it."

"She seems like a lot of fun."

"Never a dull moment with Mom around." They both stopped talking, and uncomfortable silence filled the space between them until he motioned for her to sit down. He took her mother's chair.

"There's something I wanted to ask you, June."

She nodded, then took a sip of her now-cold drink and immediately regretted it.

"A friend of mine, Isaac Meyer, owns a companion animal training facility in town."

"Oh, yeah," June chimed in. "Friends with Fur."

"Oh, so you know it. Good."

"Well, not really. I mean, I've met Isaac and his wife, Avery, but I haven't ever been to their facility, though I have heard only good things about it."

"Yes, it's excellent. Isaac and Avery are really great with animals and they do a lot of important work in the community to encourage people to rescue shelter pets. Anyway, what I wanted to ask you is, they're having an event next Sunday that I thought you might like to take the puppies to."

"The puppies?"

"Yes, well, it's an adoption event, where people can come and see rescue animals and get to know them a little—see if they want to apply to take one home."

Her heart lurched into her throat at the thought of giving away either of the dogs she'd grown so fond of after the past few days. She swallowed, reminding herself that the animals did not belong to her; soon, they would need permanent homes, and it would be her duty and responsibility to help them find forever families.

Besides, there wasn't room in her life for a pet right now, much less a brother and sister pair.

So why, then, did it hurt so much to even think about letting them go? Especially when that's what was best for them.

Ethan continued speaking, and she didn't think he'd noticed her hesitation. Thank goodness for that at least; she had no desire to explain something she couldn't even understand herself.

"I think it would be a great way for them to have a chance to find homes, don't you?"

"Yes," she agreed, her voice a little squeaky. "Of course I do."

"Good, so you'll come with me, then?"

"Sounds like a plan."

"Oh, and that's not all," he said. "What time should I pick you up tomorrow?"

"Tomorrow? What's tomorrow?"

"Don't tell me you've forgotten."

All she could do was stand there, mouth gaping open.

He crossed his arms, grinning. "You really don't remember, do you?"

She absolutely *had* forgotten.

"My niece, Neena's, birthday party. Remember, when we were at Bauer's Bakery and my parents insisted I bring you by and you seemed okay with it."

"Oh, my gosh! I can't believe I forgot. Ethan, I'm so sorry."

Mixed emotions surged through her at the thought of spending time with him around his family, at how intimate that would be considering they'd agreed that this…thing…would not get serious.

Not serious, sure. And here she was about to get introduced to the people who cared the most about him.

"My family can't wait to meet you, and after all, you did promise you'd go."

She must have looked as nervous as she felt because he gently squeezed her forearm, chuckling. "Hey, they don't bite. We don't have to stay long, but you'd be doing me a major favor. If I don't bring you, I'll never hear the end of it."

She swallowed down the nervous lump that was taking up far too much space in her throat. "I did promise, didn't I?"

He nodded, clearly enjoying the sight of her squirming far too much.

"All right, then. It's just meeting your parents." The words nearly choked her. "It'll be fine. What's the worst that can happen?"

Chapter Nine

The following Sunday, June found herself victim to the oldest curse known to woman. There she stood in front of a closet full of clothes, yet she had absolutely nothing to wear.

"I really need to give some of this stuff away, huh?" she muttered to a furry audience of two. The puppies were curled up on a towel in the cushy dog bed Ethan had given her to take home from the clinic, and when she spoke, their little heads tilted adorably.

She didn't know too much about dogs, having only ever had a cat, but she could tell that the puppies were starting to learn a few words after only a couple of days. After observing that, she'd started intentionally naming things when they were exposed to them, like their water, food and toys.

At first, trying to keep track of them had been challenging—she'd started a little notebook to record their eating and potty schedules so she could take them outside at regular intervals and to avoid accidents. Ethan taught her that it was better to try to keep those from happening altogether and instead to give the puppies treats when she took them outside and they were successful.

If someone had told her a month ago that she'd be that interested in the bathroom habits of a couple of baby border collies, she would have questioned that person's sanity.

She laughed.

Yet here she was recording everything the little ones did. Beyond enjoying their company and going through their daily routines, she hadn't thought much about the mechanics of caring for them, but it occurred to her suddenly that she'd basically become a dog mom.

And, oh, she loved it so much.

Being an only child and then working so hard all of her adult life, June had never really given much thought to having kids, but every time she cleaned up a little mess or woke up in the middle of the night to take the puppies outside, she felt a little less afraid of the idea of having a child of her own someday.

The thought of children reminded her of Ethan, whose family was large and full of kids.

Oh, gosh. Ethan!

June's eyes flew to the clock on her nightstand and then absorbed the chaotic hurricane of clothing scattered all over her bedroom. Skirts hung from the closet doorknob; tops littered an armchair in the corner; there were bras and underwear hanging from the lampshade and the unused elliptical trainer. Still, she hadn't settled on anything yet, and he was due to pick her up in less than five minutes.

The doorbell rang, sending shock waves up her spine.

Oh, God.

Her hair was still wet and she stood there wearing nothing but a towel.

That was another lesson the dogs had taught her—they always needed more time for bathroom breaks than she planned for. If they weren't so cute, she'd be tempted each time she took them out to shout at them to pick a patch of grass already—they were all the same, for goodness' sake.

But they took their time, and now she had none left.

So she did the only thing she could think of, digging through the fashion debris until she found her pale blue bathrobe with the fluffy white clouds on it. She could only hope that when Ethan saw her wearing it, he wouldn't instantly change his mind about taking her to spend time with his family.

"Coming," she called out as he pressed the doorbell one more time.

She moved as quickly as she could, wanting to curl up and die when she opened it and saw Ethan standing there, the perfect specimen of modern masculinity. Beneath his unbuttoned overcoat he wore a navy-blue, long-sleeved henley and dark jeans. His hair waved a little above his collar—she loved that it was just a little too long—and his face was clean-shaven.

There wasn't even a trace of the annoyance she'd thought she might meet when he saw that she wasn't anywhere near ready to go. Instead, his toasted-almond eyes twinkled as he looked her up and down, making no attempt to hide his approval.

Wait. Was that really what she'd seen in his expression? The perfectly put-together, insanely gorgeous Dr. Singh had just seen her at her most unkempt—wild, soggy hair that hadn't had a proper trim in months, old, ratty bathrobe that she'd thought whimsical when she'd purchased it and which now just seemed childish and not a stitch of makeup.

After looking down at herself only to confirm that, yep, it was as bad as she thought, she finally worked up the courage to meet his eyes.

"Ethan, I'm so sorry I'm running late." She wrung her hands and flicked a thumb in the direction of her bedroom by way of explanation. "The puppies…"

He crossed his arms over his wide chest—firm, too, she knew, after the closeness they'd shared the other night.

"Not what I'd expected, but I see nothing to complain about." He winked at her. "My parents and siblings, on the other hand, well, they might not be so keen on…"

"Ha, ha," she teased, opening the door wider so he could come in.

As soon as he did, two little black-and-white fuzz balls galloped over, their ears bouncing up and down.

"Well, look who it is," he said, crouching down to scoop them up.

She was tickled to see that he didn't care at all about his clothes getting hairy. That quality made her like him all the more.

"Have they been behaving for you?" he asked, moving farther inside the living room and sitting cross-legged on the floor.

June closed the door and sat on the couch, extra careful to wrap the robe tightly around her body. The way Ethan had eyed her in the doorway made her think about things she probably shouldn't. Being pretty much bare underneath the robe increased those feelings until they hovered at a dangerous level and she had to force herself to think of anything but... that. Anything but being naked and alone with a man who made her insides burn with need.

She focused on the question he'd asked.

"They've been great," she said. "I've gotten their feeding schedule down pat, and potty training them has been a cinch, thanks to your helpful tips."

"Are they eager to get treats for following through with what you ask?"

Good, she thought. If he kept the conversation along that line, she'd have no trouble forgetting her growing fantasies about what it would be like to...

"Yes, they seem to want to do what I ask as long as they know they're getting doggy snacks. Is that a good thing?"

"Definitely. It means they're food-motivated, so

as long as you're handing out the goods, they'll aim to do what you need them to."

"I've had my neighbor, Ainsley, and her dog, Max, over to work with them, as well. She's the one I was telling you about who sometimes fosters dogs, and she'll be watching the puppies tonight as soon as I text her to come on over."

"That's great, too."

"What is?"

"That they're spending time around an unfamiliar human and dog. That will help get them socialized so that when they're ready they can go to good homes even if there's already a dog living there."

Her heart lurched and she started to ask him when he thought that day might come—she wasn't even close to being ready for it—but she closed her mouth, quietly watching for a few moments as he rubbed their tiny bellies. "I'll leave you here with them and go finish getting ready."

She headed to the bathroom and closed the door, resting her back against it as she tried to slow her breathing.

Every time they were apart for a few days, and then she saw him again, things got so much worse, meaning, she wanted him so much more. The sparks between them had become more frequent and much stronger and she could feel the chance of an explosion increasing at a terrifying rate.

Since running into each other at the coffee shop, he'd called each day, often more than once, and he'd even stopped by a time or two for a few minutes to ensure that the puppies were thriving.

Each time they spoke on the phone, and when he'd come over, she could sense that he was going through the same thing—wanting to take some elusive next step with her, but afraid of what that might set in motion.

The other morning when they'd had that snowball fight, and after briefly discussing what to do with their casual, not-friendship, not-relationship thing, it had all seemed so risk-free.

Surely, if they had agreed not to let things get too emotionally serious, then they were both on the same page and that very thing would not be allowed to happen.

But then, what about all the physical longing? What about the way her body seemed drawn to his by some unseen force? What in the world were they supposed to do about that?

If they let things get too far, she couldn't be certain that she would be able to inhibit herself from wanting some kind of commitment, something more permanent. She could not promise herself that she would be able to indulge in getting physically closer to him without her heart following along.

Neither could her growing affection for him be ignored.

But she didn't think she could stand to be in the same room with him for much longer without giving in to temptation.

And that's exactly what she faced that day—hours

and hours by his side without being able to touch him the way she wanted to, tell him what she was going through every time he was around.

It would be absolute torture, she thought as she pulled on a pair of dark purple skinny trousers and a soft, silky black sweater with sparkly gems along the collar. They were the first pieces she'd put on earlier and then discarded in the bathroom, and now, with a tornado of garments covering her bedroom floor, it was of course what she ended up wearing. It was an outward testament to how little she trusted herself these days.

Her favorite outfit, the only one guaranteed to act as a confidence-builder, and along with a pair of black high-heeled boots, it would have to do.

Because Lord knew, she needed confidence that day more than ever before.

A soft knock rapped on the other side of the door and she opened it.

"I'm sorry to bother you and I don't want you to feel like you have to rush, but I just got the puppies to sit on command, and I wondered where you keep your treats."

"Oh. Of course." She passed by him into the hallway, catching that light but heady scent that hung on his clothes and skin, and started to head down the hall toward the kitchen; but Ethan caught her hand and spun her to face him.

He pulled her to his chest until her forehead touched his chin, then put a palm on either side of her face and covered her mouth with his own.

Shots of electricity buzzed up her spine as the moist heat of his tongue touched hers, deepening the kiss. Without thinking, she wrapped her hands around his hips, tucking her fingers just under the hem of his shirt, moaning when her skin made contact with the warmth of his.

Encouraged, he moved his hands to her shoulders and backed her up until she was against the wall, both of them gasping for air as they gave in to the heat between them.

Finally, she pulled away from his mouth, forcing breath into her lungs.

"What was that for?" she asked, a smile playing at the corners of her lips.

As she fought for composure, Ethan just stood back and flashed that sexy grin of his. Though his motions were smoother than hers, she could see the way his chest rose and fell rapidly, and her own swelled with pride that she'd agitated him to such a degree.

"I just wanted you to know," he breathed, "how beautiful you look today, June."

She coughed out a very unsexy laugh. "Thank you. Very much. But my hair's still wet and I haven't even gotten around to putting on makeup yet."

He stepped closer, threatening to start it up all over again. She wanted to cross her arms over her chest, to keep him at a distance, but her body wouldn't let her. It seemed to crave his in a way she couldn't control.

His eyes plunged into hers. "I meant what I said," he whispered, leaning in again.

She worried he might kiss her once more. Somehow she knew that if he did, there would be no chance of them making it to the party.

Instead, he brushed his lips against hers in the softest of touches, then let her go, padding back down the hall, leaving her breathless and shaken to her very core.

Half an hour later, standing outside an entirely different door, Ethan possessed even less control than he had when he'd arrived to pick up June.

He'd anticipated that evening all day.

Yes, he wanted to see his family, especially his niece Neena, whose tenth birthday they would be celebrating, but the bulk of his eagerness he'd have to attribute to seeing June. He'd been looking forward to a casual, fun evening and maybe an equally casual kiss at the end of it, but when she'd answered her door wearing that tattered old robe, her red hair wet and in complete disarray, she had absolutely thrown him for a loop, caught him totally off guard.

It wasn't hard to imagine her naked under that robe, and after pressing his body up against her in the hallway of her apartment, he could trace her curves in his mind's eye with no effort at all.

She was even more beautiful that way than she'd been when they first met the other night. Without any adornment, her green eyes shone clear and bright, and her hair was like satin as he'd weaved his fingers through it. She had a body that was made to be adored—ample curves for a man to hold on to, soft, creamy skin…it was such a shame he would never have the chance to be that man.

The way she'd responded to him back there, the way she'd reached under his shirt to dig her cool fingers into his burning skin and kissed him back with abandon, he knew he could have her. He knew it wouldn't take much to get her into his bed.

So why wasn't he doing just that?

He watched her face out of the corner of his eye as they stood outside his parents' front door, his heart going soft at her nervous expression.

"No worries, June. My family is a mess but they are nothing if not kindhearted. They will love you, trust me." He squeezed her hand and didn't let go.

Something knotted in his throat as he said the L-word. The last time he'd used it had been for Jessica, and he'd expected using it now to leave a bad taste in his mouth.

But it didn't. And what he'd said was perfectly true. His family would love June, which distressed him to no end.

The only time he'd brought Jessica to meet them had been awkward and uncomfortable for everyone. She simply didn't fit in, did not understand his family's warm teasing, the way they'd tried to get her to open up to them and to make her laugh. She'd been like oil to their water, everything they said hitting her the wrong way and prickling under her skin.

It was a day he'd like to forget.

It didn't escape his understanding that he was bringing Jessica's polar opposite with him this time, fully aware that she would be met with a completely different reaction.

They would love June's sweetness, her easy smile, her softhearted nature and her sense of humor.

All the things *he* loved about her.

That thought crashed into him like a sucker punch, and he thanked his lucky stars when the door opened and his mother wrapped him in a bear hug.

"Ethan, sweetheart, I'm so glad to see you," she said far too loudly into his ear.

"No need to shout, Mother. I'm right here," he said, grinning.

Melanie Singh whacked him in the side and turned her attention to the woman next to him.

"And you must be June," his mom said, folding her hands together in front of her. He knew that meant she was trying not to be too huggy and it made him cringe. Jessica had complained about his family being overly physically affectionate, a trait he'd never noticed until it had been pointed out to him. A trait he happened to treasure.

He'd grown up feeling loved and surrounded by affection. Of course, he'd apologized on their behalf when Jessica had complained, hating himself for doing so when, even at the time, he'd known it was she who'd been too cold.

A smile spread over his lips as he watched June hold out her arm, as if to invite his mother in. The two women embraced like they'd known each other their whole lives, and seeing their instant connection set off butterflies in his stomach.

"I'm so happy to meet you, Mrs. Singh," June said, holding his mother at arm's length, her eyes sparkling as she chattered easily. "Ethan's told me so much about you. I've heard lots of stories about all the places you've visited as a family, and I'd love to hear more from you if you have the time."

"Absolutely. Oh, I'm so glad. I think sometimes we embarrass our boy, and I hope you'll forgive us if we roped you into something you weren't wanting to do, but we're just so proud of him and we're so excited he's met someone new."

His mother gave him a pointed glance that said a thousand things all at once—the topmost being that she instantly liked this girl he'd brought into her home.

And though he did not like what such a thing implied, not in the least, knowing that his mom approved of June pleased him an inordinate amount.

He would have to keep that to himself. If his mother knew, she'd have the two of them married before Neena's party concluded.

"Come inside, you two, and let me get your coats. How silly of me, letting you freeze out here while I yammer away."

June laughed and followed his mom inside, tossing a smile over her shoulder as he closed the door behind them.

Inside his parents' home, after their coats were taken, they were met with a flurry of friendly chaos as siblings and their children, aunts, uncles and anyone else collected along the way descended upon them. June's eyes glowed at the rainbow of saris worn by some of the Indian women in his family. Several others wore jeans and T-shirts, but June's eyes were drawn to the rich jewel-toned fabrics of his father's place of birth.

"They're all so beautiful," she whispered when they had a second without anyone's attention on them. "I feel so plain in my outfit."

"Nonsense. You look amazing." He pulled her close so that his lips touched her ear. "I thought I made that quite clear earlier."

He loved the rosy apples that instantly blossomed in her cheeks at what he'd said. Images flooded his mind of all the other areas her skin might turn pink for him in exchange for whispered words.

She looked at him, her eyes huge under bright fairy lights that were strung all over the house. "I mean it, though. Are you sure I'm dressed okay?"

"Absolutely." He touched her elbow to soothe her. "You would look beautiful in traditional Indian clothing. Don't get me wrong. But no one expects you to wear it. I would have told you if that was the case. See," he said, holding a hand out to encompass the room. "Plenty are dressed similarly to you, so you fit in just fine."

"Good," she said. "I was a little worried I'd under-dressed."

"Not at all. Just breathe, June. They already think

you're wonderful—my mother in particular, and that's not a common occurrence."

Me, in particular, he'd really wanted to say.

She looked down at her feet. "I'm so glad."

"Ethan!" He turned from June to see his brother, Harry, hurrying across the room with open arms. Harry grabbed him, then greeted June with his usual, friendly bear hug, making her laugh.

"Is my brother bothering you?" Harry asked, sending June into giggles. If the man wasn't already happily married with two excellent children, Ethan's hackles might have risen. Harry was stupid-handsome and taller by several inches than any of the other Singh men. But he was also too sweet and goofy to invite jealousy. He teased June for several minutes until she was almost doubled over in laughter. Finally, Harry's wife, Amani, caught Ethan's eye, rolled her own and came over to join her husband.

"Take my advice," Amani fake-whispered to June, "and stay far away from this family, unless you want to become crazy like the rest of us."

As she spoke, Amani tossed adoring eyes at Harry and he gave her a big smooch on the cheek. The four of them bantered for half an hour about the couple's recent vacation, how Ethan was managing the clinic, Amani's work in civil rights law and their children, Neena and Suresh.

"Neena's having a blast," Harry said. "But I'm afraid she'll be disappointed when she finds out she's not getting the present she asked for."

Amani's soft eyes met Harry's. "She'll be all right.

I think between the cake, her grandparents and aunts and uncles spoiling her and her friends, she'll forget all about it."

Harry glanced at Ethan and then June. "Neena's been asking for a puppy since she first started to talk. I would love to look in to getting one for her, but Amani insists that she and I are too busy to take care of a pet for Neena. Between you and me, though, I think she's at just the right age to start learning the responsibility of caring for a pet."

Amani gave Harry a worried look, but he brushed off his wife's concerns.

"You worry too much, my love. The best way to teach her responsibility is to give her some. What do you think, Ethan?" Harry asked.

Ethan glanced between the two.

"Ordinarily I'd say not to drag me into it, especially when I know Amani will always win—" he winked at his sister-in-law "—but in this case, I'm inclined to agree with you, Harry."

"Well, that would be a first," his brother teased, gently punching Ethan in the shoulder.

"No, I mean it. I think you might be on to something. There are plenty of studies supporting the idea that children who are given pets to care for at a young age—with their parents' supervision backing them, of course—become more caring, conscientious and reliable adults."

Amani tilted her head. "Truly?"

Ethan nodded.

She put a finger on her chin. "Wow, I had no idea.

I mean, it makes sense, but I didn't know there was evidence to back it up. You might have to send me some of those articles, Ethan." She leaned closer to him and June. "And don't you dare tell my husband this, but if you're right, I might have to consider changing my mind," she said, plenty loud enough for Harry to hear. "Besides, you know I love dogs."

Ethan looked at June to see if she was tracking his line of thought, but her eyes were aimed down at the glass of champagne someone had placed in her hand earlier.

"And it so happens that I may have just the puppy for her."

At that, June's eyes snapped up to his.

Something wasn't right, but he couldn't read her expression. He would ask her as soon as they had a moment alone. It was possible she was just feeling a little overwhelmed; his family could have that effect on new people.

Harry and Amani seemed interested in hearing more, and he had two puppies to find homes for, so he went on. "As a matter of fact, that's part of how June and I got to know each other. It's a long story, but the short of it is that she came into the clinic during the storm the other night and was carrying two puppies with her."

Amani put a hand over her heart and her face softened as he told them about June's rescue, unable to hide his pride in her.

"Anyway, if you'd like, June and I can bring the pups by later this week and Neena can meet them."

As he spoke, Ethan's brother and sister-in-law nodding in agreement, he noticed June's skin had turned a little pale. As Harry and Amani discussed the idea of their daughter getting to see the dogs, he took the opportunity to ask if June was all right.

"Me? Oh, yeah," she said, her voice faltering a little. "I'm fine."

"Are you sure, June?" He placed his hands on her shoulders. "Look, if this is too much, being here with all these people you haven't met before… I mean, it might be too much, just let me know and we'll get out of here."

"No, Ethan, it's not that, it's just…"

"All right," Harry burst in. "We've talked it over and we think it's a great idea. As long as you don't tell Neena what the plan is. I just want you to make sure you don't say anything about her possibly getting to keep one, since my wife isn't completely sold on the idea yet."

Ethan pulled his eyes away from June for just a second.

"Hang on one sec, Harry." He turned back to her, and her features had released some of the tension that had been in her face. "Are you okay, sweetheart?"

"Yeah, um, yes." She closed her eyes and took a deep breath before speaking again. "Yes, I think I will be."

He touched his fingertips to her elbow, willing her to feel his tenderness toward her, to know that her will was his command. "Are you certain you wouldn't like to step outside and get some fresh air?"

June shook her head and he forced himself to let go of the issue, hoping that by now, she would surely tell him if he'd done something to bother her.

It shouldn't matter, he knew.

They were merely friends, destined to end that friendship when they parted ways in a short time.

But something was changing between them, something that made him believe it did indeed matter. The puppies, what she thought of his family, and of course—most of all—how she felt about him.

Warm awareness prickled up his neck.

All of it mattered.

Chapter Ten

The ride home from Neena's party was the epitome of awkwardness, and June kicked herself for being the cause of the uncomfortable silence. Ethan had asked her what was wrong more than once, but had given up the third or fourth time she told him it was nothing.

But how could she tell him what was really bothering her? He would think her silly, or worse, she might scare him off if she opened up her heart that much. What had been bugging her for the week since they'd met, since she'd been the main caretaker of two new little lives, had only become crystal clear to her as of that night when Harry had brought up giving one of the puppies to his daughter and Ethan hadn't objected.

She knew it was nothing personal, knew he wasn't deliberately trying to hurt her by rushing to find homes for the puppies—he was only doing his job and trying to make sure they were cared for—but it made her heart ache nonetheless. She'd finally figured it out, and she wanted to share her thoughts with him, but she wasn't brave enough. If he knew what she'd realized, it would be too much for him, too serious, and he'd run.

Ethan pulled his SUV to a stop outside her apartment and walked her to Ainsley's unit to pick up the puppies. Once they were back inside June's home and had put the dogs to bed, there were no buffers left; she would have to face him.

He took her hand and led her to the couch, his eyes tender as he brushed a piece of hair back from her cheek, rubbing the auburn strand between his fingers before tucking it behind an ear. The way his gaze held hers the whole time made butterflies gather in her stomach, their wings tickling her insides.

"June, look, I know something's been on your mind."

She pulled her eyes away from him and down into her lap, focusing on the sad state of her nails.

"Look at me, June, please," he said, tilting her chin up toward him. "I know that this—" he waved a hand between them and she understood that he referred to their odd pseudo-relationship "—is weird. But the fact is, well, I've begun to care for you." He swallowed, his nervousness out of character. "Quite a lot actually."

Her eyebrows lifted and one corner of his mouth kicked up in response.

"I know. I didn't mean for it to happen, either. It just did." He closed his eyes and sucked in a deep breath, and as he let it out, the impact of what he was trying to tell her pummeled into her.

"We don't have to discuss the way I feel, or if… if you're feeling something similar—" she opened her mouth to speak, but he held up a palm to give her pause "—and, in fact, I'd rather not do it tonight. There's always time for that later."

She closed her lips. They both knew there wasn't going to be time later, not if he left Peach Leaf and they both went their separate ways.

"But as I said, I care for you, June." He reached out and took her hand, flipping it over to rub a finger against her palm.

The touch resonated all the way up her arm and sped up her breathing.

"So I *do* want to know what's been on your mind that you've not been telling me."

June swallowed and took some time to gather her thoughts. She wasn't ready for this, especially after hearing his confession that he'd developed stronger feelings for her than he was supposed to have let happen. If he hadn't stopped her, the chances were high that she would have blurted out the fact that she was going through the very same thing, if not something even more.

She wasn't ready to put a label on it, was most certainly not ready to call it…*love*. But that flutter under her ribs each time she saw him, that gravitational power he seemed to have over her that made her want to get as close to him as possible—none of it could be denied anymore.

Add to that the new knowledge of how sweet he was around his family, how much she'd enjoyed watching him play with his nieces and nephews and the way he supported his brother and sister and welcomed any stranger as a new friend, and the evidence was clear. Maybe it wasn't quite love, not yet at least, but one thing was for sure; she absolutely adored Ethan Singh.

Still, she couldn't tell him the truth just yet—that she'd begun to think of the puppies as a symbol of the new life she was trying to build. That, somehow, even though it didn't entirely make sense, she'd begun to believe that if she failed the animals, she would fail herself. She knew she didn't have the resources or the time to nurture them and be there for them the way she should, but neither was she willing to let them go.

If she gave up on them, she felt, it would be as if she'd given up on herself.

Worse, selfishly, she knew that once the puppies were no longer her responsibility, Ethan would have no real reason to see her anymore.

A week ago, she hadn't known the dogs or Ethan Singh, and now the loss of all three was a real threat, a specter of darkness hanging around her future.

Imagine if she told him all of that; she wouldn't blame him for wanting to disappear from her life. And she wasn't ready to face it herself.

Still, he stared at her, waiting for a response, the question of what was on her mind hanging thick in the air between them.

Maybe it would be safe to tell him just a fraction of the truth, especially since, for whatever reason, it seemed to be almost impossible for her to lie to the man. He acted as her own personal truth serum.

"You said you don't want to talk about this tonight, and, well, I guess I'm feeling some of the same things you are. I think that this thing between us just overwhelmed me a little tonight, meeting your family and all."

"I'm sorry, June." He smoothed a hand across his forehead. "I shouldn't have pushed you into going."

She shook her head. "No, don't apologize. I agreed to go and you didn't push me. It's just that I hadn't imagined how much I would enjoy being around them and I guess the thought of never seeing them again—after you're gone, I mean—is a little sad to me."

His lips formed a thin line and his eyes narrowed as he considered her words.

"Maybe it doesn't have to be like that," he said. "But let's not talk about the future." He leaned in until his lips were mere inches from hers. "Right now, I want to know only one thing."

"Mmm," she mumbled, apparently unable to form whole words when he was that close to her.

He smiled and ran his tongue along his lower lip, moistening it. "What can I do to make you feel better tonight, in this moment?"

"Anything?" she asked.

"Anything."

Instead of spelling it out, she wrapped a hand behind his neck and slowly, tentatively, pulled him in, pressing her lips against his, relishing his signature taste—cinnamon, as always, from the chai he drank so often, layered with a hint of champagne from the party. Emboldened by his hungry response as he wrapped his arms around her waist, she parted his lips with her tongue, deepening the kiss, smiling against his mouth when he gave a soft little groan.

She moved her hands from his neck, over his shoulders and down his muscular arms, grasping his hands in hers. She moved them to her breasts and he responded by softly massaging the mounds over her sweater, her nipples rising to meet his touch.

She groaned in protest when he moved away.

"June," he said on a heavy breath. "Are you sure you want this? I mean, don't get me wrong, I absolutely, definitely do, but I don't want to pressure you. I know we're both just out of bad relationships and I don't want to…"

She held up a finger to quiet him. "Shh. Don't think so much, Ethan. Just go with it."

He smiled, lips parting to reveal perfect teeth, and she grinned in response. "I can do that," he said.

"Good. That's what I hoped you'd say."

He kissed her again and ran his hands down her sides, pausing at the hem of her sweater. When she nodded briefly, he lifted it slightly, tucking his hands under the fabric. His hot fingers against her skin, still cool from being outdoors only moments before, caused a slight intake of breath, and then she relaxed into his touch as his hands slid up her back. They slowly, expertly glided along her spine, then back down, circling around to the front where he smoothed them over her abdomen. When they trailed upward to her chest, his fingers toying with her nipples until they perked up to meet him, she closed her eyes and relished the sensation.

When she opened them again, she met Ethan's dark irises, his pupils dilated with arousal, letting her know he'd like some attention, as well.

So she moved until her back rested against the arm of her couch, pulling him until his torso rested against her. She was glad that a certain part of him was far away from her hands, though she could feel him growing when his groin came in contact with her thigh, the knowledge that she'd turned him on so thoroughly setting off her own response.

She ran her hands up his back, stopping here and there to admire the muscles before running them back down to his abs, and then to the waistband of his jeans. His mouth covered her own as he grabbed her hand and guided it to the front.

June didn't hesitate in removing his belt and unzipping his fly.

But that was as far as she got before her nerves settled in. Ethan seemed to understand that she needed to slow down a bit, and he lifted his upper body away from her, pulling her over until she rested against his chest, his arms wrapped around her. She looked up and saw that dark stubble she loved so much beginning to show along his jawline. He smiled down at her, his eyes full of desire but warm and patient. She rested her face against his chest and attempted to slow her breathing.

Was she really ready for this? Had she truly healed enough from the last person she'd been with, the person who'd so completely shattered her heart, to be able to give herself to someone new?

Even if they'd agreed that this wouldn't turn into a relationship, she still owed Ethan that much, that he would be the only man on her mind without her dwelling on the past if they went through with this; she forced herself to use the actual words—if they made love. She wanted to give him her whole self, not a broken collection of parts. He deserved that, just as she did from him.

When she looked into his eyes again, she found confirmation that she was the only woman on his mind; he wasn't far off somewhere, recalling the last time he'd held someone like that. The way he gazed at her, making her feel like she was the most beautiful, most amazing woman in the world, told her she had all of him.

And, for that night, that's all she wanted. It was enough. It had to be enough.

With renewed confidence, she placed a hand on his shoulder and pulled her body up, straddling his waist with her legs.

"God, you're gorgeous," he said, as breathless as she felt. His arousal was there between them, causing June to long for more from him. She kissed him again and again, until hunger mounted on both sides and they couldn't stand it there any longer.

In one quick motion, Ethan rose from the couch, lifting her as if she weighed nothing.

For once, she was more than satisfied with the size of her apartment, as it was so small and uncomplicated she didn't have to point out where the bedroom was.

Ethan smiled at her as he carried her there, laying her down gently on her lavender bedspread, shoving aside the clothing she'd discarded earlier.

He lifted her legs one at a time to pull off the socks she'd worn inside her boots, stopping to kiss the ticklish parts of the soles of her feet, making her giggle.

She was thankful for his lightening the mood, as intensity had begun to build and she knew they were both close to breaking. He seemed to know instinctively when she needed a softer moment before he started in again, sending desire spiraling through her.

He pulled off her pants and tossed them aside, then she leaned up until her head was at the level of his torso. His jeans were still undone, so she made quick work of removing them completely, her pulse rocketing up as she ran her hands along his firm behind, covered only by black boxer briefs.

She looked up at him and he nodded, his eyes black as night in the dark bedroom. With her eyes locked on to his, she pulled off the underwear, running her hand along his hard length until he shut his eyes and his legs slackened.

"June, I can't survive this much longer," he said, grabbing hold of her hand. "I want you."

She smiled and pulled him down onto the bed, where he relieved her of her own underwear, leaving only her bra and top. His hands worked fast but gently, pulling her sweater over her head and unhooking her very last piece of clothing.

When all of the garments were gone, they stared at each other for several seconds. June loved the contrasting colors of their skin, her lighter tone against his darker one, and she couldn't wait to blend them together into one.

Ethan softly pressed her shoulders back until her head lay on a pillow. His hands slid up her thighs until they reached her center, and he spread her legs, then bent forward to kiss her, plunging his tongue into her mouth as he caressed her heat, slipping a finger inside. When she was very wet, she grabbed a condom from a drawer of her bedside table, allowing him to slip it on before he dove deep inside her.

Everything faded away until all that was left was his pulsing, faster and faster until her core buzzed with desperate need. At his final plunge, they burst open to each other until there was nothing left to give. And when Ethan slid from her body, he lay down behind her, pulling her against his warm form.

Both of them wordless from exhausted pleasure,

he ran his fingers through her hair and along her arm, until she drifted off into the deepest sleep she'd enjoyed in as long as she could remember.

A terrible noise ripped Ethan from sleep, and it took almost a full minute for him to realize where he was, and that the god-awful sound was an alarm tone coming from June's phone on her bedside table.

He almost laughed when he looked down to find her still in his arms, her eyes slammed shut, completely oblivious to the ripping sound.

"June," he said, chuckling. "June, wake up before I throw that damn thing across the room."

One eyelid rose revealing a pretty green iris, but fell again almost immediately and it took several more tries before Ethan was able to fully wake her.

"Good Lord, woman," he said. "You sleep like the dead."

She stretched out her arms and tossed a sleepy smile in his direction. He crossed his arms over his chest and watched her, just enjoying the view. The sun wasn't up yet, but when she flicked on her bedside lamp, soft light flooded over her ivory skin and all that luscious red hair fell over her shoulders, rendering June so ethereal and beautiful that she resembled a wood nymph.

Her beauty was unique and warm, and he wanted to wrap himself in it like a blanket. As fresh thirst began to build, he reached for her, ready to quench it with her body.

But as June picked up her phone, her eyes widened and she launched out of the bed before he could catch her.

"Oh, my God, I am going to be so late for work." She ran to her dresser and grabbed clean underwear, mumbling to herself. "So late, so late, so late!"

Ethan had to get to the clinic himself to relieve the night vet tech, but he wanted to enjoy the show for a few more minutes—June's naked curves moving quickly around the room as she gathered clothing. He didn't know when he would next get the chance to see her like this, and he wasn't about to miss relishing that moment; it would be worth arriving a half hour late to work. It would also be the first time, so he was confident his father's vet tech would forgive him.

He leaned back and rested his torso against the headboard. "June," he said, but she didn't register him calling her. "June!"

This time, she looked up as if from a trance, and her eyes softened as they landed on him.

"Yeah?"

He curved a finger. "Come here for a second."

If he was honest, he enjoyed the battle raging in her eyes, clearly weighing the cost of missing work with another hour of lovemaking with him. It had been the best of his life with June, without contest. For the time being, coming off a night of it, he'd be willing to give up everything to spend another day wrapped up with her in those lavender sheets.

As it were, he would never get her out of his mind, and he could already tell that the day at work would be the longest of his life. Finally, the battle was over, and he was disappointed to realize that she'd made the mature, adult decision.

Dammit.

"I can't, Ethan. I've got to get to work."

But at least she walked over, her berry lips curved upward, and his eyes latched on to her creamy breasts as they hovered above his chest when she leaned in for a kiss.

"I really do have to go," she said, the very same moment he took her forearm and pulled her down on top of him. His heart buzzed at the giggle she gave in response.

"Ethan," she said, trying her best to be serious. "I'm going to be late for work, and it'll be pretty hard to come up with a legit-sounding excuse when Margaret's already given me a full week off."

"But I'm not finished with you yet," he argued, attempting to strengthen his case by nibbling at her neck and dotting tiny kisses along her shoulders. "There are so many spots I haven't yet kissed."

She indulged him a little, but finally pulled away. June put her hands on either side of his face.

"Last night was...amazing. It was beyond amazing," she said, echoing his thoughts, "but it can't last forever." She ran her thumb along his lip, sending vibrations all throughout his body.

"Do you know what you do to me, June?" He grabbed her hands and held them to his chest. "Do you have any idea?"

She closed her eyes as he felt his heart beat against

her fingers. "I have some idea," she answered, eyes wide and full of desire, "if it's half of what you do to me."

He grinned at that and leaned in to kiss her. She kissed him back with the same hunger that tore at his insides. Everything in his body burned to take her again, to be inside her, where he felt better than he ever had before in his life.

It was even possible that he...

"But I really do need to get out of here." She took her hands back from him and touched his face once more before rising from the bed. As she stood before him, hands at her sides, doing nothing to hide her form, he let his eyes wander from her lovely, fiery mane, past her spectacular breasts, all the way down to her purple-painted toes.

"You're the most beautiful woman I've ever laid eyes on, June." He'd thought the words might come out cheesy, and that June might rightfully laugh at him, but his voice was strong and as he spoke them he realized that no truer words had ever escaped his lips.

And then it hit him.

What the hell had he done? What had he allowed himself to get into here?

He hadn't meant for things to go this far. Obviously, he'd wanted her physically more than he ever had anyone else, but he'd sort of convinced himself that, once they'd slept together and the novelty wore off, the mystery was gone, that things would calm down between them.

He'd mistakenly believed that he could get the woman out of his system.

On the contrary, she was more present in him, had more of a grip on him, than he'd thought possible.

Instead of getting her out of his system, he'd invited her in, all the way.

And he knew now that nothing he could do or say would get her out.

He swallowed, bringing a hand to his forehead to brush off the beads of perspiration that had sprung up there.

She was right to get away from him now, and he would let her go.

He dropped his hands to his sides.

"Right," he said. "Right, you should get ready for work and I'll do the same or we'll both be seriously late."

Something in her features let him know she'd registered the sudden change in his demeanor, but she didn't have time to question it.

He offered a small smile, hoping she wouldn't ask about his abrupt decision to come around to her way of thinking.

Thankfully, she turned and left the room.

If she'd stayed, she would have seen the way he buried his face in her pillow for what he somehow knew would be the last time, inhaling her sweet jasmine scent. If she'd stayed, she might have heard him groan as he realized what a mess he'd turned their casual non-relationship into. And worst of all, if she'd stayed, she might have seen the first bud begin to grow as love—yes, *love*—blossomed in a heart he'd thought dead.

Chapter Eleven

On Saturday morning just a week after she and Ethan first made love, June's hands shook as she pulled into the drive at his parents' home. She turned off the ignition and forced herself to take ten deep breaths.

She couldn't put her finger on why she felt so nervous all of a sudden. She and Ethan had been seeing each other off and on the whole week, Ethan taking the puppies to work each day with him and bringing them to June's to spend the night. Just the puppies, though, not Ethan himself.

Maybe that was the problem.

Something had changed after they'd slept together, but it wasn't the type of thing she expected. Sure, now and then a guy spent the night with one of her friends and never called again, and it had happened to June once a long time ago, but this was something entirely different.

Ethan still called, he still visited, and if anything the two had gotten closer…but they just hadn't been to bed together again.

And it was making her insane.

This was exactly why they had agreed to keep things casual, and yet he'd gone and taken it to the next level.

She stopped herself, recalling that perfect night a week before.

Her assessment wasn't fair; she had been the one to take that first step, and she'd been more than happy when he went along with her. Without a doubt, it had been the best night of her life. Ethan had been wonderful—attentive, but not demanding, letting her take the reins, but giving as good as he got—and, oh, he was an amazing lover.

The problem was that he was also more than that. She'd seen a change in him that next morning when she'd been running late for work. He'd been so tender, so…well…*loving*. He'd been in no hurry to leave and had even packed her a lunch while she'd showered, and then had driven her to work and kissed her when he dropped her off, promising to call that afternoon—a promise he then kept.

She knew what the problem was; it was all too good to be true.

At least now she had her own car back, complete

with a big-ass bill for a new battery and the cost of a tow.

She rested her head on the steering wheel for a moment before opening the door and lifting the puppies out of the backseat in their crate, along with a tote full of baking supplies.

She slammed her car door shut with a foot, careful not to jostle the puppies too much, and then she looked up just in time to see Ethan jogging in their direction. Her heart swelled the second she met his gaze, further proof that something wasn't right.

Over the past few days, she'd had plenty of time to realize that she had been kidding herself when she'd agreed to keep this thing with Ethan casual. It would be easy to blame it on the way their physical relationship had changed, but in her heart of hearts, June knew it was so much more.

As she watched him approach, she was reminded once again just how much she genuinely liked this man, how incredibly, purely happy she was in his company. No one had ever made her come alive the way he did, and she had him to thank for bringing her natural optimism back. She'd even gotten the urge to bake again and to risk hoping that she might still someday see her dreams come true.

He was special, no doubt, and he'd gotten a hold of her in a way that no man ever had. Not her horrible ex—not anybody.

She recognized the feeling for what it was, but still she resisted naming it. Doing so would solidify it, somehow, and she wasn't ready to do that just yet.

Because she knew that, the second she did, it would all be lost. If Ethan found out what was going on in her heart and in her mind, he'd back off and possibly out of her life. And she didn't want to, but she needed him now. Though he was still as wonderful as ever with the puppies, it also had nothing to do with them anymore.

"Hey there," he said, drawing up in front of her, reaching for the tote bag and dog carrier. "Let me take those from you."

He leaned forward and kissed her cheek before leading her to the door.

Though they had seen each other since that night they spent together—doing the puppy exchange and going out to dinner a few times—this was the first time they'd be in a house together. She prayed she could keep her hands off him, keep from making a fool of herself by wanting him to sleep with her again when he'd made no motion to take her to bed over the past week.

She got the sense he was being careful with her, as though he didn't want to hurt her. But not being with him again, after they'd shared each other that way, hurt even more.

He led her through the door he'd left propped open and she followed as he brought the crate and bag into the dining room that attached to the Singhs' kitchen. He pulled a few child gates out of a linen closet and set them up. "So we can watch them while we go in the kitchen," he said.

June nodded.

Ethan glanced at a clock on the wall. "We've got about three hours until we have to be at Friends with Fur. Anything you'd like to do until it's time to go?"

June's cheeks went warm at the same time Ethan's turned a slightly darker shade and she knew he'd heard it, too. Of course there were things she'd like to do in that time, all involving clothes on the floor and lots and lots of bare skin.

He cleared his throat and looked away, disappointment clouding his features.

Her heart sank and she changed the subject before the sharp pain could do any more damage.

"I brought baking stuff, and I was thinking we could make some canine treats for the adoption fair if that sounds good to you."

He managed a soft, sad smile, but it was a smile nonetheless, and she would have to take it. "That sounds like a great idea."

He took her hand and led her into the kitchen. He asked what he could do to help and she gave him the task of measuring out the dry ingredients while she whisked together eggs and water in a small bowl.

"This isn't my recipe," she said, leaning against the granite countertop to admire the Singhs' chef-worthy kitchen. "I found it online. But I did make a few modifications that I think will make these biscuits even better."

Ethan glanced over his shoulder. "I'm sure they'll be excellent," he said, his voice sounding distracted. He stirred flour and baking powder together in silence for a bit. Finally, he turned to face her, dropping the wooden spoon to his side.

"Listen, June. I…"

She put the bowl down and held up both palms. "You really don't need to say anything."

"I would like to, though. I feel like we need to talk and we're both dancing around an elephant in the room, hoping it will go away. But, June, it won't. We have to discuss some things."

"Actually, you're completely wrong. That's the beauty of our little arrangement. You said friends only, nothing serious. So we absolutely don't have to talk about it, now do we?"

She noticed, too late, that her voice had gone up an octave, making it all too clear that she was agitated, that she cared far too much. Of course, the way they'd set things up, caring *at all* was too much.

He closed his eyes and then put down the spoon, crossing his arms over that toned chest she'd loved resting her head against. "I know that's what we said, but I don't think either of us can deny that our boundaries really don't apply anymore."

She tilted her head. "Of course they still do, Ethan." Without them, there was too much freedom. Anything could happen between them if there weren't any limits, and she just wasn't ready for that. Was she?

His brows lowered over stormy eyes. "How can you act like nothing happened between us, June? How can you stand here baking dog cookies like nothing's changed at all?"

"I don't know, Ethan. You tell me. It's probably

the same way you can take me out to dinner and then leave for the night without even kissing me goodbye."

He brushed a hand over his face. "You're right. I know I've been doing it, too." He looked up and met her gaze, his eyes burning with the same things she felt but was too afraid to speak out loud. "But don't you think it's time to cut the crap?"

She was quiet for a moment, knowing that anything that came out of her mouth had the potential to define their relationship in permanent ways.

She stood at a precipice, looking down into a pit, the bottom of which she couldn't see and held both danger and possibility. Here was her chance. Here was a guy who was willing, pushing even, to define what was going on between them, and maybe even to acknowledge that they both wanted more.

An amazing, kindhearted, hardworking, absolutely gorgeous human being obviously cared for her. Wasn't that what she'd always wanted? Wasn't that her dream? Hell, wasn't that every woman's dream?

So why would she even consider cutting their conversation short and throwing it all away, which was exactly what she knew would happen if she refused to engage in that discussion with him?

There was too much at stake. Their hearts were both still too tender from being broken by careless people. Not to mention the fact that, even if she wanted him to stay with her, or better, to go with him, she knew she couldn't have that. Could she?

"I think the crap, as you called it, is the only thing saving both of us from making a huge mistake."

The look he gave her then—that look that said all the things she couldn't articulate—nearly undid all of her resolve. It would have, except that she'd succeeded in her goal of getting stronger, of resisting the temptation to give her whole heart to someone again. As much as it hurt, she wasn't going to open her heart and tell him how she really felt. She sure as hell wasn't going to admit to him, or even to herself, that she was falling for him so fast she couldn't keep the walls from caving in on her.

"June," he said softly, unwinding the strings around her heart as he stepped toward her, "I'm not so sure anymore that it would be a mistake."

She closed her eyes so she wouldn't melt into his.

"So, how can *you* be so sure?" he asked.

She gasped when his cell phone began to buzz in his pocket.

"Aren't you going to get that?"

"No, it can wait. We're having a conversation here."

She turned away. "I think you should take the call."

Even though she was no longer facing him, June could feel the heat from his eyes blazing into her back. She felt sick. She'd been rude and awful, and she wanted to kick herself for it.

He didn't deserve this. Ethan was a great guy, willing to rehash their initial boundaries so that they could talk about their growing feelings and possibly go forward. And what was she doing?

Acting like a complete and total immature idiot.

She groaned and turned around, ready to apologize,

but was met with Ethan's broad back. He was stirring the ingredients again and the only indication that anything had changed was the forceful, angry way he beat at them with the spoon. And, of course, the thick, tense ball of terrible energy that had taken up all of the air in the room.

Her nerve endings were frayed so that June felt everything at double the normal intensity. Standing there, watching the moment slip by, with her heart hanging off a cliff, June wasn't sure if she was relieved or furious when his phone started up again.

His head tilted backward against his upper spine and then he looked back down, hands clenched into fists at his sides as if he fought to gather his composure.

He picked up his phone, voice tight as he greeted the caller.

She didn't know who was on the other end, but she was grateful for the chance the call gave her to pull herself together. Now that she'd elected to forego a conversation that could have changed her path, her entire life, all she could feel was a tight disappointment in the pit of her stomach, the absence of anything good.

She knew instantly that she'd made a severe mistake, and it would cost her if she didn't fix it. The problem was, she didn't know how.

Before Clayton, she'd been an open book, a romantic, a heart-on-her sleeve kind of girl, but he had crushed that out of her when he'd stolen her life savings and skipped town without so much as a text or a note. She'd spent the following months trying to figure out what had happened, how her dreams had seemed so clear, right at the tips of her fingers, only to disappear overnight.

It wasn't the only time her life had changed in such a short amount of time. The other night when she'd made love with Ethan, it had changed again, but this time she didn't feel like curling up in a ball and quitting; this time, it had made her want to grow wings and soar.

But she couldn't tell him, because if she did and he didn't return her feelings, didn't want the same new life with her, where would that leave her? She had nothing left anymore; if she let Ethan have her heart and he broke it, all that would remain would be a shell of a person, and June would rather not become someone she would grow to resent.

She stood, unable to get her limbs to move until Ethan finished his call.

When he turned around, all of her raw emotion was reflected in his eyes.

He fidgeted with the phone and then finally slipped it into his pocket. "I have some good news," he said, and she could see that he was trying to offer her a smile.

She put her hands in her pockets, afraid that if she didn't give them something to do, they might reach out for the man she'd begun to fall hard for. So. Hard.

"Yeah?" she asked, but the word came out more like a choking sound.

"Yeah, um…" He raked a hand through his hair "That was Harry, my brother."

"I remember," she said, folding her hands in front

of her torso, hoping he would understand that she meant she remembered far more about that night than the names of his family members.

"Right." His eyes were dark and narrow as he studied her. "Anyway, he says that Amani is on board and they want to take one of the puppies for Neena, after all."

"Oh," she said, not making any attempt to inject joy into her voice. She certainly didn't feel any, and this new revelation only made that worse. But if it would make him happy, she would lie. Just this once, because she needed to see light return to his face. "That's—" she swallowed over the pain rising in her throat "—that's wonderful. I know they'll be the perfect family for one of the puppies."

But what about the perfect family I want?

"I thought so, too. They love and respect animals and they'll take good care of a puppy." His eyes were tired now and his shoulders sunk as if he felt defeated. "We should go," he said, glancing at his watch. "Isaac will be expecting us soon."

Had that much time passed? She checked the wall clock and got her answer. No, it had not. Ethan probably just wanted to get away from the suffocating room, away from her. She didn't blame him—she wanted away from her, too.

Friends with Fur was bustling with activity when Ethan and June arrived less than an hour later. It was early—dog food and supply vendors and animal rescue organizations were still getting their booths and pens set up—but he couldn't have stayed in that kitchen with June for a single minute longer.

Seeing her struggle to talk to him about whatever it was she was feeling, and not being able to communicate himself, had been the worst form of torture. The sadness in her eyes had made him want to run, to get away from her, because what could possibly be causing it, if not his presence in her life?

When she'd come into his clinic a couple of weeks ago, she'd been like a breath of fresh air, her passion for saving those puppies only a fraction of the kindness that defined June Leavy. From that instant on, he'd wanted nothing more than to get to know her better, to get lost in her sweetness so he could forget about Jessica and his broken heart.

He'd told June that the boundaries he'd set, the "rule" that things wouldn't get too serious, were for both their benefits. But in reality, his doing so had been purely selfish. He saw that clearly now—now, when it was probably too late.

He'd tried to protect his own heart from getting broken again, but he truly had not realized that doing so might be the very thing that would cause her pain. It caused him pain, too. Keeping her at a distance had been a mistake. He realized that now. But if she wouldn't talk to him, wouldn't tell him what was wrong, how could he help her?

He hadn't thought it possible that they would end up wanting more from each other, and now that he knew that to be the case, he had no idea what to do about it.

This had not been in his plan. Their short-term relationship was supposed to be casual, a stop on their respective routes to healing from past heartbreak; instead, falling for her and not being able to do anything about it for fear of hurting her was causing more harm than good.

And still, she was sweet to him, letting him hold her hand as they walked around the open training arena inside Isaac's facility, June having insisted on carrying the crate with the puppies inside. They were getting bigger and would need their own separate crates soon.

For some unknown reason, even though he'd been campaigning to find them homes, the thought of giving them away so soon, especially to separate families, caused his throat to catch.

"Ethan!"

He turned to see Isaac Meyer, his wife, Avery, and Avery's dog, Foggy, headed toward the two of them. Isaac shook his hand and he introduced his friends to June. He couldn't help but smile as he watched June ask to pet Foggy, and Avery, who was always just a bit shy, seemed to take to her instantly.

That was his girl—warm, kind, drawing people to her like bees to honey.

"Are these the puppies you've been telling us about?" Avery asked, crouching down to peer into the crate.

June's eyes brightened and her whole demeanor changed as she regaled her new friend with stories from the past couple of weeks. She'd gotten so attached to the little guys.

And suddenly it hit him—he'd been awful about the puppies. Nonstop, he had talked only about finding them homes, giving them away, thinking it was the right thing to do. And all the while, June had been falling in love with them.

That must have been why she had become so distant the past few days, and why her thoughts had gotten so far away each time he mentioned Neena wanting a pet or bringing them to the adoption expo.

By dragging her there that day, he had, against her will, set in motion events that would break her heart yet again. He hadn't been careful with her feelings the way he so badly wanted to be, and he'd overlooked the fact that the puppies really did in fact belong to June. He didn't have the right to make decisions about them without consulting her, and now he wanted to kick himself for neglecting to put her needs first.

"You know," Isaac said, playing with one of the pups June had released from the crate, "this one could have all the makings of an outstanding service dog."

"Really?" June asked, her voice faltering so subtly that he knew he was the only one who'd caught it. He knew her so well now, and it had become more and more difficult to imagine returning to Colorado to resume his former life without her.

He hadn't realized until that moment how much he loved having her by his side.

How much he loved…her.

And yet, as he wanted to be closer and closer to

her, the thing he'd been encouraging her to do—find homes for their little furry charges—was the very thing pushing her away.

"Yes, really," Isaac continued. "He's got a calm temperament, he's alert and curious but not impulsive and he responds well to treats." Isaac beamed at June, his face full of excitement.

Ethan knew his friend was passionate about training service dogs, especially for victims of combat PTSD, and his father often donated veterinary care to keep costs down for people who needed service animals. Ethan had done the same for the time he'd been running his dad's clinic. He admired Isaac's work, but right now, all he wanted to do was to get June out of there before her kind heart let someone take a puppy, even though she didn't want to give them away.

It was so clear now. All she'd been trying to tell him was that she wanted to keep them herself. It didn't matter that she wasn't in a position to do so at the time; that could be dealt with and he would help her any way he could. All that mattered then was letting her know that he understood what was going on behind her facade of pretending to be okay.

"Isaac and Avery, would you guys mind watching the pups for a minute?"

They shared a glance and then nodded. "Of course, no problem," the two said in unison.

June set down the puppy she'd been holding and watched him carefully.

"June, would you join me for just a minute? There's something I need to talk to you about."

Her eyes narrowed but she did as he asked, taking his hand and following him to the only spot in the arena that wasn't covered in furry bodies or free dog toys and treats. He pulled her to a stop and grabbed both of her hands.

Confusion was etched into her features. "Ethan, what's wrong? Isaac was in the middle of telling me about training the male puppy to be a service dog and I…"

"How do you feel about that, June?" he interrupted. "Tell me the truth."

Her face fell and moisture sprung into her eyes. She quickly wiped away the first tear before it had a chance to fall. "It's just about the last thing I want, Ethan."

He pulled her against his chest, his heart breaking as she cried softly.

"God, June. Why didn't you just tell me that you didn't want to give them away?"

"I don't know," she said, her voice cracking in a way that made him think she wasn't telling the whole truth. "I guess it's just that you were pushing me so hard to do it, and you're the expert when it comes to dogs." She sniffed and pried her chest away from his. "I guess I felt that if you didn't think I'd be a good dog owner, then you were probably right."

"You've got it all wrong, June. If you'd have told me that what's been bothering you this whole time was that you didn't want to give the puppies up, I would have helped you find a way to keep them. I can't believe that's all it was and you kept it from me."

He thought they were having a heart-to-heart, a moment that would fix everything and get them back to normal, whatever that meant. But June was shaking her head.

He'd missed something crucial, but he had no idea what.

"No, Ethan. That's not all it is."

He was genuinely confused, and the way she was looking at him gave the impression that she was still sad and angry with him. But if that wasn't it... "Then what is it?" he asked.

More tears ran down her cheeks, making him feel like a total jerk and an idiot at the same time.

"If you can't see what's been bothering me, Ethan, then me spelling it out for you isn't going to change anything."

With those final words, she stormed off. And he knew she was very, very upset because she didn't take the puppies with her.

He wanted desperately to follow, but something in him caused him to pause. She'd made a comment in passing that morning of the snowball fight, one he hadn't paid much attention to at the time but that now stood out, marring an otherwise glowing, perfect memory.

That was it.

She'd said she needed space, time to heal from what that previous jerk did to her. And more than anything, he did not want to give her reason to lump him in with a guy like that, a guy stupid enough to let her go.

So he vowed to give her a little space, a little time, just like she asked. Maybe she would realize, as he'd begun to, that she wasn't at peace with the idea of their relationship coming to a close.

And after that passed, after her heart healed, nothing would stop him from going after her.

Nothing in the world.

Chapter Twelve

From the parking lot of her apartment building, even with tears still blurring her vision after driving aimlessly for hours, June could see her patio light blazing. The hairs on the back of her neck stood up; she did not recall flipping the switch by her back door before leaving earlier in the day.

She shut her car door and paused to grab pepper spray from her bag before making her way up the stairs to her unit. Not for the first time, but for a new reason, she wished the puppies were with her. They were still small, but their barks were deceptively loud, and lately, the little squirts had begun to put up a fuss if anyone they didn't know got too close to their mom.

Another tear slipped down June's cheek; that was how she thought of the situation. She'd basically adopted them, after all, and she still felt guilty for leaving them behind at the pet fair. Ethan would take care of them, but from the bottom of her toes all the way up to the top of her head, with every cell in her body, she hoped he wouldn't give them away that day.

But she didn't have a chance to think about regrets at the moment, because as she approached her building, June was fairly certain she caught movement on her back porch out of the corner of her eye.

She jammed her key into the lock and got in as quickly as possible, slamming the door behind her. Her back against it, she peered into her living room and down the hallway, the only light coming from a lamp on her bedside table.

"Hello?" she called, but there was no answer.

She looked out from the sliding glass door to try to see if there was someone on the patio, but the light didn't reach too far and there were shadows everywhere, so she settled for checking the lock and the dead bolt. Setting her purse on the couch, June flipped on a single lamp, checking the closets and in every potential hiding area she could think of.

But as soon as she returned to the living room and plopped down on the couch, she heard a soft knock, and it wasn't coming from the front door.

As icicles formed along her spine, she picked up the pepper spray and the golf club she kept under the couch and, one in each hand, headed over to the sliding door.

When she pressed her nose against the glass to

better see out, a face stared back at her and a blood-curdling scream erupted from her throat before she recognized who it was.

"Clayton!" she shouted, anger coursing through her veins to replace fear. Her first instinct was to call the police, but as her pulse calmed and her breathing slowed, June reminded herself that, for all his faults, he'd never been a violent man.

Clayton Miller held up his hands and turned around, showing her that he posed no threat. Convinced he didn't intend to hurt her, she dropped the golf club and unlocked the door, sliding the pepper spray into her pocket, just in case.

Hell, she thought, *I might use it just because.*

When she slid the door open, he walked slowly past her into the living room. He still stood nearly eye level with her, of course, but he'd lost weight and his thinner form didn't suit him. There were dark circles under his eyes when he looked at her, as though he hadn't slept well in weeks.

She crossed her arms over her chest, suddenly feeling a chill that had nothing to do with the January temperature. "Clayton, what in the hell were you doing on my porch?"

He cringed. "I needed to see you and my key didn't work in the lock, so I figured I'd just wait out there until you came home. Where were you, June? I've been here for hours."

She choked out a laugh, feeling sick to her stomach. "Of course your key didn't work. I had the locks changed. And after all you've done to me, your audacity continues to amaze me, Clayton. I shouldn't have to tell you this, but you don't get to ask questions like that anymore."

He looked down at his sneakers. "You're right. I… I'm sorry."

Her eyebrows rose in genuine surprise. "Well, that's the first I've heard those words since you walked out on me and took every dime I'd saved up."

"I know, June, and there's a lot I need to apologize for. I'd like to do that if you'll give me a chance."

Up until she'd found him standing on her porch, looking like something a cat had dragged up, there were a lot of things June would have wanted to say if Clayton Miller ever graced her with his presence again, and even more she'd have wanted to throw in his face. But seeing him there, she realized she no longer cared what reasons—excuses, really—he would give for leaving her and everything else he'd done.

She could finally say, with absolute certainty, that she gave less than a damn.

"I don't have anything to say to you, Clayton, and to be frank, there's nothing you can say to me that will change anything. So, if it's all the same to you, I'd like for you to get the hell out of my life for the last time."

This time, it was her choice, and she wanted him gone.

He held up a hand and she saw that his eyes were closed. "That's fine, June. I will get out of here like you asked, but there's something I wanted to give you first, if you'll let me stay just a second longer."

As he pulled an envelope from his back pocket, she tilted her chin up so she could stare down at him as though she were ten feet tall. "What's that?" she asked, not allowing her hopes to climb, not wanting to let herself wish it was what she thought it might be.

"It's…it's the money I took from you."

Her jaw dropped and she quickly pulled it closed.

"All of it," he said, holding out the paper. She stopped herself from snatching it away, opting to take it slowly instead.

"It doesn't feel like much."

"It's a check," he said. "It's not everything I took. Some of it I… I gambled away. I still owe you the rest and I plan to make good on it as soon as I can."

June rolled her eyes.

At least he'd had the courtesy to look guilty. Perhaps there was room for growth in a person as twisted as Clayton.

"Come on now, June, don't do that. It'll clear, I swear. Would I come all the way down here and give you this, knowing it wouldn't?"

"I honestly don't know, Clayton. I thought I knew you once, but then you stole everything I had and left me alone to pick up the pieces, so I really can't answer that question."

She shoved the check—if that was really what it was; she still didn't trust a word the man said—into her pocket and pointed at the door.

He gave a sad nod and turned to go.

She'd given him everything once, and he'd smashed it all, and she'd believed that if she ever saw him again, all of the rage she had felt for him would return. But standing there in the tiny living room of the only place she could afford—a place she paid for every month with hard-earned, honest money she made herself—June felt nothing but pride. Pride in herself, for putting her life back together, even if it wasn't much yet, for picking herself up off the floor and drying her tears to go to work the day after Clayton abandoned her, for telling him to hit the road when she had the chance.

She hugged herself as another chill spread through her body.

Clayton stopped, his hand on the door, and turned back. She only saw the side of his face.

"What I did was wrong, June, and you're right that it doesn't matter why. Hell, there are times when I don't even know why I did it, because some days I miss you like crazy. I know I got my own garbage to sort out, but I do want you to know that I'm sorry. I'm sorry I hurt you. If I had it to do over, I'd do things different."

With that, he opened the door. She'd thought that would be the last of him, but a second later, he was backing into her apartment as though held at gunpoint.

As he passed through the door, she saw Ethan on the other side of Clayton, shoving the man back into her living room.

"Ethan," she cried. "What are you doing?" She rushed over to where the two men stood.

Ethan's fists were curled and there was murder in his eyes. "June, who the hell is this man and why is he bothering you?"

Clayton flinched but didn't respond.

She walked over to Ethan's side and put a hand on his forearm. "It's okay. I've got this handled and you can relax."

He met her eyes. "You sure, June?" He turned to face her, jaw trembling. "I shouldn't have let you go earlier today. I should have fought for you." He tipped his chin in Clayton's direction. "I'm prepared to do that now. Just say the word."

An unexpected little flip happened in her stomach and she had to fold her lips together to keep from grinning. "I mean it, Ethan," she said, her heart going soft with tenderness toward him. "I'm fine and everything's okay. I was just telling Clayton to go on and get out."

Clayton nodded, looking relieved that he'd avoided getting punched in the face, pepper sprayed or whacked in the noggin with a golf club. Finally, the man walked out her front door, taking their dark past with him.

When June turned back around to face Ethan, even though they still had a lot to discuss, a part of her knew there would be mostly light from then on.

She walked to the door and closed it, hard, not taking her eyes off the man she loved.

"June, I have so much I want to tell you. So much I understand now that I didn't before."

"I do, too, Ethan. Oh, I shouldn't have left you earlier. Even though I was hurting, it wasn't the right thing to do, and I'm sorry."

"No, I'm the one who needs to apologize." He took both of her hands in his and led her to the couch. Recalling what had happened the last time they'd ended up there together, June's cheeks warmed and she took a deep breath. There would be time to think of that later; right then, she needed to focus on the conversation she should have had with him ages ago—the one they'd both feared, until that moment when all their walls had finally come crashing down.

For her, at least, all that remained was an exposed but ready heart, and she hoped he would offer her the same.

When they were seated, she took her time before speaking.

Ethan looked handsome, as always, but there was a little vulnerability in him just then, wearing the same hooded sweatshirt he'd put on for the pet adoption event earlier that day, his hair a little mussed, that five-o'-clock shadow she loved so much making an appearance. She longed to touch him, to reach out and run her fingers along his jaw, but there would be time for that later, she hoped.

His eyes were dark in the dim light coming from her bedroom—she still hadn't switched on any additional light, and doing so then could potentially break the spell they were under. It was one of those moments in life when she knew everything was about to change, for better or worse, and it felt as if even the quietest breath had the potential to destroy it all.

"Listen, June, I know we have a lot to say to each other, and I'd love to start if you're ready."

She offered him a tender smile, holding back from reaching out to wrap her hands in his. "No," she said, her voice firm. "Let me."

He started to open his mouth but thought better of it when he saw the determination in her expression.

"That guy that just left?" she asked, pointing a thumb in the direction of her front door.

Ethan nodded.

"That was Clayton Miller." She drew in a long breath and slowly released it. "I was in love with him for six months, so much so that I thought he would be in my life forever. We never actually talked about it, which I see now was probably a red flag, but I just assumed we would get married someday. Every moment that we weren't working, we spent together, and we both shared a dream of owning a business together."

She shook her head. "I was stupid to believe him—I see that now—but he convinced me that he'd found the perfect building for the bakery I wanted so badly, and I trusted him. I went there with him, once, to an empty store in a cute little strip mall in Dallas, and fell in love with the place."

Ethan nodded, his eyes narrowing as he followed along.

"Because I worked so much and Clay—Clayton—

had a more flexible schedule, he convinced me to transfer all of my money into his bank account so that he could make an offer one afternoon. That morning, he kissed me goodbye like always."

Ethan cringed.

"And I didn't see him again until today." Even after all that time, admitting such a thing was still embarrassing.

"Did you go to the police?" Ethan asked.

"I did, but because I'd willingly given Clayton the money and I wasn't under duress or threatened or anything at the time, there wasn't much they could do. They tried to track him down for a little while, mostly as a favor to me, I think, since this is a small town and everybody knows most of the force, but after a bit, they let it go."

She wrung her hands. "I tried to do the same, but honestly, until you came along, I was having a hard time believing that I'd ever get over that pain of being abandoned."

Ethan reached out and took her hands. "I'm so sorry he did that to you, June."

She shook her head. "And the worst part is, he made me stop trusting myself. It's a miracle I didn't extend that to everyone around me, but thankfully I didn't. I've got a lot of good people in my life that I would have pushed away if I'd have done that. But no, it was just me."

"What do you mean?" he asked, his voice gentle.

"Well, I figured that if I was that stupid once, if I trusted someone like that—someone who took everything I had without breaking a sweat—then I should never let myself get close to a man again."

"It wasn't your fault, June." The words were true, she knew, but still so hard to digest.

"So when you came along, even though I started to fall for you from pretty much the moment we met, I didn't want to let myself get too close. You seemed wonderful, but if I made such a mistake before, who was I to judge?"

"Do you still feel that way about me?"

"Of course not, Ethan," she said, willing her words to convey the extent of what was in her heart. "You have to see that."

"I do. I do see that, June, and I'm so sorry that I didn't go after you today. I'm so very sorry if I made you think I didn't care that you ran off."

"Ethan, I know you care. I can see that, even though I know you didn't really want to from the beginning."

"June, please let me explain…"

She held up a hand, then placed it back over his. "Of course, but let me finish, okay?"

He nodded, his brown eyes so warm.

"I want you to understand what happened today, when I left the pet event, I mean."

"Absolutely," he said. "I mean, I think I have some idea now, but I want to hear your story."

"Those puppies, Ethan—they mean more to me than I think you realize."

He looked like he wanted to say something but he kindly let her go on without interrupting.

"I think I've come to see them as a sort of… symbol…for lack of a more accurate word. They've come to represent some things for me that I hope make sense. If it doesn't, and you think I'm crazy, you're welcome to walk right back out that door."

"June." His voice was rigid, final. "If you'll allow it, I will never walk out that door without you knowing I'll be back. So, I'd love to hear what you're going to say, but know this—I am not that man that left here a few minutes ago. I am not him. I will never treat you like he did. I will never do what he did to you."

Ethan swallowed, his jaw ticking in that nervous way.

What he'd confessed certainly made it hard for her to continue, but it also made her heart swell with joy.

"I definitely want to hear more of that," she said, giggling, which made him laugh, too. "But what I was saying is that, the puppies are sort of like this representation of…well…us. Look, I know it's weird, but they brought you into my life, and even though we got to know each other apart from them, I always had this sort of fear that if they went away from me, well…you would, too. What I mean to say, or ask, really, is…would you still be here if it wasn't for them?"

She wanted to think she knew the answer—Lord knew she did—but at the back of her mind there was still an inkling of fear that, contrary to what Ethan said, he might just walk out that door and not come back. She hated that fear, and recognized it for what it was—Clayton's last hold on her—the last little piece of her trust he'd stolen. No apology could return it to its rightful place, she knew, but giving her heart to Ethan, letting him teach her to trust again, would be a pretty good place to begin.

Ethan leaned forward and took her face in his hands. "Absolutely, I would still be here, June. Absolutely. I *am* still here, and I'm not going anywhere if you don't want me to."

"Oh, Ethan, I'm so glad to hear that."

"Jessica broke my heart, too, not in the same way as yours but close enough. She abandoned me in a different way."

"Do you mind if I ask how?" June whispered.

"No, not at all. I want to tell you everything. After we'd been together for a while, I found out that she was engaged and had been cheating on her fiancé with me. I know it's not the same, but it hurt so much, and I really thought I'd never be able to trust a woman ever again. When I found out she'd been lying to me the whole time, that I'd been played like a damn fool, well, I decided then and there that I was done giving my heart away."

June nodded, her heart aching for him, but glad he'd felt close enough to her to share what had happened to him. Everything made more sense in light of that knowledge.

"So when I met you—" he smiled "—when you came crashing into my father's clinic with those two puppies under your coat, I was instantly attracted to you, and it only grew from there. I thought that if I put boundaries around our relationship, I could keep that attraction from becoming something more, but I was powerless from the beginning. I see that now, and my only regret is ever trying to keep you out."

He squeezed her hands, kissing her cheek before continuing. "I should never have compared you to Jessica in my heart, June." He shook his head. "You're nothing like her, in all the best ways possible. You are kind, sweet, openhearted and brave—so very brave—to have put your life back together after that asshole took everything from you. I can't even begin to tell you how much I admire your courage. I also should never have tried to keep from letting you in, because ever since I did, I've been happier and a better man than ever before."

His eyes bore into hers as her own moistened with tears of joy. He was saying everything she'd wanted to hear since she'd met him, and it was all she needed it to be.

"I love you, June. I love you with everything that I am."

"Oh, Ethan," she said through tears, "I love you, too. More than anything. And, just as importantly, I trust you one hundred percent, with my whole heart."

He grabbed her hands then and pulled her up from the couch and straight into his arms, swirling her around like a movie heroine. But it was better than a movie because Ethan was real. By being trustworthy, honest and willing to open his heart to her after having it broken so badly, Ethan Singh was all the hero she could ask for.

Finally, he set her back down and kissed her long

and hard, his lips conveying all the passion that had built up between them, stronger and fiercer than the first time they made love.

"One more thing, June."

"Yes?"

He looked down at her with twinkling eyes. "I'd like for you to give the puppies names. You can call them whatever you like, and they'll be ours to keep."

Her heart nearly burst. "I was so afraid you'd given them away at the adoption event… Wait, what about Neena?" June's hands flew to her mouth. "I love those puppies, and I feel like they're my babies, but I'm not going to be the kind of woman who takes a puppy from a child who's been promised one."

Ethan looked at her with enough warmth to heat her entire apartment building, plus the whole block. "That's something I was going to tell you. I got a call from Harry earlier today and he gave me some news."

June clenched her hands until her nails dug into her palms.

"It turns out Neena is severely allergic to dogs and we just had no idea." Ethan let out a deep laugh.

"Oh, my gosh," June gasped. "How awful!"

"No, no, sweetheart. It'll be fine. Harry and Amani are going to get her a rabbit instead."

Now it was June's turn to laugh. "So I really get to keep the puppies, then?"

He nodded, brushing a finger along her cheek. "You really do. And I'm sorry I was such a jerk. I was so focused on trying to figure out how to keep myself from loving you that I completely missed the fact that you'd fallen in love with those little fur balls. And I have to admit—I have, too."

She wrapped her arms around his neck and held him close for as long as she could stand. When she let go, he pressed his lips against hers, igniting a spark in her belly that she knew could only be quelled by spending the rest of her life with him.

"Well," he said, pulling his breathless mouth from hers. "You know what you have to do now."

"What?" she asked between the kisses she was busy dotting along his deliciously-scented neck. "Take you back to my bedroom and have my way with you?"

"Obviously that, yes," he growled, the low, throaty sound sending sparks to her groin. "But first, something else."

"What?"

"You have to name the puppies."

June threw her head back and laughed, all the tension and pain from the past flowing out of her. "What should I name them?" she asked.

"I can't tell you that," he said. "I was the idiot trying for so long to get you to give them away. They're ours now, but you're the one who gets to decide what we'll call them."

She bit her lip, looking up at the ceiling as she considered all of the possibilities.

"It's so hard," she said, grinning. "Naming one puppy would be difficult enough, but two?" She tossed up her hands. "That's going to take a while."

He looked down into her eyes, his own reflecting all of the joy that threatened to burst out of her. "That's absolutely fine, June. Take as long as you need."

He kissed her.

"We have all the time in the world."

Epilogue

One year later...

The weather for their wedding could not have been more different than the season in which Ethan and June had met.

There wasn't a snowflake in sight as June walked down the aisle toward Ethan, her smile shining brighter than the July sun. He didn't even try to contain the grin that spread over his mouth as he watched her draw nearer, going a little too fast—adorable—as though she could not wait to start their life together.

He could not have agreed more. Their hearts were absolutely on the same page.

She joined him underneath the archway her bridesmaids had covered in her favorite lilies, and he took her hands in his, joining them together forever as they exchanged vows.

The next hours whizzed by in a blur as they were congratulated by one family member after another. Even though the official ceremony was that day, the wedding had lasted far longer in his father's Indian tradition.

Ethan had enjoyed every moment, his heart alive and full to bursting, surrounded by family, friends, their two growing puppies, Salt and Pepper, and the most wonderful woman in the world, whose beauty in a sari was beyond all imagination.

But a part of him had to admit that he'd be relieved when it was all over and he could take his bride home.

They'd been discussing their next move for months, Ethan having accepted a new position as department head at a university in Montana. Although he hadn't pressured her, June had jumped at the chance to join him, sad to say goodbye to her hometown and the people that loved her there, but excited about the new chapter they planned to start together.

She still carried a dream of opening a bakery of her own, but she'd been willing to put that on the back burner so that she could be with him in his new state, which made the surprise he had for her that day all the more special. June wasn't expecting it at all, and he couldn't wait to tell her the news.

Finally, after they'd eaten dinner and had a moment of quiet to themselves amid the storm of attention, he managed to pull his new wife aside. The light in her eyes was incredible as she looked up at him, glowing even beyond their normal brightness.

"You look beautiful, Mrs. Singh," he said, taking her hand and leading her out to the gazebo in his parents' backyard. Fairy lights—numbering in the thousands, he was certain—had been strung up for the occasion and twinkled like June's eyes.

He pulled her close against his chest and held her there as they swayed back and forth in a slow dance. They had done the classic first dance as husband and wife, but that had been in front of everyone. This special moment, he wanted to share only with her.

"June, I will never be able to properly thank you for agreeing to be my wife."

She gazed up at him for a second and then tucked her face back into his chest. She felt so right, there against his heart, and he vowed, as he had hundreds of times before, to always keep her safe and, to the very best of his ability, as happy as she made him— though he wasn't sure such a thing was possible.

"You've made me the happiest man alive, my June, and thanks to you, I always will be." He felt her lips curve into a smile. "And you've already shown me more support than I've ever had the right to ask for."

She raised her head as they continued dancing. "What do you mean?"

"Everything," he said. "But right now I'm talking about your agreeing to come with me to Montana."

"Of course," she said. "But why wouldn't I, Ethan?" Her pretty ruby lips parted in a grin. "If that's where you're going, and that job will make you happy, then there's nowhere else in the world I would rather be."

"And I'm so thankful for that, June."

They moved slowly to the music as he enjoyed the warm night air, the stars sparkling above and the feel of a beautiful, happy woman against his body.

His woman, *forever.*

The joy he felt at that knowledge was almost too much to keep inside, so he twirled her around and around until she laughed for him, the sound of her voice as refreshing as a cool spring on a hot day.

"There's something else I want to share with you, though, Mrs. Singh."

Her nose crinkled adorably as she grinned at the sound of her new name.

"You like that, do you?"

"I do," she said, wrapping her arms around his waist. "Very much."

"Good, because I can't wait to say it to you when we're really alone."

She swatted him, then, moving her arms to his neck, pulled herself up so she could kiss him.

It was nearly impossible not to be aroused by the feel of her warm body against his. She was so beautiful in the ivory dress she'd chosen, the heart-shaped neckline showing off her gorgeous curves.

"I can't wait to get this incredible dress off you," he said. "But there's something else I wanted to tell you."

She stopped dancing and opened her eyes; they were like emerald gems when she glanced up at him. "What is it, my love?"

"June, I know we've been talking about you opening up a bakery someday, somewhere near my work and the home we're building."

"Yes?" Her expression was a mixture of apprehension and excitement.

"Well, I hope you won't be upset with me, but I've sort of taken the liberty of…buying you a bakery."

She jumped back, her arms flailing to her sides. "Ethan! Are you serious?"

"Completely. And, June, it's truly amazing. Ready for operation, stainless-steel, top-of-the-line appliances, the works."

Her hands flew to her mouth. "Oh, Ethan."

She threw her body into his torso and squeezed his waist. "Thank you so, so much. I've wanted this for so long."

Unable to contain his joy at her pleasure, Ethan pulled his cell phone from the back pocket of his tuxedo pants. "Here," he said, sliding a thumb over the screen to unlock the phone. "I've got pictures for you, and specs, and everything else."

She thumbed through the photos, making approving noises at each one. He'd spent ages looking for places online, calling folks in the area to see if they thought it was a good place for the kind of business his wife wanted to run. Everyone he'd spoken to had been ecstatic about the idea of a new bakery coming to their area.

And now he had confirmation that June was happy with his choice.

It wasn't possible for the day to get any better; he would have bet money on that.

"So, you like it?" he asked, needing her to put into words what he could already see on her face.

"Like it? Ethan, it's the best gift anyone's ever given me, with the one exception of this." She held up her wedding ring, tilting it so that its angles caught the light.

He'd chosen an ample round emerald circled by seed diamonds because it reminded him of her lovely eyes.

"I'm so thankful, and so happy, Ethan, but I do have one question."

"Go for it."

Her eyebrows knit. "Why did you do this, when you know I got the money back from Clayton and it's more than enough to buy a bakery?"

He'd thought long and hard about the answer to that question well before she'd asked it. He knew her money was carmarked for a bakery, and he'd taken a risk in buying the place himself, aware that she might be disappointed she hadn't done it completely on her own.

But that was just it. She wasn't on her own anymore, and he wanted her to know that without a doubt.

"I know you could have bought the bakery yourself, June, and I hope you're not angry with me for doing it as a surprise. But the thing is —I wanted you to know that I'm all in, one thousand percent. Buying that place for you, in the town we're going to call home together, was the best way I knew to show you how committed I am to this marriage."

"Oh, Ethan, how could I be angry? It's the most

wonderful thing anyone's ever done for me and I am over the moon about it."

"I thought it would be a symbol of how much I love you. Your dream was stolen before, and I wanted to give it back. I wanted you to know that you can trust me to love you well." He grabbed her hands. "Do you trust in me, June?"

"With all my heart, Ethan. With all of my heart."

With that, he swirled her around the dance floor once more.

When he set her back down, though, June looked up at him, a mischievous grin on her lips. "I have a little surprise for you, too, Ethan."

He held her out at arm's length and caught the split second her eyes flickered to her midsection.

"You're not…"

June nodded, biting her lip. "I am."

"I'm going to be a father?"

"You are," she said, bursting into tears and laughter all at once.

As he lifted her into his arms to carry her off into their future, Ethan realized he'd been wrong about one thing that night—it definitely could get better.

In fact, now that they had the promise of everything they'd wanted in a life together—it was the very best.

* * * * *

THE PUPPY
PROPOSAL

KATIE MEYER

Dedicated to:

My parents for giving me a love of books,
and my husband for telling me to write
my own already.

All the friends that supported me, especially
Jilda, Rebecca, Elizabeth, the ladies of
The Well Trained Mind, and the incredible
women of Hearts on Paper.

All the wonderful veterinary professionals
I've worked with, especially Mary C. Fondren,
DVM who supported me in countless ways
over the years.

And of course, my agent Jill and the wonderful
editorial team at Mills & Boon,
who took a chance on me.

Chapter One

He'd almost missed it. Had the setting sun been just a bit lower, the light a bit dimmer, he would have missed it, *it* being the most pathetic-looking animal he had ever seen. The dog—if that was the right word for the wet, filth-encrusted beast limping along the side of the road—was obviously in trouble. There wasn't much traffic right now on this stretch of highway, but the Paradise Isle Bridge was just ahead, or so said the tinny voice of his rental car's GPS. Crossing a highway bridge on foot, or paw for that matter, seemed a dangerous proposition. Besides, it was limping.

But limping or not, it wasn't his dog. Wasn't his problem. He was in a suit. In a rental car. On vacation—well, sort of a vacation. A working vacation. So this grimy creature was definitely not his problem.

Surely it knew the way home or would be picked up

by someone that actually lived around here. Not that he
was exactly sure where here was, GPS or no. He hadn't
passed a single town in over an hour, and the only brief
glimpse of humanity had been a roadside stand selling
gator jerky and boiled peanuts twenty miles back.

Nic Caruso tightened his grip on the steering wheel
as he approached and then passed, telling himself the
dog would be fine. But his gaze kept returning to the
rearview mirror, where he watched the muddy stray as it
slowly hobbled east. Then saw it flinch as a wave of dirty
water thrown by a speeding car drenched it yet again.

"Damn it!"

Nic swung the small SUV to the shoulder, slammed
to a stop and quickly located the emergency flashers on
the unfamiliar dash. It might not be his problem or his
responsibility, but he couldn't bring himself to just leave
the dog there. Resigned, he undid his already loosened
tie, carefully laying it on the suit jacket occupying the
passenger's seat.

"Here, boy! Come here now." He used his most au-
thoritative voice, the one that he relied on in boardrooms
across the globe.

Nothing.

The darned dog just kept going. So much for doing
this the easy way. Nic opened the passenger's door again
and retrieved his tie. A quick slipknot and he had an impromptu leash. Great. Somehow, he didn't think Her-
mès would approve.

"Easy, boy. That's it. Eaaasy…" Nic inched his way
across the muddy roadside toward the now cowering
dog, careful not to spook him any closer to the highway.

A furry ear cocked in interest. The softer approach
seemed to be working.

"Good boy. Come on, that's a good boy. How about I give you a ride wherever you're going, okay?"

A small tail wag was quickly followed by a cautious step forward. Hoping to appear less threatening, Nic crouched down, putting himself at eye level with the cautious canine. Brown eyes watched him warily, but the dog did keep moving in the right direction.

Only a foot away, cars sped by, but Nic kept his focus on the muddy beast in front of him, willing him to co-operate. Only a little bit farther and...

"Gotcha!"

Nic slid the improvised leash over the dog and held tight, just in case he bolted, but the bedraggled beast seemed to have lost his earlier apprehension. A happy, wriggling bundle, he licked and yipped in gratitude. The frenetic thank-you dance gave Nic an up-close study of what appeared to be a border collie—admittedly just a best guess with all the grime matting down his fur. He was a good size, maybe fifty pounds, but from the look of the large paws, he wasn't done growing yet.

"So what do we do now? Any ideas?"

An enthusiastic face-licking was hardly an appro-priate answer.

Nic stood and stretched while he thought of what to do. A week in the heart of Orlando on business, night-mare traffic on I-4, miles of desolate highway and now a muddy dog. When exactly had he completely lost con-trol of his life? The only thing he could think to do was to keep heading for the island, and hope there was a shelter or veterinary hospital still open. Resolved, he started walking the dog along the shoulder of the road, only to be stopped by a soft whimper. Crap. Crouching again, he gathered the grubby canine to his chest and lifted him up. Carrying him to the car, Nic tried to ignore the ooze seeping through his shirt.

"Up you go." Nic held the door open with one hand, and the makeshift leash with the other. No more encouragement was needed; the dog bounded into the rear seat easily. Hopefully, that meant he wasn't badly injured.

Rounding the car, Nic brushed the worst of the dirt and fur off his clothes before sitting behind the wheel. He checked his mirrors and pulled carefully back onto the highway, then rolled down his windows as soon as he was up to speed, hoping to keep the wet-dog smell from permeating the upholstery. He doubted rental insurance covered that particular contingency.

That was a mistake.

Tempted by the open window, the dog nimbly hopped into the front seat and shoved his muzzle into the rushing air. Nic cast a grin at the happy animal's expression—then cursed when he saw the now ruined suit jacket under his muddy paws.

Nic mumbled uncharitable remarks about the pup's parentage until the top of the Paradise Isle Bridge, where he was seduced into silence. From the apex of its span, he could see fishing boats bobbing among the diamond topped crests of the Intracoastal, then the lush green of the island, and beyond that the Atlantic Ocean, where pink-and-purple clouds flamed on the horizon, caught in the last rays of the setting sun. In his rearview mirror the atmospheric show continued, a kaleidoscope of colors, constantly shifting as the orange orb of the sun slipped further toward the horizon. The sight of all that sea and sky managed to melt the last of his workday tension, leaving him feeling, for the first time in a long time, almost free. Or he would be, once he figured out what to do with the dog.

* * *

"Yes, Mrs. Ellington, I can see how that would be upsetting." Veterinary technician Jillian Everett rubbed her temples with one hand while cradling the oversize phone receiver in the other. "But remember, Tinker Bell is only nine weeks old. It's perfectly normal for her to not be housebroken yet… Oh. Well, no, I'm afraid I don't know of any products that will get that kind of stain out of a leather handbag."

A loud snort of laughter betrayed Dr. Cassie Marshall's presence behind her.

"Yes, I agree, replacing it probably is the best idea. But, I really think you should consider waiting until Tinker Bell is older before carrying her in your purse for so long. When she's a bit bigger, she'll be better able to control where she, uh, leaves her presents. In the meantime, just stick to the feeding and training guidelines we sent home and I think she'll be fine. If you have any other questions, I'm sure Dr. Marshall would be happy to answer them at your appointment next week." Jillian mouthed a "gotcha" at Cassie, who was holding up her hands in a "not me" gesture.

"Okay, Mrs. Ellington, we'll see you next week. Have a good night and kiss little Tinker Bell for us. Bye." Jillian hung up and glared at Cassie. "You set me up! You knew what that call was about, didn't you? Why is she calling the veterinary hospital for a poopy purse, anyway? Don't those fancy dog purse things have liners for this sort of situation? Or an emergency number to call?" Shaking her head at the absurdity of the situation, she made a notation in the file and stood to put it in the appropriate place.

"I didn't set you up…exactly. After all, helping with the call tonight was your idea. But yes, Mollie may have hinted at the situation before she left, and I may have made sure that particular chart ended up with the ones you so generously took off my hands." She smiled. "Perk of being the boss, sorry."

Jillian didn't think Cassie's wide grin looked the least bit contrite. But she *was* a great boss, and Jillian *had* volunteered. Cassie had a young daughter to get home to, so when Jillian saw the big stack of files requiring follow-up phone calls, she had offered to take the majority of them. She planned to give Mollie, the receptionist at Paradise Animal Clinic, a piece of her mind tomorrow for that final absurd call, but really, it wasn't as if she had anywhere else to be. No one was waiting at home for her tonight. Or any night. Most of the time, the animal clinic was more of a home to her than her tiny apartment was.

She didn't have any family. Both of her parents had been killed in a car accident, and she'd been too young to really remember them. The last in a long line of her foster families had lived on Paradise Isle, and she had found a sense of belonging here that had kept her on the island long after she'd aged out of the system. She had never been adopted, but the people of Paradise Isle had become a kind of surrogate family. Most of the time, that was enough. But on nights like tonight, when she had nothing better to do than stay late and file charts, she couldn't help but daydream about someday having a real family to go home to.

"I'll lock up on my way out. See you in the morning," Cassie called from halfway out the door, juggling her keys, briefcase and a stack of veterinary trade magazines. She might be leaving the office, but Jillian knew she'd spend a few more hours working after her daughter, Emma, was asleep. Cassie was a single mom, and had taken over the clinic from her father, after he was permanently injured in a car accident a few years ago. Now her parents watched Emma during the day, doting on their only granddaughter, freeing Cassie to focus on the veterinary hospital. It was an arrangement born of necessity, but it worked because of their strong love for each other, something Jillian couldn't help but envy.

As she filed, the only sounds were the bubbling of the fish tank and the hiss of an overworked air conditioner fighting the Florida heat. A full day of barking dogs, hissing cats and chatty clients had her appreciating the temporary quiet, only for it to be broken minutes later by a banging at the front door. For a second she considered staying out of sight, behind the tall wall of files. People often stopped by after hours to try to pick up last-minute items, and she really didn't want to deal with that tonight. But, as always, her sense of duty won out.

Pulling her unruly black curls into a mostly serviceable ponytail, she forced a smile on her face, ready to serve whatever tardy client was making such a ruckus. Approaching the heavily tinted glass front door, she could make out, dimly, a very large man holding what appeared to be a squirming dog. Medical instincts kicked in at the sight of the would-be patient, spurring her to run the last few steps to unlock and open the door. Standing behind it was a seemingly solid wall of muscular man. Ignoring him, and her suddenly rapid heartbeat, she focused instead on the very familiar-looking dog.

"Oh, no, is that Murphy? What happened? Is he hurt?" Her voice came out more forcefully than she'd intended, but the shock of seeing her favorite patient being carried in by a stranger had her protective instincts kicking into high gear. She tried to assess the dog, but the man holding him was so tall it was hard to get a good look.

"I have no idea who or what a Murphy is, but I found this mongrel on the side of the highway as I was driving into town." He shifted the dog, holding him away from what had once been a white dress shirt. "I don't think he's hurt too badly, but he definitely needs a bath."

Jillian relaxed a bit, her mouth twitching up despite her worry. The guy, whoever he was, made quite a picture holding the pathetic dog in his arms. He was tall, over six feet, dark hair and eyes, with broad shoulders that filled out his business clothes well. The bristly stubble starting to show only added to his masculine aura. That he was carrying the nearly fully grown dog without visible signs of strain impressed her. That he had stopped to rescue the dog at all impressed her even more.

"So…are you going to help him?" the man asked, eyebrows raised. He probably wondered why she was just standing there, staring up at him like a fool.

"Oh, um, yes. Let me take a look, see if I need to call the vet back in. Just bring him in here." Jillian snapped back into work mode, chiding herself for ogling when there was an animal that needed help. Motioning him into an exam room, she told herself she was a professional. And professionals were not supposed to check out the client's rear end, no matter how nice it was.

Chapter Two

Nic carried the dog into the small, spotlessly clean room, gently lowering him onto the slick exam table. Immediately the troublemaker tried to jump off into Jillian's arms. "Oh, no you don't. Stay," he said, grabbing the squirming dog before he could take flight.

"Good reflexes," she commented, smiling that pretty smile again.

"Years of wrestling with my younger brother," he answered. "You said you might need to call the vet. I thought you were the vet." Confused, he pointedly looked at her scrubs. Scrubs that did nothing to hide her feminine curves.

"Me? No, I'm the veterinary technician, Jillian Everett," she corrected. "Cassie—I mean, Dr. Marshall— already left. But let me take a look, and then I'll give her a call if there's anything wrong." She opened a drawer below the gleaming examining table and removed a small scanning device. "But first, let's see who this furry guy is. I'm pretty positive it's Murphy, Mrs. Rosenberg's border collie, but a microchip would tell us for sure. Hopefully we'll luck out, and the scanner will be able to find one."

Upon hearing his name, the dog whimpered, wriggling in delight.

"I think you just got your answer as to who he is. And speaking of names, I'm Nic."

"You're probably right, Nic, but let's do this by the book, just in case." She held down a button and ran the scanner up and down the dog's neck, stroking his black-and-white fur with her other hand. Her affection for the dog was obvious. When the machine beeped, she wrote down a number that had popped up on the screen. "I've got Murphy's chip number recorded in his file. Let me get it and I'll be right back."

Left alone with the dog, Nic found himself hoping the veterinary tech would come back soon. He liked her smile, and the way her dark curls kept falling across her face. Liked the gentle way she stroked the dog without seeming to notice she was doing it. He wondered if those hands felt as soft as they looked. But mostly, he liked that she was focused on the dog, not him. Fawning women had become a huge turnoff.

"It's definitely Murphy," she said, striding back into the room. Murphy squirmed in glee, as if happy to be recognized. "All right, boy, I know you're happy to see me. I'm happy to see you, too. But I've got to make sure you're not hurt, okay, handsome?" She ran her hands along the dog's back and along his sides, feeling through the thick coat. "Murphy's a favorite of mine, smarter than most dogs, but as likely to get into trouble as his name implies."

"His name?" Nic looked down at the dog in his arms, confused.

"Murphy. As in Murphy's Law?" She picked up the front leg and continued to check him over for any obvious open wounds or signs of pain.

"Ah, I take it this isn't his first misadventure, then?" Nic could relate to that. He'd had his own stretch of mishaps growing up.

"Oh, no, Murphy makes trouble his hobby. It's really not his fault—he's just a smart, active dog without enough to keep him busy. Border collies are herding dogs—they need a job to do, some way to channel their energy. Mrs. Rosenberg is very nice, but she's in her seventies and just not up to giving him the kind of exercise and training he needs. So our boy here finds his own exercise. He's broken out of her apartment a few times before, but I've never known him to make it all the way over the bridge. That's quite a hike, even for an athletic dog like Murphy."

Annoyed by the owner's lack of forethought, he asked, "If she can't keep up with him, why did she get him in the first place?" His whole life was nothing but responsibilities; the idea of someone being so irresponsible, even with a pet, rankled him.

"She didn't, not exactly. Her son, who wouldn't know a collie from a cockatiel, gave him to her for a present. Said a dog would keep her company. As if she needed company—she's a member of every committee and social group in town. She tried to talk me into taking him, but my apartment building doesn't allow dogs." She paused, bent down to look at something more closely and then frowned. "Nic, can you hold him on his side for me, lying down? I want to get a better look at his paws. I think I know why he was limping."

Nic complied, concerned that she might have found something serious. Had he missed something? He hadn't stopped to check the dog over before getting back on the road. His only thought had been to find somewhere that would take the dog off his hands. When he saw the sign for the Paradise Animal Clinic just past the bridge, it had seemed a good bet. Second-guessing his handling of the situation, he gently but firmly turned the dog on his side, careful not to hurt or scare him. Then, while he held the dog in place, Jillian carefully checked each paw.

"See this? His paws are raw. He's worn the pads right off. The hot, rough asphalt acts like sandpaper on them. Poor thing...that has to really hurt." Big blue eyes the color of a cloudless sky looked away from the dog and up at him. Eyes filled with sympathy and determination. "I'm going to call Dr. Marshall. Murphy will need some pain medication, and maybe some antibiotics." She picked up a phone hung on the back wall of the small room and placed the call. "Hi, Cassie...yes, I'm still here. We've got a little problem. Murphy Rosenberg is here. Someone found him on the side of the road again. He seems to be in good shape for the most part, but he's really done a number on his paws this time. I think you'd better come take a look."

As he listened to her make arrangements, he let himself look his fill. The concern on her face did nothing to detract from her beauty. Pale blue eyes were a stark contrast to the mass of ebony curls attempting to escape the clip she'd secured it with. Her skin was fair, her cheekbones prominent, and then there was that mouth, those perfectly pink lips that she pursed when she was concentrating. A man would have to be blind not to want to kiss those lips.

That doctor had better show up soon; if he was alone with the sexy vet tech much longer, he might end up panting as badly as the dog in front of him.

Jillian hung up the phone, relieved that help was on the way. And not just for Murphy's sake. Being alone with his rescuer was making her a bit nervous. Not that she was afraid of him; she couldn't be afraid of someone willing to stop and help an injured animal the way he had. He just made her...uneasy. Especially when he looked at her with those intense brown eyes, as if he were examining her, looking inside her. Raising her chin, hoping she projected more confidence than she felt, she asked, "Can you carry him into the treatment room for me? We can clean him up a bit while we're waiting."

He easily lifted the dog, once again making the movement look effortless. "Just show me where."

Jillian held the rear exam room door open, allowing him to pass through into the heart of the veterinary hospital. She wondered how it appeared to him. To her the stretches of gleaming chrome and spotless countertops, the bank of cages filling the back wall, the tangy scent of disinfectant were all more familiar than her own apartment. However, she knew the microscopes, centrifuges and bright lights could be intimidating to the uninitiated. Some people actually got a bit queasy. But Nic, who was waiting patiently for her to indicate where to place the dog, seemed unaffected by the medical surroundings.

Pleased by his composure, she pointed to the long, shallow treatment basin covered by a steel grate. The six-foot-long sink was table height, and would allow her to bathe the dog carefully while checking for any other wounds she might have missed. He placed the dog on the grating, and Murphy, no stranger to a bath, behaved himself as she uncurled the spray handle from the end of the table, then rinsed and lathered.

Nic made an excellent assistant; he had rolled up his sleeves, exposing tanned, well-defined forearms that easily maneuvered the soapy canine according to her direction. Thankfully, she could lather and rinse the pleasant-smelling suds on autopilot, because those muscled arms were proving quite the distraction. Worried he might have noticed her staring, she bent down to retrieve a clean towel from the stacks kept below the sink. She tried to focus on toweling the dog off, rather than on the larger-than-life man across the table. But he wasn't making it easy.

"I hope you don't mind," Nic said, unbuttoning his shirt. "This thing smells like, well, wet dog." He shrugged out of the wet, muddy fabric with a grimace, leaving him standing in an almost as damp, but considerably cleaner, sleeveless undershirt and dress slacks.

Jillian nodded, eyes drawn to his broad, bare shoulders, then down to the impressive biceps that had restrained Murphy so easily. The revealed bronze skin spoke more of Mediterranean ancestry than hours in the sun. The tight undershirt did little to hide the chiseled chest underneath or the flat abdominals below. She might have continued to stare, basking in all that male beauty, if the sound of the front door hadn't snapped her back to reality.

"Jillian! Jillian! Where's the doggy? Is he hurt? Can I kiss his boo-boo? Who's that?" Emma Marshall, four years old and the spitting image of her mother, barreled into the room. Her strawberry-blond ponytail swished as she looked from Emma to Nic, blue eyes blinking rapidly.

"Emma, I told you that someone found a doggy and brought him here so I could help him." Cassie appeared in the doorway behind her rambunctious tyke. "Hi, I'm Dr. Marshall. Thank you for helping our Murphy here. I'm afraid he's a repeat offender, but we all love him, anyway."

"I'm Nic." Brushing away the compliment, he offered a tired smile and said, "He seems like a nice dog, now that he's cleaned up."

"Murphy was a mess when Nic brought him in, covered in mud and God knows what else. He helped me bathe him, but his shirt was a casualty," Jillian explained.

"My shirt, my tie and my suit jacket. But, hey, who's counting?" Nic shrugged his shoulders, and then returned his attention to the women in the room. "Can you do something for his paws? They look pretty awful."

Cassie moved to the table and gently examined each of the dog's feet. "They do look pretty bad, but they'll heal quickly. I'll give him an antibiotic injection to prevent infection, and he can have some anti-inflammatories to help with the pain. Beef-flavored tablets, he'll love them." Cassie drew up a syringe of milky-looking fluid. "You aren't squeamish around needles, are you?" she asked, cocking an eyebrow.

"Not at all." Nic eyed the syringe. "But shouldn't you be calling his owner? She's got to be missing him by now, right?" Nic looked first at Cassie, then at Jillian. "Shouldn't she have to approve treatment or something?"

"Normally, yes," Jillian answered. "But we have a standing permission for treatment in Murphy's chart.

Remember, this isn't his first time getting away. Be-sides, Mrs. Rosenberg won't be home tonight. She's over near Orlando on an overnight trip with her seniors group. She mentioned it to me when she stopped in to buy dog food yesterday. Murphy will have to stay here tonight, I guess." She grimaced. "I hate leaving him. If he scratches at the cage door, he's going to make his paws worse, and after his big outing, I'd rather he have someone keeping an eye on him. But my apartment man-ager won't allow me to take him home, and Cassie—I mean, Dr. Marshall—is currently fostering a dog at her house that doesn't get along with others. He'd beat poor Murphy up. So he'll have to stay here until Mrs. Rosen-berg gets home."

Nic's eyebrows narrowed. "You're going to just put him in a cage?"

Cassie responded matter-of-factly, "It's not ideal, but he'll be safe—a lot safer than he was a few hours ago, thanks to you. There really isn't any other option."

"Yes, there is." Nic was firm, arms crossed. "He can stay with me. The Sandpiper Inn is pet-friendly, and I can bring him back here in the morning or to wherever you say to take him. I'll keep an eye on him, give him his medication and make sure he's okay overnight." His eyes dared anyone to disagree. "I didn't go through all the trouble of rescuing him to abandon him in the end."

"I don't think that will work…we don't even know you. Mrs. Rosenberg doesn't know you…" Jillian floun-dered. In her wildest dreams, she would never have ex-pected this man to offer to play nursemaid to a gimpy dog. Knights in shining armor might be the norm in storybooks, but that kind of thing didn't happen in real life. Saviors, she knew from personal experience, were few and far between.

Cassie stepped in. "Why don't I call Mrs. Rosenberg and see what she has to say? We'll let her decide." Turning to Nic, she continued, "I'll need your contact information, and you'll have to fill out some paperwork, if she agrees. Does that sound all right?"

Nic nodded in agreement, still standing stiffly, as if ready to defend his newly found canine friend physically, if need be.

While he and Cassie worked out the arrangements, Jillian clung to the soft dog. She had lost control of this situation somehow, not something she generally let happen. Watching the gorgeous man in front her, she wondered what kind of man did this, dropped everything and did whatever it took to save the day. As if sensing her bewilderment, Murphy squirmed in her arms.

Comforting herself as much as the dog, she buried her face in his fur. The dog turned his head, straining to keep Nic in view, something he had done since the minute they'd arrived. "I know how you feel," she whispered in the smitten animal's ear. "I know how you feel."

Nic pulled into the parking lot of the Sandpiper Inn and turned the key, content to sit for a few minutes before he had to wrangle the dog and luggage. He still couldn't quite believe he had acquired a pet, yet another responsibility, even if it was just for the night. But he couldn't have left him in a cage, scared and hurt, any more than he could have left him on the side of the road.

At some point, taking on responsibility, taking care of others, had become second nature. He had always been the one to get his kid brother out of trouble, even when

it meant getting into trouble himself. Later, he had tu-
tored his sister, taking it upon himself to make sure she
passed the dreaded algebra class. Then, after gradua-
tion, it had been impossible to say no to a job working
for his father, eventually ending up where he was now,
Nic Caruso, Vice President of Property Acquisitions at
Caruso Hotels. The internationally known chain had
been his father's dream, not his, and he found no joy in
traveling from city to city, scouting out properties and
securing new locations for the ever-growing company.
He often wondered what it would be like to settle down
in one place, to meet someone that appreciated him for
who he was, rather than what he could provide.

A soft woof from the passenger's seat brought him
out of his daydreams and into the present. "Don't worry,
I'm coming. I didn't forget about you." Grabbing his
overnight bag, Nic set out with Murphy across the covered breezeway connecting the parking area to the main
house. In front of him the inn rose out of the darkness,
spotlighted by the moon against the dunes behind it.
It was hard to see details this late, but he knew from
his research that it was two stories, built in the Florida Vernacular style. The buff-colored wooden siding
would blend with the dunes in the daylight, and there
were covered, whitewashed porches on every level, designed to offer a cool spot to enjoy the ocean view. Right
now, though, all he could make out were the wide front
steps and a welcoming glow from several of the shutter-
framed windows.

Before continuing toward the inn, he took the sandy
path that ran parallel to the dunes. Whether the inn was
pet-friendly or not, he'd better give Murphy a chance
to relieve himself before going in and getting settled.

As they walked, Nic was impressed by the sheer size of the grounds, which were crisscrossed by walking paths and planted with a variety of tropical and coastal scrub plants. He stopped to lean against one of the many smooth-trunked palms, breathing in the humid air, richly scented by the jasmine that grew heavy around him. The scent reminded him of the vet tech he'd just met, Jillian. Even over the disinfectant and wet-dog smells, he had picked up on her flowery sweetness, some perfume or shampoo or something.

Straightening, he tugged on the leash and walked back to the hotel entrance. He wasn't here to daydream about pretty brunettes or to soak up the night air. He had a location to scout. Caruso Hotels was very interested in this bit of land, and he was tasked with determining if they should make an offer to the current owners.

There was plenty of room here for a modern beach-front resort once the original inn was torn down. Most of the property was underutilized, a diamond in the rough. A high-rise hotel could change the entire community—bring in tourist dollars, chain retailers and more. A Caruso Hotel would move the town into the modern age, make it a hot spot on the Florida coast.

At the top of the stairs, the large carved door of the Sandpiper Inn opened smoothly, bringing him into the lobby, an eclectically decorated but surprisingly elegant room. Native pine floors gleamed in the light of an old-fashioned chandelier. An antique table to his right served as the check-in desk, and across the room over-stuffed furniture offered a cozy place to read or chat. Bay windows with a view of the night sea were directly opposite him; a native coquina fireplace accented the wall to the left.

Bookcases held everything from leather-bound tomes to contemporary bestsellers, with conch shells and chunks of coral for bookends. The antique and modern mix was nothing like the seamless, well- planned lobby of a Caruso Hotel, but welcoming in a way no modern resort could match. For once, he felt like he was stepping into something real, a true home away from home, instead of yet another commercial space.

"Are you checking in?" The question startled him for a moment, returning him to the present business. A young girl—she couldn't be more than eighteen—had come in from a doorway behind the check-in desk.

"Yes, Dominic Caruso. I have a reservation."

She tapped keys on a slim laptop computer, concentrating on the screen in front of her. "I don't see mention of a pet in the reservation notes. Will the dog be staying with you?"

"Yes, but only for one night. Is that a problem? Your website did say you were pet-friendly."

"Oh, no problem. I'll just send up a dog bed and some bowls for him. We have a small selection of pet food, as well, if you'd like." She smiled at Murphy, ignoring Nic in favor of his canine companion, and was rewarded by a mannerly wag of the tail.

"No, thank you, that won't be necessary." Jillian had fed Murphy some kibble before they left the clinic, and had packed him some more for the morning.

"Okay, sign here, then. You're in room 206, just up the stairs and to the left. Breakfast is served on the patio from seven to nine, and coffee and tea are always available in the sitting room. If you need anything, just let me know."

"Thank you very much. I'm sure we'll be fine." He pocketed the key, a real key, not a plastic key card, and headed up the staircase he had passed when he came in. The finely carved banister was smooth beneath his hand, worn to a soft glow by generations of guests and hours of polishing. Upstairs, the hall was quiet and softly lit; most of the other guests were probably sleeping, or perhaps out for a late stroll on the beach.

Grateful for the quiet, he let himself into the compact but tasteful room she had assigned him. Too tired to note much of his surroundings, he stripped off his filthy clothes on the way to the shower, where he stood under the hot, stinging spray to rinse off the mud, sweat and stress of the day. Resting his head on the cool tile, he let the water massage his back and tried to think of nothing, to just be. Instead, his thoughts kept circling back to Jillian, to her pale blue eyes, dark ringlets and those perfect, kissable lips. In a different place, a different time, he would love to explore those lips, and maybe more. But no, he had to work. Hell, he always had to work. At least he was good at his job. Dating, on the other hand, was a series of disasters. It seemed he had a target on his back visible to every gold digger for a hundred miles. His brother adored the attention the family name brought, but as far as Nic was concerned, being single was better than being used.

Annoyed, he turned the faucet to cold, hoping to clear his head. When even that didn't work, he toweled off, then collapsed on the big antique bed. Maybe it was the soft snores of the dog at the foot of the bed. Maybe it was the lull of the waves outside his window. Or maybe he was just that tired. Whatever the reason, for once he didn't have to fight his usual travel-induced insomnia. Tonight, sleep came quickly, the kind of dreamless deep sleep that only came to him when he was home.

Chapter Three

Jillian's morning was a blur of fur and files. There had been countless puppy kisses, but she had also been bitten, scratched and peed on. And that was only the first appointment—new puppy exams for a pair of Labradoodles. Since then, she had struggled to balance her time between assisting in the exam rooms, completing vital laboratory work and counseling owners on proper pet care. Officially, the clinic closed at noon on Saturdays, but it was already almost one, and she still had charts to write up before she left.

Grabbing a diet soda from the break room, she sat at the back desk, away from the barking and hissing, with her stack of charts. But no matter how hard she tried to concentrate, her mind kept returning to Murphy and, if she was honest, to the man who had found him. Lots of men came through the clinic, but not many looked like some kind of Roman god.

And as if being gorgeous wasn't enough, his compassion toward Murphy had bumped him up even higher on the sexy stranger scale of attraction. She had forgotten to ask him what had brought him to town. She knew he wasn't a regular; Paradise was so small, she'd have heard about him if he had been here long. No, more than likely he was one of the few vacationers that occasionally found their way to Paradise.

The island definitely didn't qualify as a tourist mecca; there were no giant, high-end resorts, nightclubs or theme parks to draw people in. But the beaches were pristine, and half the island was a dedicated wildlife refuge, so they did get the occasional nature lover. Somehow, though, Jillian couldn't quite picture the well-dressed man she'd met last night as a bird watcher.

She sighed. Not thinking about him wasn't working; maybe she should be proactive instead. Mrs. Rosenberg should be home by now. If she was fast, she could pick Murphy up at the inn, get him back to his owner and still have time to grab a quick bite before the meeting of the Island Preservation Society this afternoon. Once the Murphy situation was handled, she could move on and stop thinking about the mysterious Nic.

Decided, she grabbed the phone and dialed Mrs. Rosenberg's cell phone number. "Hi, Mrs. Rosenberg. It's Jillian. I'm just finishing up here at work, and wanted to let you know I'll be by with Murphy shortly."

"Oh, dear, I was just about to call you. There's been a slight change in plans. We girls decided to stop over at the outlet malls on the way back, and then, before we knew it, we were at that all-you-can-eat steakhouse. We've given our credit cards a workout, I'm afraid. But as soon as we finish lunch we'll be on our way. I should be in town before three, and you and Murphy and I can have a nice visit then. I'll make us some sangria with a wonderful red I picked up on the winery tour."

"I'm afraid I'll have to take a rain check on that sangria, Mrs. Rosenberg. The Island Preservation Society meeting is this afternoon. I need to head there right after work." Jillian twisted the phone cord, thrown off by the change of plans. "I can bring Murphy by after the meeting, as long as that isn't too late for you. I think we should wrap up by dinnertime."

"That's fine, dear. I can't wait to see my naughty boy. I'm so glad he's okay. I do hate how he keeps getting into scrapes. Won't you reconsider keeping him? I'd feel so much better if he was with someone young and energetic like you."

The elderly woman's request tugged at Jillian's heartstrings. She loved that dog, but there was no way she could keep him. "I'm sorry, Mrs. Rosenberg, you know I'd love to, but my landlord won't allow it. Maybe when my lease is up…" But that was just wishful thinking. Paradise Isle didn't have many apartment buildings, and none allowed dogs Murphy's size. Renting or buying a house was out of the question on her current salary.

Somehow, she, the girl who had grown up wanting nothing more than a houseful of kids and pets, had ended up alone in a small apartment, without so much as a goldfish. That was why she had joined the Island Preservation Society. If she couldn't have the Norman Rockwell life she'd always wanted, she'd have to settle for protecting her picture-perfect community instead. Paradise Isle was her home, and people like Mrs. Rosenberg were her family. "I'll call you when I'm on my way. Have a safe drive back."

"I'll try, but Avril Clookie is driving this time, and you know what a flighty young thing she is."

Mrs. Clookie was at least sixty years old, and about as flighty as a St. Bernard, but Jillian let it go. After saying her goodbyes, she found the consent form Nic had signed last night. His full name was Dominic Caruso, which sounded familiar somehow, and he'd left both his room number at the inn and his cell phone number in the contact section. When he didn't answer at the room number, she dialed the cell.

"Hello?" He sounded out of breath, and she could hear wind blowing in the background.

"Hi, Nic, it's Jillian."

"Ready to pick up your patient?"

"Actually, there's been a change in plans. It seems Mrs. Rosenberg won't be back for a few more hours. I have a meeting after work, so it would probably be best if you brought him to the clinic. I can leave him here while I'm at the meeting, then take him home after that. I'm sorry to change things up on you." She hoped he wasn't too annoyed by the change of plans; his corporate look had screamed "type-A personality" last night.

"No problem. I just finished a run on the beach, figured I'd get some exercise while I was waiting to hear from you. If you want, I can—"

"Wait, you took Murphy running on the beach? His paws haven't healed! He shouldn't—"

"Whoa, slow down! Murphy's upstairs sleeping, more than likely in my bed. I've only taken him out long enough to do his business, and I even rinsed his paws off afterward." Nic's voice was harsh, and Jillian felt herself flush. She shouldn't have assumed. "I'm not an idiot—I do know how to take care of a dog."

"You're right, and I'm sorry. I'm just annoyed that I couldn't take care of Murphy myself. I'm grateful you offered to take him in—really, I am. I'm afraid I let myself get flustered by the whole switch in plans. I hope all this hasn't been too much of an inconvenience."

"It's fine. But listen, I still don't like leaving him in a cage. Why don't you just give me his owner's address, and I'll take him there myself? That way she gets her dog back and you can go to your…what was it?"

"A meeting over at the library. But really, I could figure something out. You've done more than enough already."

"I wouldn't offer if I didn't mean it. I'd like to see him safely home, if that's okay. We've bonded."

"Bonded, huh?" She felt herself smiling; he seemed to have that effect on her.

"Sleeping together does that," Nic deadpanned. "He's a cover hog—don't let him tell you otherwise."

The image of Nic in bed, dog or no dog, was one Jillian did not need in her head. "Fine, I'll give Mrs. Rosenberg your number. If it's okay with her, she'll call you and give you her address, arrange a time." Jillian paused, "I really do appreciate everything you've done for Murphy."

"Well, if that's the case, there is a way you could pay me back."

"How?" Maybe he wasn't so altruistic, after all. If he was looking for a reward, he was out of luck; neither she nor Mrs. Rosenberg had the extra cash.

"Have dinner with me."

"Dinner?" Her jaw dropped.

"Yeah, you know, the meal after lunch? I'm assuming your meeting will be over by then. I thought you could take me somewhere interesting, somewhere the locals go."

"Well…the locals mainly eat at Pete's. It's not fancy, but they have great burgers, and the seafood is fresh." Jillian tried to picture Nic in his business suit in the more-than-rustic atmosphere of Pete's. "Or we could go to the mainland. There are plenty of restaurants over there, nicer places—"

"Pete's sounds great, exactly what I'm in the mood for. Where can I pick you up?"

"I'll pick you up, at the Sandpiper," she countered. Even small-town girls knew not to get in a stranger's car. "Is six thirty okay? The deck fills up fast on a Saturday night."

"Perfect, it's a date. I'll see you then." A telltale click signaled the end of the call.

She hung up the phone slowly. A date? Since when did she go on dates with random strangers, no matter how sexy they were?

At three o'clock that afternoon, Nic was parked outside a small pink stucco house with a very eager border collie. Murphy strained at the leash on the way up the front walk, apparently as eager to go home as he had been to escape. Nic rang the bell and tried to quiet the dog. Almost immediately, the door was opened by a diminutive woman in a teal tracksuit and rhinestone glasses. Her close-cropped hair was a shade of red that was not, and never had been, anyone's natural color. Nearly blinded by the combination, he was caught off guard when she dove in for a hug, her short stature leaving her head resting just above his navel.

"Thank you! Thank you! Thank you!" Each thank-you was punctuated by a surprisingly strong squeeze.

"You saved my precious baby. My sweet boy. Such a sweet, naughty, naughty boy!" With that, she crouched down to hug the canine in question. Murphy, for his part, took the praise as no more than his due.

Finished with her exuberant greeting, she straightened to her full height, which he guessed to be no more than four and a half feet, and tugged on his hand. "Come in, come in. I'm about to open some fabulous wine that I found on my trip. You must have a glass and tell me everything that happened."

Nic followed, intrigued by the tiny dynamo. He knew Florida was known for its active senior lifestyle, but he had a feeling Mrs. Rosenberg surpassed even that stereotype. Besides, he wanted to find out how Murphy was pulling his little escape act.

The house was immaculate, and filled with overstuffed furniture in shades of mauve and teal. Paintings of tropical flowers were on the walls, and a large brass manatee served as a centerpiece atop the glass coffee table. Through the doorway to the right he could see a small galley kitchen; shopping bags currently covered every inch of counter space.

His hostess dug through the bags, removing multiple bottles of wine before finding what she was looking for. Her wrinkled but capable hands deftly wielded the corkscrew, then poured them each a generous portion. He accepted the proffered glass and took a seat on the overlarge love seat, sinking into the soft surface. His hostess's much smaller body perched on the chair across from him as she raised her glass to toast. "To Murphy!"

"To Murphy." He sipped cautiously. It was surprisingly sweet, but certainly drinkable.

"Good, isn't it? Grown right here in Florida. It's made

with native grapes. Lots of antioxidants." She winked, then drank.

He nodded, not sure what to say to the winking, booze-pushing senior in front of him.

"So you found my boy. Jillian says he was all the way across the bridge this time! I am in your debt, son—if you hadn't stopped, there's no telling what could have happened to him. A car could have gotten him, or an alligator! We have those here, you know."

Nic did know, but hadn't thought about it at the time. Which was probably a good thing. Changing the subject, he asked, "Mrs. Rosenberg, do you know how Murphy escaped? Jillian said this wasn't his first attempt. I'd hate to see him get out again."

She shook her head, neon hair flying wildly. "It's a mystery to me. I left him locked in the house, with his food and water. The neighbor was going to let him out for me at bedtime, but she says he was already gone. If he'd been outside, I might think he dug out, since he's done that before, but from inside the house? That doesn't seem likely." She frowned in thought, her bedazzled spectacles sliding down her nose.

"Do you mind if I look around, see if I can find his escape route?"

"Look wherever you like, son. I'll just sit here and finish my wine." She took another healthy swig. "You let me know if you find anything."

Curiosity getting the better of him, Nic decided to start at the front of the house. Murphy, who'd been lying happily at his feet, jumped up, eager to follow wherever he led. The front door offered no clues, and the windows appeared secure. No loose locks or broken panes. The bedroom windows were the same. Murphy, thinking there was some game afoot, pranced and barked as he searched.

When they got to the kitchen, the dog ran ahead and jumped up onto the kitchen door. Wondering, Nic stopped, and watched. Sure enough, Murphy jumped again, this time his paws hitting the lever door handle. If the dead bolt hadn't been in place, the door would have popped right open. "Mrs. Rosenberg, was the kitchen door dead bolted when you were away?"

"The kitchen door? No, the key for that lock got lost a long time ago. But I did push the button in, on the doorknob. That locks it from the inside, and it opens with the same key as the front door." She paused, eyes wide, "You don't think someone broke in, do you?"

"No, not a break-in," he assured her. "Just a breakout. See these scratches on the door? I think Murphy was jumping at the door to follow you, and his paws landed on the handle. That lock opens automatically from the inside as soon as you turn the handle. He just let himself right out. Then I imagine the storm blew it shut again. If you're going to keep him in, you're going have replace that lever-style handle with a good old-fashioned doorknob."

"Oh, my goodness. What a smart boy! Opening doors!" Mrs. Rosenberg beamed at her black-and-white escape artist. "But I see what you mean. We can't have him gallivanting around town. I'll have to ask around about a handyman—I'm afraid tools and such just aren't my area of expertise."

"I could do it," Nic said before he could stop himself.

"Would you? Oh, that would be such a load off my mind. I worry so about poor Murphy. I know this isn't the best home for him, but I'd be sick if anything happened to him." Before Nic could think of a way to extricate himself, she pressed a wad of cash into his hands. "Palm Hardware is just around the corner. You must have passed it on the way here. Just pick out whatever you think is best."

Thirty minutes later, Nic was tightening the last screw with, of all things, a pink screwdriver. Murphy had been banished to the bedroom after getting in the way a few too many times, and Mrs. Rosenberg was thrilled. Straightening, he couldn't help but grin as he packed up the pastel tool kit. Project Dog-Proof was a success, and despite his initial reluctance to get involved, it felt good to know he'd been able to help. Getting his own hands dirty was a lot more satisfying than just signing a work order.

"I have to say, I'm so glad Jillian had that meeting today, and you came instead. Not that I don't love Jillian," she clarified hastily. "Murphy adores her and I do, too. But I wouldn't have felt right asking her to change a doorknob. I'm a bit too old-fashioned for that."

He grinned. Of all the ways he might describe Mrs. Rosenberg, "old-fashioned" wasn't one of them. "What sort of meeting she was going to?" He told himself he was only interested as part of his research on the island. He certainly wasn't prying into the pretty vet tech's life. Not very much, anyway.

"The Island Preservation Society. Jillian is one of the founding members," Mrs. Rosenberg said proudly. "I don't attend the meetings—meetings give me heartburn—but I donate when they have their annual rummage sale, and attend the dinner dance they do in the spring."

His shoulders tensed. "What exactly does this society do?"

"They mostly work to preserve the historic buildings, protect the coastal habitat, anything that has to do with maintaining the way of life Paradise is known for." Her eyes shined with pride. "Our little town isn't as fancy or popular as Daytona or Miami or those other beach places, and that's just fine with us. We like things the way they are, if you know what I mean."

Nic was afraid he did know. From what she was saying, he was going to have a fight on his hands, and Jillian was playing for the other side.

Jillian walked quickly across the hot asphalt parking lot, sticky with sweat and humidity. Ahead, the air-conditioned coolness of the Palmetto County Library beckoned like a mirage, a refuge from the last gasp of summer. Stepping inside, she took a deep breath, embracing the smell of old books that permeated the air. Fortified, she climbed the single staircase to the crowded conference room where Cassie and Mollie were waiting for her.

"We saved you a seat." Mollie waved, her pixie-like face lighting up at the sight of her friend. "I was afraid you wouldn't show, and you know I only come to these things because of you." Formal meetings of any sort were definitely not Mollie's thing. Grateful, Jillian hugged the petite woman in appreciation.

"I appreciate you making the sacrifice. These meetings really are important, especially now. Rumor is that the Sandpiper's new owner wants to sell."

"Sell the Sandpiper Inn? That place is an institution! I can remember Dad taking me there as a kid for the annual fish fry and the Christmas tree lighting ceremony. And just a few years ago, he and mom had their twenty-fifth anniversary party there." Cassie's eyebrows furrowed. "It's bad enough that they don't do the community events anymore, but sell it? To who?"

"I don't know." She shrugged. "They haven't even officially put it on the market yet. I think that happens Monday. I only know about it because another one of the Island Preservation Society members, Edward Post, told me about it when I saw him at the grocery store yesterday. He was always close with the Landry family, and had hoped when their daughter inherited the Sandpiper she would bring it back to its glory days. But she's got her own retail shop over in Orlando, and isn't interested in being an innkeeper. He thinks she'll take the first good offer she gets."

Jillian's heart hurt just thinking of the stately inn being taken over by outsiders, or worse, torn down. A beacon on the Paradise Isle shoreline, the Sandpiper had stood for more than a century. Its spacious grounds had always served as an unofficial community center, the gregarious owners often hosting holiday events, weddings, even a prom or two. She'd fallen in love with the grand building the first time she saw it and had always imagined she'd bring her own family to events there, one day. Now it might be destroyed before she ever had that chance. It just didn't seem fair, or right, to let it slip away without a fight.

As the meeting got under way, she found it hard to concentrate on the details of the historic post office renovation, or a proposal for a bike lane on Island Avenue. Normally she was the first volunteer for a Society project, but right now she was too on edge about the fate of the Sandpiper Inn.

And if she was honest with herself, the issue with the

Sandpiper wasn't the only thing making her palms sweat. A good number of the butterflies fluttering in her stomach were about her upcoming date. It wasn't as if she'd never been on a date before; at twenty-seven, she'd had her share of relationships. But always with local, familiar, safe men. Nothing serious. After a few dates, they'd ended up just friends, leaving her wondering if she was even capable of more intense feelings.

But Nic, with his towering good looks and confident manner, was another kind of man altogether. One that had her squirming in her seat, unsure if she was eager for the meeting to be over or afraid of what came after it.

Finally, the last item on the agenda was addressed. Edward Post stood at the front of the room, faced the folding chairs and cleared his throat. "I know that a few of you have heard rumors about the Sandpiper Inn. I'm afraid those rumors have been confirmed. Ms. Roberta Landry, the current owner, has decided to sell the inn and return to her job in Orlando." Shifting his weight nervously, he continued, "The board of the Island Preservation Society has spoken with Ms. Landry, and she has agreed to at least entertain the idea of the city purchasing the inn for community use."

"Can the city afford to buy it?" someone from the crowd asked.

Edward pushed his glasses up his nose, to see who had spoken. "No, not without help. We're preparing an application to the State Register of Historic Places. If we can get the Sandpiper listed, we may be able to get a grant toward its preservation, which would help offset the purchase price. Our chances are good, but the process can take several months. If there is another offer before that happens, Ms. Landry is within her rights to sell without waiting for the outcome of our application."

At that point the meeting broke down, voices rising as friends and families discussed the odds of success. Everyone already knew, without being told, that with land prices finally going up, a new owner was likely to raze the inn and parcel the land up.

Heartsick, Jillian avoided the speculating citizens and quietly made her goodbyes. Descending the stairs, she vowed to contact Edward and volunteer to write the grant application herself. Tonight she'd start researching the process, figure out their best way forward. She was going to do whatever she could to increase their chances of getting that grant. This was her home, and she wasn't giving up without a fight.

Chapter Four

Nic waited for Jillian on the wide shaded porch of the Sandpiper, where a surprisingly efficient ceiling fan kept the air moving and the mosquitoes at bay. Palms and tropical plants he couldn't identify crowded up against the white railing, as if ready to take over the old inn if given a chance. Farther off, he could hear a woodpecker tapping for his supper, and under all of it was the hypnotic lull of the ocean moving against the shore. He'd traveled the world, stayed at the most luxurious resorts in the most exotic locations, but he couldn't remember ever enjoying an evening more than he was right now.

Something about the seclusion of the location, nestled as it was against the wildlife sanctuary that made up almost half the island, allowed him to let down walls that he'd spent most of his life putting up. The friendliness of the island people was a part of it, as well. He'd wandered up and down Lighthouse Avenue, the main street through town, and every person he'd seen had greeted him openly, willing to talk about the town, their businesses and their families. He'd learned that the mayor had held office for forty years, and was running again in the spring. The streetlights came on at dusk and the shops closed soon after, but the local diner opened early for the fishermen and commuters. He'd also been warned, with a wink and a nod, that alcohol sales were banned on Sundays, so if he wanted to pick up a six-pack to watch the game with, he'd better get it today. The traditional pace of life here was worlds away from the life he'd known, but right now, sitting on a porch swing waiting for a pretty girl, it definitely had its perks.

Tires crunching over gravel signaled a car pulling into the lot hidden by thick green foliage. Leaving the sheltered sanctuary of the patio, he took the steps two at a time, then followed the winding footpath to the large gravel and sand parking lot. A bright blue compact car was in the first spot, its engine still running.

As he started toward it, the door opened, long legs swinging out. Then she stood, facing him, and he was stopped in his tracks, paralyzed. He'd remembered her as pretty, but now, in the light of day, she was stunning. Gone were the shapeless scrubs. Today she wore snug-fitting jeans and a casual but fitted navy tank top that clung to her generous curves. She'd left her hair loose, a mass of ebony curls tumbling down her back. Her striking blue eyes sparkled in the sunlight, framed by dark lashes he knew his sisters would kill for. But it was her smile, innocently seductive, that nearly knocked him over.

"Hi," she said softly, gripping the door handle. "I hope I'm not late."

"No, right on time." He forced himself back into motion, heading for the tiny car. "I heard you pull in, thought I'd save you the walk up."

"Ah, okay. Well." She started to walk toward him, then stopped. "Guess we should be going, then."

"Right, you said it fills up fast, and I'm starving. I think it's all the fresh air." He opened the car door and folded himself carefully into the seat. Although roomier than it had first appeared, it was still a tight fit for his six-foot-two frame. "Is it far?"

"Nothing's far on Paradise Isle."

"Right, I keep forgetting." He grinned. "Here on the beach, it seems the sand goes on forever. It's hard to remember that the actual town is so small."

"Most of the island is taken up by the wildlife sanctuary and public beach access. Only a small portion is actually developed." Her tone indicated that she liked things that way, and he tried not to think about how things would change if Caruso Hotels built a resort here. Instead, he focused on the view as they wound their way down the coast along the beachfront road. Pelicans dove and rose, searching for their evening meal, disappearing and reappearing from behind grass-covered dunes. Some kind of vine also grew on the dunes, with big purple flowers soaking up the evening sun.

"I didn't know flowers could grow in sand," he said, pointing to the tough-looking vines.

She smiled, either at his interest or at the flowers themselves, he wasn't sure. "That's railroad vine. They call it that because it just keeps chugging along the dune, sometimes growing a hundred feet long. The roots help hold the sand in place, protecting the dunes. Best of all, it flowers all year-round. The tall, grasslike plants around it are sea oats—not as pretty, but just as important for the dunes."

Intrigued, he had her point out a few other interesting species as they drove. By the time they reached the restaurant half a dozen names, like coco plum and wax myrtle, were spinning through his head. Impressed, he told her so.

"It's my home. To protect it, I had to learn about it," she said simply.

Another stab of guilt knifed through his stomach. At this rate, he'd be too knotted up to eat a thing. Changing the subject, he focused on the rustic, almost tumbledown appearance of Pete's Crab Shack and Burger Bar—serving the "coldest beer in town," if the worn sign above the door could be believed.

He could see what looked like a small dining area inside, but most of the patrons were sitting on the spacious, covered deck, enjoying the ocean view along with their baskets of food. Jillian led him to one of the few empty tables and passed him a plastic menu. Scanning the offerings, he quickly decided on the grilled snapper BLT, fries and a sweet tea.

"A man that knows what he wants," Jillian commented, raising her head from behind her own menu.

He met her eyes and sparks flew, hotter than the heat lightning flashing in the clouds behind her.

He knew what he wanted.

And it definitely wasn't on the menu.

Jillian felt her cheeks become flushed from the heat in Nic's eyes. Somehow, her innocent comment didn't feel so innocent anymore. Embarrassed, flattered and more than a little confused, she bit her lip and tried to think of something to say. His eyes caught the movement, narrowing on her lips. Oh, boy. Her previous casual dates had not prepared for her this level of...intensity.

Desperate to ease the tension she turned away, hoping to signal the waiter. Instead, she saw Mollie, weighed down by a giant paper sack, cutting across the deck to their table. Knowing there was no way to stop her, Jillian waved her over.

"Hey, Jillian, who's the handsome stranger?" Mollie batted her eyelashes theatrically at Nic.

"Mollie, this is Nic. He's Murphy's most recent savior. Nic, this is Mollie. She's the receptionist at the clinic, and a good friend." She gestured to the overflowing bag. "Stocking up for a hurricane?"

"Picking up dinner for Emma and me. Cassie got an emergency call, and her parents couldn't babysit, some concert or something. I said I'd swing by and pick the munchkin up, take her home and feed her. I wasn't sure what she likes, so I had Pete throw in a bit of everything." She shrugged. "I figure Cassie can eat whatever is left over when she gets home."

"An emergency? That's odd—I didn't get a call from her." Jillian dug in her purse for her phone. Cassie usually called her for assistance in emergencies.

Mollie grabbed her hand. "Chill out. She didn't call because she said you were, and I quote, 'on a hot date.'" She scanned Nic from head to toe, slowly. "I guess he qualifies." Jillian kicked her under the table. "Seriously, no worries. She said she had it handled, something about a pug having an allergic reaction. She just wants to observe it for a while at this point, make sure the medication is working."

"Oh." Somewhat appeased, she put the phone down. "Well, I'm available if she needs me."

"No, you aren't," Mollie said, winking at Nic. "Hot date, remember?" Avoiding another kick from Jillian, she took her paper bag and strolled out, obviously pleased with herself. Nic, for his part, looked incredibly amused by the entire situation.

"Something funny?"

"Nope, just enjoying myself. And the view," he added, looking pointedly at her.

Those butterflies were rapidly morphing into pterodactyls. Thankfully, Nic's flirting was curtailed by the arrival of the waitress. Jillian ordered the crab cakes, and Nic his sandwich.

The perky waitress, in shorts that covered less than most bikini bottoms, couldn't take her eyes off him, and really, who could blame her? He looked every bit as masculine and commanding in jeans and a casual button-down shirt as he had in his professional clothing the night before. If anything, the more relaxed attire highlighted his chiseled features and hard body.

Annoyed with Ms. Skimpy Pants and irritated with herself for caring, Jillian drummed her fingers on the paper placemat. Nic smiled at her frustration, but to his credit kept his eyes on her, not the scantily clad waitress, who thankfully was called away to another table.

By the time the red plastic baskets of food arrived, Jillian felt a bit more relaxed. Nic, despite his tendency to make her breath catch and pulse race, was a pleasant dining companion. They chitchatted about the weather, which was still warm, even in October, then he relayed the story of his rendezvous with the eccentric Mrs. Rosenberg. His description of her enthusiastic greet-

ing and the way she had bamboozled him into changing her doorknob had her breathless with laughter. "I'm
sorry. I should be thanking you instead of laughing at
you." She shook her head. "Seriously, thanks for helping her. I'm sure she didn't give you much choice, but
thanks, anyway."

"She was definitely persuasive." He sipped his tea,
then continued, "But I would have done it, anyway. I'm
sure she's very capable for her age, but she's not up to
replacing doorknobs. And it needed to be done."

His simple answer spoke volumes about him. Most
single guys didn't go around acting as handymen for little old ladies. That Nic didn't realize how uncommon his
charitable streak was made it even more appealing. She
found herself wanting to know more about this mystery
man, and how he'd come to be so chivalrous. "Where did
you learn how to change a doorknob, anyway?"

"My dad taught me. That, and a lot of other things.
He didn't believe in paying someone else to do what you
could do yourself. So he taught us about household re-
pairs, car maintenance, that kind of thing."

"Us?"

"I have a brother and two sisters. I'm the oldest."

"He taught the girls to do that stuff, too?"

"Definitely. No gender discrimination there. And we
all learned to cook, too, no exceptions."

"Your dad cooked?" Jillian was flabbergasted. None
of her foster fathers had, of course, but most of their
wives hadn't, either. She'd grown up on frozen dinners
and boxed mac and cheese.

"Of course he cooked, he's Italian. But my nana is
the one that taught us kids. When Mom and Dad were
in the kitchen, they were busy, you know, trying to get

food on the table in a hurry. Nana had more time and patience, so she taught us all. We would start with tossing salads, easy stuff, and then move up to more complicated things when we were ready. By the time we were in high school, we could all cook reasonably well." He popped a fry in his mouth. "Except for my brother, Damian. He does more than reasonably well. He just finished culinary school, and now he's in Italy getting advanced training. He's a magician with food."

"What about your sisters...what are they like?"

"Smart," he answered without hesitation. "Both are really smart, but complete opposites. Claire is a total bookworm. She's studying for a masters in English at NYU. Isabella is more practical. She has an MBA and works for a big investment firm."

His pride in them was obvious; she could tell just from his tone how much he cared for his family. A small stirring of envy clawed at her, but she pushed it away. She'd spent much of her childhood wishing for a family like his, with siblings and parents and grandparents. But she was an adult now; she'd had plenty of time to learn that wishes didn't always come true.

Nic enjoyed talking about his family, but the questions about their careers made him nervous. He knew it was dishonest, but he didn't want her to ask what his father did or what *he* did. He'd had too many women want him just because of his family, or rather the family fortune. Of course, in this case, his family being the driving force behind Caruso Hotels didn't seem like news she'd be happy to hear, with the Sandpiper being up for sale. If she knew he was here to look into buying it, well, that would definitely wipe the smile off her face.

And it was a knockout of a smile. Her whole face glowed, and her nose scrunched up, just a little, in the most adorable way. In the end, business would have to stay business. His father and the whole company were counting on him to make this deal. If he was going to take over from his dad one day, he needed to prove he could handle the job. But in the meantime, he couldn't help but want to spend some time with a woman who seemed to like him, not his money or his glamorous lifestyle.

Hoping to change the subject, he asked casually, "So what about your family? Do they live around here?" Her face blanched, just briefly, and he saw a flash of pain in her eyes that had him reaching for her hand as she caught her breath. Caught off guard by her reaction, he kept silent as he waited.

She looked down at their joined hands, then into his eyes.

"I don't have any family."

When he didn't react, other than to squeeze her hand reassuringly, she continued. "My parents died in a car accident when I was two years old. They were caught in a bad storm and lost control of the car. I'm told they died on impact, but paramedics found me buckled in my car seat, not a scratch on me."

He didn't know what to say, had nothing to offer, other than "I'm sorry."

Smiling at that, she said, "Yeah, so am I. They—I— didn't have any family, at least that anyone knew of. I ended up in foster care, moving every year or so. Eventually I ended up here, on Paradise Isle. When I was in high school, I got an after-school job at the clinic, back when Cassie's dad was still running things. Later, when my foster parents moved to Jacksonville, I convinced the social worker to let me stay here. I had some money saved up, and I got some financial assistance from the state. I finished out my senior year living in a motel room. After I graduated and could work full-time, I found an apartment and started classes at the community college. A few years ago, I passed my State Board exams, and got certified as a veterinary technician."

"You've been on your own since high school? With no help?"

"I had my friends, and Doc Marshall, Cassie's father, helped by convincing the case worker not to put me back in foster care. I was almost eighteen and with foster homes so scarce, it wasn't a hard sell. But without him backing me, and giving me a job, it never would have worked."

Nic couldn't even imagine that kind of self-reliance. His family had always been involved in his life—sometimes too involved. But as much as their expectations and demands could feel like an albatross around his neck, they had always been there for him when he needed them. They were the only people he could truly count on.

No wonder Jillian was so attached to the community—it was all she had. The guilt he had pushed aside began chewing a fresh hole in his gut. If he green-lighted the Caruso Hotel project, it would completely change the island, and although he'd assumed that change would be for the better, he had a feeling she wouldn't agree.

Carefully, he tried to feel her out on the subject. "So why Paradise? Of everywhere you lived, what made you stay here?"

Jillian smiled. "Because it felt like home. Nowhere

else ever did. Here, the people I met really seemed to care, to want to know me. No one brushed me off as just a foster kid, or acted like I was a lost cause. The town is small enough that people really get to know each other—there are no strangers. And everyone looks out for each other. It's the closest I've ever come to having family." Her voice quavered at her last few words, leaving no doubt as to the extent of her loyalty.

Nic wanted to argue, to offer some counterpoint, but he couldn't. Even in his short time on the island, he'd seen the camaraderie she was describing. Her friend Mollie's willingness to give up her Saturday night to help a friend was just one more example. He wished he could say there were plenty of places like Paradise, but if there were, he'd never seen them.

Of course, small towns, isolated from the fast pace of modern life, weren't his usual haunts. Caruso Hotels were found in the busier tourist destinations; some of their larger resorts became cities unto themselves. On paper, Paradise Isle had seemed like a blank canvas, waiting for development. Choosing an unknown place wasn't their usual mode of operation, but he'd thought it a brilliant and cost-saving strategy, one that would pay handsomely when they transformed Paradise Isle into a tourist hot spot.

Now, seeing the town for himself, he realized how arrogant he'd been. Paradise might be small, but that didn't mean it was insignificant. A revelation that was a bit too late in coming. How could he tell his father, the CEO of a world-renowned business, not to purchase a prime piece of property because "the people are really nice"? It was absurd. He'd just have to figure something out.

And find a way to live with himself afterward.

* * *

Jillian hadn't meant to go on and on about her childhood; she hated it when people felt sorry for her. But Nic didn't look as if he pitied her. If anything, he looked thoughtful as she talked about Paradise, her adopted hometown. She found herself wondering what his hometown was like, but before she could ask he was signaling the waitress for the check. "No, I'm buying," she protested. "We agreed. I'm treating you, to thank you for being Murphy's knight in shining armor. And for helping Mrs. Rosenberg. "

"I changed my mind." He handed his credit card to the waitress without even looking at the check. "What kind of knight lets the princess foot the bill? Besides, I'm the one who should be grateful. You stayed late to help a stranger—"

"Murphy isn't a stranger—" she objected.

"No, but I was. And you didn't know it was Murphy when you let me in. And you've kept me from eating alone or worse, falling prey to our waitress over there." The woman in question was still making eyes at him, none too subtly.

"A fate worse than death," she teased. "Better watch out, she's headed our way."

He just grinned, and signed the offered receipt without taking his eyes off Jillian. The waitress, realizing she was being ignored, practically stomped off. *Not so perky anymore*, Jillian thought, more pleased than she had a right to be.

She knew she had no claim on this gorgeous man, but she was enjoying his company, and the way he made her feel. He listened to her, really listened, and when he spoke, he was funny and engaging. And of course, he wasn't exactly hard on the eyes. Several times she had embarrassed herself by staring at him; thankfully he didn't seem to have noticed. She'd never been so quick to be attracted to a man before, but Nic had intrigued her from the first minute she'd seen him.

When he took her elbow to guide her down the steep stairs she didn't object, nor did she protest when he opened her car door for her after she unlocked it with the remote. His actions were quaintly old-fashioned, and that appealed to her more than she would have expected.

She turned on the air conditioner as soon as she got in, hoping to relieve the oven-like temperature, zooming the windows down to let some of the hot air escape. Once on the road, she put them back up, cocooning them in a car that suddenly seemed quite claustrophobic. His scent permeated the air, some kind of aftershave or cologne that smelled clean yet spicy.

As she merged onto the main road, he reached over and rested a broad hand on hers where it gripped the gearshift. An innocent touch, but it had her pulse racing. All at once the drive to the Sandpiper felt too long and yet not long enough. She was still debating how to handle things when she pulled into the Sandpiper's secluded parking lot.

Should she take her hand back? Kiss him? Let him kiss her? Or maybe she was misreading the whole thing, and the attraction was completely one-sided.

Confused, she turned to find him watching her, searing her skin with his gaze. Energy was radiating off him in waves. Frozen, she could only blink as he reached to brush a lock of hair from her face, twirling it around one finger. They both seemed to hold their breath as he gently tugged, then untwined it curl by curl.

She moistened her lips, and he shifted his attention to her mouth. Sensuously, he traced a finger over the swollen nerve endings, the sensation causing her eyes to flutter closed. There was a whisper of air as he leaned toward her, and then his mouth was on hers.

His kiss was gentle at first, a request, not a demand. But when her lips parted on a sigh he accepted the invitation, deepening the kiss. As his tongue teased, she reached for him blindly, finding his broad shoulders, clutching him to her, not wanting him to stop, not able to stop. Never had she experienced a connection like this. This was so far beyond a kiss; it was some kind of magic, and she never wanted it to end. Straining toward him, but trapped by the seat belt, she whimpered in frustration.

Immediately he let her go, backing away to his side of the car. "Did I hurt you?" His worried eyes darted over her, obviously mistaking her whimper for a sign of pain.

"No," she managed, her voice shaky. "No, that definitely didn't hurt." Finding her composure, and realizing he really was concerned, she explained, "The seat belt was in my way."

"Oh."

She could see now that he was breathing as hard as she was. So she had affected him, too. A bit of feminine pride crept over her.

"Tomorrow. What are your plans tomorrow?" His tone was insistent, compelling her to respond.

"Um...I usually go to church in the morning, the early service, but otherwise, I'm not sure. I don't really have any." Until now, painting her nails and catching up on reality TV were generally the highlights of her weekend.

"Spend the day with me." When she hesitated, he pushed. "Show me your island, give me the grand tour."

She considered. She certainly wanted to spend more time with him, and it was an innocent enough request. But this man was trouble wrapped up in sin. If he could get her this worked up over dinner and a short car ride, who knows what would happen with a full day together? He knocked down walls she didn't even know she had, and she wasn't sure she was ready for that.

As if sensing her hesitation, he withdrew as far as he could in the small confines of the car and said, "I'll be a perfect gentleman, I swear."

He really was cute. Giving in, she nodded. "All right, what time do you want me to pick you up?"

"How about ten thirty? And no offense, but I'd rather we take my rental. More legroom."

He had a point; he barely fit in her little compact. But she knew enough about basic safety to avoid giving out her address to a man she barely knew. "Let's meet at The Grind, a coffee shop on Lighthouse Avenue, a few blocks from the clinic. They've got great coffee, and they carry pastries from the local bakery if you want something sweet."

"I think I just had something sweet."

She felt her cheeks heating again at his casual innuendo. Flashing her a very male, very satisfied smile, he let himself out of the car. She watched him walk confidently toward the inn, as if he hadn't completely rocked her world.

Dear heavens, what on earth did she just get herself into?

Chapter Five

The cool dimness of the All Saints sanctuary never failed to soothe Jillian. The scent of incense clinging to the walls and the flicker of dripping candles made her feel as if she'd stepped out of the ordinary world, and into someplace timeless.

Most of the old wooden pews were empty this early in the morning—the eleven-o'clock service was much more popular. Which was the main reason she avoided it. Seeing all those happy families squeezed into the pews, children whispering, parents trying to keep them quiet, made her ache for what she had missed out on. So she came early, and then had the rest of the day for errands and chores.

Today, the stillness of the old building was particularly welcome. She'd had a restless, sleepless night, tossing and turning while reliving Nic's kiss. Of course, now, in the light of day, she felt silly getting so worked up over a single kiss.

As she prayed, waiting for the service to start, she felt the bench shift, signaling that someone had joined her in the pew. Her peripheral vision caught the familiar motions of the sign of the cross. Finished with her own prayers, she eased back into her seat and turned to greet her pew mate. *Nic?* "What are you doing here?" she whispered.

"Praying?" he whispered back, all innocence.

"No, seriously, what you are doing here? Are you some kind of stalker or something?"

"What, I can't just be here for my own redemption? Remember, big Italian family, church attendance comes with the territory." At her narrowed brows, he admitted, "Okay, so I'm not going to win any attendance awards. But I did grow up in the church, was an altar boy and everything."

She tried, but could not picture this wickedly sexy man as an altar boy. He might have been an innocent child once, but you'd never know it now. When she continued to glare at him, he confessed, "I talked to my mom on the phone last night, and it came up that I was meeting you after church. I thought I would score big points by saying I met a nice girl." He rubbed his neck ruefully. "But she just wanted to know why I wasn't going to church, too. By the time I got off the phone I had promised I'd go, and that I'd say a prayer for Aunt Irene's cataract surgery."

Jillian stifled a chuckle, aware that their conversation was starting to draw attention. Nic might be a grown man, but he obviously still respected his mother. Definite bonus points. "So, did you pray for Aunt Irene yet?"

His answer was cut off by the processional hymn. Standing, she stood shoulder to shoulder with him, his masculine presence impossible to ignore. He held out his hymnal for her to share, and although she appreciated the gesture she was flustered enough to stumble over the words more than once. He had no such issue, his rich baritone voice carrying the notes clearly. She was still feeling unsettled when they sat to listen to the readings, but eventually was carried away by the familiar readings, songs and worship. By the end of the service she found she was actually enjoying his company, and told him so as they filed out into the sunlight.

"Sorry I acted so startled in there. I'm not used to having company in church, but it was nice."

"How long have you been going here? It seemed everyone in there knew you by name."

"Most of them do. When I turned eighteen, my case worker gave me a packet with all my information in it, including my baptism certificate. I was so young when my parents died, I don't have any real memories of them, but I do know that my mom attended church, and that religion was important enough to her to have me baptized. Saying the prayers she said, singing the hymns she sang, it makes me feel closer to her somehow." She stopped, wary of oversharing. "That probably sounds silly."

"Not silly. It makes perfect sense. I'm sure she'd be very proud of you." He stopped, looked at his watch. "So we have most of the day left to play. Do you still want to hit the coffee shop? Or something else?"

She squinted at him; the bright sun overhead had already heated things up considerably. She sized him up and made a decision. "You go get the coffee, and I'll meet you there—I just need to run home first. Cream and sugar, please. Oh, and pick out some muffins or scones or something." She paused. "And get a couple of bottles of water. You're going to need them." Then she walked off before he could ask any more questions. This time, she was in charge, and she liked it that way.

Nic had no idea what Jillian was planning, but he might as well go with the flow. Tomorrow he had to meet with a city council member to discuss infrastructure plans, look into possible traffic and utilities issues, and then write up his findings before getting on a cross-country flight to Las Vegas. So today, he was going to enjoy himself as much as possible. He'd promised himself that much. Everyone and everything else could wait.

He stretched out his legs beneath the small sidewalk table outside the coffee shop. The sun was hot enough that he had chosen khaki shorts and a golf shirt instead of slacks this morning, deciding that was dressy enough for church, given the steamy weather. As he sipped from the eco-friendly paper cup he watched the Sunday morning street life ebb and flow around him. Children with dripping ice cream cones and sticky smiles, parents with shopping bags or grocery lists, all smiled or nodded a greeting to him as they passed. From his shaded vantage point under The Grind's awning he could see quite a bit of Lighthouse Avenue.

Across from him was the Sugar Cone, an old-fashioned ice cream parlor. Treasures of the Sea, a gift shop of some kind, abutted it on one side, and a used bookstore called Beach Reads was on the other. On his side of the street, there was a pharmacy to his left, and beyond that Framed, which looked to be some kind of art gallery and photo studio. To his right was a bicycle shop, and farther down were restaurants, a grocer and a clothing boutique.

On his drive over he had also passed a post office, medical clinic and the hardware store. There were no big box stores on the island, no shopping malls or dance clubs. There was one bar, more tavern than nightclub, over on the beach side, near Pete's, but there was not much in the way of nightlife. That would mean that a Caruso Hotel built here would need an on-site nightclub to satisfy its usual customer base. Recognizing he was still in work mode, he gave himself a mental shake. Surely he could spend one day focused on pleasure, not business.

Recommitted to that goal, he munched on one of the donuts he'd picked out and went back to soaking up the beach town ambiance.

Spotting a woman approaching, he blinked in surprise. Was that Jillian? She'd changed into tight athletic shorts, a spaghetti-strap tank top the color of daisies, and had her hair pulled through the hole in a white ball cap. Struggling a bit, she was pushing a metallic-green bike with oversize tires.

"What is that?" he asked, pointing to the odd-looking bike.

"It's a fat bike, for riding on sand. And it's yours, for the day, anyway. Here—" she shoved the bike at him "—hold this, I'll be right back with mine."

Bemused, he propped the bike against a pillar and waited while she went back into the bike shop. She soon came out with a similar, if slightly smaller, blue version of the first bike. Leaning it with his, she plopped down in the seat across from him and snatched one of the donuts. "Those are easier to ride than push," she commented, before taking a large bite of the sticky confection.

"I certainly hope so. It's been a while since I've ridden a bike, other than the stationary one at the gym."

"Well, you know what they say—you never forget how." She tasted the coffee next, and he got to see her eyes close in a look of pure bliss. "Best coffee on the island."

"So what's the plan?" He eyed the bike uncertainly. He hoped she was right about not forgetting how to ride. The last real bike he'd ridden had been a ten-speed in junior high. And that had been on pavement, not sand.

"First, I'm going to eat another donut and finish this coffee. Then sunscreen—don't make that face, because the sun's brutal here and even tough guys wear sunscreen—then we bike down the avenue, and take Palmetto. That's the way you would have come in on, over to the coast road. We'll take the ramp down to the beach and ride all the way to the Sandpiper." She grinned. "If you're a good boy, we'll stop for lunch along the way."

"Oh, I'm very, very good," he responded, rising to the bait. While she finished the last donut he disposed of the trash and secured a water bottle to each bike. He noticed she had an insulated bag attached to the rear rack of her bike, and wondered what other surprises she had in store.

He'd wanted something different, something outside of his normal routine, and he was getting exactly that. He even let her mount and ride ahead of him—although it chafed his ego a bit—since she was the one giving the tour.

"Follow me, watch for pedestrians and holler if you need to stop," she called over her shoulder, merging into the meager Sunday traffic.

He immediately realized there was a definite upside

to taking up the rear position. Namely, the good view he had of her rear end. Shapely and athletic, it was more than enough to take his mind off his rusty biking abilities. Watching her ride, her black curls blowing in the wind, firm legs pumping up and down, he was so distracted that they had ridden several blocks before he remembered he was supposed to be taking in the scenery. Forcing himself to look away, he made himself notice the tidy storefronts as they continued down Lighthouse Avenue. He'd seen only one franchise business, and that was a gas station. All the other stores were obviously run and owned by locals, and seemed to be thriving despite any problems in the larger economy.

Paradise Isle might be a small town, but it certainly was flourishing. Not having a direct connection to I-95 had kept it isolated, but the town didn't seem to be hurting from the lack of exposure. As they turned into a more residential area, passing picturesque Spanish-style stucco homes alongside the small wooden "shotgun"-style cottages, he couldn't help feel that the people he saw mowing lawns and walking dogs were not going to be eager to have the floodgates of Florida tourism thrown open. Normally that wasn't something that he would even think about. But now, every time Jillian turned back to smile at him, he felt his sense of duty pulling him down like a weight, one he didn't know how to escape.

By the time they reached the beach, Jillian was sweating, but exuberant. The sight of the ocean, as common as it was to an islander, never failed to thrill her. Nic had been a great biking companion, staying far enough behind for safety, but close enough to hear if she needed to give directions. Not that she had doubted his athleticism, not with that body.

Stopping to rest under the shade of the sea grapes that grew around the access ramps, she freed her water bottle from its rack and drank her fill. Nic did the same, his head tilted back, tanned skin gleaming with sweat as he gulped the cool water. Watching, Jillian's mouth went dry. She raised her own bottle again to cover her slack-jawed staring.

He finished drinking and looked around. "This was a great idea—definitely more fun than the bike at the gym."

"Not much of a compliment, but I'm glad you're enjoying it. But before you get too enthusiastic, remember, we still have the beach ride."

"I'm game if you are." Daring her, he pushed off and started down the beach, leaving Jillian to catch up. She laughed out loud, and stood on the pedals to get more speed. When they hit the hard-packed sand near the water, he paralleled the coast and slowed for her to catch him. Nodding, acknowledging his win, she pulled abreast and set a more leisurely, and safer, pace down the fairly crowded beach.

Just like every other weekend there were bronzed teenagers, slick with suntan lotion showing off for their friends, eager children digging in the sand while their parents watched, and surfers on colorful boards fighting for the perfect wave. But even as everything looked the same, it felt different. She felt different. She felt…happy.

Being with Nic made her happy in a way that nothing else ever had. There was a warmth deep inside that was filling her up, as if the sun's rays were somehow penetrating all the way to her heart. In such a short time this one person had filled a hole in her life, in her heart, that she had spent years trying to ignore.

But as wonderful as he made her feel, she was scared to death of what that feeling meant, and what would happen when he left town. She'd lost her heart too many times in her life to be willing to risk that kind of pain again. Her parents, foster parents, foster siblings...they had all left, and she had the emotional scars to prove it. Sure, someday she wanted a family of her own, but getting attached to a tourist was a bad bet. Of course, that didn't mean they couldn't have a good time today, enjoy some food and activity, and then part as fond acquaintances, if not friends.

Resolved, she turned and smiled, shoving down the tingling that shot through her when he grinned back, boyish enthusiasm lighting up his face. Unlike a lot of the guys she had dated, he had nothing to prove, and was secure enough to be silly and have fun without worrying he'd look less manly. A refreshing change, one that made it hard to keep her guard up.

They cruised along, eventually leaving the populated part of the beach for the deserted stretch between the public access area and the Sandpiper. Awed, as always, by the pristine beauty, she slowed her pace to take it all in. White sand stretched for miles in either direction, marred only by the tracks of the industrious little sandpipers the nearby inn was named for. Even the ocean was at peace here, swelling slowly and stretching to the shore in a smooth arc, rather than crashing and foaming against the beach.

Signaling to Nic, she slowed, and then stopped. "I'm ready for a break, if that's okay with you."

He wiped the sweat from his forehead and ran a

hand through his damp hair, his fingers mussing the dark waves. "Sure, you're the boss." He drank from his water bottle and looked around at her chosen resting point. "This is amazing. I've been on beaches all over the world, but this is something else. I feel like we're on a deserted island. I can't believe how close this is to the main part of town. It feels so far away."

"I know. It's amazing to have something this pristine only a bike ride from home. And the Sandpiper is only a little ways around that bend. They don't get busy enough to disturb this part of the beach." Sitting down on the sand, she removed her tennis shoes, stuffing her socks into them. "Come on. Let's get our feet wet, cool off a bit."

After a moment's hesitation, Nic followed suit, toeing off his boat shoes and following her to the ocean's edge. The water was perfect, just cool enough to be refreshing but not cold. "Wow, that feels amazing."

She walked a little ways down the shore, splashing like a kid. There was nothing better than sun, sand and surf to clear the mind. Nic strolled with her, gradually easing closer. Trapped, she couldn't move away from him without getting into deeper water.

When he took her hand, she knew she should say something, remind him that they were just friends. But her voice caught in her throat, and she reveled in the touch of his warm, calloused palm, swinging their arms as they walked.

She was so focused on that point of contact that it took her several moments to realize how far they had strayed from the bikes. Stopping, her hand tugged on his, turning him to her. She wanted to tell him that they should go back, but his eyes locked on hers, and the words wouldn't form. He used their linked hands to pull her toward him, close against his chest. His left hand was still tangled in hers; he buried his other in her hair, anchoring her as she stood in the swirling water. She felt her heart tumble as if buffeted by the waves around him, all of her arguments washed out to sea. Logically, this was a bad idea, but she had left her good sense on the beach with the bikes and their shoes. Instead of pulling away, she arched up to him, ready to meet his kiss.

Splash!

Sprayed with water from head to toe, Jillian jolted, stepping back as far as his grip on her hair would let her.

"What the heck?" Nic let her go and wiped the salty water from his eyes. "What on earth just happened? Is this some kind of practical joke?"

"A pelican." Jillian, now free, retreated another step. She shook her head at the dumb luck of it. "He was diving for a fish. Usually they don't come so close to people, but a few get enough handouts from fishermen to make them pretty bold. I've never been quite that close, though." Heart pounding from the near miss with the bird, and the even nearer miss with Nic, she headed for the bikes, her steps quick and precise. She was going to have to be much more careful from now on, if she wanted to keep her pride, and her heart, intact.

After the pelican's untimely interruption, Nic found straddling a bike to be a tricky business. Luckily, his baggy shorts camouflaged the extent of his response. But discomfort aside, it was best they move on, putting the near kiss behind them. He was leaving tomorrow, and when he came back, if he came back, it would be to buy the inn she was so desperate to save. Under those circumstances, kissing her, sleeping with her, would be unethical. He had been raised better than that.

He'd never lied to a woman to get her into bed; hell, he'd never needed to. Not once they found out he was an heir to the Caruso fortune. And although he hadn't exactly lied to Jillian, he wasn't being honest, either.

There was no way around it—she and that hot body of hers were off-limits. Not that she was chasing him down; she'd all but run once he'd let her go. Something he should be grateful for.

"The Sandpiper's just ahead. We'll have lunch there on the back deck, if that's okay." Jillian pedaled easily alongside him, as if nothing had happened. Fine, if she wasn't going to bring up their near kiss, he certainly wasn't going to.

"Sounds good to me." He figured they'd order in or get something from the small kitchen at the inn, but when they parked their bikes, she unstrapped the insulated bag from hers, tossing it to him.

"Lunch is served."

Intrigued, he carried the bag up the stairs to the wide, covered deck of the Sandpiper. Shaded by an upper-level balcony and boasting several paddle fans, it was at least ten degrees cooler than the beach below. Cushioned lounge chairs at one end and an outdoor dining area at the other looked out over the water below.

He set the bag on the table and started fishing out the contents. Instead of the typical sandwich and chips, he found several plastic containers filled with obviously homemade food, as well as a small loaf of crusty bread and a thermos of lemonade. "This looks a lot better than the soggy peanut butter and jelly sandwiches I remember from picnics as a kid." He held up one of the containers. "What is all this stuff?"

"The smaller container is a smoked fish spread, made with locally caught amberjack. There are crackers to go with it. Then those two have salads in them, greens with cold chicken and a citrus dressing. And that last one has a couple of slices of key lime pie in it." She opened the smoked fish and spread some on a cracker for him. "Try it, it's good stuff."

Starving, Nic shoved the cracker in his mouth. Smoky and sweet, the flavors exploded across his taste buds. "Wow…that's seriously good," he managed to get out around the mouthful of food. "I wonder if I can buy this stuff at home." Not that he was ever home long enough to bother grocery shopping. Ignoring that depressing thought, he reached for the dish and began loading up another cracker.

Jillian sorted out the rest of the food, and he eagerly accepted his share of salad, a hunk of the crusty bread and a paper cup of lemonade. Chewing, he ate in silence, determined to keep his eyes on the view of the ocean and not on the way her shirt, damp now from the pelican encounter, clung enticingly to curves he wasn't supposed to notice. A losing battle if there ever was one.

"Penny for your thoughts."

Had she seen him staring? She was chasing a piece of lettuce with her fork, and didn't seem upset, so maybe not. "Just thinking how impressive the view is." And not just of the beach.

"It is. It's been a while since I've sat back here." Her eyes went soft, as if she was seeing something he couldn't. "Lots of memories here."

"You've stayed at the Sandpiper?"

"As a guest? No. But before the last owners died, they would host all sorts of community events. Fish fries to raise money for the fire department, Fourth of July fireworks displays, a big Christmas tree lighting party, that kind of thing. The place was pretty much the heart of the island for decades. Toward the end they were too frail to run things the way they wanted to, and when their daughter inherited, she was too busy for that sort of thing." Her mouth curved into a small smile. "Some of us are hoping to get it listed on the register of historical places. That would mean grant money, which would allow the city to buy it when it goes up for sale. I'd love to see it back in the center of things."

She paused, as if weighing if she should continue. "The thing is, when I was a kid and came here alone, everyone else was with their families. I'd always hoped to bring my own family here one day. So I offered to write the grant proposal myself. Saving the Sandpiper would be a way to hold on to that childhood dream."

The creamy pie turned bitter in his mouth. The hope in her eyes tore at him. The better part of him wanted to respond to that innocent dream, to help her achieve what she so obviously wanted. But it was impossible. His duty was to his family, to his company, not to this siren of an orphan, no matter what spell she had cast on him.

So he would do his damn job, do what he had to do. But that didn't mean he had to keep lying to her about it. He'd just have to find a way to explain things. Even if it made her hate him.

Chapter Six

Nic had been quiet ever since their picnic at the Sand-piper. He'd definitely seemed distracted on the bike ride back into town; she hoped he wasn't still upset about the kiss. Correction, the nonkiss. She'd been about to jump into his arms, and then had practically run away. Talk about mixed signals. Not something he usually dealt with, she was sure. He probably had his pick of women back home, wherever that was. She needed to get him talking about where he was from, to remind her brain that he was just a temporary distraction. Maybe then the weird tingling sensation running through her body would go away.

"So, where are you from, anyway? You never really said." Watching him out of the corner of her eye, she baited her hook with a piece of squid and executed a near perfect cast over the pier's guardrail. Fishing at the Paradise Isle Pier was a favorite way to relax, and something she'd wanted to share with him, ridiculous as that was. She really knew so little about him, other than that he wore expensive suits, cared for stray dogs and old ladies, and was way better looking than any man had a right to be.

"I'm from New Jersey, at least originally. I've got a place in Manhattan now, but I still don't think of it as home."

"You don't like New York?"

"I like it fine. You know, it's true what they say—it is the city that never sleeps. There is always something to do—anytime, day or night. I just never seem to find the time to actually do any of those things." He rubbed the stubble on his face, as if just noticing it. "I work a lot. Pretty much all the time. Spending a day like this, just enjoying myself, going with the flow... I can't remember the last time I did that." He cast his line out almost as well as she had her own. "It's a curse for a lot of us in the city. We move there for the culture, the plays, the museums, the nightclubs, and then work so damned hard we never actually see any of it."

"That sounds awful." She worked hard to support herself, but even back when she was taking classes at night and working days at the clinic, she'd always had time for walks on the beach, or a few hours fishing on the weekend.

"I shouldn't complain. I do well for myself, and a lot of people would kill for my job. And it's not like I'm working every day. But I'm out of town more than I'm home, and the rare times I am there and have a day off, I feel like I need to spend it with my family." He turned to her, earnestness shining in his eyes. "I realize I probably sound like a jerk, complaining about family, when I should just realize how lucky I am to have them. But I don't mean it like that. I love my family, and I love spending time with them. It's just…"

"Overwhelming?"

He flinched at her word choice. "That's pretty terrible, isn't it?"

Was that shame she saw in his eyes? She put a hand on his arm. "No, I think I understand. You want to be there for them, but you want a life that's your own, too." She'd always romanticized the idea of big families, but maybe it wasn't always picture-perfect.

"Right. I just feel like I have so much responsibility at work, so many people counting on me, and then there's my family, counting on me, as well. Keeping everyone happy is a nearly impossible job." He turned back to the water, watching his line with more intensity than it probably warranted.

Sensing he was uncomfortable revealing so much, she kept her tone casual, her eyes on the water. "Wanting your own life, your own destiny, that isn't terrible. You just need to find a way to do it."

"It's not that simple." He tugged hard at his line, reeling it in and then whipping it back out.

"Why not?" She stopped pretending to watch the water, and faced him head-on. "Why can't you work less, or just tell your boss you need more time off?"

"Because I work for my family. It's a family business. If I don't get the job done, I'm not just slacking on the job, I'm betraying my family." The muscles around his eyes were tense, his jaw hard. "My parents raised me to believe that family comes first. Loyalty matters. My dad always wanted me to take over one day, or at least play a significant role in the company. He started it from scratch and built something he could be proud of. I need to live up to that. I won't let him down. I owe him."

"Wow. Okay, that does complicate things." She was in over her head here; she had no experience balancing family and work, let alone managing them both together. But it was easy to see that he was both intensely loyal and proud. With no advice to give, she was better off just listening. "So what kind of business is it, anyway?"

Nic set his pole into one of the holders screwed into the railing, and faced her, shoulders squared as if preparing for a blow. "Hotels. My family owns Caruso Hotels."

"But…" She tried to think, get her bearings. Caruso Hotels? They were one of the biggest hotel chains in the country, catering to high-end tourists. There was even one opening in Orlando soon. She'd read something about it in the paper, and from the sketches it had included, it was going to be a world-class resort. "The Caruso Hotels? The ones with the fancy resorts all over the East Coast?"

"We're expanding out West, too. I'm flying to Vegas tomorrow to handle some issues with a land deal out there." His voice betrayed not a single shred of emotion.

"Wait—land deal?" Her heart sunk. Bits and pieces of their conversations coalesced, forming a picture she didn't want to see. She had to physically force the question past the lump in her throat. "What exactly is it you do for Caruso Hotels?"

"I'm Vice President in Charge of Acquisitions." He hesitated.

"Go ahead, tell me." She wasn't letting him get away with anything less than the whole truth, late though it was.

"I scout out new locations for our hotels, negotiate sales and make sure the building process goes smoothly."

"So you aren't just here on vacation, are you?" she accused, the words like acid in her mouth.

"To be fair, I never said I was." His denial was too little, too late. As if he realized it, he continued. "I came here to check out a potential new location, a property that recently came up for sale."

Her stomach clenched; she knew what he was going to say, but she had to hear him say it. Fisting her hands, she asked, "What location? What property are you looking to buy?"

"The Sandpiper." She rocked back as if he'd hit her. He was here to buy the Sandpiper? The city didn't stand a chance against a corporate giant like Caruso Hotels. At least now she knew why he'd been wearing a designer suit when they had first met; he'd probably been wheeling and dealing all day. And now he was here to do the same.

She'd trusted him. Told him about her childhood, her dreams for the future. And all the while he'd been planning to crush those dreams like so much sand beneath his feet. How stupid was she, to imagine he felt something for her? Here she was, thinking how he was the first man to make her heart beat faster, and he'd just been looking to get the inside scoop on the island.

Tears stung her eyes, but she refused to let them fall. "So today was just another day on the job for you, huh? Market research or whatever?" She swiped at her face. "So glad I could be of service."

Hurt flashed in his eyes before he composed his features. As if he had the right to be hurt. She was the victim, not him. "What, can't stand the truth?"

"Today wasn't about business. Hell, it's probably the first day I've had in almost a year that I didn't work." He shook his head, pacing the pier. "I have meetings scheduled for tomorrow, but this weekend was supposed to be an attempt at some downtime. Maybe try on the idea of a personal life for once. You were a part of that. This place was part of that."

"Right. Well, excuse me for thinking that a tour of the island's best tourist spots might be of professional interest to someone intent on exploiting the town for his financial gain. I might not have been part of the original plan, but hey, sometimes you just get lucky."

"Seriously? I don't want to exploit anyone. I'm just trying to do my damn job. People are counting on me. My family is counting on me."

"Right, it's all about family. How could a poor little orphan understand something like that? Obviously, I have no idea what it's like to care about people." The anger and the pain tangled within her. How could she have been so naive? How could he have been so deceitful?

"That isn't what I meant. None of this is what I meant, what I wanted to happen." He reached out toward her, grasping her arm. "You have to believe me."

Locking down her heart, she shook him off. "Tell it to the fish. Maybe they'll believe it."

Nic watched her storm off, mired in guilt. He'd totally screwed up. Yes, his hands were tied, but that didn't justify the way he'd hurt her. And he had hurt her; he could see the pain shimmering just beneath her anger. He didn't blame her; he'd behaved badly. But it *was* business.

He should let her go before he made things worse. Just move on, get back to work and do what needed to be done, like always. Somehow, though, that didn't feel right. He had gotten this far in life by going with his gut, and right now his gut said he needed to make this right. Not because he thought he had a chance with her—he knew that was out of the question—but because, business or not, she'd gotten to him. The whole damned place had gotten to him.

Mind made up, he started after her. His own stride was twice the length of hers, and he was able to catch up before she was even halfway down the long wood-and-stone pier. "Hey, wait."

"No." She quickened her pace.

"Let me make it up to you."

"What? Now you want to bribe me? Maybe that works in New York City, but here we put people before profit. I don't want your money." Her shoulders shook. "I don't want anything from you."

"What if I help you with the grant?"

"What?" She stopped, faced him, eyes wide, brows raised.

Uh-oh, where had that idea come from?

Not one to go back on his word, he scrambled for mental traction. "Well, I could help you write the grant. If you get it, I'll back off, let the city buy the property."

"Why would you do that?" Her steady stare bored into him, daring him to lie.

"Because if the Sandpiper is listed as a historical site, it could mean a legal battle when we tear it down." Which was true.

They had the legal means to fight any challenges, but the press would be ugly, making it a huge hassle none of the executives would want to deal with. Of course, they also wouldn't want him to help write the grant proposal, but that didn't matter right now. "Listen, I've got some connections, and a lot of background dealing with properties of various importance. I'll help you however I can, and if the grant goes through I'll find somewhere else to build."

"And if it doesn't?"

"Then Caruso Hotels will make an offer." He wasn't going to lie. He was already kicking himself for his earlier misrepresentation. He'd always been a man of his word, and any hint of dishonor disgusted him. For his own sake, as well as hers, he wanted to make it up to her, and to do that they had to trust each other.

Appearing to consider his offer, she bit her plump bottom lip, forcing him to look away before he forgot this was about business, not pleasure. Thankfully, even if she took him up on his offer, they'd be collaborating long-distance; he obviously had control issues when it came to her.

"How would you even do this? You're leaving for where? Reno? The application process isn't something that can be done in one night."

"Vegas, and no, I'm not planning to do this tonight." In fact, he planned to stay far, far away from her tonight. "I work on the road all the time. Between video conferencing and email, we should be able to get it done without any real face-to-face contact." He should be relieved that there would be so much distance between them, but instead an odd heaviness settled in his bones. He drew a deep breath, suddenly exhausted. "I'll leave my contact info with the Sandpiper before I go. Just email me the forms and I'll take a look at what we're dealing with."

Shading her eyes against the setting sun, head cocked, she asked, "Who *are* you?"

"I thought we just covered that. Nic—technically, Dominic—Caruso. Do you want to see my identification or something?"

"No, I mean, I don't know. I just don't get it. One minute you're saving puppies, then helping old ladies, and now you are going to help me try to save the property you came here to buy. I don't understand. Why are you doing all this?"

"Honestly? I have no idea."

Chapter Seven

Nic was still trying to understand his own motives when he got back to his room that evening. Yes, he'd felt guilty about withholding his true intentions from Jillian, but that wasn't enough to explain his impulsive, and honestly reckless, offer to help her. The last thing he needed was another person looking at him to fix everything; he got enough of that from his job. And yet here he was, taking on exactly that. Maybe he was just a masochist. What other explanation was there? Sure, he was attracted to her, but attractive women weren't exactly in short supply. So why was he willing to risk a business deal for one? Maybe it was because, unlike his family or the women he tended to date, she didn't have any preconceived expectations of him? She'd certainly been shocked when he offered to help.

Pushing away his muddled thoughts, he entered the

room and absently noted that it had been tidied and the
bedcovers turned down. After tossing down his wallet
and keys on the nightstand, he headed straight for the
shower, where a stack of clean white towels awaited him.
He certainly couldn't fault the service at the Sandpiper,
or much else about it, for that matter.

He turned the shower knob to hot and stripped down.
When the temperature was sufficiently close to scald-
ing, he stepped in, letting the water pound his knotted
muscles. High-stakes deals, red-tape snarls and near
constant travel made tension his normal condition, and
he'd long ago found that a hot shower did more to relieve the stress than a bottle of whiskey. Of course, the
whiskey was more fun, but with meetings back-to-back
tomorrow, he couldn't afford the hangover.

He braced his hands on the cool tile and lowered
his head, letting his mind wander as the jets of water
worked their magic on his neck and back. Behind his
closed eyelids he saw Jillian again, how she'd looked at
the pier with the setting sun burnishing her skin. How
she'd leaned in for the kiss that hadn't quite happened,
how her tank top had clung to curves that shamed every
bikini-filled billboard from here to Miami. Frustrated
in more ways than one, he gave up on relaxing and shut
off the tap.

As he toweled off, he caught the familiar ring of his
cell phone. Crap, he'd forgotten. He always called his
parents on Sunday evenings, just to touch base. It kept
his mom happy and out of his hair, and let him and his
dad do a bit of strategizing before the workweek started.
Normally, he called around seven, and it was after nine.

Grabbing the phone, he perched on the edge of the
bed, still dripping despite the towel around his waist.

"Hi, Mom…sorry I didn't call, I just got back to my room a little bit ago." He shifted farther onto the bed as they talked about his sisters, his grandmother and whether he had in fact gone to church. Suitably pacified, his mother turned him over to his father, who, like always, was ready to talk business. Nic half listened as his father reiterated the issues with the Vegas deal, issues they'd already discussed several times this week. But Lorenzo Caruso took the Boy Scout motto of "be prepared" seriously, and wanted to make sure they'd covered every contingency. Normally Nic was just as obsessive as his father, but tonight he just didn't have it in him.

"So what do you think of the Sandpiper property?" his father asked, grabbing his wandering attention.

Not the conversation Nic wanted to have right now. "It's got a good view, and most of the property is undeveloped. I'll know more after I meet with the people at City Hall tomorrow."

"We already knew all that, son. What I wanted to know were your impressions of the place. Is it good enough to be a Caruso property?"

"It's got potential," he hedged.

"Something wrong? Any problems down there I should know about?"

"Just some rumblings in town. It seems the Sandpiper is something of a local landmark. People aren't very happy about the idea of it being sold." One person in particular.

"They're just nervous about change. When they see the sketches for the resort, they'll love it. People always do. And the tourist money it brings in will shut down any complaints."

"Maybe."

"You okay, son?"

"Yeah, I'm fine. Just tired. It's been a long week-end." He explained about finding Murphy, helping Mrs. Rosenberg and touring the island. He left out any mention of his attraction to Jillian, or her feelings about the sale of the Sandpiper.

"So the dog's okay now, right?"

His father was a shark in the boardroom, but a big softie when it came to animals of any kind. "Yeah, he's healing up fine, according to Jillian."

"And this Jillian, she's a pretty girl?"

"What? Where did that come from?"

"You don't expect me to believe it was your mother's persuasive powers alone that got your butt in a church pew this morning, do you?" His father's chuckle carried over the line easily, despite the miles.

"Listen, it's not like that. Besides, have you ever tried telling Mom no?"

"Absolutely not, I'm no fool. But don't change the subject. This is the first time I've heard you talk about someone or something not related to work in longer than I can remember. I can only assume there's something special about her."

A mental picture of Jillian came unbidden. He rubbed a hand across his eyes and tried to sound disinterested. "She's pretty enough, and we had a good time. Nothing wrong with that."

"Agreed, nothing wrong with that at all. In fact, I'm happy to hear you had some downtime. Your mother and I worry about you. You work too hard."

"I do what needs to be done," he answered, hating how defensive he sounded.

"You do, and I'm grateful, and proud of your work ethic. But there's more to life than work."

"I do date, Dad. I'm not a monk." Although, come to think of it, he couldn't remember the last time he'd been out on a date. He'd given up on the idea of a real relationship years ago after the last in a string of girlfriends let it slip that she was more into his money than him. He wasn't willing to be anyone's sugar daddy.

For a while after that, he'd contented himself with casual flings. There had been a time when he'd been more than happy to pick up a girl in a hotel bar, but somehow he'd outgrown that lifestyle without really noticing. No wonder he was reacting to Jillian like she was a pool of water after a summer drought.

His dad laughed, triggering a wave of latent homesickness. Since when did he get homesick? "No one could accuse you of celibacy. But I didn't mean…dates. I'm talking about family, love, kids. The things that are really important in life, just as important as the job. I couldn't have gotten as far as I have without your mother by my side, you know that."

"Geez, Dad. I take it Mom's pining for grandkids again?"

"It's not just her, you know. I'd like to have a chance to get to see another generation of Carusos before I'm in the grave."

"You're not exactly elderly yet. But I'll make a note that providing the next generation of Carusos is another of my obligations to the family." He couldn't help the bitterness that crept into his voice. It was just never enough.

"Obligation? Hell, what's gotten into you? You think your mother's an obligation to me? Or you kids? Something I put on the schedule like a meeting with my broker?"

Now he'd stepped in it. He knew that his father adored his mother—he'd never seen a couple more in love. And they had raised their kids in that same love. Which was why he refused to settle for anything less now. "No, sir. I know that's not how it is."

"Damn straight. Love, family, those aren't obligations, they're blessings. The best part of life. I thought we'd raised you to know that. Your mother and I don't want you to miss out on that. We want the best for you, for all you kids."

Nic cleared his throat. "I'll keep that in mind." Good Lord, this was all too much right now.

"See that you do."

After exchanging goodbyes, Nic hung up the phone without getting out of the bed. Stretching out, still in nothing but his towel, he let his eyes drift closed. He'd get up and work on some reports in a few minutes.

But the exhaustion of the day had caught up with him, and he soon fell into a restless sleep, his dreams cluttered with barking dogs, bicycles and a blue-eyed siren he was forbidden to touch.

"Hey, Jillian, you there?"

Her head snapped up; she'd been daydreaming again. "Yes, sorry. Cassie, did you need me?"

"Just wanted to know if you were going to eat out back with Mollie and me. It's too nice to stay inside today." Cassie tossed her lab coat on her desk, and left by the rear clinic door, not waiting for an answer.

A break in the heat was rare this early in the year, and always welcome. Shaking off her lethargy, she closed up the chart she'd been working on and headed for the little seating area Cassie's father had built when he owned the clinic.

Stepping outside, she took a deep breath, relishing the lack of humidity for a change. By tomorrow the weather would probably be back to the normal sauna-like conditions, but today was pleasant and mild, with a taste of fall on the breeze. Cassie and Mollie were already sitting at the old-fashioned picnic table, a pitcher of iced tea between them as they ate their lunches.

Jillian set her own lunch on the table with the others, leftovers from the picnic she'd made for Nic yesterday. Remembering their uneasy arrangement had her stomach tumbling like a Tilt-A-Whirl. Unable to eat, she sipped some of the sweet tea instead, readying herself for the interrogation to come.

"So, spill it. How'd the date with Mr. Tall, Dark and Handsome go?" Mollie never was one to mince words. She called it like she saw it, usually an endearing trait. Not so much right now.

"Yeah, give us all the details so I can live vicariously through you," Cassie demanded, waggling a carrot stick at her.

"It wasn't a date. Just a...thank-you dinner."

"No hanky-panky?" Mollie asked.

"No!"

"Not even a good-night kiss?" Cassie prodded.

Jillian felt the heat rise in her cheeks.

"You're blushing!" Cassie clapped her hands in excitement. "You *did* kiss him! Was it amazing? God, I miss kissing."

"I am not blushing. I just got a lot of sun yesterday." As if they were going to buy that excuse. Her face was always a dead giveaway. "And yes, if you must know, we kissed. But it was just once...well, almost twice, but really just once."

That piqued both women's interest, the questions coming fast and furious.

"Whoa, slow down. There's nothing really to tell. We had lunch, he kissed me goodbye and then the next day, we did some biking and fishing."

"Two dates in two days, but there's nothing to tell? What happened?" Mollie's eyes crinkled in confusion. "I would have sworn I saw sparks flying when I ran into you at Pete's. Did he end up being a dud?"

Remembering the way she'd felt pressed against him, the way he'd made forgotten parts of her anatomy tingle, had her shaking her head. "No, not a dud. But things got...complicated."

"It's been a while since I've been with a man, but I don't remember it being that complicated. Slot A, Tab B, that kind of thing," Cassie countered.

"Cassie! Seriously? Get your mind out of the gutter. What I meant is, he isn't who I thought he was. He's not here on vacation, for one thing." At their blank looks, she added, "You know Caruso Hotels, right?"

"Of course," Cassie answered. "They've got that giant resort and casino down south, and I heard they're building one in Orlando, too. It's supposed to have its own water park and two nightclubs." She stopped, mouth dropping open. "Wait, Nic Caruso...he's one of *those* Carusos? What's he doing here?"

"He's here to see about buying the Sandpiper, that's what. They want to tear it down and use the land for one of their mega-resorts." The thought still stung. Sure, for him it was a job, not a personal attack, but the idea of her home being turned into some kind of twenty-four-hour tourist trap sure felt personal. At least being angry about it felt more useful than the tears did.

"What a lousy piece of—"

"Hold on, Mollie, it isn't settled yet. He says Caruso Hotels won't buy it if the grant goes through—they don't want the bad press of tearing down an historical site. And…he's going to help me with the grant application."

That bombshell had even Mollie speechless for once. Cassie regained her composure more quickly. "Wait, why would he help you if it would mess up his own plans?"

"Honestly, I'm not sure." She had lost hours of sleep trying to figure that one out. "He said he felt bad about not telling me who he was, but… I just don't know."

"I wouldn't trust him," was Mollie's response.

"Don't worry, I won't." Trust was earned as far as she was concerned; she'd learned that the hard way, growing up in foster care. Too many times she'd counted on someone, trusted them, only to have them leave without a backward glance. Better to rely only on yourself than to have your heart broken. She would never let someone shatter her that way again. No matter how tempting he was, she planned on keeping Mr. Nic Caruso a safe distance from her heart.

Chapter Eight

Jillian had overslept again today, after another night of tossing and turning. In fact, she hadn't slept well in weeks, not since she'd started working on the grant to save the Sandpiper. So much was riding on that application; she felt she had to get everything just right. If it wasn't for Nic's help, she would have gone crazy by now. She'd tracked down important events in the building's history using the library, but most of the technical work had been on his shoulders.

He had brought in an architect he knew to help them make sure they were describing all the building's attributes correctly, and then arranged for the land survey required. She just hoped it was enough. There was only so much grant money to go around, and as beautiful as the Sandpiper was, looks alone wouldn't cut it. Without any ties to important historical figures, the odds were long at best.

She'd mailed off the paperwork this morning, so now it was a waiting game.

That Nic was coming into town tonight hadn't helped her nerves, either. Having him call or chat on Skype every single night had been bad enough. The application didn't really require daily communication, but not a night had gone by that he hadn't spent time talking with her, asking her about her day, getting under her skin in a way that she hadn't expected.

Then he had offered to take her to dinner to celebrate the completion of the grant paperwork. She'd told herself it wasn't a date, not really. Just two friends marking the end of a business relationship. If she'd spent extra time choosing a dress to wear tonight, well, that was just because she didn't often get a chance to go somewhere as nice as Bayfront, where he'd made reservations. The sheer black dress had been a fun splurge, one both Cassie and Mollie had approved of when they had seen her hang it in the break room this morning. And the queasy feeling in her stomach was because she'd been too busy to eat lunch, nothing more.

At least after this it would be over. She'd gotten a bit too comfortable with their routine, snuggled into the couch, talking to him for hours every evening. That kind of closeness wasn't a good idea with someone like him, someone from a world so different from hers. She'd miss their chats, she could admit that, but that was all the more reason they needed to end. She'd have dinner with him tonight, but that would be their last contact until there was news of the grant, one way or the other.

Hoping to take her mind off the Sandpiper—and Nic—she grabbed the chart for the final patient of the day. She'd worked through lunch, and hoped this would be a quick case. She was eager for dinner, and still needed to change before Nic arrived. Before she entered the exam room to get the patient's vitals, she skimmed the notes Mollie had made.

Oh, God—no—this couldn't be right. The patient, Bailey, was a favorite at the clinic, a young beagle who'd never met a stranger. His owners, newlyweds in their late twenties, were just as friendly. Jillian always looked forward to their visits, which until now had consisted of routine checkups and the occasional ear infection. But, according to the notes in the chart, this was something altogether different.

It seemed that Bailey had been injured when jumping off the bed a few days ago, and at first he had been only mildly stiff. But instead of getting better, he'd gotten worse, and now was dragging both hind legs. Apprehensive, Jillian entered the room, hoping the young owner had exaggerated the symptoms. Maybe Bailey was just limping a bit, a little sore. One look, however, confirmed the worst. The normally exuberant pup was crouched in the corner, shaking instead of prancing for a treat, as was his normal habit. Elle Hancock, the beagle's mistress, was red-eyed from crying, and obviously struggling to hold it together.

Jillian felt like crying herself, but fought down her own emotions. She needed to project confidence for Bailey's sake, and Elle's. Gently lifting Bailey onto the table, she checked his temperature, pulse and respiration rate while Elle watched with concern.

"That's a good boy. You sure got yourself in trouble, didn't you, buddy? Don't you know better than to scare your mama like this? That's it, easy now." She finished her tasks and, reassuring Elle as much as she could, went to fetch Cassie. She found her in the lab, looking over an earlier patient's blood work results.

"Cassie?"

"One minute." She finished reading the report, then set it on the counter. "Who's next?"

"It's Bailey, and it's bad." She forced herself to be clinical. "I'm worried it's his back. You're going to need to take a look, but if we want to catch Dr. Rainer before he leaves for the day, I should have Mollie call as soon as possible." Dr. Rainer, the best veterinary neurologist in the state, was at least an hour's drive away. If they were going to transfer the paralyzed patient they'd need to start the process soon, or he wouldn't make it there before closing time.

"Oh, no, Bailey? Is he ambulatory?"

"Nope, totally down in the rear, not able to stand or walk at all."

"In that case, yeah, go ask Mollie to give Dr. Rainer a heads-up, then come join me in the exam room."

Cassie's very thorough exam was not encouraging. She tried to offer some hope, but cautioned that, with cases like this, there was a possibility the paralysis would be permanent—or worse—progress further. The prognosis wasn't good, and everyone in the room knew it.

With an increasing sense of dread, Jillian carried the patient beagle to the car. Elle followed with a copy of Bailey's medical records and driving directions to the specialist. As if sensing her unhappiness, Bailey squirmed, angling himself to lick her face in reassurance. The sweet creature was trying to comfort her, when he was the one so gravely injured. Touched, her tears spilled silently down her cheeks, soaking into the soft brown fur. Settling him on the seat of the car, she turned and hugged Elle, who had tear streaks of her own on her face. "Good luck. He's a strong, healthy dog, and Dr. Rainer's the best. You'll like her, I promise."

Elle simply nodded and got into the car. Jillian watched her drive away, then walked back inside, her legs almost too weak to carry her. Dazed and overwhelmed, she stood in the empty waiting room, unsure of what to do next. Intellectually, she knew that weeks of sleep deprivation and a skipped lunch were as much to blame for her reaction as concern for her patient, but the fear and grief were like a living thing, crushing her from the inside. On autopilot, tears still falling, she headed for the treatment room. There were patients that needed medications and lab equipment that needed to be taken care of before she could leave. She just had to get through the next half hour or so, then she would curl up somewhere and let the numbness swallow her.

For once traffic was cooperating, and Nic was fairly confident he could catch Jillian at the clinic before closing time. Maybe a smarter man would have stayed in Orlando after finishing his meetings, instead of heading for Paradise again. But being so close to Jillian without seeing her would take a stronger man than he had ever been or could ever hope to be. It was like he was addicted, and she was the drug. She'd slipped into his system somehow, and now he couldn't get her out. More surprisingly, he didn't want to get her out. Or let her go.

Of course, there was a chance that after seeing her in person, he'd find that she was just a woman like all the others, looking out for herself. Not the near-angel he'd come to think of her as during their nightly conversations. It had been her looks that caught his attention, but what had him reaching for the phone every night went deeper than that.

As they had worked on the complicated government forms, he'd found she had a sharp intellect tempered by an easy wit. Even more impressive was her determination. She had grit, and there was nothing he admired more. She certainly had to be tough to have made it through foster care, then living on her own and putting herself through school. He couldn't think of a more independent woman, and he'd certainly known his share, growing up with his mom and two sisters.

It was her independence, as much as anything, that made him feel comfortable getting as close as they had. He'd avoided entanglements for years, unable to handle being responsible for even one more person, as weighed down as he felt by work and family already. He hated that he sometimes resented the long hours and constant travel that he felt obligated to do. Even worse, he was starting to think of his family only in terms of the job, lumping them in with the rest of his to-do list.

Having one more person pushing him to be more, do more, might send him over the edge. And that's what women he dated always wanted: for him to work harder, make more money, gain more power for them to bask in. He didn't think Jillian was like that, but only time would tell. The more jaded part of him said that finding out wasn't worth the risk of being used again.

So why was he, even now, crossing over the Intracoastal, on his way to see a woman he had no business seeing? Because he couldn't do anything else, that's why. Being this out of control was a new feeling, one that didn't sit well. At least driving to Paradise Isle was taking action, and action was always better than inaction.

He'd see her, take her to dinner to celebrate the grant process being over, and maybe even get her out of his system for good.

Keeping that in mind, he pulled into the clinic parking lot just before six. He noted her tiny compact in the lot. Good, he hadn't missed her. Pleased that things were going according to plan, he locked his rental, the same style of SUV he'd rented before, and examined the building in front of him; he'd been in too big a hurry last time to notice many details. The low-slung building was in the same Spanish-style stucco as many of the other buildings on the street, with large glass windows lining the front, tinted against the brutal Florida sun. A nicely landscaped path took him to the front door, where he chuckled at a discreetly placed container of doggy pick-up bags. Swinging open the heavy door, he strode to the front desk, where Mollie and the doctor— Cassie something—had their heads together, whispering worriedly. He didn't see anyone else in the waiting area; from the state of the parking lot, he assumed the last clients must have already left.

"Hello, Mollie, Doctor. Is Jillian still here?" He'd seen her car, but it seemed presumptuous not to ask.

The two women looked at each other, as if conferring silently. The hair prickled on the back of his neck. Something wasn't right here. Something to do with Jillian. "What? What's going on? Where's Jillian?" Fear made his voice harsh, but damn it, how did they expect him to react?

The veterinarian spoke first, silencing Mollie with a gesture. "Jillian is in the back, finishing up with some overnight patients." She paused, as if she wasn't sure how to phrase what came next. "She…had a hard day.

She might not be up to dinner tonight. Maybe you could postpone?"

"Not possible. I'm only in town one night. I flew in this morning to finish up some details on our Orlando project, and I fly back out in the morning." What was going on here? "We've got reservations in an hour." He'd secured the seats at the elegant restaurant on a whim, one he was seriously rethinking. "Listen, if she doesn't want to go, or has other plans, just say so."

Mollie stood up, ignoring the other woman, and quickly made for the doorway to the next room. "I'll tell her you're here."

Nic turned back to the doctor. "You still haven't answered my questions, Doctor. So either you tell me what's going on, now, or I can force my way back there and see for myself. Either way, I'm not leaving until I know Jillian's okay. You choose." Someone was going to give him some answers, fast.

"Please, call me Cassie." The petite woman smiled, not in the least intimidated by his assertive demands. Oddly, that made him like her more, but he wasn't going to back down on his threat. "Jillian's a bit upset, that's all. One of her favorite patients just came in, critically injured. We've transferred him to a specialist, but his chances aren't good. It hit all of us hard, but Jillian particularly so. She's…not herself right now. I'm a bit worried about her being alone, so all in all, it's probably a good thing that you're here."

"Murphy?" He swallowed hard.

"Oh, no, not Murphy. Another patient, a sweet dog with really nice owners."

Hearing that the rascally border collie was safe had him relaxing the fists he hadn't known he'd been clenching. "But don't patients get hurt all the time? I mean, I get it, it's sad, but isn't that kind of business as usual?"

"Sure, and usually everyone handles it very professionally. You learn to keep your emotions in check, to be kind, but not get drawn into it. You have to. But sometimes…sometimes something happens and it's like all the pain is there at once, all that emotion you've managed to ignore over a hundred different patients swallows you up for a time. It happens to all of us, when we're tired, or stressed out, or just not up to par. A pint of rocky road and a good cry are the usual treatment, and then, when you finish crying, you're ready to do it all over again, see that next patient, face whatever the next challenge is." Her smile was weak, and couldn't hide the strain on her face.

He'd never really thought about how hard a job like this could be. It made his issues with zoning boards and contractors seem petty. That these women dealt with this kind of emotional trauma on a regular basis had him in awe. He'd be a basket case trying to deal with all that. So tonight he'd make sure to keep things light, cheer Jillian up, show her a good time. No problem.

Nic heard the treatment room door open behind him, and turned, a smile in place. Then he saw her, and his heart stuttered in his chest. Her face was tearstained, her normally pale skin blanched an unnatural white. He had to grip the counter in front of him to keep from picking her up and carrying her out of there.

Instead, he let her come to him. Gently, he placed a palm on her cheek, needing to touch her, but afraid she might shatter like a crystal if handled clumsily. She didn't so much as blink, just pressed her own palm against his hand, holding him to her. Her eyes, red from crying, pleaded with him, but for what? What could he do?

"She's been like this how long?" He kept his attention on Jillian, but his words, bitten past the lump in his throat, were for Cassie.

"About twenty, thirty minutes. She'll be okay. She just needs a little TLC."

"I just want to go home." Her words were clear, if quiet.

"I'm going to get you out of here, okay, honey?" He moved his hand down to her waist, steering her toward the front door. "Are you hungry?"

"She skipped lunch. We got swamped today, so I know she hasn't had anything since breakfast, if then," Cassie interjected, concern showing in the lines on her face.

"I…I didn't have breakfast, I overslept. But I'm not hungry right now. I'm fine, really."

Her voice sounded stronger, but he could see what the effort was costing her. She was ready to collapse, no two ways about it. No way was he letting her go home by herself. Cassie was right; she was in no condition to be alone right now.

Or to go to a fancy restaurant.

Fine. Problems cropped up in his work all the time; this was no different. He'd just come up with a new plan. Gears turning, he accepted the small purse and slinky black dress that Mollie retrieved for Jillian, then waved a brief goodbye as he escorted her out of the building.

When she stumbled, he held her tighter, half carrying her slender form by the time they reached his car. Using the button on the key fob to unlock it, he used his free hand to open the door, then simply lifted her up and into the seat. She was like deadweight in his arms, and her lack of protest scared him. She just sat there, eyes closed, so he reached over and buckled her in himself. Careful not to catch her hair in the door, he closed her in and ran around to the driver's side, starting the car with no real idea of where to go or what to do.

He headed for the Sandpiper. He'd reserved a room earlier, and they'd be able to get food there. Besides, it was as close to a home turf as he had right now.

Driving carefully, ridiculously afraid to jar her, he kept one eye on the road and one on her pale face. She appeared to be almost asleep, probably the best thing right now. His panic abating, he wanted to shake her for letting herself get so run-down. He'd known her to be resilient, practically invulnerable; seeing her this fragile made his heart ache in a way he didn't want to acknowledge. Instead, he focused on the task at hand, getting her to the inn, getting some food in her and then giving her hell for scaring him like this.

Plan in place, he pulled into the closest spot he could find in the Sandpiper parking lot. Rounding to her door, he touched her arm, again struck by how cold she felt. Her eyes opened at his touch. "Hey, honey, we're here. Can you get out?"

She nodded, taking in their surroundings without a word. If she was surprised he'd brought her to the inn instead of her apartment, she didn't show it. She could question his motives later. Right now, he just wanted to get her to his room safely. After that? He didn't have a clue.

Chapter Nine

Jillian wandered the lobby of the inn while Nic checked in with the front desk. It had been a while since she'd seen the inside, but not much had changed. The natural orchids in the coquina fireplace caught her eye; it must be too early in the year for a fire. Too bad, she would appreciate the warmth right now. She was cold down to her bones. Served her right for skimping on meals and sleep. Nic must think she was an idiot, acting like some kind of trauma victim over an injured dog. She would have tried to explain in the car, but she was just too tired. Just thinking about putting that many words together was exhausting. She desperately wanted to flop down in one of the lobby chairs, but if she sat down, she might not get back up again.

Finished at the desk, Nic motioned for her to follow. Maybe he wanted to drop his stuff off before taking her back to her place? Why else would he have brought her here? Or did he bring her here so she could change into her dress? Did he still want to go out to dinner? Nothing made sense to her frazzled brain, and trying to figure it out made her head hurt. Better to go along with whatever he was planning, and figure it all out later.

He led her up a flight of stairs, catching her elbow when she almost missed a step. At the landing he went right and opened the last door off the hallway. Watching her, he paused, then gestured for her to go in.

Of course, ladies first. Always the gentleman. An absurd giggle threatened to bubble up, another sure sign she was way over her emotional limit for the day.

Inside, he locked the door, set her purse on the nightstand and strode directly to the bathroom. Left to wait again, she checked out the room. She'd never been in one of the Sandpiper's guest rooms, and this one was certainly worth seeing. A king-size sleigh bed dominated the room, its carved cherry headboard an art piece in itself. A small sitting area with two wingback chairs sat in front of the balcony doors, and a low dresser with a flat-screen television on top completed the furniture. Turning to take it all in, she found Nic standing at the bathroom door, watching her.

"I ran you a bath, put whatever bubble stuff they had in it. It should warm you up. I'll order the food while you're taking your bath." His words were clear, but she couldn't wrap her head around his meaning.

"You want me to take a bath?"

"You're cold, and you're upset. My sisters swear by long baths when they're upset. My mom, too. I thought it might help."

"I don't know..."

"Just take the bath. Then we can talk, or not talk, whatever." He scrubbed a hand over his face. "Listen, I'm not trying to seduce you or anything, okay? Just take the bath, please?"

It was the "please" that got to her. She knew adding it on had cost him. And really, a bath did sound wonderful. Her apartment only had a glassed-in shower stall, no tub. Stretching out in the big claw-foot one behind him would be heavenly. And warm, so very warm. Giving in, she nodded. "Okay."

He stepped aside so she could pass, saying nothing, but looking relieved when she went into the bathroom and shut the door. Stripping quickly, ignoring her appearance in the mirror, she sank into the fragrant bubbles. The scent of lavender and honeysuckle rose up on the steam, making her feel like she was floating on flower petals instead of water. Heat seeped into her, releasing the muscles she had been clenching in a desperate attempt to keep from falling apart. Letting herself slide down the tub, she submerged to her ears, and tuned the world out for a few blessed minutes.

Cocooned in the fragrant water, her thoughts turned to the man that had brought her here. Who would have thought a straitlaced corporate executive would have such a sensitive side? She would have bet money he was going to bail when he saw her falling apart like that—she'd seen the fear and confusion in his eyes—but instead he'd rushed to her side, supported her, been there for her.

Nothing in her background had prepared her for that kind of reaction. No one had ever really been there for her, taken care of her. The Marshalls, Cassie's family, had tried, but she'd been too distrustful to let them get close. So they'd mostly let her take care of herself, which was exactly what she'd wanted and needed. Foster care and living on her own so young had taught her to be independent, no matter what.

As much as she said she wanted a husband and a family someday, the idea of actually letting down her guard, being that close, that dependent on anyone, had always terrified her. But with Nic it felt natural. Easy. Safe. Who knew that giving up a bit of control could feel so right?

Creak...

She sat bolt upright at the sudden sound, only to immediately slosh back under the bubbles when she saw Nic at the door. "What are you doing in here? Get out!"

"I knocked, but you didn't answer. I was afraid you'd fallen asleep in there." He had one hand over his eyes; the other was clutching a stack of clothing. "I brought you some sweatpants and a T-shirt. I thought you might want to change when you were done, and that dress didn't look very comfortable."

She wouldn't have heard his knock with her ears submerged. But still! "Just leave them there and get *out*." Mortified, she slid farther under the water, hoping everything was covered. She didn't trust him not to peek between his fingers. Just the thought of him seeing her nude warmed her blood, despite the rapidly cooling water. Nic Caruso definitely heated things up, that's for sure.

When she was sure he was gone, she jumped out of the tub, then darted to the door to lock herself in. Heart pounding, she grabbed a towel and dried herself hurriedly, feeling exposed despite the locked door between them. She threw on the too-big clothes, the soft shirt falling nearly to her knees. The pants she cinched with the drawstring, and then rolled up the legs so she wouldn't trip.

Fully covered, she stopped to catch her breath and mop up the water she'd sloshed onto the floor in her mad dash to lock the door. She ignored the fogged-up mirror; a quick finger comb of her curls was the best she could do appearance-wise, anyway. Her makeup was in her purse in the other room. Not that she was trying to impress him. They both knew that anything between them was completely impossible. No point in getting worked up over what was, in the end, just a business relationship.

After closing the door, Nic sank down onto the edge of the bed. He really had been concerned she might have fallen asleep in there. But his brotherly compassion had flown the coop when she'd jolted into a sitting position, suds streaking down her slick skin. He'd covered his eyes as quickly as he could, but not before he'd seen more than he should, more than was good for him. The image of all that creamy skin, slick and rosy from the bathwater, was going to be branded in his brain forever.

Adjusting his suddenly too-tight pants, he debated calling down to room service again to ask for some whiskey, something to take the edge off. On the other hand, if he was going to have any hope of taking care of her needs, rather than focusing on his own less honorable ones, he needed to stay sober. Otherwise, he was liable to forget what a bad idea being together was, and in her weakened condition that would be unforgivable. He might be a hot-blooded guy, but he knew not to take advantage of a woman; his father had drilled that lesson into him by the time he hit puberty. Which meant he needed to keep his libido locked down, even if it killed him.

The click of the bathroom door signaled her return. She edged out around the door, and he knew he was doomed. Seeing her in his shirt, his clothes, was like a sucker punch to the gut. The soft material clung to her curves, her hair was damp and curling around her face, and her big eyes were even darker against her still-too-pale skin. She was softness, and vulnerability, and everything he thought he didn't want, didn't need, all bundled up in a package hot enough to melt steel. Absently, he pressed a hand against the aching in his chest. Dear God, what was he going to do with her?

Worse, what was she doing to him?

"I'm sorry."

Her voice jump-started his stalled mental capacities. "What?" Yeah, that sounded brilliant.

"I said I'm sorry. I don't know what got into me. I'm never like that." She fiddled with the drawstring to his too-big sweatpants. The innocent movement had his hormones swirling again. The lady was killing him slowly and she had no idea she was doing it.

"Like what?"

"Weak." Her eyes dropped at the word.

Crossing to her, he lifted her chin, his fingers burning where they met her skin. "Not weak. Human. We all have a breaking point, honey. Today, you hit yours."

She offered a shy smile, then broke contact by stepping past him, toward the sitting area. "I shouldn't have skipped lunch, it was stupid. We were just so busy and—"

"And you were taking care of everyone else but yourself. Am I right?" He cocked an eyebrow, daring her to contradict him.

She raised her chin, defensiveness radiating off her.

"That's my job. It's not like I was doing my nails or something. I was busy."

Good, she was getting her spunk back. "I get that. I get busy, too. But you've got people and their pets depending on you, so try for some balance, okay? Stock some snacks in the break room for when you're busy, or protein shakes, whatever. Being busy doesn't have to mean letting your blood sugar crash. You're smarter than that." He really did hope she would listen; she'd scared the crap out of him. If pushing her buttons would get her to take better care of herself, he was more than willing to do it.

Looking chastened, she shrugged. "You're right. It was dumb."

"Like I said, we all have bad days."

"I bet you've never cried on the job."

The image of him crying in the middle of some business deal had the corners of his mouth twitching. "No, I guess not. But I do yell, and I bet you don't do that."

"No, I guess I don't," she conceded. Her stomach rumbled audibly. "I'm too hungry to keep arguing. I think I could eat a horse."

"Well, horse wasn't on the menu, but hopefully burgers and fries will work. I'd planned to take you out for steak and champagne, but comfort food and a movie on pay-per-view seemed like a better idea, given the circumstances."

"A burger sounds heavenly right now. Then we'll see about a movie."

A knock at the door signaled the arrival of room service. Nic opened the door for a teenager pushing a wheeled cart with an assortment of covered dishes. The food was transferred to the sitting table, along with two sodas, napkins and tableware. Nic signed the receipt, gave a generous tip and closed the door. Turning back to the table, he let Jillian choose her chair, then settled in the one opposite. "I hope soda is okay. I thought it might help get your blood sugar up quickly, in case you weren't ready for a meal yet."

"It's fine, and I'm more than ready to eat, trust me."

Trust. She threw the word out casually, but they both knew it wasn't as easy as all that. Trust had to be earned, and even then you could still get burned. He trusted his family, sure, but he'd seen too many handshake deals gone wrong, seen too many wealthy men used by women as nothing more than a meal ticket, to be willing to accept anything or anyone at face value. That Jillian, sitting there, barefaced, in his old clothes, could make him want to let down his hard-won barriers was absolutely terrifying. He'd been worried about not hurting her, but now he realized she held the power to hurt him, as well. And that was something he could not allow.

Jillian attacked her burger with a vengeance. She felt like her stomach was turning itself inside out, she was so hungry. Her embarrassing outburst had sapped her remaining reserves, leaving her hollowed out in more ways than one. The juicy burger would fill some of that emptiness, but not all of it. Work, her friendship with Cassie and Mollie, her church, the animals, they helped, but at the end of the day there was still a dark hole deep down inside. One she hadn't been aware of until she met Nic.

Rolling her eyes at her own melodrama, she concentrated on the good food in front of her instead of the man across the table. He must think she was some kind of basket case. No need to make it worse by mooning over him. Only when the last fry was gone, and as much of the burger as she could stuff in, did she risk conversation.

"So I never did ask why you had to come back to Orlando. I thought you were working over in, where was it—South Carolina—this week?"

"I was able to wrap up that deal yesterday, but there were some environmental issues to address at the Orlando site, so I flew in this morning. I met with the landscape architect and the environmental group, got them to come up with a compromise that provided the drainage we need while protecting the native species in the area. And of course, I wanted the chance to celebrate with you."

"I'm sorry we missed our reservations." Her burger suddenly felt heavy in her stomach. He'd had such a long day, then driven all the way out here to treat her to dinner, and instead of a celebration he'd ended up playing nursemaid.

"Hey, I told you, you have nothing to be sorry for." His deep voice brooked no argument. "Besides, I'd rather eat burgers in a T-shirt than lobster in a suit any day."

He did look content, and all male, leaning back in that big chair, long legs sprawled out in front of him. His T-shirt—he must have changed while she was in the tub—stretched across his broad shoulders and well-defined chest, making him look more like a male model than a businessman. But the casual clothes did nothing to detract from the energy that radiated off him. Men like him didn't need power suits to be intimidating; they were just born that way.

Watching him, mesmerized by all that maleness, she didn't even notice the buzzing coming from her purse.

"Is that your phone?"

"My phone? Oh, crud, yes, my phone! I forgot to turn it off vibrate when I left work." She dove onto the bed to grab her purse, retrieving her phone before the voice mail could kick in. Spotting Cassie's number on the caller ID had her burger threatening to come back up. *Please, please, don't be bad news.*

"Hey Cassie, do you have news on Bailey?" She listened to Cassie's report, tears stinging her eyes, heart in her throat. "Are they sure? Oh, thank God! Does Elle know? Wonderful! Okay, let me know if there's anything I can do." She gave Nic a quick thumbs-up when he sank down on the bed beside her. "All right, see you Monday. And thanks again for calling."

She hung up and turned, the tiredness gone, her smile stretching so wide she thought her face might break in half.

"Good news, I take it?"

"The best. His test results looked better than expected, and he's already responding to the intravenous medication they're giving him. It will take a while, but they think he'll make a full recovery. He's going to be okay!"

Overwhelmed, she threw her arms around him, hugging him in celebration. Her face pressed to his shoulder, she inhaled his clean, spicy scent as he returned the embrace. He felt strong and safe, his muscles hard beneath her hands. Then his arms tightened around her, and that quickly the moment shifted. Her breathing quickened as one of his hands began to rub sensuous circles up and down her back. Melting, she yielded to the pressure, arching into him, her head bowed back to the kiss she craved as much as her next breath.

He met her halfway. His mouth came down over hers, tasting and then plundering as he lifted her into his lap.

Her hands roamed his body, testing the muscles beneath. His fingers wrapped in her hair, pinning her in place as their tongues danced to a silent rhythm.

Head spinning, she clung to him, fists bunching in his shirt as heat pulsed beneath her skin. Every cell in her body was screaming that this was right, he was right. Deep inside, something clicked, as if the tumblers of a lock were falling in place.

Greedy, hungry for more, she pressed even closer, swept up in the magic he wove with his hands and lips, knowing now that she needed him, more than she'd ever needed anyone.

Holding Jillian was like holding a live wire, her soft curves lighting up his body wherever she pressed against him. Her hands electrified nerve endings everywhere she touched, daring his body to respond. Nuzzling his way from her lips to her slender neck, he tumbled them both to the bed, angling her so her compact body landed on top of his own hardness.

"Ouch!"

A sharp pain shot through his back, just below his rib cage. "What the…" Moving Jillian to the side, he rolled and reached for the unseen weapon. "A fork?"

"What? Oh, no, I must have dropped it when I was grabbing for the phone. I was so worried it would be bad news, I forgot it was in my hand." Giggling, she bit her bottom lip. "Are you okay?"

She was laughing? The most intense kiss in his life ends with him being stabbed in the back, and she was laughing at him? Lobbing a pillow at her head, he grunted out, "It's not funny. I could have been seriously injured."

"Uh-huh."

"This is serious." He tried to sound stern, but knew he'd failed. The truth was, it was serious, way too serious, given that he was leaving first thing in the morning. They'd come very close to crossing a line, one he had promised himself he wouldn't cross, not while she was weak and vulnerable.

As if trying to diffuse the situation, Jillian scooted up to the top of the bed, carefully keeping to her side, and grabbed the remote. Eyes averted, she focused on the flat-screen television across from the bed. "You promised me a movie, didn't you?"

Willing to play along, knowing this wasn't the time to push things, he stretched himself out next to her, plumping a pillow under his head. "Yes, ma'am. Lady's choice."

Less than an hour into the movie, Jillian's slow, even breathing told him she had fallen asleep. Should he wake her up, take her home? She didn't have to work tomorrow; he knew it was her one weekend off this month. It seemed a shame to disturb her when she was so tired. If she stayed, it would be torture to lie beside her all night, without touching, but the idea of waking up beside her was oddly tempting.

Ignoring the warning bells in his head, he kissed her forehead and pulled the covers over her, settling himself in for a long night. Despite the lingering sexual tension, listening to her breathing proved more relaxing than he would have predicted. He was on the verge of drifting off himself when he heard her cell phone ringing.

Please, not more bad news, not now. Teeth clenched,

he grabbed the phone from the table and answered it himself, as she slowly stirred beside him.

"Hello?"

"Who's this? Where's Jillian?" The voice sounded oddly familiar.

"This is Nic. Jillian's right here. Can I tell her who's calling?" Jillian was sitting up now, reaching for the phone, rubbing her eyes.

"It's Vivian Rosenberg, that's who! Now let me talk to Jillian!" Handing the phone to Jillian he made the connection. Rosenberg? As in Murphy's owner? Had something happened to the dog? Listening to Jillian's reassurances that she'd be right there, wherever *there* was, he quickly found and put on socks and shoes, handing Jillian hers, as well. Keys in hand, he was ready to go when she hung up.

"Murphy got away again. Mrs. Rosenberg had the senior group over tonight for cards, and in the confusion of everyone leaving, he slipped out." She slipped on her shoes, then grabbed the plastic bag he'd given her to put her clothes in after her bath.

"We'll find him," he assured her, already unlocking the door.

"We? Oh, Nic, you don't have to come. You can just drop me off at the clinic. I've got my car there."

"No way. I'm going with you. It's late, and however safe Paradise is, you shouldn't be running around in the dark by yourself."

She rolled her eyes, but didn't protest. "Fine, let's just hurry."

They made for the car and were on the road within minutes, both of them scouring the streets for signs of Murphy on the way to Mrs. Rosenberg's. As they entered her neighborhood, he remembered something he'd been wondering about. "Why did she call you, not the clinic, or animal services or something?"

"Well, I've been going over there every day to take Murphy for a run, do some training with him. She knows I love him just as much as she does, that I'd want to be the one to look for him. Plus, he knows me, so he's more likely to come if he hears me calling."

"You go over there every day?"

"Well, not tonight, obviously. But yeah, either before or after work, ever since his last escape attempt. She still wants me to keep him, but since I can't, this is the best I can do, and the exercise keeps him out of trouble. Usually." She smiled, but it didn't reach her eyes. "It's almost like having my own dog."

They rode in silence the rest of the way, him wondering at the bond she'd forged with Murphy, and the dedication it took to go take care of yet another animal after a full day of doing just that at the clinic. Every time he thought he knew her, she impressed him again. That someone so dedicated to pets couldn't have one of her own struck him as incredibly sad, but she had made the best of it, like she did with everything. Hopefully, she'd be able to do the same if Caruso Hotels bought the Sandpiper.

Sobered by the thought, he let Jillian take the lead when they reached Mrs. Rosenberg's. The elderly woman handed out flashlights, clutching a fuchsia robe around her, seemingly unconcerned that Nic was with Jillian at this late hour. He'd wondered if she'd say something, and was glad when she didn't. He didn't want Jillian having to deal with small-town gossip about their relationship. Especially since he hadn't figured out how they could ever have a relationship. He had a job to do, and he couldn't ignore it for the sake of one woman, no matter how bewitching she was. Which meant he'd keep the Caruso legacy moving forward, and hope it didn't push her out of his life entirely.

Chapter Ten

Flashlight in hand, Jillian tried to figure out where to start looking. Her head was such a tangle right now, she wasn't sure she could find her way out of a paper bag, much less locate a stubborn pup with a nose for trouble. "I always use the same route when I take him on his run, and dogs can be creatures of habit. Maybe he was frustrated because I didn't come today, and followed it on his own."

"Makes as much sense as anything. Lead the way." Nic held a flashlight, a bottle of water and Murphy's leash. Jillian had dog treats and the other flashlight. Together they started down the quiet suburban street, taking turns calling for the dog. At each clump of trees, she'd stop and check the shadows before moving on to the next bush, the next yard, the next block.

The moon was bright above the horizon, creating a

silver-tinged landscape that would have been romantic under any other circumstances. Jasmine blew on the breeze, sweetening the evening, despite the fear that gripped her. Poor Murphy. His training was progressing, but with the limited time she had to spend with him, he still wasn't trustworthy around doors. And Mrs. Rosenberg, bless her heart, wasn't up to the challenge he presented. If he was hers full-time, she could have had him well under control by now, but her landlord wasn't budging. Just one more dream that wasn't going to come true.

Watching Nic as he checked yet another hedge, she sighed. He was another dream that wasn't going to be realized. The past few weeks, she'd gotten to see the man behind the business suit, and she liked what she saw. His workaholic nature was driven not by blind ambition, but by a desire to do right by his family. She knew he looked up to his father, that he was determined to live up to the trust placed in him. That kind of family loyalty was rare, and she couldn't help but respect him for it. Even though that same family loyalty could mean the destruction of her little island sanctuary.

"Do you think he would have gone this far?" Nic asked as they crossed yet another deserted street.

"I honestly don't know. He's fast, so he could have covered a lot of ground pretty quickly if he wanted to. On the other hand, if he was sniffing every fence post and fire hydrant, it could take him all week just to circle the block." She huffed to blow her hair out of her face. She hadn't thought to grab a hair tie when they ran out of the hotel. "If it was daytime, we could ask if anyone had seen him, but as it is…" Her voice trailed off.

"Yeah, this place really does roll up the streets after dark, doesn't it?"

They hadn't seen anyone since they'd started their walk. Most of the houses were quiet, the warm glow of porch lights acting as sentries against the night. "I guess Paradise is pretty boring after Vegas and New York City, huh?" She kicked at some mulch that had spilled over onto the sidewalk from its assigned flower bed. This might be her idea of perfection, but to him it was just some Podunk town. No wonder he was so eager to bring in tourists and nightclubs, to make it another Daytona or South Beach.

"Boring? No, that's not how I would describe it. Peaceful was more what I was thinking. It's actually kind of nice to be somewhere where everyone goes home at night, has dinner with the family and turns out the lights. I'd forgotten people still lived like this."

His wistful tone took her by surprise. Had she been wrong to assume he couldn't see what she saw? "Before I moved here, I didn't know people could live this way. I love seeing kids playing in the yards every evening, old men hanging out at the hardware store in the morning. Life on the mainland is always changing, but here on the island, they've managed to hold on to what's important. That predictability makes me feel…safe, I guess."

The rhythms of Paradise Isle were like a security blanket she tucked around herself to help her sleep at night. After so many moves, changes and families, she had finally found a place where she felt secure. That he could tear that all apart was the elephant in the room, a fact both of them were unwilling to confront.

"The town I grew up in was like this, but I guess I

thought that because I had changed, everyone else, everywhere else, had changed, too." He looked directly at her, as if holding her with his gaze. "I'm glad I was wrong."

Before she could decide exactly what he meant by that, a faint sound had her attention shifting. "Did you hear that?"

"What?"

She heard it again…a high-pitched whine, almost a whimper. "That!"

"Maybe…yeah, I hear it. Think that's Murphy?"

"I don't know, but it doesn't sound good." Pacing, she tried to locate where the sound was coming from. Maybe it was a bit louder, a bit stronger in that direction. Maybe.

Frustrated, she walked more quickly. "Murphy! Is that you, boy?" An answering bark and more whining had her running, Nic's footsteps heavy behind her. The distressed sounds grew louder, coming from behind the last house on the block.

Ignoring Nic's protest, she darted right into the yard and around the side of the house. At this point, she could hear two animals; the whining one was, hopefully, Murphy. But what was that hissing, growling noise? A possum? They could really do some damage; a raccoon would be even worse. Heart in her throat, she scanned the small backyard, hoping the poor dog wouldn't be too injured.

There, in the corner, she could make out Murphy's white patches in the moonlight. Approaching cautiously, Nic at her side, she brandished the flashlight like a weapon, hoping desperately she wouldn't have to use it.

Nic grabbed Jillian's arm, slowing her before she could barrel headfirst into whatever had Murphy cowering in the shadows by the fence. Didn't she understand how dangerous this was? They were in a stranger's yard late at night, chasing what might be some kind of rabid beast. And she was ready to jump in without thought to her own safety, an idea as foolhardy as it was admirable. "Let me go first, see what we're dealing with."

"No way. I'm the one with the animal background, and I'm more familiar with the wildlife around here," she snapped, trying to pull away from him.

His instinct was to argue, but before he could come up with something that sounded like more than macho rhetoric, the clouds parted, letting moonlight flood the yard. There, only a few feet away, standing guard on top of a large trash can, was Murphy's would-be attacker.

"Oh, Murphy…" Jillian's reproach dissolved into a full-fledged laugh.

A cat. The creature they'd heard hissing and screeching was nothing more than a big old tomcat, defending his territory from the hapless canine.

Shaking his head, Nic ignored the angry sentry and went to the trembling dog. "Big tough dog like you, afraid of a little pussycat? You should be ashamed of yourself." He gave the dog a good-natured pat and reached for the bag of treats Jillian had brought. "Here you go, liver treats. Maybe they'll give you some courage." The cat, assured of its victory, stretched and then proceeded to carefully groom itself. Still, Nic gave it a wide birth, if only to spare Murphy any further trauma.

"We'd better get out of here before whoever lives here comes out to investigate," Jillian warned, her eyes darting to a light that now glowed in an upstairs window.

"Good idea." Explaining this ridiculous rescue mission to a half-asleep homeowner didn't sound like fun. And they really needed to get Murphy back to Mrs. Rosenberg before the poor lady made herself sick with worry. "Let's move."

They'd made it a full block before his pulse settled down, and he was able to appreciate the humor in the situation. Murphy was back to his normal carefree self by then, as well, and he danced at the end of the leash, eager to be home.

As he walked with the happy dog down the quiet street, Jillian by his side, he was struck by the normalcy of it all. The longing behind that thought surprised him. Sure, he'd become disillusioned with the constant travel of his current lifestyle, but did that mean he wanted something so completely different? Lately, he had toyed with the idea of shifting some travel responsibilities to other people in his department, spending more time at his office in the city. But would that be enough? He had thought it would be. But then why did he feel more at home, more at peace, here on this tiny island, than he ever had in New York City?

Shoving away the questions that circled him like hungry sharks, he chose to focus on the here and now. Right now he was strolling under a starry sky with a beautiful, intelligent, courageous woman. Reaching out, he caught her hand in his, letting them swing together as they walked. She accepted the gesture without hesitation, perhaps trapped by the same magic that had him wishing for things that weren't his to wish for. If there was a way to freeze this moment, keep it and take it out whenever he wanted, he would.

They reached the street that Mrs. Rosenberg lived on

far too soon, his steps slowing as they approached the house. When they reached the walkway, Jillian slipped her hand away, a shy smile on her face. The spell that had entangled them was unraveling, taking a part of him with it.

"Is that you, Jillian? Did you find him? Is he okay?" Mrs. Rosenberg called from her front porch, peering out into the night.

"Yes, Mrs. Rosenberg, we have him. He's fine, other than some bruising to his ego. He got cornered by a cat over on Hibiscus Street."

The elderly woman waved them over, eager to be reunited with the dog that gave her so much trouble. "You poor thing, was that cat mean to you? Mama will make it up to you, don't you worry." Murphy accepted her praise and subsequent petting with a big doggy grin, tongue hanging out one side of his mouth. "You two, do you want to come in and have a drink or a snack? I've got plenty of cookies left from our little card party."

Jillian responded first. "No, but thank you. It's been a long day, and I really need to go home and get some sleep."

The older woman scrutinized the younger and then nodded, apparently accepting her excuse as valid. "You do that then, and sleep in tomorrow, too, if you can. Murphy can wait for his run until later. I'll keep him locked down until then."

"Sounds good," Jillian replied.

"And you, young man. Don't think I'm not wondering why you were with my Jillian at this hour. I'm just too well-mannered to say anything about it. But I'm watching you, and you'd better have the right kind of intentions, if you know what I mean."

The right kind of intentions? Who said things like that? He might have laughed if she didn't look so very serious. Not wanting to hurt her feelings or dig himself any deeper, he decided to play it safe. "Yes, ma'am. I understand." Which was a bold-faced lie. Right now, he didn't understand anything, least of all his intentions toward Jillian.

Jillian settled into the comfortable bucket seat as Nic drove her home. She was exhausted, too many near catastrophes in too short a time, but the energy crackling between them kept her alert. The passionate embrace at the inn had ignited more sparks between them, and the walk with Murphy had layered a new element of sweetness onto the sultry feelings he inspired.

Chemistry was crazy that way. She'd been on numerous dates with totally suitable men, men from her own neighborhood with similar lifestyles and goals, and felt nothing more than curiosity. But Nic, who was all wrong for her, and completely unattainable, made her pulse throb and her knees weak every time he came near. Totally unfair, and at the moment, incredibly disturbing.

Would he expect a kiss when he dropped her off? Or more—would he want to pick up where they'd left off before an errant piece of silverware had so pointedly interrupted them?

Of course, the most likely scenario was that he was berating himself for that lack of judgment and trying to figure out how to let her down easy. After all, this was just one stop in his busy schedule. For all she knew, he had dinner, and maybe more, with women at every job site. Not to mention that currently she and the Island Preservation Society were a huge thorn in his side with regards to his business dealings. And with Nic, nothing was ever just business; it was always personal, always about how best to impress his family. Which meant if the grant fell through, his connection to her wouldn't be enough to stop him from buying, and destroying, the Sandpiper. For him, it was a matter of family loyalty, something she would never begrudge him, no matter how it affected her personally.

Hoping to avoid an awkward scene, or the lack of one for that matter, she had a hand on the door handle, ready to jump out the minute he pulled up to the clinic. "Thanks for the ride, and dinner, and helping with Murphy and, well, everything," she fumbled, nerves getting the best of her. "I'll, um, talk to you later."

Nic, with his quick reflexes, bounded out of the car and was at her side before she finished extricating herself from the SUV. He reached into the backseat, retrieving her purse and dress, both of which she'd nearly forgotten in her cowardly bid at a quick getaway. He ignored her attempt to take them from him, instead carrying them to her car, where he took the time to put them on the passenger's seat before opening the driver's door for her. His automatic chivalry gave her weary heart yet another jolt. His touch, a soft brush of his knuckles against her check, nearly broke her.

Their eyes locked, heat and longing and something more spilling into the stillness between them. She watched, helpless to stop him, not wanting to stop him, as Nic leaned into her, then closed her eyes against the sudden, sharp sting of tears when he only placed a gentle, chaste kiss on her forehead.

"We need to talk about us, Jillian. Not tonight, but soon. I'm not done here." His voice was husky; hers had abandoned her entirely. A simple nod was the best she could manage before retreating into the relative safety of her car. She somehow shut and locked the door in a single motion. Locking him out, or herself in?

Chapter Eleven

It had been a full week since Murphy's last escape and everything that had happened that night. She'd spent much of that time dodging Nic's phone calls. Now that the work on the grant proposal was over, there was no reason for him to contact her, but he still called every night, like clockwork. What had he meant when he said he wasn't done? What more was there?

It was not like they'd been dating, or even friends really. They'd had a moment of passion, some tender moments. They both knew that wasn't enough to build a relationship on. So any lingering emotion was misplaced and should be ruthlessly ignored. To that end, she'd agreed to meet Mollie for an afternoon at the beach; a few hours of sun and sand could fix pretty much anything. And just in case, she'd picked up Murphy on her way over. Now that his paws were healed, he was in need of some playtime, and his high spirits were guaranteed to chase any blues away.

She held the leash tight and let Murphy sniff each weather-beaten stair step on the way down to the sand. His nose quivered with delight at all the new smells, and his black-and-white plume of a tail wagged high over his back. His enthusiasm was impossible to resist. Happier already, she kicked her flip-flops off and left them at the base of the stairs before breaking into a jog over the hot sand, heading for the cooler, hard-packed sand closer to the water. Murphy barked with delight, happy to chase the pipers and gulls that skittered along the shoreline.

At Murphy's bark, Mollie, comfortably situated in a low-slung beach chair right at the water's edge, looked up from her book and smiled. "I didn't know you were bringing this handsome guy. Has he been behaving himself lately?"

"More or less, depending on the day. But no more escape attempts. I figure a few hours at the beach should wear him out enough to keep him home for a while." She passed the leash to Mollie so she could put down the chair she'd been carrying, unfolding it and situating it next to Mollie's. From her bag she withdrew a rubber ball. Murphy spotted it and immediately crouched down in the famous border collie stance, ready to leap the minute it was tossed. Unsnapping the leash, she threw the toy into the waves before settling into her chair.

"So has he called yet?" Mollie asked.

"Who?" Jillian feigned ignorance.

Mollie wasn't fooled. "You know who. Mr. Caruso Hotels himself. Have you heard from him?"

"Yes. I mean, no." At Mollie's raised eyebrow, she continued, "He's called. A lot. I just don't answer. He'd promised to help with the grant, and he did, but that's over now. There's no reason for us to talk now."

"No reason at all, except the guy is crazy about you."

She dropped the dripping ball she'd been about to throw, her fingers unresponsive. "What? You're crazy. It was just business."

Mollie lifted her sunglasses to scrutinize her friend. "Are you telling me nothing happened between you?"

Jillian looked down to watch the water creeping closer to her chair. "There's some…chemistry. I won't deny that. But he's probably got women throwing themselves at him all the time. A girl in every port, you know." Just saying the words hurt, but she might as well face the truth.

"I don't buy it. If just any girl would do, he wouldn't have driven all the way from Orlando to take you to dinner." The petite brunette shook her head, her short hair swinging. "No, that wasn't some booty call. The man cares about you. Otherwise, he would have ditched you the other night when he saw what a basket case you were."

"I was not a basket case."

"Sweetie, you were in rough shape. Most men would have run fast and far from that kind of drama. Instead, he went all protective alpha male —I swear I thought he was going to pick you up and carry you off. I may have even swooned a little."

The image of tomboy Mollie swooning made Jillian smile. "He *was* awfully sweet," she conceded. "But the fact is, there's nothing going on between us, and no reason to keep in contact. At least not until we find out about the grant."

Mollie frowned. "What do you think the chances are of saving the Sandpiper?"

"Not great." She sighed, absently rubbing Murphy's ears. "We applied late in the year, so there won't be much money left, even if they like the proposal. And although the Sandpiper is certainly old enough and still reflects the original architecture, most of the buildings that are selected have some kind of tie-in to Florida history or to a famous person. The Sandpiper is meaningful to us, but that isn't enough to impress the committee."

"If it doesn't go through, will Nic really buy it and tear it down? Even though he knows how much it will upset you?

"It's not really his call. Caruso Hotels is a giant corporation. He's just doing his job." Why was she defending him?

"But he has to have a say in it. He's a vice president, isn't he? Can't you get him to back off?"

"What, ask him to set aside a multimillion-dollar project because it would hurt my feelings?" Jillian scoffed.

"Yes! I'm telling you, he cares about you."

"Even if he does—and I don't think that's the case, at least not the way you mean—but even if he does, he cares about his family more. When push comes to shove, he's going to do right by them, and if I get hurt in the process, well, that's simple collateral damage."

After all, family always came first, and she wasn't anyone's family.

Cold pizza and a lone beer of unknown age. The state of his refrigerator was pathetic. He could order some Chinese takeout, but he didn't want to wait for it. Resigned, he grabbed a slice and the longneck bottle.

Twisting off the top, he leaned a hip against the counter, content to eat standing up after ten hours hunched over a desk. This was not turning out to be a stellar Saturday.

He'd gotten into town yesterday morning and had spent the whole day in various meetings at Caruso headquarters. Today he'd been stuck at his desk, dealing with the inevitable paperwork that those meetings generated. Somehow, he'd managed to put off any questions about the Sandpiper, but he knew it was only a matter of time before his father would expect a status update. Burying himself in reports and sales figures was nothing more than the urban version of hiding his head in the sand. If he kept busy enough, he wouldn't have to think about how to handle the Sandpiper or, worse, how to handle Jillian.

He had tried calling her at least a dozen times in the past week, but had gotten her voice mail every time. She'd obviously started screening his calls, and it hurt more than he wanted to admit.

Hearing her voice, discussing his day with her, had become second nature. Somehow she'd become the person he bounced ideas around with, the person he went to for advice, or just a listening ear. Obviously she didn't feel the same way. He should have expected this. Once the grant proposal was denied, and despite their best efforts, he knew it probably would be, Caruso Hotels would buy the Sandpiper and Jillian Everett would kick him out of her life for good. Maybe she was just trying to do him a favor by ending their friendship, or whatever it was, now, before things got really ugly.

He understood her reasons for fighting against Caruso Hotels—hell, he was actually starting to agree with her. Which just made everything more complicated. His instinct was to fly down there, make her see him, but that was the last thing she seemed to want. Which left him standing here, alone, trying to figure out a way to go on with his life. Or, more accurately, get a life.

A check of his watch showed it wasn't even eight yet; he could still go out. He was young, single and had money to burn. A night out was just what he needed after yet another long week.

Before he could change his mind, he pulled his cell phone from his back pocket and dialed his brother. Damian was supposed to have gotten back from Florence sometime last week, but he'd been too busy to call and ask him about his trip. A lame excuse. Tonight he'd make it up to him. Buy him a drink and listen to all the ways European cooking was superior to anything in America.

Three rings in, Damian picked up. "Hey, wow, was wondering if you'd call. Are you in town?"

"Yeah, sorry… I've been busy. Got in yesterday and just came up for air."

"Dude, you work too much. Seriously, you've got to live a little."

"Agreed. Starting now. Want to meet me for some drinks at Dry?"

Damian was silent for several seconds. "You want to go have drinks? At a club? Who are you, and what have you done with my brother?"

"Ha, ha, very funny. What's wrong with wanting to go out on a Saturday night?"

"Nothing, bro. It's just not like you. But, yeah, I'm up for it. Meet you there in an hour?"

That should be plenty of time to shower, change and get a cab over to the trendy bar, named for its famously dry martinis. "Yeah, that works. See you soon."

He called down to the doorman to request a cab, then took a quick shower. The scruffy look was still fashionable, right? No need to shave. Searching his seldom-used closet, he found designer jeans and a button-down dress shirt. The owner of Dry, Andrew Bennet, was a family friend, so getting in wasn't an issue, but he didn't want to look out of place, either. Keys in hand, he headed out the door, ready for whatever the night might bring.

Nic made it to Dry before Damian, so he elbowed his way to the main bar and sent his brother a text to meet him there. Music pulsed from hidden speakers, enticing the more adventurous onto a dance floor commanding most of the exposed second level. Spotting the bartender, he ordered a scotch on the rocks and then surveyed the action. Lots of what were probably young professionals, looking to unwind after working way too many hours. And of course, lots of people looking to hook up, men as well as women. Skintight and low-cut seemed to be the trend of the day, the couture clothes designed to showcase bodies perfected by spin classes and personal trainers. He had never realized how frenetic it all was, with everyone rushing to cram as much fun as possible into the meager downtime their lean-in lifestyle permitted.

By the time Damian appeared at his elbow, he had an empty glass and a full-on headache. Damian placed his own drink order and motioned to Nic, asking if he was ready for another. "Sure." Maybe the booze would drown out the pounding in his skull. Had this place always been so loud?

"So why are we here?" Damian asked, skipping over the usual pleasantries.

"To drink." He tipped up his glass, taking a large swallow of the fiery liquid. "Why else?"

Damian's eyes roamed the room, then came to rest on a particularly well-endowed blonde enthusiastically sucking on a lime. "There are other reasons. Thought maybe you were ready to come off whatever self-imposed dry spell you've been on. This place is practically dripping with possibilities."

His brother had a point. There was no shortage of attractive women, including the bombshell doing the tequila shooters. He certainly could appreciate the display, but nothing about her or the other women that had attempted to make eye contact drew his interest. They were trying too hard, making him feel like a conquest, a prize to be won. Not that he could explain that to his brother, so he just shrugged. "Maybe."

Damian quirked up an eyebrow at that, but didn't comment, content to drink and listen to the music.

One hour and three drinks later, Nic's head was a bit fuzzy, so he was slow to react when a leggy redhead with surgically perfect features moved in a little too close. He had nothing against a bit of harmless flirting, but she seemed to have more ambitious goals in mind. When her roaming hands started heading south, he realized he'd had enough.

Turning to Damian, he shouted over the music, "I'm leaving." Damian looked questioningly at the handsy redhead, but shrugged and followed him out.

"What happened? She seemed into you."

"What she was into was my pants pocket, with her hand. She was trying to get a grip on the goods, if you get my drift."

"And?"

"And I like to know a girl's name before she starts massaging the family jewels. I'm old-fashioned that way."

"Damn, Mom was right. I hate it when she's right."

"What the heck are you talking about?"

"Mom. She said you'd fallen for someone, some girl down in Florida. That she had you going to church and everything."

Great. "I haven't fallen for anyone, not like that." He scowled, hoping to intimidate his younger brother into dropping this line of questioning.

Damian was undeterred. "She says that you talk to her all the time—that you even hung up on her so you could talk to this chick."

"It's business, that's all. I'm helping her with some real estate stuff." That the help he was giving was in direct opposition to the goals of Caruso Hotels didn't need to be mentioned. "And I didn't hang up on Mom, for crying out loud. I'd already talked to her for half an hour, so when Jillian called on Skype I told Mom I had to go."

"Skype? What is she, some kind of cybersex babe?"

Damian barely had the words out of his mouth before Nic had him shoved against the brick wall of the club, one arm across his throat. "Don't talk like that about her, understand?"

Damian, eyes wide, nodded, unwilling or unable to speak while his trachea was being crushed.

Nic stepped back, breathing hard. Crap, what was he doing? He scrubbed a hand over his jaw, feeling the bristles, taking the time to calm down and think clearly, or as clearly as the alcohol would let him. "Damian, I'm sorry, I had too much to drink, I shouldn't have—"

Damian's hoot of laughter cut him off. "Oh, boy, you

are totally messed up over this girl." His idiot brother was grinning from ear to ear. "No worries. I'll even be your best man, just let me know when the wedding is."

"Very funny." Great, if this got back to his parents, he'd be signed up for a tux fitting before he knew what hit him. "Like I said, she's just…" Hell, he didn't know. A friend? A colleague? The woman that kept him up at night, aching? "She's just someone I met. Besides, that's all over with. I haven't even talked to her since I was down there last week." Mainly because she wouldn't answer his phone calls.

"Wait, you saw her last week? I thought you were in Orlando last week?"

He was never drinking again. Ever. "Yeah, well, I drove over to Paradise Isle while I was there."

"Orlando to Paradise Isle? That's quite the booty call." Damian ducked this time; he was smaller and more sober, and easily eluded Nic's drunken punch. "Sorry, dude, that was just too easy."

"You're a jerk, you know that?"

"Yeah, I know. But I'll buy you a late dinner to soak up that booze, to make it up to you. Let's get out of here."

"Fine."

"Oh, and Nic?"

"Yeah?"

"Mom was definitely right." Nic glared, but didn't have a response, at least not one that Damian was going to buy. Not after seeing how riled up he got over a few remarks about Jillian. He was still hot about it, could still feel the temper simmering within him.

Which told him, more than Damian's taunts had, that his mom was right. He was really falling for Jillian. Maybe it was time he let her know it.

Chapter Twelve

A long afternoon at the beach with Murphy had scorched her skin but cleared her head. She'd even let Mollie talk her into dinner, and then drinks, at Pete's. Her canine buddy had been worn-out when she'd dropped him off, and now, climbing the stairs to her apartment, she felt about the same way. It was a good kind of tired, though, and she was glad she'd taken the time to catch up with Mollie. Sure, they saw each other at work every day, but it wasn't the same. Chatting with her friend had reminded her she had people in her life that cared, that she wasn't dependent on Nic Caruso or any man to keep her entertained.

After unlocking the door, she crossed the small living room and headed straight for the bathroom. She stripped off her tank top, shorts and bathing suit, leaving them in a pile on the floor, and turned the water on full force.

Nothing felt better than a hot, soapy shower after a day at the beach.

She took her time, using her favorite deep conditioner to rehydrate her curls after the salt water. A tingly, ginger-infused body wash got rid of the sticky sunscreen residue and left her feeling refreshed. She chose one of her biggest, softest bath towels for her body, and another for her hair. An orange-and-ginger-scented body lotion slathered on from head to toe finished her mini home spa treatment. She really should do this more often; she didn't need to wait for a big date to pamper herself a little. Feeling soft and pretty was its own reward.

A glance at her cat clock with the waggling tail told her it was already late, but after the beer she drank she should hydrate before going to bed. So she slipped into her favorite old nightshirt and went to the kitchen to pour a giant glass of water. Minutes later, she was perched on her hand-me-down couch, scanning the channels and sipping her drink. An old sitcom marathon was the best she could find, unless she wanted to watch endless infomercials for products she'd never heard of.

By the third episode her eyelids were sagging more than the punch lines. She really should go to bed, but getting off the couch sounded like a lot of work. Easier to just curl up right where she was. She snuggled farther into the cushions and snapped off the flickering television. Drifting off, she was in that lovely not-quite-asleep haze when the phone buzzed.

"Hello?" she managed to mumble, answering it without thinking to check the caller ID.

"Hi, Jillian. It's Nic. Did I wake you up? I didn't realize it was so late." His deep voice rumbled through the phone, a wakeup call to every sleeping nerve in her body.

"Um, no. I mean, well, not quite. I'm camped out on the couch and was just kind of dozing. Too lazy to get up and go to bed. I don't even know what time it is."

"Oh. It's almost midnight, I think. I shouldn't have called so late. I'll let you get back to sleep."

"No!" She scrambled to a sitting position. Now that she could hear his voice, she wanted him to keep talking, to ignore all the reasons she'd been avoiding his calls. "No, I'm awake. Really, it's fine. What's up? Did you hear something about the grant?"

"The grant? No, not yet. I'm sure you'll hear something soon."

"Hopefully." Why did he call if it wasn't about the grant? Did he just want to torture her, string her along a little longer?

"Yeah. Hopefully."

The silence echoed, stretching her nerves until she couldn't take it any longer. Maybe she would regret asking, but she had to know. "Nic?"

"Yeah?" His soft, husky voice sounded only inches from her ear, tempting her heart into wishing for things that weren't there.

"Why did you call?" Breath held, she waited.

"Because—well, I just wanted to talk to you, but you've been kind of hard to get ahold of lately. I care about you, you know."

Guilt formed a knot in her throat. Swallowing past it, she forced some cheer into her voice. "Oh, I'm fine. Went to the beach today with Mollie. I took Murphy. You should see him chase the ball in the waves. He's a real fiend about it."

"Yeah, I bet that's something." He cleared his throat. "In fact, when I come down there, maybe—"

"Maybe what, Nic?" Her embarrassment and guilt fused into anger in the space of a heartbeat. "Maybe when you're down here directing the demolition of the Sandpiper, you'll find some time to hang out on the beach? Show me where you're going to put in the first high-rise, and the water park, and who knows what else? Maybe you can take me on a tour this time, show me the new and improved vision for Paradise Isle, with all the tacky T-shirt shops and after-hours nightclubs? Is that what you think, Nic?"

His words were low and controlled when he spoke. "I wasn't thinking anything of the kind, Jillian."

"Good! Because I don't think anything of you or your plans to ruin the only home I've ever known." She was sobbing now, her voice cracking. "So stop pretending we're friends, or that you're going to come down here and we'll have some kind of romantic reunion, you, me and Murphy. Stop acting like you care, and stop calling me." She pressed the end-call button and threw down the phone, mortified.

Where did that come from? Hadn't she told Mollie just this afternoon that she agreed with Nic's motives, if not his plans? And yet here she was, throwing it all in his face, acting like a crazy woman. Because he was going to destroy the Sandpiper?

Or because he was going to destroy her heart?

Was she angry with him or with herself for letting her guard down, letting someone in?

Not that it mattered. That display of theatrics was guaranteed to keep him out of her life. Too bad it was a bit too late. No matter what she told her friends, this pain in her heart could only mean one thing. Somehow, she'd managed to fall in love with Nic Caruso, a man destined to destroy her world, and her life.

Sunday was usually Nic's chance to sleep in, at least on the days he didn't have an early flight. And since he'd lain awake for hours last night, trying to puzzle out his disastrous phone call to Jillian, he really needed the extra rest. A detail that his sister Isabella didn't care about in the least. When he'd ignored her phone call, she had just sweet-talked the doorman into letting her in. At least that's what she said. Eyeing his take-no-prisoners sister, he figured she'd most likely bulldozed whatever unlucky man had gotten in her way.

Right now she was standing in his dining room, towering over him while he slowly drank a cup of much-needed coffee. She was wearing jeans and a tailored blouse instead of her usual designer suit, but she still oozed the kind of confident power that had made her successful in the male-dominated world of investment banking. But if she thought that kind of power play was going to work on him, she was sorely mistaken.

"I'm assuming there is a reason you barged in so early?"

"It's only early to people that were up late getting drunk."

Great. Damian didn't waste any time tattling. "It wasn't that late, and I wasn't drunk." At least the first part was true; he had been home at a decent hour.

"You were drunk enough to shove Damian around."

"Since when do I need to be drunk to want to mess around with Damian?" He certainly felt like beating on his brother right now. How much had he told her?

"Okay, you have a point." Dropping the tough interrogation act, she sat down next to him, her golden eyes filled with concern. "But seriously, what's going on with you?"

Oh, boy. He could stand up to her tough-girl talk all day long, but he couldn't resist his sisters when they turned mushy. "Listen, it's not a big deal, okay? Some girl hit on me at the club, and I turned her down."

"Why?"

What, did all his siblings think he was some kind of playboy? Was turning down a girl that earthshaking? "No real reason, she just didn't do it for me."

"Maybe." She watched him closely; she had always been too perceptive for her own good. "Or maybe she was the wrong girl. Maybe there's someone else you're interested in."

"Yeah, well, sometimes the right girl is still all wrong," he muttered, shoveling in another bit of cereal.

"Aha! So there is a girl. Okay, well, by 'wrong,' do you just mean it might take some actual effort on your part? 'Cause, big brother, I have to tell you, you have gotten lazy."

He nearly choked on his cornflakes. Lazy? She had to be kidding.

"Don't you look at me that way, Dominic Caruso. I know you work hard, but when it comes to women, you've never had to lift a finger. They just throw themselves at you, and the most you have had to do is decide which one you want. I'm betting that for once, you've found one that won't come running when you snap your fingers. Am I right?"

He didn't want her to be right. He definitely didn't like the picture she was painting of him, but there was some truth to her words. "Let's just say that when I tried to talk to her last night, she hung up on me, crying."

Isabella's smug smile seemed completely out of place. "Oh, that's nothing. Just give her some flowers and grovel. Totally fixable."

"I don't think it's that easy."

"That's because you've never really groveled. Trust me, it works." The glint in her eyes told him she'd seen her share of such men.

"There's more to it than that. There are other…complications."

"So tell me about them. You know you're dying to tell someone. And unlike Damian, I won't go running my mouth to the rest of the family."

That much was true. Isabella's brain was like a vault. Nothing spilled out without her express permission. And maybe talking it out would help him to make sense of things. Drinking hadn't. So he explained, as best he could, the situation, telling her about the town, Jillian, the Sandpiper and Caruso's plans to transform the island. By the end of his story, his sister had tears in her eyes and a sappy smile on her face. "What? Why are you looking at me like that?"

"Because it's so romantic," she gushed, fanning her face to stop the tears from ruining her makeup.

"It's not romantic, it's a mess." Standing, he carried his dishes to the kitchen, loading them into the dishwasher with more force than necessary.

"Well, yeah, it's a mess. But it's romantic, too. The two of you are star-crossed lovers, like Romeo and Juliet."

"And look how they ended up."

"Okay, bad example. But seriously, it has to be fate

that the two of you met. If you really have feelings for her, if you love her, you have to find a way. You can't let anything stop you."

"Whoa…who said anything about love?" He staggered back, knocked off-kilter by the idea. "We've only known each other a few weeks, nowhere near long enough to be throwing the *L* word around."

"Oh, yeah?" Isabella advanced on him, coming in for the kill. "And exactly how long did Mom and Dad know each other before they got married?"

"Three weeks." *Oh, man.* "But that was…different."

"Not so different. And you know they're just as much in love now as they were then."

Nodding, he rubbed his chest, struggling to even out his breathing. His parents *were* very happy, but he'd always thought their whirlwind romance was the exception to the rule. Certainly nothing that could happen to him. His father was undeniably a risk taker in every facet of his life. A whirlwind romance, a risky business idea: that was Lorenzo Caruso's modus operandi. Nic, on the other hand, was methodical to the bone.

Someday he'd planned on falling in love, preferably with someone he was already friendly with, and only after a long courtship. They'd date casually at first, then more seriously, then after a year or so announce an engagement at just the right time. That was the right way to go about things.

Isabella interrupted his tumbling thoughts with a dilemma of her own. "I actually didn't come by here just to give you a hard time. I wanted to ask you to put out some feelers for me."

"You're looking for a new job?" He knew she'd been

under a lot of stress, working longer hours than even he did, but he hadn't thought she was that unhappy.

"Yeah, it's time. I took this position as a stepping stone, a chance to get experience in a big company. But I'm tired of doing grunt work. The pay is great, but I want a chance to make real decisions. Instead, I'm spending all my hours crunching numbers, just for some executive to ignore them and do whatever he wants, anyway. I need a new challenge, a different way to use my skills. Maybe something with some travel. I've always envied you, getting to stay in all sorts of interesting places, meeting new people. Me? My biggest adventure is getting a new flavor of nondairy creamer for my coffee."

"It's not all glamorous, trust me."

"Nothing is, but I didn't come here to complain, just to ask you to keep an ear out. Let me know if you hear of anything that sounds interesting."

"Sure, I can do that. I don't have a lot of contacts in finance, but if you're looking for a change, there are lots of businesses that would jump at a chance to have someone with your experience. It's just a matter of who has openings."

"Thanks, I know it will take some time. Just fix your woman problems, and by then I'll probably have my dream job all lined up." As confident of her success as ever, she let herself out, leaving him alone with his thoughts. And if any of what she'd accused him of was true, he had plenty of thinking to do.

Chapter Thirteen

Jillian regretted her angry outburst at Nic, but what had her nerves twanging like a tautly strung banjo wasn't the fight, it was discovering how deep her feelings for him ran. He might think he was interested right now, but she was realistic enough to know that any feelings he had couldn't last, not long-term. Anyone could see they were all wrong for each other. Even without the controversy over the Sandpiper, there were so many reasons they could never work as a couple. He was a rolling stone, constantly traveling. She was a homebody, with a need to plant deep roots. He was wealthy, with powerful family connections. She was happy to finally be able to afford rent and her own car. And of course, his life centered on his family, and she was an orphan who didn't know the first thing about those kinds of blood bonds.

Added all up, it equaled disaster. And yet, somehow

she'd managed to fall for him, anyway. Hook, line and sinker. The only bright point was that he didn't know how she felt. In fact, after that last phone call, he probably assumed she hated him. Better that than to face humiliation on top of rejection. This way she could nurse her wounded heart in peace, with no one the wiser. Surely, after a while, it would heal. She'd lived through worse. She'd live through this, too.

Her coping strategy of the moment was to spend time with Murphy, her wannabe dog. She'd increased her training sessions with him, and he was really turning into an obedient little guy. He loved the extra attention, and she found comfort in his furry friendship. Mrs. Rosenberg had asked a few times about Nic, but when Jillian refused to talk about him, she had backed off. Even Cassie and Mollie had stopped asking about him, instead focusing on the future of the Sandpiper and Paradise Isle. The first thing anyone asked when they saw her was if she'd heard about the grant decision yet. The stress of waiting for news was almost worse than the heartbreak over Nic. Almost.

Arriving home after another long day at work and then an hour working with Murphy, she was ready to call it a night. Out of habit she stopped at the row of metal mailboxes, using her tiny key to access a stack of what looked like bills and junk mail. Shoving them in her purse, she climbed the stairs to her second-floor apartment, trying to decide on dinner. Sandwich? Soup? What the heck? Might as well have both.

Once inside, she tossed her purse and mail on the kitchen counter, the envelopes fanning out across the tan Formica. She found a can of alphabet soup and heated it up on the stove, letting it simmer while she made a quick ham sandwich. Cooking didn't seem worth it when there was no one to cook for, so this would have to do.

She ladled the soup into a bowl and started nibbling the sandwich, sitting at the breakfast bar that extended from the counter. Too tired to read, she let her mind wander. She ought to wash her car this weekend. Organize the pantry. Oh, and clean out the mail basket; there were ads and coupons and bills all mixed together in a jumble. She had a tendency to just pile it up, and then she didn't have the coupons when she wanted them, and it was a pain to find the bills and pay them. Really, she should start that now. Go through the stuff she'd just dropped on the table, sort it out. It would at least be a start.

She put her dishes in the sink and scooped up the scattered mail, taking it to her desk in the entryway. Pulling out the wastebasket she kept under the desk, she began sorting. Advertisement, bill, craft store coupon, bill, political brochure and a plain brown envelope with the State of Florida seal on it. Her hands trembled. Maybe she shouldn't open it. Maybe she should give it to the Island Preservation Society, let them open it.

"Don't be such a baby," she scolded herself, ripping open the envelope before she could chicken out again. She unfolded the single page, holding her breath as she quickly scanned the typewritten lines. *We regret to inform you...*

None of the other words made sense after that, or even mattered. There would be no grant money. The city wouldn't be able to purchase the inn; it wouldn't be listed as an historic place. It would be torn down, and in its place would be some mega-resort with everything the busy traveler could want—for a price. They'd overrun the beaches, crowd the streets and take over the restaurants. The Paradise Isle she'd come to love would no longer be the quiet sanctuary of her dreams. And there was absolutely nothing she, or anyone else, could do about it.

Sinking to the floor, she tucked her head against her knees and let the tears come. She cried for the sheer ugliness of what was going to happen, for the upheaval sure to come, but mostly for the loss of yet one more place, one more dream. Would she ever find a safe haven of her own?

A good cry helped to wash the pain out of head and heart, leaving an empty numbness in its place. Soon, she'd have to figure out the details and set up a meeting of the Island Preservation Society to break the bad news. For now, though, there was an even bigger hurdle to clear. She needed to let Nic know. And then face the consequences, whatever they were. She was sure he'd be nice about it, of course. He didn't want to hurt her, of that she was sure. But hurt her he would, and she couldn't even work up any righteous anger about it.

As much as she hated what he was going to do, deep down she admired his devotion to his family, his loyalty. She couldn't ask him to betray the trust his family had placed in him when they brought him into the company. Which meant that there was nothing left to do but move on and make the best of it.

Unfolding herself from her cramped position on the floor, she stood tall, bracing herself for the coming conversation. She needed to be strong—she wouldn't, couldn't, let him hear her pain. No, she'd be professional, impart the information he needed, and that would be the end of her dealings with Nic Caruso.

She dialed with steady hands, calming herself through

sheer force of will. She could do this. The phone rang. Her stomach flopped. She hadn't talked to him since their big fight. What if he didn't want to talk to her, wouldn't answer? Another ring. Just as she lost her nerve and started to hang up, he answered.

"Jillian?" He sounded cautious, but not angry. That was a good sign. At least he wasn't going to hang up on her.

"Hi, Nic. I'm sure you're wondering why I'm calling. And I won't keep you. I just wanted to inform you that I received a letter from the State Registry of Historical Places, and they were not able to grant us any funds."

"Oh."

She tried to finish quickly, get it over with. "So, just thought you should know, so you can make arrangements, do whatever it is you do. So anyway—"

"Hey, listen, for what it's worth, I'm sorry."

She didn't want to hear that. She wasn't going to be able to hold it together if he started pitying her. "Well, be that as it may, the fact of the matter is, you win. You get what you want."

"Jillian, I need to talk to you—"

She hung up. She'd told him what she had to tell him; she wasn't going to torture herself by staying on the line, making small talk, pretending things were just fine between them. How could she? He had stolen from her the one thing she'd come to count on: her home. She had wanted to raise a family here, on the quiet and safe streets she'd grown to love. But now those streets would be overrun with tourists, the small shops replaced with chain stores and after-hours nightclubs. She'd lived in other places where tourism had taken over, and had no desire to repeat the experience. She knew some people thrived on the hustle and bustle, but she craved peace and a sense of community that those busy cities couldn't provide.

And, beneath that hurt, there was a deeper, sharper pain, one that tore at her battered heart.

How could it hurt this much to lose a man she should never have fallen for in the first place?

Chapter Fourteen

As much as Nic had come to dislike the constant traveling his job required, he had never actually dreaded a trip before. Of course, it had never been so personal before. Boarding the plane to Florida, all he'd been able to think about was Jillian and how badly he'd messed things up. Not that he could think of a different way to have handled things, other than never meeting her at all. He couldn't have prevented the bond that had formed between them any more than he could prevent his next breath. Heaven knew he'd tried. But she'd gotten stuck inside him somehow, and now he was trapped, forced to either hurt the woman he wanted to protect or betray the man that had given him everything. He couldn't do that to his father.

So his only option was to try to minimize the impact of the hotel on the island and hope that would be enough to show Jillian how he felt. It wouldn't be easy, and most of the changes couldn't be prevented. But he had to try. He only hoped that would be enough for Jillian to forgive him. Maybe then he'd have a chance with her. It wasn't a great plan, but what else could he do?

The flight, for once, felt too short. In what seemed like no time he was loading his luggage into yet another rental car. The motions were familiar, but the anxiety chewing through his gut was not. He'd always been a confident person, and years in the field had assured him he had the skills needed to complete the task at hand. So it wasn't fear of failure that nagged him now. It was the cold, hard fact that this time, he didn't want to succeed.

Shrugging off his melancholy mood, he concentrated on navigating the horrendous traffic that Orlando was famous for. Caruso Hotels would definitely have to arrange for some kind of shuttle from the airport, so vacationers didn't show up to the resort already in a bad mood. Maybe even a helicopter service for the VIP guests; they'd love that. The noise would be an issue, but in the scheme of things, the prestige would be worth it. He'd send a memo to the development team so they could work a landing pad into their plans. Focusing on the details let him avoid thinking about the ramifications of what he was about to do.

That strategy worked well until he approached the spot where he'd rescued Murphy, and all the memories of that first weekend came flooding back in Technicolor clarity. Her gentle touch with the injured dog, her eyes so big and blue, her lips and how right they'd felt on his own. Just thinking about it had his body responding, his blood pressure rising.

Damn, if he was this wound up just thinking about

her, how much harder was it going to be to see her? And he was going to see her. Even if he couldn't convince her of his feelings, he didn't want to end things like they had, with her angry and hanging up on him. He wanted a chance to explain, to apologize, to tell her his plans to make the transition as easy as possible. And, if he was honest with himself, he just couldn't stay away.

Which was why he found himself climbing her staircase as dusk was falling, knowing she would, most likely, slam the door in his face. When his knock was met with silence his first assumption was that she was, in fact, avoiding him. It was only when he scanned the parking lot and didn't find her car that he realized his mistake. She was probably taking her nightly run with Murphy; he'd somehow forgotten her commitment to the pet she couldn't have. He could sit and wait for her, but his growling stomach gave him a better idea.

There was a diner around the corner; he could pick up food for the both of them, a peace offering of sorts. Deciding to walk rather than drive, he once again noted the Norman Rockwell quality of the town. Everywhere he looked, he saw kids playing in the twilight, families gathering in neat little houses, older folks rocking on front porches, as they probably had every evening for decades, watching the comings and goings of their neighborhood.

Even Mary's Diner was picturesque in its own way, a throwback to the 1950s, with red booths and chrome accents everywhere. A few single men sat at the bar; the tables were filled mostly with young families grabbing a bite out after a busy day. The service was quick and friendly. A matronly woman wearing a frilly apron took his order, and within minutes he had two meat loaf dinners and a lemon pound cake packed up and ready to go. The aromas tantalized him as he made his way back; hopefully she'd be hungry enough to let him in, at least long enough to eat.

She arrived a few minutes after he did, pulling into the parking lot directly across from where he sat at her front door. He knew the minute she saw him; her eyes narrowed, as if just the sight of him caused her pain.

What had he been thinking, coming here?

It was too late now. He only hoped he could reassure her somehow, make things even a little bit right for her. Because as much as he knew he should just walk away, he couldn't do it. Not yet.

The last thing Jillian had expected when she finally got home that night was Nic Caruso at her door. They had no business left to discuss, and she thought she'd hinted pretty clearly that she wanted no personal contact with him, either. Obviously subtlety was lost on him. She'd just have to tell him, politely but firmly, to go. Whatever he thought he wanted, he wasn't going to get it from her. She wasn't equipped to deal with the emotional maelstrom he triggered—she was too raw. The sooner she got him out of her life, she sooner she could pick up the pieces of her broken heart.

When she had stomped up the last step, she saw the bags of food. Damn him. She was starving; no way was she going to turn down food from Mary's. Fine, they'd eat—quickly—and then he could leave. Whatever he had to say, he'd have to say fast, before she finished devouring whatever was behind that wonderful aroma.

She refused to ask him why he was there as she pushed past him to open the door. It didn't matter, anyway. "Put the food on the counter. I'll get plates and drinks."

He did as she instructed, opening up Styrofoam containers to reveal savory meat loaf, mashed potatoes and carrots. Her stomach rumbled, betraying her interest in his culinary olive branch. She assumed that's what it was, and it annoyed her that it had worked. Just having him in her apartment was a major mistake, one she wouldn't have made if she had been thinking with her head instead of her stomach. The irony was that now that she'd seen him, the only thing she had an appetite for was him.

Get a grip. She couldn't let him see how much she wanted him. She couldn't lose her pride on top of her heart.

She forced herself to set the plates down on the breakfast bar rather than slam them, not wanting to show more emotion than necessary. Crossing to the refrigerator, she considered the options, then closed it again and grabbed a bottle of red wine off the counter. A little liquid courage to get her through this. She silently handed him the bottle and corkscrew, then fetched the wineglasses. He poured generously, then clinked his glass against hers. "Salute."

She looked up, unfamiliar with the toast, and her eyes met his over the raised glasses. She read regret there, and concern, emotions a little too close to pity, and she wouldn't be pitied. Not again. She'd gotten over being the poor little orphan girl long ago, and didn't need him feeling sorry for her. He might as well pour salt on her wounds.

"So, I assume you're here to buy the Sandpiper, tie up all the loose ends or whatever. Then you'll be off to your next conquest." *Soon*, she added silently. The sooner he was gone, the sooner she could try to forget the way he made her feel. Even now, knowing what he was here to do, she found herself wanting to let down her guard, recapture the closeness that had sprung up so quickly between them.

"Not just yet. I need to schedule more land surveys, have various inspections done, that kind of thing. And I'm going to order an environmental survey, as well. It isn't strictly required, since the zoning won't change, but I'm going to do my best to limit the impact to the beaches and wildlife. I want to make this work, and I want to do right by Paradise Isle. I want to do right by you."

"So that's why you're here?" She gestured to the apartment around her. "You came to my home, knowing how I feel about all this, to tell me it won't be so bad, after all?" She didn't know if she should laugh or cry at his brazenness.

"Well, yeah. And to bring you dinner." He smiled cockily, melting her defenses in the space of a heartbeat.

"That was a dirty trick." But she took a bite of the meat loaf, anyway. She *was* hungry, and heaven help her, she couldn't keep up the bitch act around him. She liked him too much. Liked him? Who was she kidding? She was head over heels for him. Just watching him sit in her kitchen, in faded jeans and an old band T-shirt that stretched enticingly when he moved, had her hormones working on overdrive.

But it was more than his looks; it was who he was as a person that had gotten her to let down her guard. Even when they should have been enemies, they still slipped into the easy banter that had become so natural between them. She loved hearing about the exotic places he had traveled, and he always seemed genuinely interested in the stories she told him about the animals at work. They'd found they also shared similar views on politics, religion and literature, but were, of course, rivals in football and baseball. His family was another frequent topic of conversation, one that often had her crying tears of laughter as he told stories of his childhood.

"Is Damian back yet from Florence?" she asked, reaching for more wine.

He filled her glass, and topped off his own. "Yeah, he got back a few weeks ago, even more arrogant than he was before."

She grinned. A certain level of self-confidence was a trait the brothers shared, whether Nic acknowledged it or not. "So I take it you got a chance to see him the last time you were home?" With his crazy schedule, he didn't always get time for family visits on his brief trips to New York.

"Um, yeah…sure, I saw him," Nic mumbled, suddenly very interested in the last few carrots on his plate.

"What? What happened?" She smelled a story here. When he didn't answer, she grabbed his arm, spinning his bar stool toward her. Facing him, she demanded, "Spill it!"

"Nothing happened, really. I had a few drinks and, well, things got a little tense. But it's fine now, no big deal."

Jillian had heard enough about the family to know that a scuffle between the brothers was nothing new. But something about his reaction had her curiosity piqued. "What was the fight about?"

Again, he didn't answer. Now she had to know. She

slid off her stool into the space between them. Taking his face in her hands, she pulled him down so she could look into his eyes. "Hey, seriously, what started it this time?"

Sighing, he knocked back the rest of his wine. "It was just a misunderstanding. He was trying to get a rise out of me, and it worked. I mentioned that you and I had been talking on Skype a lot, and he insinuated I was using you for cybersex."

Speechless, she felt the blood rise in her cheeks. She wasn't a prude, but wow, she hadn't expected that. Unbidden, seductive images streaked across her mind's eye.

"Don't worry. I made it clear to him that's not the situation. At all."

"That's...good." Suddenly she realized how close she was standing to him; only inches separated them. There wasn't enough oxygen, not enough space. She needed more distance, physically and emotionally. She tried to clear her suddenly dry throat. "Obviously that's not the kind of thing that would happen with us."

"Oh, I don't know," he answered, reaching out to brush a stray curl from her face. "I can't say the idea *never* occurred to me."

Her mouth parted in shock and Nic took full advantage of the offering, lowering his lips to hers, tasting, testing, gently seducing. His tenderness was her undoing. Time stopped, the world spun away. Distantly, she knew this shouldn't happen, but there was no way she could stop it. Nothing else mattered, just him. Just this moment and this man.

He'd never paid much attention to descriptions of heaven, but it couldn't be better than this. She was warm and soft in his arms; her lips were a silken seduction tempting him to explore and linger. Holding himself back, ignoring the fire in his body that demanded to be fed, was like holding back a raging river. It took all his willpower but he kept his touch light, sampling rather than devouring the mouth she so innocently offered up for him.

When his resolve was strained nearly to the breaking point, he forced himself to pull away. Panting, he leaned his forehead against hers. "I didn't expect that."

Her eyes were glazed, but she shuttered them quickly, turning away at his words. "I'm sorry." Her voice trembled, plucking at his guilt.

When she tried to walk away, he grabbed her arm, stopping her. "Don't be sorry—I'm not."

Shaking him off, she pulled out of his grip, backing into the living room, putting as much space between them as was possible in the small apartment. "This can't keep happening." Her eyes pleaded with him, pain reflecting in the smoky depths.

"It can, if you'll just let it." He shoved his hands through his hair. "Damn it, I can't force you to admit what you feel, but I'm done hiding how I feel. And I'm sure as hell not to pretend I'm sorry, that I regret kissing you. And I don't think you regret it, either."

"I think you should go now." Her arms were wrapped around her body, her gaze refusing to meet his.

"Don't do this. I know you want—"

"What I want is for you to go." Her voice cracked with emotion. "Please...just go."

Damn it. Look at what he was doing to her. He'd been a fool to think he could see her and keep his hands off her. All he'd wanted was to make things a bit better, a bit easier for her. Instead, he'd made of mess of everything, leaving her worse off than before. But he'd told her the truth; he didn't regret that kiss, or any of the others for that matter. He only regretted hurting her. His instinct had been to protect her, but for now the best way to do that was to leave.

"I'll go." He'd brought nothing with him other than the food; there was nothing to collect, no way to stall on his way to the door she held open for him. He wanted to stay and fight, to make her let him stay, but the tears spilling onto her cheeks stopped him when no argument or harsh word would have.

"Goodbye. And Nic? Please don't come back."

Her final words haunted him as he drove through the night. He had reserved a room at the Sandpiper, but he took the highway back to Orlando instead. He didn't trust himself to stay away with so little distance between them. Even now, knowing how badly he'd hurt her, he had to fight to keep from turning around and forcing her to let him back in.

Maybe he'd been wrong about them, about making it work. She obviously wasn't going to forgive him. And he didn't blame her; he'd attacked the one thing she held dear—her community.

Being without her might kill him, but if seeing him was going to hurt her, then the only solution was to leave the island, leave the project. He'd have to find someone else to take over; there was no way he could be there, day after day, and not see her, even if only accidentally. He'd never walked away from an assignment before, but right now his reputation was the least of his worries. He'd turn over his notes to one of the up-and-coming executives, give them a chance to prove themselves. He could spin it that way, make it sound like he was mentoring someone, helping them move up in the ranks.

His father would be a hard sell, but certainly by now he'd earned some discretion. The project would go forward, and Jillian would get the space she'd asked for. He should have done this weeks ago, as soon as he started getting involved with her. But he'd always managed to keep his business and personal lives separate before; he hadn't expected it to be a problem.

But there was no way to compartmentalize his feelings for Jillian. She permeated every facet of his life; he'd even started dreaming about her. Right now he should be thinking about work, about finding the right person to take over the project, and figuring out how to streamline any collaboration. Instead, he kept seeing the tears on her face, each one another slice at his soul.

He'd dated dozens of beautiful women, so why did this one bring him to his knees?

The answer was obvious. He was in love with her. Only he'd figured it out way too late.

Furious with himself, with fate, his job, he pounded his fist on the steering wheel, relishing the sting. Physical pain faded quickly. Much worse was this throbbing ache in his chest, threatening to consume him. Maybe with some distance he'd be thinking more clearly and would find a way out of this mess. Because the alternative was unthinkable.

Chapter Fifteen

Jillian knocked quietly on Cassie's door, not wanting to wake Emma if she was already asleep. What time did four-year-olds go to bed, anyway? Not that she knew what time it was. She'd spent longer than she should have indulging in tears after Nic left, then had gone on a cleaning spree, taking her angst out on her kitchen. She now had gleaming tile and the beginnings of a plan. Talking to Cassie was the first step to putting it in motion.

Her friend opened the door, ushering her into the small but cheery 1950s cottage she'd purchased when Emma was born. Soft throw rugs were scattered on the terrazzo floor, creating a welcoming and child-friendly space. Family photos and pictures of various pets intermingled with books on the large, built-in bookcases, the only real decoration other than a few jewel-toned throw cushions. Jillian kicked off her shoes at the door and sat cross-legged on the taupe microfiber couch. Cassie joined her, settling slightly sideways so she could face her friend.

"Thanks for letting me in, I know it's probably late. I hope I didn't wake Emma."

"You know you can come by anytime. And Emma sleeps like a rock—a five-piece band wouldn't wake her up. But it is late, at least for you, so I assume it's important."

Jillian took a deep breath, steadying her nerves. She'd practiced a speech on the way over here, but now it seemed so scripted. Maybe she should just lay it all out there, and then deal with the aftermath. "I'd like to tender my notice of resignation."

"Excuse me? What did you just say? I must have misheard. I would have sworn you just said you were quitting."

"That's exactly what I'm saying. I've stayed in Paradise a long time, longer than anywhere else I've lived. I stayed because of the kind of place it is, but that's all changing, so there's no reason I shouldn't move on, try something new."

Cassie narrowed her brow. "Funny, I would have thought your best friends being here might be a reason to stick around."

Crap. She didn't want to offend Cassie, but she had to move. She couldn't stay in Paradise with Nic parading in and out of town constantly. And once the resort was built it would be a constant reminder. She would never be able to put him behind her if she stayed here.

Maybe she just wasn't meant to have a real home. Some people never settled down; they moved whenever the urge hit them. Just because she'd always dreamed of putting down roots didn't mean it was the right thing or that this was the right place. She knew better than most that dreams didn't always come true. "I love you guys, you know that. But just because I won't live here doesn't mean we can't still be friends. I'll call, we can talk on Skype, email, text. And when I'm settled you can come visit me."

"Settled where?" Cassie threw her hands up in the air. "Do you even know where you want to go?"

She'd anticipated that question. Unfortunately, she hadn't come up with an answer yet. "Not yet. But I will. I'm going to start checking ads, see who's hiring. Maybe try somewhere up north for a change."

"So let me get this straight." Cassie had shifted to what Jillian thought of as her doctor voice. "You have no idea where you want to go, nothing planned out, and yet you are quitting your job—a job I was reasonably sure you liked—leaving your best friends, and deserting the town you love. And you are doing this why?"

"When Caruso Hotels buys the Sandpiper—"

"Ah, Caruso, that's what this is about. Nic Caruso, to be specific. Damn him. What happened? If he hurt you, I know how to castrate—"

"That won't be necessary." She managed a smile at the image, pleased by the show of solidarity if not the dramatic suggestion. "He didn't do anything, really. Other than be the wrong man at the wrong time." She needed Cassie to understand. "He came by tonight. He's in town to start negotiations to buy the Sandpiper. He wanted to tell me he was sorry things turned out this way, that he would try to make the transition as painless as possible, even though we both know there isn't much he can do to minimize the impact of thousands of new tourists." She focused on her hands, resting them carefully in her lap. "He brought me dinner."

"What a bastard," Cassie said drolly.

Jillian continued without pause. "We talked, and for a while it was like before. Then it got...tense, sort of. And then he kissed me."

"And?"

"And it was wonderful, okay? The best kiss I've ever had. But then I stopped it. I can't go there when I know it can't work, not long-term." She swiped angrily at her eyes, refusing to cry over him anymore. "I get that he has to do his job, has to build the hotel. I fell in love with him, anyway. I'll find a way to get over him, but I can't keep seeing him. It hurts too much." Her voice cracked, but she didn't break down this time. No more. She'd learned to be strong a long time ago, and no man was going to break her. Not even Nic Caruso.

"Oh, Jillian...I'm so sorry."

"Don't feel sorry for me, okay? Just help me move on. Accept my resignation."

Cassie started to say something, then stopped. Getting up, she moved to the desk in the corner where she kept her computer. "Well, come on. Let's start searching those job databases. We need to find you somewhere fantastic, somewhere fun for me to visit."

Nic sat in one of the leather chairs facing the oak desk where his father conducted all his business. He'd waited until the end of the day to approach him, not wanting to chance their conversation being interrupted. Even still, he'd found Lorenzo Caruso tied up in a conference call with the marketing department.

Tapping his fingers on the leather, he took another swallow of the whiskey he'd helped himself to, trying to contain his nerves. He was generally given free rein with business decisions; as a vice president, he technically didn't need approval to hand off the Paradise Isle project. But his father would be curious, and it was better to head off any questions, rather than be put on the defensive later. At least, that was the plan.

His father waved a finger at him, signaling he would only be another minute. Good: the sooner this was over, the sooner he could get to work on something else, anything else. A new place, a new challenge—that was what he needed. Hopefully Dad would have something ready for him, something meaty that would take all his concentration. Something to get his mind off his impossible situation with Jillian.

Finally, his father hung up the phone, circling the desk to envelop Nic in a crushing hug. "What are you doing here? I didn't think I'd see you until next week!"

He returned the embrace, happier to see his father than he would have expected. The older man returned to his desk, settling on the edge of it rather than sitting behind it.

"Were there any problems?"

"No problems, Dad. As expected, the grant I told you about didn't go through, so there's no issue there. In fact, it should be a straightforward enough project that I'm going to have Mike Patrullo head this one up. He's been doing good work, and I think it would be a positive experience for him."

His father pursed his lips, swirling his own, mostly empty glass of whiskey, the golden liquid dancing in the light. "You've never turned an assignment of this magnitude over to someone else before."

"No, but this seemed like a good time to try it, let someone else take their shot."

"And this decision wouldn't have anything to do with a young lady your mother was telling me about, would it?"

Great. Was his whole family obsessed with his love life?

"And don't go blaming your mother. You know she just wants you to be happy," his father added before Nic could voice a complaint.

Cornered and not willing to lie to his father, he conceded the point. "Yeah, I guess it does have to do with her. I messed things up, badly."

"So you're running away? I thought I raised you better than that."

"I'm not running. She asked me to leave. Staying there would just make things harder for her, and—"

"And you're willing to make a sacrifice if it means you can help her out, is that right?"

"Yes." He relaxed a bit more into the buttery leather; he should have known his father would understand. He might be a savvy businessman, but he had raised his boys to be gentlemen, as well.

"Do you love her?"

The blunt question ripped through his careful posturing, resurrecting the headache he'd almost managed to forget about. Knowing his father wouldn't leave it alone, he gave the only answer he could. "Yes." Dropping his head back, he closed his eyes against the overhead lighting. "But that doesn't seem to matter."

"Dominic, love is the only thing that does matter."

Those were not the words he'd expected to hear from his ambitious father.

"You don't understand. She deserves things I can't give her. She needs someone that wants the same things as her, someone that can be there day in and day out, home for dinner, with kids and a dog in the backyard."

"Ah, I see." His father rested his hands together, steepling his fingers. "And that's not the kind of life you want."

"No. I mean, I don't know. But either way, it's not the life I have. Heck, I'm barely home long enough to read my mail, let alone have a relationship."

"True. And after investing so much time and effort into your work, you wouldn't want to change things now."

"It's not about what I want. It's about what needs to be done. I've got responsibilities. You know that—you're the one that taught me about responsibility."

"Yes, I did. And I've always been proud of your work ethic. But maybe I didn't do a very good job of teaching you about priorities."

"What's that supposed to mean? I should just drop everything, run off to Florida because I met a pretty girl?"

"No, not if that's all she is. But this isn't about playing beach blanket bingo with some random girl, is it?"

Nic shook his head, then got up and walked to one of the large windows overlooking the street far below. From this distance, the frantic pushing and shoving of evening commuters looked almost choreographed. Were any of them as twisted up inside as he was?

His father stepped up behind him. "You won't find the answers out there, son, and I don't have them, either. You're going to have to do some hard thinking. But

I trust you to find your way in this, just as you have in everything else."

Nic stayed at the window long after his father left, hoping for some inspiration in the place where so many pivotal decisions had been made.

A knock at the door found Jillian elbow deep in a box of books, trying to figure out the best way to arrange them for maximum space. Happy for a reprieve, she stretched out her aching muscles. Packing was harder work than she remembered, although really, this was the first time she'd ever had much worth packing. Increased pounding hurried her to the door. "I'm coming. Keep your pants on."

Impatient as always, Mollie had already let herself in by the time Jillian got there. Taking in the boxes, packing paper and all-around mess, she let out a long whistle. "You didn't waste any time getting started, did you?"

Jillian huffed at a curl that had escaped the bandanna she'd used to cover her hair. "No, I want to be ready to go as soon as I hear back on a job. And if you're here to talk me out of it, you can just leave now." Hands on her hips, she silently dared her friend to challenge her.

"No, I said I'd help, and I will. That doesn't mean I have to like it, or that I agree with what you're doing, but it's your life."

"Exactly."

Kneeling next to the box again, she gave up on efficiency and just piled the books in however they fit. It wasn't like boxes were hard to come by—the clinic got enough shipments of dog food and medications to keep her well supplied. "I'm doing the bookshelves first, then the pictures, then we can start on the hall closet."

True to her word, Mollie pitched right in, grabbing another box and a stack of books. "So, any leads yet?"

"A few nibbles. I have a phone interview with a place in New Mexico on Tuesday."

"New Mexico, huh? What about New York? Did you find any openings up there?"

"I didn't really look," Jillian lied. She'd spent quite a bit of time and ink printing job ads for New York City, only to toss them in the trash.

"Well, you should. If you're going to be selfish enough to move away from us, you should do it for a good reason. Moving to be with the man of your dreams qualifies. Running away, on the other hand, does not."

"I'm not running away, I'm getting a fresh start."

"You say to-*may*-to, I say to-*mah*-to."

"Juvenile."

Mollie stuck her tongue out, undeterred.

"And I'm not moving to New York City. First of all, Nic has given me zero indication that he has any interest in making things work between us."

"Maybe that's because he thought you would never agree to relocate. You made such a big stink about how Paradise Isle is the only place you've ever felt at home, he probably never even considered asking you to be near him. And yet here you are, moving away, leaving everything."

Mollie had a point. She had made it sound as though she would never leave, for anything. Until just a few days ago, she hadn't thought she ever would. But that didn't mean anything, did it? "It would be pointless, anyway. Even if I did move up there, which I won't, he's almost never home."

"Maybe he's never had anything worth going home for?"

"Right...gorgeous guy, lots of money, apartment in the city. He's been starved for female companionship, I'm sure." Her eyes rolled so hard she almost sprained something.

"Maybe not. But love is different, it changes things. If love is powerful enough to make you pick up and run from the one place you've always said you'd never leave, don't you think it would be enough to get him to spend more nights at home?"

All Mollie's talk of love was making her head spin. "He's not in love with me. Anyway, I'd probably hate a city that big. I've always said I want to start a family somewhere small, with a hometown feel to it. You know that."

"Sure, and that's a great dream. But it seems to me, you're looking at this from the wrong angle. What's important about a home is the people in it, not what zip code it's in." Shrugging her shoulders, Mollie went back to packing the box in front of her.

Jillian looked into her own box, then at the things still waiting to be packed. She'd spent so much time and energy searching out things that would make this apartment feel special, feel homey. But no matter how she decorated, it never had the kind of inviting vibe she was going for. Sure, she'd been burned by people in the past, but had that somehow taught her to invest her emotional energy into a place, instead of people? Was she so afraid of being hurt again that she'd ignored the importance of love in her search for the perfect home? So many times she'd prayed and hoped for a real family, but when had she stopped believing that wish would come true? Had she traded her dreams of love for security?

If that was her coping strategy, it wasn't working very well. Wasn't that why she tended to stay at work late, or go by Mrs. Rosenberg's in the evening? She thought about the houses she'd envied growing up—all were filled with people that cared about each other. Even the clinic, with all its sterility, felt welcoming because Cassie and Mollie were there. Despite herself, she had wonderful people in her life. Was she really going to let her old insecurities drive her into leaving them, running away from everyone that mattered, in a misguided attempt to protect herself?

Was that hidden fear the reason her romantic relationships had never gone anywhere? Because she was afraid of being abandoned again? Had she pushed Nic away, too, because of her distrust? Maybe she had been too quick to assume things between them could never work out, too quick to shut the door on what could have been. She had missed her chance to fix things with him, but that didn't mean she had to keep repeating the same pattern.

Energy rising, she stood, dumping the half-filled box, the books thudding to the floor. "You're right."

Mollie nodded, her short hair bouncing. "Always. But in what way, specifically?"

"About me, about people being more important than places. I've always said that I'd stay in Paradise forever, right? So leaving just because things are changing is crazy."

A smile filled her friend's face. "Totally insane. And stupid."

"Don't go overboard." She smiled. "But moving isn't

what I really want. Paradise might be different, but my friends are the same, and I'm not going to give them up." She felt her own grin growing. "I'm staying. Which means—"

"That we need to unpack all these boxes." Mollie sighed. "Do you have any wine? This is going to take a while."

Nic wasn't sure how long he had been in his father's office, alternating between pacing the floor and staring blankly out the window. Long enough that the offices had grown quiet other the bustle of the janitorial staff somewhere down the hall. He really should leave, but instead he sank into his father's worn desk chair. In front of him a small city of photographs populated the desk, as if guarding the stacks of paperwork enshrined there.

One, older than the rest, caught his eye. The frame was a plain, wooden square, aged but sturdy. The picture inside was faded, the sepia tones revealing two men, one middle-aged and bearded, the other young and clean-shaven with an adventurous gleam in his eye. Father and son shared similar dark features, features that Nic had inherited, as well.

He hadn't thought about his grandfather, his *nonno*, in quite some time. His health had kept him from visiting the past few years, but before that he had made a point of staying in touch with his descendants in America, despite the distance. Picking up the picture to look more closely, Nic could make out the bow of a boat in the background, one they had probably built together. Nonno had been a shipbuilder, as had his father before him. Lorenzo, Nic's father, had been taught the craft at a young age, with the expectation that he would continue the family tradition.

But the youngest Caruso had had other dreams. He'd worked for passage to America, sure his destiny was there. And it had been. He'd used his business expertise and natural charm to find jobs, saving until he could buy the rental home he'd been living in. He might have never owned more than a property or two, but wise investment and a healthy dose of luck had allowed him to channel his legendary determination into what was now one of the premier resort chains in the country.

And no one was more proud than Lorenzo's own father, who had made it his personal mission to stay in every single Caruso Resort. If he'd ever been upset about his son's choice to immigrate, Nic hadn't heard about it.

The family ties that spanned the two continents hadn't broken or strained over time, only strengthened. That was an accepted fact of Nic's family history, but one that he was now seeing through new eyes. There had been no disloyalty in his father's decision to leave the family shipbuilding tradition or the country of his birth. Maybe it had caused some tension; surely there had been concerns, but never hard feelings. So why did he feel so trapped by his own relationship with his father? Had he confused his connection to his father's business with his connection to the man himself?

Yes, his father had wanted a son to take over the business—he'd made no secret of that—but he'd also never indicated his love for his children hinged on it. No, the blame was his own. Success in business had become a way to prove his loyalty to his father, a way to earn his respect. And that was still important; it always would be. But following blindly in another man's footsteps, even a man as wise as his father, wasn't a life. It was time to make his own decisions. He needed to respect himself enough, trust himself enough, to follow his own heart.

His father had left part of his family on another shore, but in doing so he'd expanded the family in other ways. Vision finally clear, Nic grabbed the desk phone. Dialing from memory, he waited for her to pick up, fingers absently tracing the faded photograph.

"Hey, Isabella? We need to talk."

Chapter Sixteen

"Up you go." Jillian lifted the elderly schnauzer into a cage lined with clean, soft towels. Mr. Snappers was recovering from his dental extraction, and was still a bit loopy from the medication. She checked his IV again and adjusted the fluid rate, then placed a hot water bottle wrapped in a soft cloth next to him. The warmth would help him recover more quickly and would feel good to his old bones.

Finished with her midday patient checks, she washed her hands, then walked to the front desk to see if the first afternoon patient had arrived. Dan Jameson was there, talking to Mollie, his dalmatian focused on the cat cowering in a carrier a few feet away. "Hey, Dan, how's Flash doing?" The lanky, white-whiskered man was a security guard at the county courthouse, but volunteered with the small island's fire department and considered it his civic duty to keep the fire station mascot in good health.

"Right as rain, Miss Jillian, right as rain. I just stopped by to pick up his special food." Flash had a genetic condition that caused bladder stones; a prescription diet helped keep them at bay.

"Wonderful! And you're only giving him the special prescription treats now, right?"

"I keep a jar of them at the station house and some in my pocket for when we're out and about. The kids like to make him do tricks, and he likes to show off, don't you, boy?" He patted the handsome animal, pride showing in his face. They were a great pair, and an example of everything she loved about Paradise. How could she have even considered moving?

Mollie handed Dan his receipt and then turned to Jillian. "Dan was just filling me in on some news. It seems the sale of the Sandpiper is moving forward."

Her stomach tumbled as if tossed by a rogue wave. Counting to ten silently, she steeled her spine. If she was going to stay in Paradise—and she was—she would have to come to terms with the sale and the changes it unleashed. "Well, that was to be expected."

Dan shook his head. "Maybe so, but it sure seems to be happening fast. A lady over in the clerk's office told me that the survey was already ordered, and the seller is hoping to be done with it and back in Orlando within the month."

"I didn't think it could happen that quickly." She swallowed and reminded herself that the sooner it was done, the sooner Nic would be onto the next project and out of her life.

"Me, either, but I guess when you've got money, the wheels turn a bit more quickly than they do otherwise."

"I guess so." Rubbing Flash's silky ears, she sighed. Gesturing to the bag of food on the counter, she asked, "Can I take this out for you?"

Eyes wide, he shook his head. "No, ma'am, I can't have a lady carrying my things for me. The boys at the station would never let me live it down."

She laughed, recognizing the truth in his words. "I'll get the door for you, then, if it won't hurt your reputation too much."

"Just don't tell anyone." He winked, then hefted the bag without letting go of the waiting dog's leash. She beat him to the door, swinging it open for him, then took a minute to appreciate the breezy fall afternoon. A light wind stirred the palms that dotted the street and carried the smells of the Sandcastle Cakes with it. "Hey, Mollie, when's the next appointment due? Do I have time to run and grab a coffee?"

"You've got five minutes, but I just made a full pot, so why do you need to run out?"

She grinned ruefully. "Because I like my coffee with a side of pumpkin spice scone. I can smell them from here."

"Ooh, yum. Get me one, too. But hurry."

"I'm already gone. Tell Cassie I'll grab her one, too."

"Grab me one what?" Cassie asked, walking in past Jillian, returning from her lunch break.

"A scone and a coffee. The smell of pumpkin spice is too much to resist."

"Ooh, perfect. I knew I had a light lunch for a reason. Whose turn is it to buy?"

"Mine," Jillian answered. "I'll be right back."

Heading for the sweet shop across the street, she felt

her shoulders slide down, her tension over the discussion of the Sandpiper soothed by the normalcy of the errand. The new influx of tourists might make her daily coffee run take a little longer, but surely places like the Sandcastle would stick around, at least until one of the national donut chains chased the crowds and opened up shop. Grimacing, she entered the quaint storefront, where the warm aroma of sugar and spice reminded her of her mission.

"Something wrong?" Grace Keville asked, pausing from wiping down a gleaming display case chock full of decadent desserts.

"Nothing one of your delicious scones won't fix. Three pumpkin ones, please, and some cappuccinos to go with them." Sandcastle Cakes didn't offer the variety of coffee creations that The Grind did, but the freshness and sheer number of drool-worthy treats made it her favorite place for an afternoon pick-me-up. Her mouth watering, she scanned the glass cases. Scrumptious muffins, cookies the size of her hand, layer cakes dripping with buttercream. How did Grace stay so skinny? Just the scent of all that yumminess was probably adding an inch to each of her own thighs.

Seeing her order was ready, she tore herself away from the wonderland of confections. "Thanks, Grace, this is just what I needed."

"If only all my customers were so easily pleased." She wiped a smudge of flour from her face with the edge of her apron. "I've had to do three mock-up cakes for one of my wedding clients. If it's this hard to decide on a cake, I don't see how she ever managed to pick a groom."

Laughing, Jillian pocketed her change and took the cardboard drink carrier and white bakery bag. "Good luck with Ms. Indecision. I'd better go before Cassie sends out a search party for me."

Walking as quickly as she could without spilling coffee, she pondered how to protect small business owners like Grace from the influx of commercialism that was on the horizon. She'd bring that up at the next Preservation Society meeting; there might be zoning issues or other changes they could make if they hurried.

Unfortunately, it was too late to protect her heart; that was a restoration project with no end in sight.

Nic adjusted his tie for the umpteenth time, hoping his impatience wasn't overly obvious to the man on the other side of the desk. He'd dealt with dozens of mortgage officers at banks across the country, and they all seemed to move in the same lethargic time warp as this guy. The minute hand on the large wall clock ticked by with maddening precision, a metronome for the musical shuffling of papers and clacking of keyboards. No other deal had been this nerve-racking, but he'd also never had a deal with so much riding on it.

He needed this to go through smoothly, without any last-minute changes or red-tape snags. He'd spent hours going over the business plan, the revenue projections, the zoning regulations. Everything was there; he just needed this one poorly paid employee to stop overestimating his own importance and sign off on it. He'd seen the glint in the man's eye—he was enjoying making someone with the Caruso name wait on tenterhooks. It might be the only time he got to be in a position of power with someone like Nic, and he wasn't letting it go sooner than he had to. Recognizing the situation for what it was, Nic had forced himself to smile, to make small talk. And now, he forced himself to wait.

"Well…it seems everything is in order." The mousy man with thinning hair and an ill-fitting suit looked up. "I know you've called in some favors to fast-track this. I find that highly irregular, and not the proper way of things. But Mr. Ackerman, the bank president, has instructed me to proceed. Everything will be ready for you at the closing, as you arranged."

Thank heaven for small favors and the connections his father had made over the years. He needed this deal to close as soon as possible. He shook the man's limp hand and was out the door, on to his next appointment. He had a meeting with an architect in twenty minutes, and then a landscape specialist after that. If all went well, he'd have the big items on his list checked off by late afternoon and be back in New York by nightfall. He had some shopping to do, and the limited options on Paradise Isle just weren't going to cut it for this particular task.

He was almost to the architect's when he saw her. She had darted across the street, almost directly in front of where he was stopped for a red light. She hadn't recognized him in a different rental car, but he'd know her anywhere. Her dark curls bounced as she walked, and her cheeks were reddened by the wind. His body hardened as he watched her. Would it always be like this? Would he always want her, need her so badly, that just the sight of her nearly drove him mad?

A car honked behind him. The light had turned green without him noticing. He drove through the intersection, fighting the urge to turn around, to go to her. But that wasn't part of the plan. He had things he needed to do, and he couldn't let his hormones, or his heart, distract him.

He pulled into the small parking lot in front of Island

Architecture with five minutes to spare. Time enough to make a quick phone call.

"Hey, Dad, just finished up at the bank. Your phone call did the trick."

His father's voice rumbled back. "Are you sure you want to go through with this?" Concern echoed over the airwaves.

"I'm sure. The numbers make sense."

"It's not the numbers I'm worried about. You're more important to me than any of that."

"I know, Dad." And he did know. They'd had a long talk, late into the night, after he'd met with Isabella. They were on the same page now, and that felt good. Really good.

"I'll call you after the closing, let you know when everything's settled. And Dad?"

"Yes?"

"Thanks again for understanding."

"You got it. Now, get back to work. You've got a big project on your hands."

"You're right, I do. Bye." He hung up and did what his father had advised, what he did best. He got to work.

"I wish I had better news for you, but if there's a way around this, I can't find it."

Jillian absorbed the Preservation Society president's words, knowing they were no more than the truth. She and Edward had been poring over zoning regulations, municipal codes and city ordinances for hours, hoping to find something they could use to stop the spread of the large chain stores they both were felt was inevitable. It wasn't that she was averse to commercialism—she liked to shop as much as the next girl—she just wanted to protect the small businesses that gave Paradise so much character. She'd hoped there would be something already on the books, but it looked as though they'd have to start from scratch. A process that would take more time than they had.

She shouldn't have gotten her hopes up. She had been so sure they would find a way to protect the charm of Paradise amid the changes the new resort would bring. But the town's elected officials had never anticipated this kind of rapid progress; no one could have predicted this.

Heart heavy, her neck stiff from hunching over the conference table so long, she stood and stretched. "You're right, Ed. There's nothing more we can do about it tonight, anyway. I knew the Caruso lawyers would have triple-checked everything as far as the hotel itself, but I had wanted there to be something we could do about all the other changes coming." She started stacking up the books and reams of paper they'd torn through. "Looks like we don't have a leg to stand on."

"Don't give up just yet. I'll ask around, see if there's anything else we can do."

"Thanks, Ed. I'll try to stay positive.

"That's the way. Remember, the people here won't change, not just because there are a bunch of new stores and tourists crowding up the place."

"Good point, and exactly what I needed to hear." On impulse, she hugged him, making him blush like a schoolgirl instead of the middle-aged man he was. This learning-to-trust business was hard, but he was right. She needed to remember that the people wouldn't change just because everything else did. Maybe someday expecting the best from people would be second nature, but for now she appreciated the reminders. She'd probably need a lot of them as construction got under way. Leaving Ed flustered, but smiling, she said her good-byes and left the small library room that served as the society's headquarters.

At least she hadn't run into Nic yet. She was on pins and needles every time she left the house, certain she would bump into him on the street or in a café. The constant anxiety was draining her; she needed to relax. Maybe she'd check out a book before she went home, something lighthearted. Romance was out, but maybe one of those funny vampire books, where everyone wore designer clothes twenty-four hours a day. Something to take her out of her head for a bit.

Browsing the stacks, she found a few that looked interesting, and started for the checkout area. Reading the back cover of one of her picks, she walked right into one of the other patrons in line. "Excuse me, I wasn't looking where I was—"

"Jillian."

"Nic. Wow. I didn't expect to see you here. I mean, here, the library, not here, Paradise." Off-kilter, she tried to look anywhere but at his face. The book in his hand caught her attention. "*Native Florida Plants for the Landscape Beginner*, interesting choice. I hadn't pegged you as the gardening type."

"Just some research. How about you?" He gestured to the paperbacks she was clutching.

"Some pleasure reading." She tried to hide the covers from him. Why did all the novels have to feature such erotic images on the front? He was going to think she was sex-crazed if he saw them. Which admittedly was pretty accurate where he was concerned. They were in a library, of all places, and he still had her blood thrumming through her veins, her body warming in all the right places. At least the sudden jolt of lust offered a bit of a distraction from the ever-present ache in her heart. Hormones beat heartache any day.

"Good, you deserve a bit of relaxation."

"Seemed like a good idea. Things have been a bit stressful."

He winced at her not-too-subtle indictment. "I suppose I deserved that."

"Yes, you did." If only she could really hate him, that might make things easier. But she couldn't.

Moving forward in line, he handed his book to the librarian at the desk, presenting a Paradise Municipal Library card. When had he gotten that? The library did issue short-term cards to nonresidents for a fee, but not many people took advantage of the service. It seemed like a lot of trouble for a short-term business trip.

He wasn't planning on extending his stay, was he? He had to go. Soon. Being this close to him, and not having him, was agony. Even breathing hurt. He had to go so she could try to forget him and move on with her life. Every run-in would be like ripping off a newly formed scab. She needed space and time for the wounds to close, for her heart to mend.

He'd finished with his transaction, and was watching her, his eyes soft. "I had planned to call you tonight."

Keeping her face averted, sure he'd see the turmoil in her eyes, she handed her books to the impatiently waiting librarian. "I don't think that would be a good idea."

"No, I can see that." He hesitated. "Have a good night, Jillian."

Not able to trust her voice, she only nodded. Accepting her silence, he turned and walked out of her life once more.

Chapter Seventeen

Nic paced the whitewashed boards of the Sandpiper's wraparound porch. After that last run-in with Jillian, it was obvious that a straightforward approach wouldn't work. Hell, the way she'd treated him had him rethinking his plan altogether. Maybe he'd done enough damage and should cut his losses and run.

Except he wasn't built that way. For better or worse, he didn't quit, and he didn't walk away, not when it mattered. He might be making some changes in his life, but he was, at heart, still the same guy. Which meant he needed to find a way to get Jillian to listen to him, no matter how angry or hurt she was. She might push him away forever after that, but at least he would know he tried.

Frustration spurred him down the stairs and onto the soft sand of the beach below. Maybe a walk would clear his head. Leaving his shoes by the steps, he started for the shore. Then he went back and moved his shoes farther out of sight, under a step. He knew it was ridiculous—crime was almost nonexistent in Paradise—but New York habits died hard. It was going to take a while to adjust.

Satisfied he wouldn't be the victim of a random shoe-napping, he started off at a brisk pace. Most of the young families had already packed up for the day, and in their place were older couples walking hand in hand, enjoying a simple Friday night. He knew from the local paper that the beach was also a favorite of the high school crowd, come the weekend. He had read that one student had broken his arm on this beach, trying to play tackle football by moonlight. If that was the worst trouble the young people got into around here, he figured they were doing pretty well. This place really did seem like a tropical version of a 1950s sitcom.

His feet kept time with the waves, carrying him farther down the coast. Ahead, he spotted a dog chasing seagulls, barking in delight as they kept just out of reach. Smiling, he wondered what Murphy thought of the birds. He knew Jillian took him for regular runs on the beach; maybe they were old hat by now. He still couldn't get over how dedicated she was to that dog, caring for him better than many people did their own pets.

He stopped. Murphy—that was his answer. Jillian might not be willing to meet with him, but she'd do anything for Murphy. It was a dirty trick, but he just needed it to work once. Hopefully she'd agree the ends justified the means. And if not, well, he wouldn't be any worse off than he was now.

* * *

It turned out Mrs. Rosenberg loved his scheme and was happy to lend Murphy to the cause. When he'd spoken to her last night, she'd agreed to have the dog ready at five thirty today. She had already called Jillian to tell her not to stop by to exercise Murphy, saying she had family coming by that wanted to see him. All the other details were taken care of, and, checking his watch, he decided it was time to head over to collect the dog.

He had directions with him, but felt pretty confident he could find her house without them. He'd become much more familiar with the island over the past several days. Driving along the coast, he marveled yet again at the constantly changing view. Today he saw nothing but blue sky and a single osprey silhouetted darkly against it. The big bird was perched on a light post, where he, or she—he had no idea how to tell the sexes apart—had built an enormous nest. He'd seen quite a few of the precariously balanced constructions, and every time wondered how they kept the things from tumbling to the water below. Maybe he should pick up a book about the local birds the next time he hit the library. He'd never been much of a reader, but he'd been doing a lot of new things lately. Given the scope of his plans, it made sense to continue to research the area.

Turning onto one of the main thoroughfares, he kept an eye out for any businesses that might be interested in putting together vacation packages, things that could be bundled with a hotel stay. The dive shop seemed like a good bet, and maybe the kayak outfitter, as well. He was also hoping to work out some arrangements with local restaurants for picnic baskets to be delivered directly to the beach for lunching families. Driving by the photography studio's window display had the gears turning in his head, and he made a mental note to drop by with a business card and proposal next week.

Soon he was past the last of the commercial buildings and navigating the residential neighborhood where Mrs. Rosenberg's house was. The houses here were older than on the other side of the island. Most were small, single-story bungalow types with stucco or siding to protect them from the harsh Florida sun. Mrs. Rosenberg's was easy to spot, the pink paint standing out among the more neutral colors of her neighbors' homes. A few plastic flamingos were the only thing keeping her house from being a Florida cliché.

Shutting the car door, he started up the walk. At his knock, Murphy's enthusiastic barking greeted him, followed by Mrs. Rosenberg's muffled voice as she shushed the eager border collie. Once she opened the door for him, he held up a treat he'd stashed in a pocket. Murphy, knowing the routine, plopped his furry rear end on the floor, then accepted the treat with dignity. Nic ruffled the dog's fur and took the leash that Mrs. Rosenberg had already secured.

"Thanks again. I really appreciate you letting me borrow him."

Her brightly painted lips turned up as she regarded man and dog. "I'm happy to do it. I don't usually condone sneaky behavior, but it's for her own good. She has some issues with change, I know she does, but sometimes you have to embrace change if you want to move forward. Besides, if you don't take him, he's liable to drive me crazy, with her not coming to play with him tonight."

"Well, I'll take good care of him. Any particular time you want him back?"

"No rush. I went ahead and told the girls in my senior group to come over—didn't want to be lying to Jillian. We'll wait up together to hear how things go."

He had no doubt they'd be gossiping about it all night. Heck, there might even be bets placed. But at the end of the night, he would be the one taking the risks, and the stakes were high.

Jillian put the final coat of polish on her freshly manicured nails. The pretty golden color was unlikely to last, given how hard she was on her hands during the workweek, but it was a Saturday, and she figured she deserved a bit of pampering, even if she had to do it herself. The meticulous process also gave her something to focus on other than Nic Caruso, Caruso Hotels and the entire mess that had become her personal life.

Since she'd run into him, she had cleaned her apartment, decluttered her closet, baked and frozen more muffins than any one person could ever hope to consume, and gotten an early start on her Christmas list, thanks to the wonders of online shopping.

But no matter what activity she threw herself into, the pain was still there, gnawing away at her. There was an empty spot inside of her, a deep hole that no amount of manic cleaning or self-improvement could touch. Even when she closed her eyes, exhausted and desperate for sleep, she saw him. His dark eyes, chiseled jaw and teasing smile followed her into her dreams, dreams that left her needy and restless.

It seemed there was no cure for heartbreak, other than, hopefully, the tincture of time. She'd gotten through other disappointments, but this time was different. She had finally learned to open her heart, only to have it squashed like one of the many lovebugs stuck to her windshield.

Still, the hurting couldn't last forever. She'd just have to keep her chin up until then. She could do that. Focus on work, and her friends, and maybe take up a hobby or twelve. Reading hadn't worked; every hero in every story had reminded her of Nic. Maybe knitting or golf. Golf was popular.

She was searching golf lessons on the internet, and becoming increasingly intimidated by the prices, when the phone rang.

Desperate for a new distraction, she grabbed the phone without checking the caller ID. "Hello?"

"Hey, Jillian, it's Nic. Please don't hang up."

"Why not?" This was crazy—how many times did she have to tell him to leave her alone? Her stupid heart was beating a happy tune just hearing his voice, but her head knew there was only pain down that path.

"Because I need help, or rather Murphy does. He's here, running on the beach. I don't know if I can catch him on my own."

Well, crap. This was really starting to get old. She'd have to talk to Mrs. Rosenberg again about being more careful. "Fine. I'm on my way. Keep an eye on him until I arrive, and keep your phone on. I'll call when I'm there."

Fuming, she got her keys and stomped down the stairs. She was supposed to be pampering herself. Now, she'd be torturing herself instead, teasing her heart yet again with the one man she wanted but couldn't have. Maybe she needed to get away. Not move, she'd ruled that out as cowardice. But there was no reason she couldn't take a long-overdue vacation, maybe go camping in the state forest or drive up to St. Augustine for a few days. Anywhere would be better than here, if being here meant constantly running into Nic.

By the time she got to the Sandpiper, she had a vacation itinerary mapped out. She parked and noted that other than a few cars in the employee section, and a single rental car that must be Nic's, the place was empty. Odd, but then again, with the sale so soon, maybe they'd stopped taking reservations. Crunching over the gravel, she punched Nic's number into her phone. It rang three times before she got a breathless answer.

"Hey, are you here?"

"Yeah, walking up now. Are you still on the beach?"

"No. Yes. Just…come around to the back." And the phone clicked off.

He'd sounded a bit off; maybe Murphy was giving him trouble? Or maybe he wasn't thrilled to have to see her, given how she'd treated him the past few times. She'd blown hot and cold so often she felt like a hair dryer on the fritz. He had every right to be a bit wary of her mood. Or just frustrated to once again be saddled with a delinquent dog. Either way, she'd get Murphy, and herself, out of his hair as quickly as she could. Her pockets were stuffed with liver treats, more than enough to guarantee the canine's cooperation.

If only the human male could be wrangled so easily.

She took the steps two at a time, ready to get this over with so she could continue with the business of getting on with her life. The front door was right there, but it was just as easy to go around via the wraparound porch. Between cleaning, baking and pampering, she'd been cooped up inside for too long, and the longer route gave her a few more minutes to brace herself before she saw him.

Skirting potted orchids and patio furniture, she made the trek around the stately building. Not a single guest to be seen—in fact, if it wasn't for the murmur of voices drifting up from the beach, she would have sworn she was alone on the island.

Reaching the final turn, she saw Nic in one of the wicker lounge chairs, Murphy sitting expectantly at his feet. Surprised, she watched as Nic tossed the dog a treat, then ruffled his fur. Man and dog looked completely at ease, as if they were just enjoying the afternoon air. If there had been any kind of crisis here, it was long over. So why had he called?

Chapter Eighteen

Nic felt like a suspect waiting for a jury verdict. He'd prepared his case, would make his arguments, but in the end the decision was out of his hands. At least he had Murphy as a character witness.

Wait, was he really so far-gone that a dog was his best chance of success?

Sadly, yes, yes, he was. If an actual dog would keep him out of the proverbial doghouse, he wasn't going to fight it. He stroked Murphy's coat, more to calm his own nerves than settle the animal. In fact, Murphy seemed perfectly content. He figured the continuous consumption of liver treats probably had a lot to do with that, so he tossed the happy dog another one.

"You're going to make him sick if you give him too many of those."

Busted. "They're really small."

"And very rich. We'll take him home in your car. If he yaks, you can deal with it."

Nic looked down at the mostly empty bag of treats in his lap. Maybe he had been a bit overgenerous. Murphy nosed his leg, maybe to show support, more likely to search for more treats. "You heard her, no more."

"So, I thought you needed help. Seems like you're doing just fine on your own."

"I don't suppose you'd believe that I just now got him under control?"

"You're not sweating, he's not panting and it doesn't look like either of you have any sand on you at all."

Sand. He hadn't thought about that. Oh, well, the ruse had gotten her here, so it had served its purpose.

"Are you going to tell me why you dragged me over here?"

Her blue eyes were like icicles, her lips pursed in righteous indignation. She was angry as hell, and still knock-you-on-your-butt gorgeous. Her mood didn't matter when it came to his feelings, or his libido. He wanted her, in his arms, in his life, in his bed. But wanting didn't mean having. If he didn't play his cards right, she was going to walk out of his life, leaving him right back where he started. And he wouldn't, couldn't, let that happen.

"I had to show you—and tell you—some things. If you give me this, I promise I won't bother you again. I'll leave town tomorrow if that's what you want."

She narrowed her eyes. "If I listen to you now, you'll leave town? No more running into each other, no more emergency phone calls, no more anything?"

"You have my word. You tell me to leave, and I'll go."

Sweat trickled down his back. Everything was on the line—there would be no second chances.

"Fine. Let's get this over with."

Not exactly a vote of confidence, but he'd take it. "Come with me, we'll walk Murphy while we talk."

"While *you* talk. I don't have anything left to say."

"Either way." He started to reach for her hand, but figured that would be pushing it. Instead, he grabbed Murphy's leash and headed around the side of the building, hoping she would follow. She did, and his lungs loosened a bit. Drawing a deep breath, he spoke. "As you can see, the structure of the building is sound, but a lot of the siding needs to be replaced, and in several places the porch railing shows signs of dry rot." He gestured to an area where the weathered boards, bleached by the sun, were peeling away. "The good news is I've found a contractor who has experience working on buildings from this time period. He should be able to match everything, make it look just like the original."

Jillian stopped dead. "Replace? What's the point of replacing stuff when you're just going to tear it—"

"No questions yet. I'm not done, and you promised to listen."

Jillian's mouth opened, then closed. He definitely had her interest now.

"There are obviously some improvements that can be made inside as well—a new computer system, some upgrades in the kitchen, that kind of thing. More updating than remodeling. But really, what I wanted to talk to you about are the grounds." He chanced touching her, taking her elbow to steer her down the stairs to the walking path below.

"The majority of the land is undeveloped. Other than

a few fruit trees, and of course the benches and paths, nothing had been touched out here."

"Right. Your point?" She was still prickly, but he could tell she wanted to hear more.

"Well, I'm thinking we can add some interest to the landscape and still keep the natural feel of the place. For instance, a butterfly garden with a gazebo at the center. There's a nursery on the mainland that can set one up using native plants. It will add some color, but blend in with the natural surroundings."

"A gazebo?"

"Yes, I think it's exactly what we need, if we want to hold weddings here again. Didn't you say this used to be a popular place for them?"

"Yes, but wait—what about the giant resort?" He could almost see the wheels turning in her head. Grinning, he ignored her question and continued walking, taking her past the parking lot to the south side of the inn.

"Take a look at this spot." He pointed to a shady clearing amongst the scrub pines. "What do you think of a playground here, the kind made mostly of wood, so it doesn't stand out too much? Maybe some picnic tables or benches for the parents."

"Playgrounds. Gazebos. Weddings. New siding. Am I crazy or are you? Because I don't see how any of this makes sense when you're just going to bulldoze the place."

"Maybe I'm crazy, maybe I'm not. But I one thing I can say for sure, no one is bulldozing this place."

"Excuse me?" Jillian felt as though she were on some kind of carnival ride, her head was spinning so fast.

Nothing made sense. She had to have heard him wrong or misunderstood. "I could have sworn you just said you aren't going to tear down the Sandpiper."

He gave her a smug little grin and tucked his thumbs in his pockets, as if there was nothing strange about her question or the whole situation. "That's right. I'm not tearing it down. It's got good bones and a history. I don't want to lose that."

"But, then, what are you going to do?" She suddenly understood how Alice felt when she fell into Wonderland. Up was down, down was up and the man in front of her was mad as a hatter.

"That's what I've been trying to talk to you about. For starters, we'll remodel the inn itself, repair what we can and replace what we can't. That's the easy part."

"None of this sounds easy."

"Easy in that we already have a blueprint and the contractor just has to replicate what's already here. No big changes. It's the rest of it that I wanted your input on."

"My input?"

"That's right. I want to bring the Sandpiper back to its glory days, and to do that I need to know more about it. I need to know what the community is missing, what it needs and wants. You know Paradise better than anyone, so I thought you would have some insight into what needs to be done."

She had some thoughts all right, but getting them sorted out would take a while. "Let me get this straight. You are not going to tear down the Sandpiper or build some giant luxury hotel?"

"Right."

She plowed on, trying to grasp what was happening. "And you called me—tricked me, in fact—to come out here, so that I could tell you where and how to build a playground?"

"Among other things, yes."

He really was insane. It was the only explanation.

And now he was walking away, veering off the path and cutting through the clearing he'd designated for the playground. She scrambled after him, catching up to him in a grassy area that backed up to the bluffs, with a view of the beach below. Grabbing his arm, she spun him toward her. "You said other things. What other things?" How much more bizarre could this get?

"You said there used to be community events here. What kinds?"

"Well, charity stuff, mostly. They used to sponsor a yearly fish fry benefit for the library and a chili cook-off for the fire department." She tried to think of what other events she had attended over the years, as well as the ones she'd heard about from Cassie from before she'd moved here. "There used to be a big Christmas tree lighting every year, with caroling and hot chocolate. And I think there was a fall festival, too, but that was before my time." She looked out over the ocean, spotting a cruise ship against the horizon. "They would do the fireworks here, too, on the Fourth of July. Sometimes there was a pig roast or a clambake first."

She turned back to him, and realized he was actually taking notes on a small notepad. "Did you get all that? Or should I repeat it for you?" She tried to infuse as much sarcasm as possible into her voice, but he either didn't pick up on it or tuned it out.

"I got the basics. But thanks." He tucked the pad into the back pocket of his slacks. "Next question. What do you think about this spot for a house?"

"Whose house?"

"The innkeeper's house, of course. There's a suite in the Sandpiper, but I'm thinking that a house makes more sense. It opens more room up for guests in the main inn and offers some privacy for starting a family."

"I can't imagine Caruso Hotels makes a habit of building custom homes for the management staff."

"No, but Caruso Hotels doesn't own the Sandpiper. I do. And I want a house."

Her knees buckled, and she leaned against a well-positioned pine. The rough bark scraped through her thin T-shirt, grounding her. He bought the Sandpiper? Not Caruso Hotels? He was staying? Permanently? There would be no way to avoid him, not if he was running the inn. And what was that he said about starting a family? Was she going to have to watch him date, get married, have children? She'd said she would stay in town, but how could she do that when Paradise was turning into her own personal version of hell?

Jillian looked as though she'd been sucker-punched. The color that had heated her cheeks while they argued had vanished, leaving her as pale as the white clouds floating overhead. Eyes wide, she stared at him. Maybe he shouldn't have blindsided her, but she hadn't left him much choice. She never would have come if she'd known that he, not his father's company, was the new owner of the Sandpiper. Still, her silence had his gut churning. "Are you okay?"

She nodded, straightening almost imperceptibly against the tree she was braced against. "You don't mean you bought it for yourself, right? You must mean you bought it on behalf of Caruso Hotels."

"No. I couldn't do that if I wanted to, since I'm no longer an employee of Caruso Hotels. I turned in my resignation the last time I was in New York."

"But…you can't just quit. You're a vice president, for crying out loud. "

"Not anymore. My sister Isabella now has that title, and good luck to her."

"Your sister? I thought she worked at some fancy Wall Street investment firm."

"She did, but she hated it. She was tired of doing work in the background, never getting to make a decision. She wanted something different, and with her business background and her degree, she'll do a great job."

Jillian threw her hands up, more flustered than he'd ever seen her. "But, it's not just about the job—it's about who you are."

"Who I was. I don't want to be that person anymore." He shoved a hand through his hair. How could he explain this to her, when he was just starting to figure it out himself? "I wasn't living my own life. I was just doing what I thought everyone wanted me to do, what I thought I had to do. But that's not a real life, and it's not what I want. I need to do something for myself, find my own path."

"And that means being an innkeeper?"

"It's as good a job as any. I can use what I know about the industry, but be truly involved. I won't just be setting things in motion. I'll get to follow through. I can create my own vision, instead of following someone else's. And I'll get to put down real roots. I'm tired of living out of a suitcase."

The shock and horror on her face were easy to read, but hard to accept. He had planned on her being surprised, but the anguish on her face, that was something else entirely. Had he misunderstood everything? Imagined her feelings in order to justify his own? He'd convinced himself that she was fighting the same losing battle he was, but maybe she was already over him or had never really wanted him in the first place.

No. He couldn't think like that. Couldn't go there. He'd second-guessed everyone he loved too many times, trying to live up to expectations they'd never really had. If he'd learned anything in the past few days, it was that the only real freedom came from honesty. He had to act on what was in his own heart and then let the chips fall where they may. At least he would have no regrets.

"What about your family?"

"My family wants me to be happy. I don't know how I convinced myself that the only way to make them proud was to be a part of the family business, but I know now that isn't true. I did some hard thinking about our family and what has kept us all together. It isn't the business or a set of expectations. It's love."

He took a deep breath to steady his nerves. His eyes searched hers; he needed her to see the truth in his words.

"I stayed in the job because of love. And I left it for love, because love is the most important thing in the world. I bought the Sandpiper for love, for you. Because I love you."

He saw the tears coming, and before he could stop and think, he took her in his arms. She clung to him, her shoulders shuddering as she sobbed. At a loss, he stroked her hair and let her cry herself out, wanting nothing more than to keep her protected in his arms forever.

* * *

Jillian couldn't believe she was blubbering all over Nic, but she was powerless to stop. All the worry and pain and sadness had built up, and now, hearing his words, she couldn't hold it back anymore. It flowed out of her on a river of tears, clearing the path for the warmth that was taking over, everywhere her body touched his. Was it possible? Pushing away, she wiped her blurry eyes. She had to hear it again, had to know he'd really said it, that it wasn't her emotions playing tricks on her. "You did all this because of me? Because you love me?"

"I did it for us. I bought it for us. I wanted to show you how I feel, and the Sandpiper seemed like the perfect way to do that. You love it, and I love you. Pretty simple."

"But…you really love me?"

He laughed. "Were you not paying attention?"

"I just need to hear it again." Her voice was shaking, one more thing out of her control. "I've never heard it before."

He smiled. "That's because I've never said it to you before. But I'll say it again. I love you."

Something fluttered inside, breaking free. She felt the tears starting again, but this time she laughed through them. "No, I meant I've never heard that before, from anyone." She smiled. Were her feet even touching the ground? "I'm glad you were the first."

Taking her trembling hands, he pulled her against him. "I'm so sorry, I didn't think… With foster care, your parents. I just didn't think. I should have said it before now, but I promise I'm going to make it up to you. I'm going to say it so often you'll get sick of hearing it."

Stopping, he tilted his head to the side. "Wait, does this mean you love me, too?"

She stretched onto her toes, angling for a quick kiss. Lips nearly touching, she whispered against his lips, "I love you—"

He took her mouth, silencing her. She responded eagerly, no longer afraid of the feelings he triggered. When his tongue teased, she parted for him, letting him explore her mouth, answering him with her own bold invasion, needing to taste and feel and love the way she had wanted to since she first saw him standing at the door of the clinic. She held nothing back; she gave him everything. Heart and soul went into that kiss, and he met her passion moment by moment, until her head was spinning and the only thing keeping her upright were his arms firmly wrapped around her body.

Slowly, gradually, he gentled the kiss, nibbling at her bottom lip before putting a few inches of distance between them. "I have more I want to show you, tell you."

"More?" She felt half-drunk; how much more could there be? She had everything she wanted right here, in him.

"Plenty more, of everything," he answered, his husky voice sending shivers through her body. Practically giddy, she let her imagination paint pictures of what could be.

"But for now, let's start with where we should put the gazebo. I want you to pick the spot."

"Me?"

"Didn't I say I bought this because of you? You're the one that knows it, that loves it. You should be the one that helps it come alive again. Besides, a gazebo is all about romance, and as the female of the species I'm willing to bet you have more expertise in that particular area."

"Hmm, I suppose that's true." She grabbed his hand, dragging him with her as she looked for the perfect spot. "You said it would be used for weddings, right?"

"Right."

"Okay, so you want a good view and enough room around it for guests to gather." She nearly floated across the grass, heading for what she knew would be the ideal location. Tucked away, just off the walking path, was an open area framed by towering palms and a clear view of the ocean. "Here," she declared confidently.

"You're sure?" He squeezed her hand.

"Positive. It's the perfect setting. The sea as a backdrop, plenty of room for folding chairs, easy access from the parking lot—this is the spot."

"Well, if you're sure." He walked to the center of the spot she had chosen, Murphy following at his side. Pulling a small box out of his pocket, he knelt down on one knee and looked up at her.

"Wait…what are you doing?" He couldn't be… could he? Even Murphy looked confused, his gaze going from her to Nic and back again before finally laying his head on Nic's bent knee, as if waiting to find out what was happening.

"I told you, I want to start holding weddings here again. And I want the first wedding to be ours, if you'll have me." He held out a ring, the large diamond scattering rainbows as it caught the setting sun. "Jillian Everett, will you marry me?"

Her throat closed over another round of tears, stealing her voice. Pulling air into her lungs, she swallowed and tried again. "Yes." And then, offering a shaking hand, "When?"

He laughed, the hearty laugh she'd learned to love, and slid the ring over her trembling finger. "As soon as we can get the gazebo built, if that's what you want."

Tugging on their joined hands, she pulled him back up, leaning into his body. "Nic?" She slowly kissed her way along his jaw, letting her hands roam his back, his chest, his arms.

He groaned; whether in frustration or pleasure, she wasn't sure. "What?"

"Build fast."

Chapter Nineteen

Nic figured he'd probably broken a world record in gazebo construction, if there was such a thing. He had ended up having to order most of the supplies—there wasn't much of a lumber selection in Paradise—but once everything had arrived he had attacked the project like a man possessed.

He had spent years supervising construction, massive projects with hundreds of crew members. But this was the first time he had actually built something from the ground up on his own. When the last board was in place and the last coat of paint applied, he was as proud of it as he ever had been of a high-rise hotel.

Of course, it turned out that planning a wedding involved more than just building the gazebo. Thankfully, Jillian was handling most of the other preparations. He was much more at home wielding a hammer, however

inexpertly, than he was in a florist's shop. He'd be forever grateful that his main contribution was preparing
the physical surroundings.

With the gazebo finished, he had turned his ener-
gies to the Sandpiper itself. The previous owners had
canceled all the reservations, and the hotel was isolated
enough that there was no one to disturb as he hammered
and sanded and painted until the wee hours. They were
going to hold off on the grand reopening until after the
wedding, but he wanted the old building to be at its best
when his family came for the ceremony. His parents, siblings, aunts, uncles and maternal grandparents would be
on hand, filling the Sandpiper to capacity. His father's
parents weren't able to make the transatlantic trip on
such short notice, but they had insisted the happy couple
visit while on their honeymoon tour of Italy. He had been
so afraid of losing his family, but the upcoming wedding had only brought the generations closer together.

Checking his watch, he decided he had enough time
to shower before the last of them arrived. He'd just finished moving his things into the suite he and Jillian
would be living in while their new house was built. Construction was slated to start next week, but for now this
little grouping of rooms would be home. Their home.
The irony of living in an inn after protesting his suitcase lifestyle for so long wasn't lost on him. But now,
instead of moving on, he'd be putting down roots, becoming part of the community.

More important, he'd have Jillian at his side—and in
his bed. She'd suggested, since they had already waited
so long and the wedding was so soon, that they should
wait to make love until after they had said their vows.
Something about heightening the anticipation. He, as a

gentleman, had agreed, but after three weeks of sleepless nights and countless cold showers he was regretting that particular act of chivalry. As far as he was concerned, anticipation was highly overrated.

At least they wouldn't have far to go. They had decided to spend their wedding night here at the Sandpiper before catching a plane for Rome tomorrow afternoon. The less time between the saying of the vows and the consummation of the marriage, the better. If he had his way, they'd skip the reception entirely and go straight to that part, but that wasn't going to fly with Jillian or their guests.

Forcing himself to think of something other than getting his soon-to-be wife in bed, he stripped down in the large bathroom they would soon be sharing. Waiting for the water to heat up, he eyed the shower stall. They could probably both fit in there, with some creative positioning. Steam rose as he contemplated the possibilities.

But this was no time for fantasizing; he had a wedding to get to. Resigned, he braced himself, and turned the faucet to cold one last time.

"All set?" Cassie asked, straightening Jillian's veil.

Jillian nodded. She'd been ready since the moment Nic had asked the question. But as excited as she was to marry him, she hadn't wanted to give up her girlhood idea of a dream wedding, either. So, with Cassie and Mollie's help, she had crammed months of wedding preparations into a few short weeks. Now, after what felt like a mad dash to nuptial bliss, she was more than ready to get to the "I do" and become the newest member of the Caruso family.

She had worried that Nic's parents would resent her,

blame her for him leaving the company. Instead, she had been inundated with offers to help with the wedding. Both of his sisters and his mother, Marie, had flown down as soon as they heard of the engagement to take her dress shopping. Then, while everyone else was ooh-ing and aahing over her final choice, Marie had quietly made arrangements with the shop owner to pay for it herself. She'd insisted that it was her honor, making Jillian cry for what was probably the hundredth time since Nic had proposed.

Now they were all waiting for her, seated around the beautiful gazebo Nic had crafted. She just had to walk down the path and her new life would start.

Taking a deep breath, she watched Cassie and then Mollie, dressed in simple pastel gowns, walk down the aisle to the strains of a single violin. Then Emma, in the pink flower girl dress she'd picked out herself, started down. She held a posy of flowers in one chubby hand and Murphy's leash in the other. The canine ring bearer trotted beside the pretty girl, trained to home in on Nic, his new master. Mrs. Rosenberg had given them the dog as their first wedding present. There was a mountain of gift-wrapped boxes waiting for them inside, but nothing else could compete with him.

When the music shifted to the traditional wedding march, Doc Marshall, Cassie's father, gave Jillian's hand a squeeze. "We're on, sweetie. Your fella's waiting."

Taking his arm, she let him guide her out of the trees and into the clearing. Nic, in an elegant linen suit, waited for her in the gazebo he'd worked so hard to build. As she started down the aisle he smiled, the love in his eyes unmistakable.

The officiant said the standard words, and she was

sure there were readings and hymns and all the usual things. But all she heard were the vows they said to each other, and the declaration that they were man and wife. And then even that proclamation was wiped from her mind when Nic's mouth met hers in their first kiss as husband and wife.

The rest of the evening was a blur of tears and laughter, new family and old friends. Finally, as the stars came out, the guests began to make their farewells.

"Miss Jillian, you forgot!"

Jillian looked down from her plate of cake at a very sleepy Emma. "What is it, honey? What did I forget?"

"The flowers. You forgot the flowers."

Jillian looked around at the garlands artfully decorating the wraparound porch. "There are plenty of flowers, Emma, enough for you to take some home even, if you want."

The little girl furrowed her eyebrows. "No, not these flowers. The ones you throw. So someone else can get married."

"Oh, the bouquet. You're exactly right, princess. I did forget the bouquet. Were you hoping to catch it?

Wide-eyed, she shook her head, curls swinging. "No, I don't wanna get married. I wanna help you throw it."

Laughing, she tucked the child's hand in hers. "Okay, let's do it."

She found Cassie quickly and told her the plan. Then, upstairs, she led Emma out onto the main balcony, handing her the bouquet of tropical blossoms. "Here you go, Emma. I'll pick you up, and on the count of three, you throw it as hard as you can, okay?

The little girl's eyes beamed. "Okay."

Shouldering the girl, she saw Cassie and Emma, Nic's

sisters, and even Mrs. Rosenberg gathered on the lawn with the other single ladies. As soon as the crowd spotted the duo on the balcony they started the countdown. "One—two—three!"

The cheer that went up almost drowned out Emma's shout of "Mama, catch!" But everyone saw her smile when the bundle of flowers landed directly in Cassie's hands.

"Now it's all over, right, Jillian?" the tired girl asked, stifling a yawn.

All but the best part, Jillian thought, suddenly as eager as Emma to move the guests along.

It took another hour, but finally they were standing on the front steps, waving goodbye to the last of their guests. Even the cleaning crew had finished, leaving only Nic's family, most of whom had already retired to their rooms.

"Good night, Jillian, and welcome to the family." Lorenzo Caruso, the last to go up, gave her a crushing hug, squeezing a laugh from her.

"Thank you so much. And do let us know if you need anything during the night."

"Are you kidding? It's your wedding night. My wife and son would kill me if I even thought about disturbing you."

"You've got that straight," Nic agreed, wrapping his arms around her. "Now go, before Mom comes looking for you."

"Nic!"

"No, he's right. He's waited long enough to have his bride to himself. We'll see you in the morning." He patted her arm, then retreated into the inn.

The minute the door was shut, Nic swung her around,

pressing her against the railing, his mouth coming down hard on hers. A throbbing hunger rose up at his touch, and tasting him only made it stronger. His hands crushed her dress as he molded her to him. Maybe she should care that he was ruining the lace, but she was too desperate for his touch to stop him.

Her own hands sought skin, pulling and pushing at the layers of formalwear. "Nic, I need—" she panted in his ear.

"I know, baby." His husky voice vibrated along her neck, sending chills zinging along her skin. In an instant, she was in his arms, being carried across the threshold and up the stairs, into the master suite.

They somehow managed to undress as they tumbled onto the bed, buttons flying, mouths nipping, hands seeking. He expertly teased her to a fast peak, leaving her gasping and aching for him. "Now, Nic, please, now."

And then they were one, and it was everything she had ever wanted or needed. He whispered words of love as she met his pace, then urged him on. Perfectly matched, they raced for completion together, each swallowing the other's cries as they climaxed.

Afterward, he rolled her on top of him, so her head rested on his chest. Hearing his heart galloping, she smiled and snuggled closer.

"Don't get too comfortable, Mrs. Caruso. That was just the opening act," he rumbled, stroking lazy patterns up and down her bare skin.

"So was the wait worth it?" she teased.

"Let just say we have a lot of work to do, to make up for lost time." As if to punctuate his words, she felt him growing ready again.

"Speaking of time, I know it probably makes more sense to wait to start a family until the house is built—"

Cutting her off with a kiss, he flipped her beneath him. "I can build fast, remember? Nine months should be plenty of time."

* * * * *

LET'S TALK
Romance

For exclusive extracts, competitions
and special offers, find us online: